Xionflight

by

PATRICIA WEBER

PACIFICA EDITIONS

La Jolla, California

ISBN
Library of Congress Cataloging in Publication Data

PUBLISHED BY: PACIFICA EDITIONS

Make inquiries to: Pacifica Editions
P.O. Box 412
La Jolla, California 92038-0412

PRINTED in the U.S.A.

2 3 4 5 6 7 8 9 10

TYPESTYLE: Plantin, 10½ point on 12 leading

TYPESETTING AND PRODUCTION:
Moog & Associates, Inc. c/o Arlene A. Machado, Supervisor

ARTISTS:
Mary Louise Coman
Yves Andres

DISCLAIMER. Circumstances in this story are imaginary and none of the characters who play a part throughout the plot exist in real life, nor are they patterned after persons living or not living. The setting is a composite of several related towns.

Foreword

Gregor Morghann is at his best when he is beneath the surface of the ocean photographing sharks, whales or shipwrecks. The strength of his character is put to a severe test by the constant and mystifying visits of a gifted woman who complicates his other loves. Claiming access to a spectacular new science, she induces him into the basics of XIONFLIGHT.

It is 1960, an era shadowed by the fighting in Vietnam. Gregor lives in a charmed place called Sunday Village, a modern Camelot where aging is discouraged and tears are forbidden, a pastoral settlement that has been a century of haven for its affluent notables. Time and progress, like over-zealous surgeons, have sculpted and gouged and grafted the cozy village until its charisma begins to fade into memories that are preserved in these pages.

Like the bewitched children of Hamlin following the Piper's flute, let yourself be drawn into a sense of knowing this utopian surfer's cove. Escape into unique fantasy. Ponder over exciting and exotic passages. Let dreams haunt you as they haunt the heroes of Sunday Village.

Acknowledgments

Grateful acknowledgment is made to the following
whose interest and encouragement
was deeply appreciated:

Charles E. Weber, M.D.
Nancy Jean Smith
Pamela Jane Moitoza
Richard Scott Weber
Marjorie Zittau
James P. McGowan
Louis H. Gessay, M.D.
Judith Lynn Petty
Joyce Tullis
Nancy Sayeedi

Dedication

To My Husband

As these pages come to view,
I dedicate this book to you,
Wonder-doctor, physician-god,
Of whom the woman world is awed
Because your help made dreams come true
That would not be except for you,
For you made angel voices sigh,
And with your touch, begin to cry.

I stand in shadow til I dare
To do some work a fraction fair.
You watched me write this lasting song,
Through hours tedious and long,
And constant, loving vigil kept
While I often floundering stepped.
You stretched me when my reach was shy,
And answered when I wondered why.
You very often helped me see
When sometimes shadows blinded me.

Wonder-doctor, heaven blessed,
To you I dedicate my best.
My book is done, my very own
From the marrow of my bone.
May happiness surround you long
While fifty thousand read this song.

Contents

Chapter 1	*"..I will come to find you..."*	1
Chapter 2	*Flashback to the Day of the Shark*	11
Chapter 3	*"..some kind of international intrigue..."*	54
Chapter 4	*"..maybe a girl with red hair will marry me..."*	58
Chapter 5	*"..leave the surf clean for the seventy scene..."*	61
Chapter 6	*"..half-a-dream hamlet..."*	66
Chapter 7	*"..to be a bird when I come back to earth..."*	73
Chapter 8	*"..air was almost exhausted..."*	76
Chapter 9	*"..the pot-bellied statue...Hot Curl..."*	78
Chapter 10	*"..it might be Pandora...has amnesia..."*	82
Chapter 11	*"..metaphysics and ontology..."*	87
Chapter 12	*"..huddled against the body of his friend..."*	91
Chapter 13	*"..fog circled the tall evergreen..."*	98
Chapter 14	*"..she just materialized out of thin air..."*	102
Chapter 15	*"..telling me not to fall in love with him..."*	107
Chapter 16	*"..no horse's ass would go down on a day like this..."*	118
Chapter 17	*"..a broken bottle came flying through the air..."*	129
Chapter 18	*"..try not to get stuck in yesterday..."*	141
Chapter 19	*"..Rex sprang...nursing a bitten arm..."*	146
Chapter 20	*"..a time barrier broken..."*	149
Chapter 21	*"..no magic word for him..."*	158
Chapter 22	*"..communing in the fog with her ghost..."*	160
Chapter 23	*"..Vanessa's crying didn't come to him..."*	164
Chapter 24	*"..Riptide! Riptide!..."*	167
Chapter 25	*"..everyone who isn't a stereotype..."*	179
Chapter 26	*"..Poseidon rejoiced...despite the hordes of mortals..."*	181
Chapter 27	*"..the gallery heaved like a huge animal laboring..."*	187
Chapter 28	*"..everything turned to blackness and oblivion..."*	197
Chapter 29	*"..my pad is big enough for two..."*	207
Chapter 30	*"..stop hating one man...stop loving another..."*	213
Chapter 31	*"..the shark incident was a hoax..."*	221
Chapter 32	*"..go home and forget him..."*	225
Chapter 33	*"..throw the damn tie away..."*	228
Chapter 34	*"..she had been made a prisoner..."*	237
Chapter 35	*"..he reached for the scalpel..."*	242
Chapter 36	*"..Kelley is on the critical list..."*	253
Chapter 37	*"..the infant was barely alive..."*	260
Chapter 38	*"..it went out with bobby socks and swing..."*	264
Chapter 39	*"..dabble in the brook..."*	268
Chapter 40	*"..to hell with Gregor..."*	272
Chapter 41	*"..autonomic responses..."*	284
Chapter 42	*"..put a face on your dream..."*	290
Chapter 43	*"..a cap of diamonds for your Sunday Village..."*	310

Prologue

Imagine a point of land, serene and sunbathed, jutting into the ocean at the foot of a lofty hill, a Shangri-La guarded by the souls of the Sea Indians who haunted the crooked trunks of the tortured pines that grew over their sacred grounds.

When enchanted breezes passed, the Indian ghosts awoke and crept from their sepulcher trees to ponder whether the land would be pristine for them once again after men passed through.

However, if the Village disappears, those who loved it will be remembered because these pages will record their unique vision and exquisite passion, just as Camelot is remembered by the recording of its gladness and its despair.

Such memories would be lost if no document seals into history the tales of man's spoiling and his sadness and joys. If it were not for the telling, Atlantis would be an unknown place in a shallow sea, neither with a name. There would be no Eden, but just another green valley. Another lazy river would have met uncharted seas if people had not written of the romance of the Nile. There would be no land of the Amazons, no Bali Hai.

Neither will Sunday Village be remembered unless this story is spun because some day the Indian ghosts will claim their pristine ledge of land.

I

"...I will come to find you..."

With hurricane velocity, the storm flogged the village that nestled below the lonely hill. Buildings vibrated like bass drums as thunder roared through them. Sheets of rain flailed the roof of the old clubhouse where Gregor Morghann shouted into the telephone above the clatter of the onslaught.

"Chris, we can't find Pandora! Chris? Can you hear me? We can't find her anywhere. She must have left the Club and she's out somewhere in this hurricane. I've even searched some of the fairways. Can you hear me?" Gregor tried to suppress a deep cough that surfaced nevertheless.

The storm's growl blotted out part of the answer that came over the line. "...as soon as I can. Are you okay?"

"Hell, no, I'm not okay!" Gregor exploded. "I didn't get to eat one bite of my dinner because the committee practically carried me on stage and made me dance the soles off my damned shoes! You should have told me about that. All hell seems to have broken loose here and Pandora's out somewhere in this tornado! How could anyone be okay? I'm sick! Wouldn't you be?"

A streak of lightning blinded Gregor for a few seconds. He dropped the phone as thunder cracked like splintering wood. Pain shot through his ears and he clapped his hands over them. Cold sweat bathed his body. He backed away from the club manager who had entered at that moment and was tugging on Gregor's arm.

"That's Pandora's voice, Bob!" he shouted to the manager over the fury of the storm. "Can you hear it? It's coming from the hall. Pandora! It's about time! Pandora?" Gregor pulled away from the grip on his sleeve and almost fell over a chair as he stumbled to the hallway. "I can hear you," he screamed again. "Where are you?"

There was nobody there and he stared, aghast, at the empty corridor.

"Oh, my God!" he muttered as the frantic manager pulled him back into the lounge. More lightning flashed and Gregor watched, open-mouthed, as the carpet began to loosen and flutter. The building must be falling, Gregor thought. Get under something, he told himself. Get under something. A shrill sound shot through his eardrum as he dove under a table. The floor flew up to meet him. The roof opened. Instantly, he felt himself engulfed in water. Then everything faded.

The fatherly figure of Christopher Holliss and the manager were bending over him as consciousness returned. Gregor tried to lift his head. Furniture came into focus and he could see that the room was untouched. Nothing was out of place!

1

"What the devil—" he began. He raised up on one elbow. "Chris, what the hell happened?"

"Easy does it fella," Christopher said as he wiped some blood from Gregor's temple. "You got cut when you fell. Hold still while I get this bandage on. Bob says you tackled a table leg."

Gregor turned to the manager. "But—but the building was shaking! I thought the tornado hit us. You were pulling me, uh, pulling me to—"

"I was trying to get you to sit down, Mr. Morghann. You were white as a sheet. Just as the lightning struck, you crumpled to the floor and crashed into the leg of the table."

As memory of the scene returned, Gregor's features contorted. "Oh, my God!" He sat upright and pointed. "I heard Pandora calling me from the hall. Did you see her? Was she there?"

"Easy, easy." Christopher reached out to help him to his feet. "That's a nasty bump you got on your head. Here, Bob brought you some coffee. Drink it while it's hot."

"Chris, did you see her? Didn't anyone see her?"

"The whole place has been searched. She just isn't here," Christopher insisted with a shake of his head. "Here, try your coffee. You'll feel better."

However, Gregor scowled at the two men who were watching him anxiously. "Look, Chris, don't tell me that. I heard her voice as clear as if she stood in this room."

Throwing Bob an uneasy glance, Christopher repeated, "Every inch of the place has been searched. There was not anyone in the hall, Gregor. You didn't see anyone, did you?"

As he arose unsteadily, Gregor shook his head. "Dammit-to-hell, how could I hear her calling if she wasn't there? I heard her. I swear it!" His fist struck the table. The coffee cup rattled.

"Hmm. Well, uh—" Christopher scratched his graying temple. "Well, tell me, didn't the doctor say that you might have trouble with that eardrum you ruptured on that deep dive? Could it be playing tricks on you? Now, now, don't get upset. Just think about it for a minute. Is it possible?"

Gregor flinched and was silent. He stroked his sunbleached hair, sighed, then faced his friends. "No way. No way! I couldn't make a mistake like that. She screamed my name." Stepping to the window, he stared out at the fine drizzle left by the passing storm.

Nervously, Christopher buttoned and unbuttoned his sweater as he joined Gregor at the window. His usual tie was missing. His square chin seemed broader as he pressed his lips together tensely. "Come on, drink your coffee and I'll drive you home."

"Chris, I can't do that. I've got to figure out where she is," Gregor insisted.

"Well, how far could she go? How much time has gone by? About what time did you leave her alone?"

"I left her alone at the table for about twenty minutes. She was gone when the stage contest was over. Only twenty minutes!"

"It was more like forty minutes," the manager interrupted.

"Well," Christopher deliberated, "there's no point in staying here. The place is closed. Pandora must have driven home with someone. She's done this before, remember?" He turned to Bob. "We'll leave Gregor's car here."

2

"Better park it close in by the light, Mr. Holliss."

Hand in pocket searching for his key, Gregor's brows lifted suddenly "Uh? Oh! Pandora put the key in her purse. Dammit!"

"Well, okay, I'll just make sure that your car is locked up." Christopher held up his hand. "No, no, you stay here, lad, and finish your coffee."

Left alone, Gregor drained his cup and paced the floor muttering, "Little minx! It's time she got over these tantrums. She's worse than a kid. When I find her this time, I'll put her over my knee and spank her really good. What a hell of a thing to do to me!"

In a few minutes, Christopher returned. "She took your car," he announced sourly. "I phoned Vanessa and she's going to call around. We'll go over to Pandora's place right now. Let's not panic. I guarantee that she'll turn up in the morning."

"But, uh, don't you think we'd better—" Gregor hesitated and bit his lip.

"Call the police?" Christopher shook his head. "No. No real reason to call them. You know what they'd say? Your girl left the party because she was angry with you. That's about the size of it, isn't it? Come on, let's go."

Again, Gregor hesitated. "But, she was out in that downpour and that lightning, Chris. I called her place. She's just not there."

"She just isn't answering her phone. We'll go over there to check."

"But, Chris, isn't it strange that—"

"Well, it would be if she hadn't done this before," Christopher interrupted. "Come on. We'd better go. The fog is getting thicker than soup."

They had barely stepped through the door when the checkgirl rushed after them.

"Mr. Morghann! Mr. Morghann! Your lady's wrap! I wouldn't leave it here. Looks to me that it's embroidered with real pearls and gems." The girl held up a delicate shawl of gossamer fabric encrusted at the edges with tiny jewels. "It doesn't look like just a costume that people would wear to a luau."

"It isn't," Gregor replied as he retrieved the shawl. "It's a gift from some wealthy sheik. She has clothes from all over the world."

The girl's eyes lit up. "I know. I've seen some of them."

Gregor surveyed the girl curiously. "How did you know my name?"

"I saw you at the Beach Club dance last week and at the Surf Club picnic."

"You have a good memory. Would you remember if the lady left some time tonight?"

"She didn't come past me, Mr. Morghann."

"You're sure you'd see her if she had?"

"Oh my, yes! I couldn't miss her. She was the prettiest lady here tonight. I couldn't forget her or you, either." She looked away, slightly embarrassed. "I mean lots of people are hard to remember the minute they are out of sight."

She was right. *Nobody ever forgot Gregor.* Always, the image of him haunted the beholder's afterthought. It was not because he was tall and incredibly handsome. It could have been because of the calm strength in his features or their rare symmetry, or even the combination of his olive skin and his color-free hair. Even more likely, it was the perturbing beckoning in his eyes. They were gray and seemed to have no pupil because the inner perimeter of the iris melted into a vortex that left the onlooker with a feeling of seeing deep into a tunnel. Then came the sensation of being trapped, the strange desire to remain captive coupled with the struggle to break away. Women often confessed to having a moment of giddiness when Gregor left their presence, followed by the feeling of searching for a fleeting remnant of a sweet dream. It was true. *Nobody ever forgot Gregor.*

"I'll get my car, lad," Christopher said. "You stay here. No point in both of us getting wet."

After driving to Pandora's apartment only to find it empty, Christopher suggested a plan. "Let's reconstruct the whole evening from the beginning. Remember how we used to do this when you were a kid? Like the time I gave you twenty dollars to get a car part for me in the Village?"

"Yeah, and I stopped to do some diving with the gang and forgot which rock I hid my wallet under."

"Well, we found it by re-tracing every step. We'll do it again. Maybe something will surface. Start with the telephone call."

With a sigh, Gregor began. "Funny thing, Chris. The last place we expected to be tonight was the luau at the Club. We were going to stay in tonight. Pandora was waiting for a call from the war zone."

"Did she tell you she was waiting for a call?"

"Not in so many words, Chris. You know how I read her mind sometimes."

"Yes, I know. The extrasensory exchange that the two of you have. I know."

"Then you called. Vanessa had a headache. I explained to Pandora that you couldn't leave her and that someone had to take your place at the party to see that the changes in the show came off right."

"Bob said it went off fine. Thanks, lad. I'm sorry that the evening had to end so badly for you. Go on."

"Well, Pandora got this island beach costume together for me." Gregor fingered the hopsack pants, cut off and shredded at the knees. He loosened the sash that bound his beachcomber's shirt around his middle. The woven hat that he had worn so rakishly earlier had been discarded. "We didn't have much time, so she just threw on one of her sari outfits. She did her hair up like a genie from Aladdin's magic lamp and ..." He sucked in air and exhaled suddenly. "...and, God, she was beautiful, Chris! Everyone stared when we came in."

"She has a rare beauty, no doubt about that. I'm sorry I called so late."

"Well, when we finally got there, I told her to go in to check out our table number while I parked."

"But we had valet parking."

"Oh, I like to park my Porsche myself because it has such a touchy clutch. Anyway, Kamehameha held the door open for her but she didn't go in."

"Who?"

"Al, the old waiter, was the doorman dressed like King Kamehameha. Pandora stood talking to him and watching me while I parked. Could she have planned to take my car, Chris?"

"Could be. Could be. Then what?"

"I came in and saw her talking to a man at the top of the stairs. He left as soon as he saw me. I just grabbed Pandora and hurried to our table. Everyone was finished with the main course."

"Was the whole committee there?"

"Uh-huh. Everybody showed. Browns, Mignon, Dolly, even J. T. and the

4

Captain. Your committee did a great job. They got that catamaran into the pool, filled it with flowers and even had a girl in it singing Hawaiian songs. But that statue! Who found that weird carved tiki god on the stage?"

Christopher shrugged. "Someone unearthed it in his attic. The luau is our best party and we go all out for it. We've never missed one."

"Vanessa talked about it a lot."

"Too bad Vanessa was sick. I think it was the heat. The weather report said it was the hottest Saturday that Sunday Village has had in thirty years."

"And that tornado we had tonight! That's one I'll never forget."

Nor would Gregor ever forget that night of the luau in Sunday Village in 1961. If Vanessa had not been ill, Gregor's life might have been different, but maybe destiny had already laid out a special plan for him and had used any device to implement that plan. Tonight, that device was Vanessa's illness.

Gregor went on to say that he had taken two bites from his plate when he was called to the stage to take his part in the program. When that ended, he hurried back only to find Pandora gone from his table. His search for her began leisurely and ended in a panic as the deluge began.

"I've never seen a storm like that come up so unexpectedly," Gregor said. "The whole place was a shambles in five minutes."

The evening had indeed ended in chaos. Costumed guests had scurried for cover. Tables had toppled into the pool. Chairs and dishes were scattered over the fairway. Cars were blown against the retaining wall of the steep exit.

The scourging gale had descended like a living thing bent on destroying the town, bringing with it a fire flinging dragon spitting forked flame as it scrambled to scale the hill. Only the carved mahogany deity with the derisive smile remained standing on the bare stage, perhaps exulting over the party's tumultuous conclusion.

"Funny thing—there wasn't even a storm predicted," Gregor added. The place looks like it might qualify for federal disaster relief."

"By the time I got there, the waiters were trying to recover evening wraps and purses. Could Pandora have left her purse at the table?"

"Not a chance. She carries some little computer gadget in it that she won't let out of her sight."

"Curious. Anything to do with her, uh—her science, whatever she calls it?"

"She calls it Xionflight. I don't know exactly what the gadget is. She tells me it's a calculator, but it could well be a receiver of some sort. I don't pry."

"Is she doing much with her science any more?"

"Yeah, some," Gregor answered. "Why do you ask? Do you think it might have something to do with tonight?"

"You'll have to answer that." Christopher shook his head. "She's like something out of the space age, if I do say so myself. And you aren't exactly the ordinary person yourself, lad, with all your unusual pursuits."

Gregor sighed thoughtfully. Given free choice, he would have wanted to be like most any other man. He would not have chosen, if he had been able, to be the descendant of a Nilotic wizard, nor the spawn of a Poseidon-like water god, nor the bewitched progeny of one who came from a frozen outer emerald sphere a hundred millenia ago.

He would have reasoned that his birthright owed him the same potential as any other Earth-born man with the same bodily passions, the same mental prowess and physical limitations. He preferred to believe that this was so and he shelved any thought to the contrary, particularly on this August night in the quaint coastal community called Sunday Village.

In the morning, after a brief fitful sleep, Gregor began his search again with the help of the Holliss family. Vanessa manned the telephone. The Holliss girls, Kelley and Karla, combed the local beaches that Pandora frequented. Their older brother, David, checked all the places that Gregor had listed. Christopher questioned all the waiters and the parking attendants who had worked at the Club the night before. By noon, neither Pandora nor the car had been found. The next day passed in much the same way. Nevertheless, at Gregor's apartment, it was decided that it was premature to file a missing person report. Afterward, as Christopher poured coffee at the bar, Gregor heaved a deep sigh and his shoulders sagged. The jangle of the telephone jolted him upright. Vanessa's soft voice drifted over the line. He let his body go limp again as he listened.

"Hello? Hello? Are you there Gregor?"

"Just dead tired, Vanessa. Is there anything new? Anything?"

"We've checked every lead. There isn't anything. Is Chris still with you?"

"Yeah, he's still here."

"Dinner is about done. You probably haven't had a good meal all day."

"Chris is starving, no doubt, but I don't have much of an appetite."

Vanessa's voice chided him. "You shouldn't go much longer without food."

"Yes, I know, but this thing has me so riled that I could...I could vomit!" Gregor wiped the sweat from his brow.

"If she wasn't in the habit of doing things like this, there'd be more to worry about."

"Yeah, I know Vanessa, but I could crawl up a wall every time she does this. This time, there's gotta be a reason—something!"

"Did Pandora say anything to you about...?"

"About what, Vanessa?"

"...about going to Vietnam?"

Gregor leaned forward, suddenly alert. "Did you say Vietnam?"

"Yes, Greg. She spoke of it that day you were in Mexico, that day she gave her talk on the campus, remember?"

"But you're sure she said Vietnam?" Gregor asked tensely.

"Yes, Gregor, she did. She talked at length about her visit to South America and she said she wanted to go into the war zone."

"Damn it all to hell!" Gregor drummed impatient fingers on the bar. "She promised me she would stop running around the globe! Now it's Vietnam!"

There was another pause. "I know it's upsetting."

"Upsetting? Good God, yes! Why didn't someone tell me sooner?"

"We didn't take her seriously, I guess, or we would have mentioned it."

"Okay, okay. I want to know everything she said, Vanessa, line by line."

"Chris was there. He'll remember better than I will. Better ask him."

With a sigh, Gregor thanked Vanessa and slowly replaced the telephone. Absentmindedly, he drew his index finger over a faint scar on his right jaw. The white mark was a reminder of the time many years ago when his spear gun had become entangled in a kelp bed. When Gregor was ill at ease, he had the habit of drawing his hand over the scar almost as though he sought comfort in its being there. However, he was not ill at ease often. He had mastered a complacency that was almost a detachment in the face of stress. This calm in his nature was regarded by his friends as an enviable secret inner strength.

Today, his calm was gone. Worry darkened his features with a heavy frown as he turned to question Christopher.

"What's this about Pandora's going to Vietnam, Chris?"

"They need interpreters. She said she might have a job there."

"I wish she had told me." Gregor ran nervous fingers through his unkempt hair.

Christopher's shaggy brows arched. "She told us that she had. H'm. She also said that someone in India asked her to translate a book for him. She was going to ask you about that."

"No way! No way! She knows damn well I wouldn't let her go."

There was a pause. Finally, Christopher shook his head. "It doesn't make any sense. None of those reasons explain why Pandora would run off in the middle of a rainstorm with your car. It's absurd."

"You don't know her, Chris. I do, but I still don't understand her. Just when I give up hope of making her settle down, she comes back from one of her jaunts around the world, devil knows where, and again she agrees to quit traveling. She promises. We make plans. Hell's fire, Chris, I don't know what to think! I agree with you. There's no reason for her to run off. Yes, it's absurd. Did she say anything else?"

Christopher stared at the ceiling in thought. "Oh yes! I heard her talking to Kelley about some kid at the University who caught her car with his bumper. I was reading my paper. Wasn't really listening."

"She didn't tell me about that either!" Gregor banged his fist on the bar top.

"Better ask Kelly about it." Christopher reached for the pack of cigarettes on the bar, changed his mind and took up his pipe instead. He chewed on it, unlit, while he concentrated on the man seated before him. His strong jaw made a toy of the heavy Kaywoodie. "I figure she would have said more if it had been important." He sighed as he tightened the Windsor knot in his tie and put on his gray suit coat.

Gregor arose, paced the room, then sprawled full length on the sofa. "Man, am I tired!" he said, rubbing his eyes. "Look, Chris, call the phone company tomorrow again, will you? They should know whether that call to Pandora came from India." He yawned loudly. "I'm gonna drive to L.A. tonight."

"Sure thing, I'll call first thing in the morning. Do you think you'll feel up to driving that far tonight?"

"Yeah, after I grab a couple hours of sleep. Cripes, I feel like I've been run over by a Mack truck, I'm so tired. But I'm going tonight. Bill is helping me to do some checking up there. You know how to reach me. I'll be back in a day or so."

"Do you need our car?"

Gregor's answer came as a bare murmur. "Thanks anyway, but I have a key to Pandora's car."

Heavy lashes had closed over deepset eyes and lay softly on his flushed cheek. His nostrils quivered at the tip of a finely chiseled nose. The stress of the day was forgotten and his handsome features were tranquil once again.

Christopher stared for a moment more at the shock of flaxen hair, observing how it deepened at the temples to meet the olive of his skin. Then he sighed, bent over to remove Gregor's shoes and quietly left him sleeping.

It was difficult to say when the day had begun, for who can define the moments of dawn? However, it was without a doubt a moment just when the sun climbed high in the eastern sky to clear Mt. Soledad and to thrust a splinter of light into the sea's depth. A hush seemed to fall over the water as a sunbeam danced on the rim of the hill. The waves seemed to poise in anticipation. Then the rays of light met the crest and the sea hesitated no longer. It crashed itself upon the sand with added tumult over the birth of another morning. As though it were self-willed, with an identify of its own, the white water augmented its own song for the day.

Gregor stood watching the ocean from the porch of his small apartment. He swam every morning about this time. The surf was rough this morning, but a rough surf or a choppy swell discouraged him very little, nor did the many riptides, for there was frequently an outgoing rip current from the bay.

Gregor knew the wiles of this stretch of ocean. He had been born in the Village and the ocean had been his playground since he could swim. Never had the water outwitted him, although there was to be one time in question. It was to be a time when, of his own free choice, he would succumb to the riptide with a wish to stay forever in the sea. Some other man might drown, but not Gregor. The sea was to spit him out, hissing, "Do not soil my depth with your tears and sorrow. Your solace is not written in my duty because my purpose is ageless and my comfort is for eternity, not for you alone." A wave was to seize his body and carry it high until it was thrown on the beach.

Today, Gregor didn't think of swimming. He locked his door, made his way to Pandora's car and started toward the highway.

It didn't occur to him to stop at his grandfather's old farm until the cutoff appeared. He veered into it, crossed the little bridge, and eased his car eastward down the rough dirt road. When he came to the gate of an old ranch house, he stopped. All was still in the yard except for the soft neighing of horses in the corral and for the song of the birds. Gregor noticed that the trees had grown tall almost hiding the barn and the hothouse from view. From the thick branch of one tree, the swing that his grandfather had made for him still hung, limp and lonely. Through the shrubs, he caught a glimpse of the fountain in the garden. The statue of the young boy was still there, commanding the dolphins at his feet. He remembered the idle times when he pretended that he was the boy standing in the splash of water, commanding the mammals to obey him. He remembered the feeling that they responded to his will. Then he commanded the animals in the yards and found that they were prisoners to his whim. To a degree that was frightening to his grandfather, Gregor had the same sway over his small friends. He remembered overhearing his grandfather talking to Christopher Holliss.

"Chris," Grandfather Jonathan had pondered, "what shall I do with that blue stone on the chain? Vanessa said that Gig used to fall asleep with it when you were raising him."

"Oh, yeah, I remember it used to have him completely mesmerized. Put him to sleep like a charm! Much better than a security blanket," Christopher answered.

"Did you ever decide what the inscriptions meant?" Grandfather asked.

"No, not really," Christopher said. "Van always thought they were sacred designations. *Chi* is found as a god-reference in some old cultures. *Re* is an Egyptian deity. *Myah* could be a form of *Mary.*"

"Hmm," Grandfather continued to muse. "Curious, to say the least."

"Van meant to have the stone appraised, but she never got around to it. Why don't you have it done and stick it in a safe somewhere, if it's worth anything, until he's grown up." There was a pause. "This place is the greatest thing for a growing boy. He is very happy with you."

"Chris," his grandfather had said, "he puzzles me. He seems to have some exceptional talent. I swear that he had the Brogan boy hypnotized the other day."

Christopher had only laughed. "Kids play with a lot of imagination. Probably just pretending."

"No, Chris. No. It seems to be more than that. He really has some exceptional ability. Didn't you notice it during the years you and Vanessa had him?"

"He was just a baby then, but very bright, I'll agree."

"I'm wondering whether we should encourage his talents."

"Hmmm. Have you had him tested?"

"Not especially. Just the regular thing at school. His teacher wants to advance him a grade. Now just listen to this, Chris. She says that—" Grandfather continued in a lowered tone that drifted off.

"Are you considering it?" Christopher's voice came finally after a few minutes.

There was a pause while Gregor's grandfather deliberated. "Do you know what I want for him, Chris? I want him to be a normal, fun-loving kid, and not some misfit genius. I want him to be happy."

"He is," Christopher answered. "He is the best diver in his crowd, the best fisherman, and he knows the ocean better than the streets of the Village. His friends like him, he is popular with everyone he meets, and one can't ask for more. You are raising one hell of a nice kid." Their conversation shifted to other subjects.

One hell of a nice kid. One hell of a nice kid...nice kid....

These were the words that stayed with Gregor and did much to add to his feeling of worth. He trusted his capabilities all the more. He felt secure about himself with one exception. He experienced times of inward confusion when repeated questions about his parents remained unanswered, and he finally realized it was not to be discussed. Any serious doubts about himself were warded off to a subconscious level. Then he compensated until he displayed a degree of outward poise and stature beyond his years.

At this moment, as Gregor stared at the old house in the early morning light, he visualized his grandfather's tall figure crossing the court toward the small hothouse where he grew his roses, his heliotrope and rare herbs.

Just then, a light appeared in the farmhouse window. Someone peered out at him. Gregor guided his car quickly out of the circular driveway and back to the highway.

Traffic was light at this early hour and the monotony of the drive allowed Gregor's thoughts to drift repeatedly to the first memories he had of Pandora. They had met two summers ago on a day similar to this day and it was almost as though time had reversed itself. Submerged in thought, Gregor began to relive those two years from the very first day.

II

Flashback to the Day of the Shark

t had all begun with a drive like this one to Los Angeles. How well he remembered the trip that day two summers ago! He and his partner, Roy McClouder, had just finished filming a sunken treasure ship. The film was made into a travelogue. A commentary had been added which was translated into several languages by a Greek interpreter whose name was Lion. On that morning, the film was to be previewed. Despite the haze that hung over the city, the air was invigorating and the traffic noise was music. His step was light as he left the car and made his way to the lobby of a tall building. The elevators were on the far side of a court where a giant fountain of water rose and fell, whispering as it splashed over statues of humans and mammals cavorting in the sunsoaked foam. Through the spray, Gregor thought he saw the form of a young woman, or was it a statue? He stopped and stared.

A heavy braid of pale hair crowned her head. Even from where he stood, Gregor could see a round, almost childlike face that was dominated by over-large, dark eyes. Her sensuous lips appeared to be pouting. Folds of white gown draped her petite figure. It was as though one of the nymphs from the fountain had come to life.

She did not appear to be looking casually across the court. Gregor felt that her gaze was directed at him like some kind of sonar-sent beam that penetrated and pinned him. He faltered for a minute. His pulse quickened. His vision blurred. He had the feeling that the dolphins in the pool were from his grandfather's fountain; that they were cowering in obeisance, not to him this time, but to the woman on the other side of the pond.

Gregor rubbed his eyes and blinked. The sound of the elevator echoed in the courtyard. The waiting crowd congealed around the open doors which swallowed them together with the figure in white.

With giant steps, Gregor circled the fountain, but the elevator doors closed. A faint trace of heliotrope hung on the air. He scaled the steps of the nearby stairwell several at a time in an effort to overtake his enchantress. Four flights later he swore softly and gave up the chase. Tired from his exertion, he went to the penthouse conference rooms where his partner, Roy, towered over people jamming the entry.

Roy was elated. His flaming mustache twitched as he talked excitedly.

"Wait till you hear the commentary, Gig! Man alive! This one really turned out to be a winner! Could have used that extra footage after all even though it was a bit blurred. We shouldn't have edited so much. Oh, man! I'm ready to do another one like this tomorrow. Come on." He squinted and stared. "You aren't listening to me, Gig. Say, have you been running?"

"Just ran up four flights of stairs," Gregor answered.

Roy lifted one eyebrow. "What's wrong? Don't ya like elevators? Well, come on. The rolls and coffee are over there." He pointed across the room. "You're not all that late, just twenty-five minutes."

It was then that the faint scent of heliotrope drifted to him as he came face to face with the beautiful woman whose head was crowned with a braid of gold and whose expression was that of a wistful child. Their eyes met and held each other in speechless rhetoric. Neither of them really heard Roy as he began an introduction. "On this great occasion, allow me to—" The stupefied expression on his friend's face made him pause.

"Gregor, are you listening to me?" Roy said for the second time. "Miss Lion is our commentator and the interpreter for the foreign version. Her style really fits the film." He paused, looking from one to the other and waited for a response. None came. "Pandora, Gregor and I have been partners for five years." He hesitated and squinted again. Then he placed his hands on his hips as he added, "Ah-hah! You don't have to tell me. You two have met before."

Pandora was the center of attention but Gregor hardly left her side. In the course of their conversation he found that she had an assignment to interpret for a foreign dignitary visiting San Diego. Her plane reservation was for the following morning.

"Drive down with me!" Gregor begged. "It is just a two hour trip down the coast, beautiful once you get out of heavy traffic. At Newport, the Pacific Highway runs along the ocean, and we can drive with the top down, if you like. Cancel your reservation right now. Here is a phone." He watched the wistful expression on her face as he groped for the instrument.

"You will have to go out of your way? I will accept only if it is on your way." Her voice betrayed a faint, provocative accent.

Gregor felt a strange strength course through his frame. In his mind's eye, a painting on the wall melted, then dripped and congealed again in violent colors. The ocean floor suddenly drained dry and covered itself with blooming trees. A star spun in descending spirals and became a disc playing a symphony.

A search for the telephone book served to hide the tremor that passed through his body. "No, no, it isn't out of my way," he insisted. "My place is only ten minutes from San Diego. Which airline has your reservation? I'll make the call."

Pandora was deep in conversation when Gregor finished.

"...and the second time I went to China," she was saying, "I took my twin sister with me so that she—"

"Holy smoke!" someone interrupted. "She's got a twin sister!" Listeners continued to comment. "Wow! Two of them, yet!" "Hey, does she look like you?" "Does she ever come to California?"

"But, no," Pandora answered with a saucy toss of her head. "She is in Russia now, dancing with the ballet. You shall have to be satisfied with me."

Roy leaned forward. "I'm satisfied," he sang out. "Oh, man, am I satisfied! I have tickets to the ballet and the symphony, Pandora. You'll come with me?"

"Aw, come on, Roy, when did you ever go to the ballet?" someone mocked. Another snickered, "Or to the symphony?"

Pandora laughed softly. "Thank you, Roy, but I must meet an Indonesian ambassador in San Diego tomorrow. Gregor has offered to drive me there."

An expression of disappointment passed through the crowd. "Aw, nobody has a chance when Jeedge is around," complained the man seated next to Pandora. He arose and wandered off. Roy promptly put his foot on the edge of the empty chair to keep Gregor from sitting down. He propped his elbow on his uplifted knee and stood towering over the crowd, enjoying his vantage point and Gregor's discomfort. Roy enjoyed attention, not that he didn't get it because his language was loud and colorful. He wore expensive Western clothes. His wiry hair was as bright as his flaming mustache. When he grinned, he favored one side of his mouth.

"Don't let Gig bore you with all that talk about his experiments, Pandora," Roy said. "He'll talk about it all the way down the coast."

Smiling, Pandora looked from one to the other. "Everyone seems to call Gregor by a different name. You called him Gig."

"That's the way he spells it! Suits him fine, too. A gig is a kind of wagon drawn by horses. He is kind of a drag when he gets to talking about the alpha waves."

Although Gregor generally took Roy's put downs lightly, today he was annoyed. "A gig is a type of fishing spear," he said calmly. "My grandfather had one."

Roy ignored him and kept talking to Pandora. "Say, did I tell you about my next project? I'm going to do a film on shark feeding. Take my word for it, that takes a lot of guts! In order to—" Roy removed his foot from the chair, intending to sit beside Pandora.

Gregor timed his kick to the second. The chair shot out from under Roy who went sprawling to the floor. Quickly, Gregor took Pandora's hand.

"Come on, let's get away from this macho character." He guided her toward the band. "Good music. Wanna dance awhile?"

She shook her head. "I broke my leg recently."

"Okay, okay, you probably won't enjoy just watching. Why don't we go out on the balcony? It's cooler there."

"I'm glad you understand." She appeared relieved. "I hope Roy is not angry. He fell so hard and I see he is limping a little."

"Oh, cripes, don't worry about him! Roy is absolutely indestructible. He's tough and mean. Unpredictable. Rough taskmaster. And he doesn't watch his language. You wanna stay away from him. He's good to dive with, though. Working underwater, you gotta be tough. His discipline pays off when we are down there on the sea floor. I respect him for that and we work well together. He lets me do most of the camera work."

"The shots you took of the old ship are spectacular."

"I work with a Nikonos. It's the only kind for the type of underwater shots that we're doing right now. Roy says there's a new model coming out. Right now, we have to make our own housing out of plastic sheeting and it doesn't withstand the pressure of deep dives. No matter how you make them, they explode under pressure."

"The ship in your film was not in deep water?"

"Not really. As you could see in the film, it was on a nice flat shelf with a southern exposure which gave us lots of light. We had a ball doing this assignment. Do you know what our worst problem was? Big fish getting in the way of the camera."

Huge, inquisitive fish wanting to check us out, not the least bit afraid of us after awhile. Let me tell you more about this one in particular, the one that you noted in your commentary. On the first day, this great big grouper came from....''

When Gregor finished he grinned and said, "Now, let's talk about you."

"Not now, later," she answered. "I want to hear about the alpha waves that Roy said would bore me. I don't think it will. Please tell me what it is."

"Oh," Gregor said with a shrug. "He was referring to some research in optic conditioning that a friend of mine does. That's all. By the way, I like that super ending you put on the commentary. Gave it real class."

Again, with a saucy twist of her head, she said, "Optic conditioning? *Qu' est-ce que c'est?* What is that? I never heard of it."

Matter-of-factly, Gregor answered her, "Oh, well, you wouldn't have if your major was languages."

Pandora sobered. "I majored in physics, phenomenology, astronomy and ontology. Languages come to me naturally. I speak twelve languages fluently." To prove her point, she repeated *I like you* in several tongues, but she stopped in a moment and stared at Gregor.

Suddenly, he found himself studying every line of her face as though she had just come into focus. For Gregor, the moment never passed. It became a vacuum in time as though some imperfection in a cosmic force permitted him to slip freely forward or backward in time. He felt lightheaded and Pandora's voice seemed far away as she continued hesitatingly. *"Paracerce a usted. R'wyn dy garu di. Vous me plaisez."* Finally she stopped. "You aren't listening, Gig. You're thinking of something else. More alpha waves?"

"Maybe," Gregor answered with a grin.

"Bien, bien!" Pandora said spreading her palms wide. "Perhaps if you told me about this, it could be my thirteenth language, because I suspect that it is a method of communication. Am I not right?"

"You're close. It's kind of complicated. Right now I'd rather talk about you," Gregor said.

Pandora persisted. "I am quite curious. Please tell me about it."

Gregor stretched his arms, delaying his response as he remembered how Roy had warned Pandora. "Well," he began. "Well, okay. You were correct. Communication does play a part, but not in the ordinary sense. In a nutshell, alpha waves are brain waves that are produced, harnessed and channeled in a way to produce changes within the body. The scientists I work with call it optic conditioning. They have developed ways to measure electrical activity in the brain and they can train subjects to produce waves of a certain length in order to alter some function." He paused and waited. "Are you with me or have I lost you?"

"C'est fascinant! Je voudrais en savoir davantage." Then, bobbing her head from side to side, she continued apologetically. "When I am excited, I forget my English and speak in French. All this fascinates me. I must know more. Why does Roy say this is dull? It is not boring."

"Oh, I suspect because he's heard me talking about it so much."

"He mentioned alpha waves. Are there more?"

"Yes, several, and then there are combinations. However, alpha waves are present when you feel contentment or pleasure or elation." Gregor grinned roguishly.

14

"Now, tell me all about yourself."

"*Non! Non!*" She stamped her small foot. "I want to hear more."

"Tomorrow," Gregor promised. He leaned forward, his elbow on the balcony rail. "Do you like the view of the city from here?"

"Cities!" she said with a sigh. "Cities were never meant to be." She leaned on the rail and stared out over the scene.

Gregor didn't know what to say. He cleared his throat and watched the evening lights reflect on her thick braid of gold hair. The impulse to reach out to touch it as a child would reach to touch a new doll passed. He thrust his hands into his pockets, cleared his throat again and waited for her to continue.

"You seem to have three names. Which shall I call you? The masculine of Gigi?"

He shook his head. "Not if you give it that much French flavor!"

"You do not like the name Gregor?"

"Oh, yeah, I like it fine! It was my grandfather who thought it was, to quote him, 'Too proud a name for a small boy'. He preferred the name I gave myself."

"Then I shall also." She whispered his name softly.

Man, oh man, Gregor thought, how I'd love to hear that—day and night—for the rest of my life.

"I wonder," Pandora continued, "just what your grandfather would call me if my name had—ahh..." The pouting lower lip broke into a slow smile. "...too much weight."

Gregor scratched his temple. "Well, my grandfather was a romanticist. He thought all beautiful women were rightly queens. He probably would have called you Princess."

"How delightful! I like that." She clapped her hands together.

"Maybe I will, too, in that case."

The noise inside had grown louder. Roy's angular form appeared in the doorway. "The food is out of this world," he announced. "Filet mignon. Baked russets. Caesar salad." He looked from one to the other waiting for a response. "How about Dutch apple pie? Say, you aren't talking about those feedback experiments, are you? Pandora, I warned you! Why don't you come inside with me? All the action is in here." Roy hesitated. "It's a party, Gig," he reminded. "The hard work is over. For Pete's sake, relax!" He grinned his lopsided smile and motioned for them to come.

Gregor nodded and they followed Roy through the crowd.

The next day they started later than they had intended. It was about noon when Pandora found a map in the dash of the car and began to study it. Finally she said, "I can't find your Village anywhere on the map. You said it was within ten minutes of San Diego, Gig. Is it, then, south of the city?"

Gregor laughed. "It has a funny Spanish name, actually spelled one way and pronounced another. It gives some people such a hard time to get it right that it has become equally well known as Sunday Village."

"Sunday Village," Pandora repeated. "Now why do you call it that?"

Gregor thought for a few minutes. "Well," he said. "You know how everyone enjoys a beautiful, bright Sunday?"

"Yes."

"And there are only fifty-two of them in a year," Gregor added.

She nodded her head. "Of course."

"Well, we have three hundred of them here," Gregor said.

"A village of three hundred Sundays!" Pandora exclaimed. "How charming! But what of the other sixty-five days?"

"Then we have fog," Gregor answered. "Now hold up that map so I can show you where it is."

"This tiny point of land? I see it now," she said. "Yes, it is an odd name. It makes no sense to me. What does the name mean?"

"No one is certain. Some people say it means diamond pirates because there is a cave in a cliff with a funnel-like hole that was used long ago by pirates and smugglers."

Pandora's eyes grew wider. "Pirates and smugglers? How exciting!"

"The tubular opening is still there. There is a curio shop at the top, and you can walk down some steps to the cave at the ocean level," Gregor explained.

"I should like to see it, considering that the Village is named for it."

"Well, some of the Villagers don't agree about the meaning of the name. There are some who think the name means *cap of diamonds* or something close to that."

"It's probably better than to call the place after a nest of jewel thieves." She studied the map again. "How large is the Village?"

"Strangely, it doesn't have any clearly defined boundaries."

"Then how does one know when he is there?" Pandora asked.

Gregor chuckled. "Well, let's put it this way. Imagine yourself going to Mars or some new planet. Okay? Now suppose that being in the gravitational pull of the new planet brought about some change of feeling, like lightheadedness or goose bumps."

Pandora's eyebrows raised slightly like those of a confused child as she interrupted him. "Gooz boomps," she repeated with a touch of pleasing accent. "What are gooz boomps, *mon ami?*"

This time, Gregor laughed outright. "Goose bumps," he repeated. "Your skin tingles. Okay?"

"Okay," she replied. "I will feel lightheaded and have goose bumps!" she said proudly.

"That, and a slightly accelerated pulse, and then you will know that you are in the Village!" Gregor explained. "It is a very individual experience."

Pandora pondered over this for a moment. "You make it sound like a *charmante* place," she said softly. "I lived in such a place in Greece when I was a small girl. It looked out over the sea."

"My Village does, too. It seems to me sometimes like a huge shelf of rock that hangs out over the water. There is only one place where the water comes in over a shallow ocean floor. There is a nice beach and a pretty bay with only one bad pocket in it that sometimes fills with a heavy backwash. I can chart the pattern of the riptide."

She tilted her head and eyed him curiously. "You speak as though you know every mile of the ocean floor!"

"You bet I do! I know every valley and fault better than I know how to get from the market to the barber shop," Gregor said with a smug grin. "Sometimes

16

I feel that I know the fish better than I do people," he added with a short laugh. "Sometimes I like them better, too!"

Deep in thought, she appraised him for a brief moment. "You have clefts in your chin when you laugh like that," she said. Then, afraid that she might have embarrassed him, she added quickly, "Yes, yes, we can learn much from the nature of God's wild creatures. They can speak to us if only we listen."

The words flung themselves at Gregor like shots from a pistol and echoed in his brain...if only we listen...if only we listen...she knows the secret of co-existence...few people do or they wouldn't shoot dolphins any more than they would shoot surfers...she understands...what is there about her...she can read my mind...I get this strange feeling....

Gregor looked in her direction and stared as long as he dared to keep his eyes from the road. The dark eyes under the braid of gold blinked at him and blinked again. The provocative lips that seemed to be pouting suddenly parted as she smiled at him. His throat froze when he tried to swallow. He turned his attention to the road again. A flurry of thoughts continued to flood his mind.

Half a minute passed before she spoke again. "Are you going to tell me more about the brain waves?"

"Well," Gregor began, "we're getting close to the Village. Not really enough time to start a serious discussion." Then, noticing that she was patting her damp forehead, he added, "We'll be driving along the ocean soon. It'll be cooler. This wind today is a desert wind."

"Then it is not always like this?" she asked. "A desert wind, you say?"

"We call it a Santa Ana because it comes through the pass from that direction. Very nice when it comes in October and November."

"It is good to know the weather so that one packs the proper clothes," Pandora said. "I must tell you about the one time I went to India in the—"

High above them, a small, solitary cloud traveled in much the same direction, appearing as insignificant from below as the small convertible must have appeared from high up, a spot of lapis lazuli dashing broadside of the foaming water ridges, down a long slope, up a tedious hill and past tortured pine trees to a fork in the road.

It was an unassuming fork in the unpretentious, so-called highway of two badly paved lanes. A tacky, small gas station appeared. The road dipped and followed a gorge downward toward sea level. Gregor had already pulled his tie off and loosened his collar. He inhaled deeply and glanced at his companion. Her hands were over her head pulling the hairpins from her hair. A sudden thought struck him. That beautiful hair! It's got to be real. Seconds later, a cascade of soft gold had fallen over her shoulders and was fluttering in the breeze. There was a sparkle in her eyes as she smiled at him, and then they both broke into a ripple of laughter, not really knowing why.

"I think we must be in your Sunday Village," Pandora said.

"Right! We are children of the sun and master of our own whims for a while." Gregor pointed seaward. "I live right down there at the end of the row of palms."

Pandora leaned forward in her seat. "I was thinking, Gig, that I could stay at the hotel right here in the Village, rather than make you take me all the way into town. The people I work for tomorrow will come to get me here. You have been kind enough."

"Great!" Gregor exclaimed. "Maybe while you're unpacking, I'll go down to catch a few waves. With this off-shore wind, surfing may not be so good today. Gotta check the beach first."

"Oh, please, Gig, take me with you!" Pandora pleaded. "I want to see where you surf!"

They turned onto Prospect Street, then to a lane hugging the edge of the cliff that hung over the ocean. The great expanse of water beyond heaved gently. Shades of blue and emerald extended to the horizon except for the silvery-purple patches near the shore. Here, appearing much like the slimy back of a gigantic sea monster, the kelp beds stilled the motion of the water.

Pandora pointed to the stairs that led to a small cove. "Look, Gig. There are steps down to the beach. Let's go down for just a few minutes."

Their shoes were abandoned in the car as they threaded their way down to the circle of beach that was protected from the sea by an arm of layered rock. At the bottom of the stairs, they passed a young man whose friends were assisting him up to street level. Despite a towel pressed to a laceration on his thigh, he left footprints of blood on the concrete steps.

Gregor paused to allow them to pass. "Seems that he cut himself on a rock. Must be deep to bleed like that." Pandora was not listening, however. She ran ahead, splashing in the surf, finally returning. Her blue tunic was soaked.

"You're drenched to the waist," he said.

"Can we come back tomorrow? I know that you want to surf today."

Gregor motioned toward the stair. "Yeah. The big swells are just starting to come in. This is the best time of the year for surfing."

"Do you mean to say that the waves change during the year?"

"Storms in Mexico this time of year send up the big swells. The coast bends just enough to catch the force."

"Do you think I could learn to surf? Even with a bad leg?"

"Maybe, if I let you use my chip. The old boards are much too heavy for you. But not where I surf at Boomer. That beach is not for beginners. Slope is too steep. Strong undertow. It's better to start on a sandy beach with a gradual slope. We'll catch some clean swells at the Shores or maybe at Moonlight."

"Someone said that there were seals playing around that small boat out there."

"I'll get my binoculars from the car."

Pandora watched for a moment. *"Oh, oui, oui! Je le vois.* They seem to be swimming away." She turned the glasses over to Gregor who scanned the cove.

Pandora's accent had become more pronounced, and Gregor thought about it as he watched two teenage girls splash through the surf toward deeper water. Pandora is comfortable with me, Gregor thought...off guard...being herself...that's good...it's the kind of day that relaxes...has the feeling of Sunday...the feeling that there is trust among creatures...and sharing...sharing the coolness...that lazy pelican...the gulls...the seals...the divers...the fish...all in harmony...same with the moray eels...the girl has a steady stroke...her friend turned around toward the beach again...not half as good a swimmer....

Gregor looked again at the girl with the steady stroke. She had stopped swimming and was treading water. Suddenly, directly in her path, a figure in a wet suit seemed to leap upright out of the water, waving his hands wildly above his head.

Gregor heard a faint cry. He stiffened and steadied his binoculars.

"There's a man in trouble out there," he said to Pandora, pointing. "Out there. See? Beyond that girl. The diver came straight up out of the water to his waist, like something was lifting him. His face mask was off. Then he went down. There's another skin diver going after him."

"It couldn't be a seal that bothered him, could it? See, a couple of men on that rock out there are shouting something, and two more are swimming out to help," Pandora said.

"Seals don't bother anyone." Gregor pressed the glasses to his face. "Someone is shouting–waving everyone else back." Gregor continued to watch while groups of bathers on the beach stood tensely staring seaward.

The feeling of Sunday was suddenly gone, replaced with an apprehension. A shadow fell over the day, fear-filled and threatening. Beach sounds died, one by one, leaving only frantic shouts from guards and would-be rescuers.

A man behind them asked, "Someone have a heart attack?"

"Don't think so," replied Gregor. "The way he came straight out of the water at such an odd angle, something had to be pushing him up. It's strange. Everyone is clearing the area."

A cry sprang up from the group on the beach. *"Clear the water!" "Get the swimmers in!" "There's a shark! Shark! Shark got one of the divers! Right here in the Cove! Shark! Shark!"*

The peaceful scene of a moment was gone. A fearful murmur arose as the crowd began to congeal. Bathers scrambled out of the surf, pulled by others. Gregor watched for a few more seconds, then let out a grunt as he handed the glasses to Pandora.

"You wait for me here," he directed. In another instant he was at the foot of the steps, making his way through the throng of bewildered people. Above, on the street level, sirens sounded as police were already clearing the sudden traffic jam. Gregor, however, dashed through the surf and struggled into the swell to the teenager he had been watching from above. He reached her at the point where the sandy bottom of the Cove dropped away. She gasped and went under, but he had already grabbed her hair. In a few strong strokes, the sand was beneath his feet again and he carried the limp girl to the beach. She coughed and sputtered when he put her down, then began to sob hysterically. Scooping her up again, he made his way through the crowd to his car where he deposited her gently on the seat. He patted her head and pushed back strands of her long hair which hung dark and wet over the velvet tan of her pretty face and supple shoulders. Not many girls in their early teens, Gregor was thinking, had as good a figure as she had: long tapered legs and a tiny waist. It was then that he noticed a cut on her leg.

Sobbing and shivering, she took the towel that Gregor offered to put on the gash. Tears still tumbled down on lightly freckled cheeks as the car inched its way out of the confusion.

"This kid is Kelley Holliss, daughter of a friend of mine," Gregor explained to Pandora. "We'll take her home. Hope you don't mind. The poor girl is practically in a state of shock. The guard said she was right over the spot where the shark must have turned around. With that sand bar, I just don't see how it came in."

In a few minutes more, Gregor guided Kelley through her front door and to the sofa. Then he turned to face her surprised parents.

"There was an accident down at the Cove, Chris, and your daughter—" He paused to clear his throat.

"An accident? Good Lord, look at that cut on her leg!" exclaimed Kelley's father. "Was it a boat accident? A fight? Quick, Vanessa, get some medicine and bandages."

"Why, she's shaking like a leaf, Chris," Vanessa said as she covered Kelley with an afghan. "I'll get the bandages." She hurried to the kitchen.

Christopher Holliss bent over the cut on his daughter's shin. His heavy brows lifted and settled into a scowl. "Whew!" he said. "This may require stitches." He straightened his sturdy figure to face Gregor. "Any broken bones?"

"I don't think so, Chris. She's just scared." Kneeling beside Kelley, he said softly, "Take a couple of deep breaths. There! That always helps a person to stop crying. We want you to tell us what happened."

"Yes! What happened?" Christopher asked. "Someone tell me what happened."

"Well, Chris, you won't believe this, but—" Gregor began, but hesitated as Vanessa appeared in the doorway to listen. David and Karla entered at the same time from the patio.

Seeing the blood, Karla squealed, "Ooh-ooh! Dad, I told you that the kids were starting to jump off the Clam again!" Karla was not as pretty as her older sister who always seemed to get more attention.

"She didn't jump off the Clam, Karla," Gregor said softly. "She was swi—"

"Or did she fall off a cliff?" Red pigtails bobbed as Karla danced around the sofa.

"Or was she attacked by an eel?" David asked. "Or scraped by a sea bass? That looks like a rough tear, not a cut. Like it was done on a piece of coral."

"Well, you're close," Gregor said. "Kelley was swimming near where a shark attacked a diver in the Cove."

"A shark?" Christopher stared, aghast. "Did—did you say a shark? Good God!"

Vanessa let out a cry and hurried over with a mug of tea for Kelley. "My poor girl," she murmured. "What a frightful thing to happen."

"Oh, Jesus!" David exclaimed. "What about the diver? Did he get away?"

"The report on the beach is that the diver was swallowed," Gregor answered.

"Oh, yuk!" Karla winced and held her hand over her stomach.

"I'll go down to the beach and find out," David volunteered promptly. "Come on, Karla, you can go with me."

"Call me later," Gregor said. He noticed the sparkle in Karla's eyes as she left with her big brother, hand in hand.

Meanwhile, Christopher and Vanessa confronted each other, dumfounded. "A shark? A shark in our Cove? One big enough to swallow a man? Incredible! Are you sure? How was Kelley involved, Gregor?"

Again, Gregor hesitated. "Kelley seemed to be swimming just where it happened. I was watching with my binoculars from the street above. Maybe Kelley can tell us more."

All eyes turned to the girl on the sofa who wiped her nose and sniffed once more. "Just like Greg said, I was swimming past the flat rock and suddenly there was a lot of foam and turbulence like I was inside a wash machine. I think something passed under me. It almost sucked me under. Someone started screaming something about a shark and waving me back. I had a hard time treading water. I–I got so scared!" Kelley wiped her nose again. "I got so scared that I don't–don't remember much. The beach seemed awful far away all of a sudden. I think I must have panicked and passed out in the surf."

"Oh, she would have made it in okay." Gregor gave the wet head a reassuring pat.

"Dad, I know better than to panic. You've always told me to—" Kelley sniffed again.

Christopher knelt by his daughter's side. "Well, did anyone see the shark? Did you see it, Kelley?"

"No, I didn't Dad. Maybe Gregor saw it."

Gregor shook his head. "All I saw was the diver coming straight out of the water to his waist, arms thrashing like mad. Then he went straight down. His buddy dove down after him, surfaced, and gave a shark warning. I thought Kelley was swimming strangely, but she was already almost in when I reached her."

Patting a bandage in place, Vanessa turned to Gregor. "But how do you explain this cut?"

Gregor shrugged. "You'll have to ask Kelley more about that." He looked toward the door. "I'm going to have to run. I have a guest waiting for me in the car."

As Gregor drove away, he reflected on his close bond with Christopher's family. The thought was brief, however, because the mood of the Village itself dissolved languor and preoccupation. Like a hive of busy winged things, it hummed with a provocative pace. The motor of a speedboat throbbed in the distance where the swells of the ocean seethed and threw their own sounds up against the hill. Serious bicyclists, geared for a long trek, filed past Gregor's car in a curious line. The air sparkled with late afternoon sunshine and carried pungent fragrances like honeysuckle and sage. A place with a charm put upon it, apart from the world about it, the Village oozed with enchantment.

After Pandora finished registering at her hotel, she turned to Gregor. "I feel that I stood in the way of your surfing."

"No problem! I'll go tomorrow," he reassured her. With his hands on his hips, he added, "You said you'd like to see the Village. We'll drive around a while. What would you like to see most? Take your pick—shops, bars, beaches, historical spots, our famous Torrey Pine trees, the aquarium or the polo field."

"Oh, everything!" she interrupted. "I want to see everything!"

"That's great!" Gregor said as he took her hand. "We'll start right here at the Whaling Bar with a daiquiri, then we'll catch the end of the glider meet, and I'll show you where they broke ground for the new university, then the park, and the Tennis Club." They wound their way through a small, outdoor cafe as he continued. "We'll catch the sunset and the bird's-eye view of the Village from the top of Mt. Soledad before it gets dark."

"That sounds like a full day."

"Oh, no! Not by a long shot! We'll have dinner at the German restaurant, after which we can walk to the pier and then top it all off with my special Margaritas on my seaside patio. And tomorrow—"

They were finally at Gregor's apartment, a small place that had probably been a guest house for an expensive structure that was built above it. The entrance to it was down a flight of stairs to Gregor's front door. From there, the steps continued down to a small patio that was protected from the high tides by a concrete wall. A small balcony jutted out over this patio, closing it to everything except the afternoon sun and an occasional wave that stole around the wall at high tide.

Late in the evening, they sat here at the edge of the enclosure. The sand held the afternoon's warmth. The ocean waves spoke in broken murmurs. The Margarita glasses lay empty on the ground.

During the course of the evening, Gregor had talked of the Village, his love of the ocean, and his knowledge of its wayward ways. He spoke of his boyhood days in his grandfather's home in the little valley on the other side of the highway, and in turn, Pandora confided in him how much the Village reminded her of her life on an island in the Mediterranean. However, she talked mostly about her travels and the dignitaries she had met in the course of her work. Always the discussion seemed to shift back to talk of the sea, and it was no wonder, for the sea was not to be ignored. This huge water that filled half the hollow of the earth, this forceful entity that propelled its body for thousands of miles in rage and fury, this churning thing that now tossed itself at Gregor's feet in mild obeisance—this sea was not to be ignored. Tonight, its voice was a mesmerizing whisper that said, "I am timeless. You are insignificant. You are here for a moment. I am *forever*."

"It is too bad you missed your surfing today," Pandora said again.

"Oh, I'll go tomorrow morning while you are busy."

"Non, non! Please wait for me, I want to watch you on your board. You said that the newest thing is bodysurfing. As much as I have traveled, I have not seen much surfing."

"There aren't many beaches in the world with the right kind of waves. Makaha, in Hawaii, is the best for me. Then, the Wedge at Balboa Peninsula. It takes the right kind of swells and the correct slope to the beach to make a perfect surfing beach. I'll show you tomorrow." Gregor studied her face in the faint light. He fell silent in thought...man alive...she is so beautiful...class...real class...never knew a girl like her...I'm afraid to touch her...damn...no one has ever done this to me before...is this real....

Gregor reached out to smooth the cascade of pale hair, silver in the fading light. "Why are we wasting time talking about surfing?" he asked in an undertone, but she did not stir or answer. He waited while seconds passed.

"Pandora? Did you hear me?"

She turned to him slowly. "I'm sorry, Gig. I wasn't listening. It seemed for a minute that I was home again on the island. It was so clear that I felt I could reach out and touch things. It happens to me sometimes, as though I have been transported elsewhere, out of my body. Has this ever happened to you?"

"Hmmm—" He paused. "Well, looking out into such limitless space, I begin to feel myself infinitesimal, non-existing, drawn to feel a oneness with nature, losing the center around which I pivot to a large one. Is that what you mean?"

She sighed. "Something like that, only more so." She shifted her position and became tense. "I feel as though I was actually there for a moment. Does that sound crazy to you?"

Gregor reflected for a brief time. "Have you ever heard of astral projection?"

"Yes, of course," Pandora answered.

"There is such a thing. Researchers have established that it exists, that some persons have a mental capacity to project themselves—usually while in a trance or state of half-sleep or deep concentration—to a different place, communicating with other people. It calls for a different state of consciousness, not a wakeful consciousness, something more like when you are coming out of anesthesia perhaps." He toyed with her hair, rearranging the strands to fall like a rivulet over her chest. "Have I told you that you have a beautiful voice? It fascinates me."

"I wish that I could drop the accent," Pandora said, pensively.

"No, no! Don't do that. Leave it just as it is. If you changed it, you would sound just like a hundred other people. I like it just as it is!" Gregor assured her.

"*Tel quel?* Tell me if you think this projection can really happen."

He stared at the ocean, deep in thought. "The tide is starting to come in. Hear how loud the surf is now?"

"You didn't answer my question, Gig," Pandora prodded.

"I thought you might want to talk about something lighter. I don't want to get so serious."

Pandora persisted as though he had said nothing. "It is a very provoking idea. Do you think it is credible?"

"Well, I know that experiments have been conducted, and cases have been documented. Yes, I can believe it can happen, but with a certain type of mind, a certain kind of capacity. Perhaps you have this capacity. Would you like to be tested? I know of a psychologist who tests apt subjects. He has even documented cases in which persons have traveled back and forth in time."

Pandora nodded. "It is incredible, is it not?"

"Well, have you heard stories of persons foreseeing a catastrophe before it happens?"

"That goes a little too far. It is easy to have premonitions, some of which are bound to materialize. However, I do go along with the idea that the mind sometimes has a unique potential to travel and to exist in other places. Has this ever happened to you?"

Gregor fingered the line of her halter top. A sigh escaped him before he answered. "Not really, I suppose. I'm not sure. There is one dream in which I go back to my grandfather's house. I can feel him there, and I can touch him, but he isn't there. Then I dissolve into a cloud that moves across an empty sky, just expanding. That isn't astral projection, however. Probably just a desire to be a boy again."

"You were happy with your grandfather?" Pandora asked.

"Yes. He was a neat guy. I lived with him until he died." Gregor leaned back on his elbows and looked up at the sky. "Everyone has a recurrent dream. You must have one," he continued.

"Yes, I have one. I walk among people, naked." She laughed at the look of surprise which crossed Gregor's face.

He laughed, too. "Is it fun doing it, or do you feel uncomfortable?"

She shook her thick hair back and forth over her shoulders. "I walk about not caring in the least—proud, happy, not the least bit concerned or apologetic."

"You have no reason to be apologetic."

"But I have. Didn't you notice that I limp a little?"

"No." He hesitated. "I might have thought that your shoe was tight."

"Well, I do limp. The bone in my lower right leg has been broken five times. It breaks with any kind of pressure. It has never calcified properly. I have to wear a brace on it when I do strenuous things, sometimes when I drive a lot."

"Nothing to be sensitive about," Gregor assured her.

"I am, but when I dream, I walk so very evenly that people remark about how beautifully I glide along. It is simply the greatest feeling! I wish it were possible to walk like that all the time." Strands of her hair tumbled forward as she reached to clasp her knees.

"Possible to walk naked all the time, you mean? Sure! Sure, you can!" Gregor insisted. "Don't let me stop you!" He reached playfully for the tie on her halter top, but she sprang up and ran off protesting. Gregor chuckled and rolled over on the sand. "Really, you ought to do it some time. All joking aside. Get it out of your system. Get it out of your dreams."

Pandora laughed gaily. "Gig, you know what I mean. And I don't mind the dreams."

Gregor scooped up a shell and threw it deftly into the surf. "You are overworking your superconscious."

"My what?" Pandora asked, dubiously.

"Here, let me explain it to you in French. *Par où dois-je commençer? Je—*"

She cupped her small hand over his mouth. "No French," she said. "You must explain it to me in English. Now, you were saying, my super—"

Gregor's eyes twinkled. "Your superconscious. Your overall consciousness, or call it what you will. That's the part of you that has to work out a compromise between what you actually do and your subconscious which wants to do something else. You are overworking it. It is forced to prepare a situation in your dreams wherein you no longer conceal your leg. You are able to disclose your concern. You are relieved and happy. Now, if you really did walk naked, the result might be the same, and your superconscious would be relieved of the responsibility."

"Sounds as though you might approve of nudist colonies."

"Yes. Some out-of-the-way place. Lots of people have hang-ups and it might be one way to get rid of them."

She handed him a shell to throw. "You are serious, aren't you?"

He gave no answer. He had turned and was lying on his stomach in the sand, his fingers tracing lines in the damp earth. "Okay! Can you tell me what that is?"

She, too, had stretched herself beside him on the sand. "Let me see. It's a—dolphin, isn't it? You didn't finish the tail."

"I can't. It's broken." He started to explain, but the sound in his throat turned to a howl as a wave swept away their cocktail glasses. Reaching for them, they lost their balance in the shifting sand. Sputtering and laughing, she was light in his arms as he carried her to the shelter of the wall where he put her down, his arms still about her. Meeting no resistance, he bent toward her, placing his lips softly on hers. Then he took a deep breath, smoothed the drenched locks that fell to the sides of her upturned face, and kissed her again and again.

After a moment, bewildered and breathless, he listened to a voice which spoke loudly inside himself...I've kissed a lot of women in my life...but she is different...what is it...why am I shaking....

He hardly trusted his voice as she bent suddenly to gather her belongings. "Do

24

you have to leave?" He reached for her arm to detain her. "You can't go now. You can't just leave as though all this hasn't happened! Please!"

"My appointment is quite early in the morning, remember? I have to interpret a political paper. That is why I'm here. Anyway, dawn will be breaking over that hill in a few hours." She pointed to the sky. "I have stayed too long already," she said firmly.

Reluctantly, Gregor took her to her hotel. When he returned, he sat for a few more moments on the sand, elbows propped on his knees, chin in the palms of his hands. Almost shouting to the sky, he cried, "You, out there, water, moon, all of you! Something is different tonight! Help me figure it out. What is it that I want? A night with her? No! Like the rest of them? No! Then what? Love? I've never been in love! What is it? What am I looking for?"

Tossing and heaving, the sea answered Gregor. Never content in its seeking of the shore, the sea spoke. "You wait for something, a conversion to reality, a place in time ahead of the moment that you are now passing through, but you will never reach it because the moment remains always before you. When you think it has come, it goes tantalizingly before you so that there is never fulfillment. Your struggle for the ultimate will never end. Look at me. In my longing to caress the sand, I throw myself upon it in ecstacy, in tumult. Yes, even with passion! Yet, when I do, there is one more wave to toss, one cap of white left behind, one more bank of water to send crashing into a million circles of singing foam. Where is my fulfillment? When can I reach the moment of my ultimate ecstatic perfection? *Perhaps not until I have thrown my most poignant caress upon the sand and all my water is on the shore!*"

Gregor lifted his chin and tossed his head backward as he laughed loudly. "Now, how can all your water be on the shore? That is a stupid thing to want. What would it accomplish?"

The wind came and soothed Gregor's brow. "Don't listen to the sea," it whispered. "The surf is always murmuring. If she wishes, she can link the moments and make the ultimate reachable. You can, too. At the very moment that your thought is born, when the mordant second makes you realize the intensity of your bond with universal force, then your seconds will fuse and you will conquer time and come into the perfect state." The breeze wandered into the still night, but it returned to whisper, "If that is what you want."

Gregor closed his eyes. "Do you know what I want? I want everything there is to be, triple-strong and double-deep, like I was two men instead of one. I want *fire on top of fire!* How can I make you understand?"

The sky of graying velvet answered him, "Do not fear. The moment of perfection will come when the very core of you will be everything and even the earth will fall away leaving nothing but you. The universe will disappear and you will expand to occupy it alone. *Indeed, you will be it.* There is no higher perfection."

Somewhat bewildered, Gregor asked, "What are all of you telling me?"

"You know," the sea groaned. "You know, you know, know–know."

Gregor pondered over this and sighed. "Are you saying that a man is perfect only in close union with nature? Then time stands still? Are you speaking in parables? I hear you talking, but I still don't understand!" Gregor protested. "How can the sea put all its water on the shore?"

"It would mean a tremendous displacement of elements," the sea said.

"An unimaginable osmosis," the sky added. "A blend of willing forces."

"A phenomenon of passion," the wind gasped.

Still puzzled, Gregor asked, "Are you describing love?"

"What is love?" they groaned in unison. The air grew still, the sky faded and the ocean became a mirror, but their words were stamped into Gregor's mind.

Gregor slept restlessly until the sun was well over the hill. He went for his morning swim a little later than usual. Even so, the morning seemed endless until Pandora finally called him shortly before noon.

"Oh, Gig!" she said. "I have been talking to so many people here, and they gave me lists of things to do! They told me about the imports in the Green Dragon Colony. And I should stop at the library for a book for my translation."

"I'll be there to get you in ten minutes," Gregor replied.

"And, Gig, could we—could we—" There was a long pause.

"Yes?" A twinkle stole into Gregor's eyes.

"Could we barbecue again tonight and walk on the beach again?" she asked timidly.

"Great," Gregor answered. "But before we do, I have to drop in to see a friend of mine. I promised I would. I want you to go with me."

"Where will we go?" Pandora asked.

"To Nichole Vincett's deb party. We won't stay long."

Hubert Vincett, an oceanographer at the Institute, met Gregor at the door at eight o'clock that evening.

"Come in! Come in, both of you. The band is just warming up out on the patio," he said. "Haven't seen you in any of our classes lately, Gregor. Got some good ones coming up. I'll see that you get the schedule."

"Fine," Gregor answered. "Didn't I see Nichole at the door here as we came up the path?"

"She must have just now stepped away," Mr. Vincett answered as he looked about. "You'll find her on the patio."

As they proceeded, many eyes turned in Pandora's direction, many conversations stopped in mid-sentence and a few of the debutantes looked annoyed at the intruder. When Gregor left Pandora to search for Nichole, she was immediately surrounded by admirers.

However, Nichole was nowhere to be found and Gregor was about to give up when he saw the blond head of a young girl peeking at him from behind the gazebo. As he approached, the girl turned to leave.

"Wait! Wait, Lisa," Gregor entreated. "I'm trying to find your sister. I've looked everywhere for her. Will you tell her? I want her to know that I kept my promise to come."

Lisa brushed her yellow hair from her temple nervously. "I'm not supposed to be out here, Gig. The party is just for debutantes. Nicki will tell on me if she sees me here. I just wanted to take another peek at the movie actress you brought with you tonight."

"Lisa, she knows a lot of movie people, but she really isn't an actress."

"Well, Nicki said she was."

"Actually, she has an international reputation as an interpreter. Did you say you saw her somewhere before?"

"Well, yes, but I'll get into trouble if I tell."

"You can tell me, Lisa. You know I'll keep your secrets. It was on the beach yesterday, wasn't it?"

The blond head bobbed in agreement. "But don't tell Nicki. I'm on restriction and not supposed to be on the beach this week. Nicki tattles on me and gets me into trouble." Lisa clenched her teeth. "She can be so—so—"

"So what, Lisa?"

"So mean. So darned mean. Sometimes I get awfully mad at her. I'm glad you did it to her tonight."

Gregor looked puzzled. "Did what, Lisa?"

Lisa chuckled. "You brought a date. You wouldn't believe the snit she is in because of it. She was expecting you to be her date tonight."

"I told her not to count on it. Anyway, Rex is here tonight, so I'm sure she understood me."

"Gig, you *know* that he is second choice. You *know* how crazy she is about you," Lisa insisted.

With a wry expression, Gregor sighed and scratched his ear. "Where is she now? Can you find her for me?"

Lisa shook her head. "She is having a big showdown with Rex in the bath house. Rex told her that she is making a damned fool of herself over you, and she slapped his face, and he shook her awful hard. She is crying."

Gregor raised his eyebrows. "How do you know all that?"

Lisa looked uncomfortable again. "Well, I'm supposed to be watching TV next door with my girlfriend, but I wanted to see what was going on. Dad doesn't think I'm old enough to be at Nichole's parties."

Gregor pursed his lips in thought...pretty little thing...even better looking than her sister and that is saying a lot...I remember Nichole saying that they were step-sisters...nice kid...maybe she won't have Nichole's temper....

"Lisa," Gregor said, "Let's keep this between you and me. Just tell your sister that I was looking for her." Then, with a twinkle in his eye, he added, "and I think you are old enough to be at parties."

"Do ya really?" Lisa asked, smiling proudly. She turned and left, whistling with the music.

Gregor wandered back to where Pandora stood in a circle of men. He pulled her away and guided her toward the door, followed by David Holliss and a plain-faced girl whose nose seemed too long for her round face.

David placed a staying arm on Gregor's arm. "Gig, you can't leave yet! You just got here. This is the best part of the party. This is Kimberly, Gig. Best dancer on the floor. I have a hard time getting her away from all the other guys." He put a protecting arm around Kimberly's waist as another youth approached her to ask for a dance, but she waved him off.

"I want to ask Pandora a few more questions about her beautiful sari."

Pandora picked up the edge of the shimmering fabric. "As I was saying to the group in there, Kimberly, it was made for me in India and the design on the border has a significance."

Kimberly ran her fingers over the delicate embroidery. "What pretty jewels!"

"They are all real," Pandora explained. The two of them drifted off into their own conversation.

Meanwhile, Gregor had turned to David. "What did you find out about the shark?"

"Oh, man!" David exclaimed. "That damned fish really ate that diver! Crunched him through the middle and swallowed him! Couldn't even find his abalone iron. No hoax!"

"Someone saw the fish?"

"Yeah! The man's buddy dove down to help him and found the shark on his back forcing his catch down his gullet!"

Gregor stared openmouthed. "Good God! He saw his friend being swallowed?"

"Yeah! He said there was so much blood in the water that he couldn't see past the guy's middle, but he was sure that the other half of him was in the shark's mouth, and hanging together with strands of gut. The shark had to take two bites."

"That had to be a hell of a big fish." Gregor whistled. "Was it a Great White?"

"From the diver's description of the fins, it had to be a Great White, maybe a Tiger. Holy smoke, this one had to be at least twenty-five feet long to eat a man like that." David stroked his chin and grimaced. "There's something weird about it, though. Big ones like that just don't come in close to shore."

"Or this far north, either, but warm water brings them. The water has been up to seventy for the last two summers and not much below sixty last winter."

"Yeah, and the shark could have been trailing that hurt whale that came in on the Shores Beach. Blood in the water stirs sharks into a frenzy."

"Well, don't forget the skindiver who came in with the bad cut on his leg just as I got there. He probably left a trail of blood right in to shore."

David whistled softly. "Whew! It's just a good thing that Kelley wasn't the first thing in his path."

"Is Kelley feeling better today?"

"Yeah. Still a bit scared but enjoying all the publicity. Dad won't let her back in the water. Gee, the beaches are almost deserted. What do you bet that the Town Council will cancel the Rough Water Swim?"

"That's possible." Gregor looked at his watch. "Look, kids, I hate to leave, but it's time for us to split. I'm getting too old for this crowd. Tell Nicki I'm sorry that I missed her." He took Pandora's hand and they made their way to the car.

Once again, it was late and the beach sand held its warmth. They had walked to the pier and now they turned to start back.

"Did I hear someone say that David is related to you?" Pandora asked.

"Oh, distantly. I'm not sure just how," Gregor answered.

Content to clasp Gregor's hand, Pandora walked for a while listening to the sound of the waves that broke in chiding bursts on the deserted beach.

"David is a handsome man. Strong features. He has eyebrows like yours," Pandora said.

"Handsome family, the Holliss family. But I can't say much for the girl David was with tonight. Maybe if her nose was shorter, she'd be pretty."

"Yes, but..." Pandora paused, tilting her head in a saucy way.

"But what?"

"...but I was struck with her charm and affability. She said she was David's blind date at one of the other debutante parties. She has such a beautiful smile."

"And a fortune. Her family owns Chemwell Weldin Consolidated. Everyone knows the name. You see it in several places in the Village."

Pandora nodded. "The local names are easy to find. I noticed that the pier and the park have the same name as the hospital. The town must have had a fairy godmother."

Gregor continued the list. "Lucky for us that someone had forethought long ago. As a rule, people don't concern themselves with generations to come. A fast buck is all that counts. We owe a lot to the Villagers who planned our parks and preserved our beaches, and who provided libraries and cultural centers. That's what makes this place a Shangri-la and gives it magic."

Pandora shook her head. "No, no, it's the people that give it its magic, Gig. You have a charmed populace. They live under a spell, a lovely enchantment that makes it a sin to grow old."

Gregor eyed her curiously. "You noticed it?"

"Yes, yes. It is true. An enchanted village! It came to me so clearly when I had lunch today in the outside cafe near the eucalyptus grove. I could feel it each time the wind rustled the leaves—like they were whispering something to me."

Gregor smiled. "My grandfather helped to plant those trees. Those and the ones all over the mesa above the pier. Some railroad builder thought the eucalyptus trunks could be used for railroad ties and the trees grew fast, but the wood proved to be too soft for ties. However, that's how all those trees got there. Before that, there was only chaparral over the hills and in the barrancas."

"The Village is delightful!" Pandora said with a sigh. "I could spend another day there. Everyone was so friendly. I am reminded of the shops in my village back home."

"Most of our shops are still owner-operated. Lots of them in the Green Dragon Colony were there when I was in grade school. Along the main street, too. I can remember back when the Feed Store had a room at the back where they kept the town drunks because there wasn't any other jail." Gregor chuckled. "That's when the Village was real small."

"Is there a jail now?" Pandora asked.

Gregor shook his head. "Never was, other than the back room of the Feed Store. Nothing much happened here. We kept the game warden busy, though, when we brought in shorts and abalone over our quota." He slowed his footsteps and pointed. "This is where I learned to surf. Now that the tide is low, you can see how gradual the slope is. See where the waves are breaking? Those waves are about three feet high, so we know that the water there is only about that deep. A four-foot wave breaks in four feet of water and so on. Otherwise it's a shore break."

"What is a shore break?"

"That's when a four-foot wave comes up a steep slope and crashes dangerously in very shallow water."

Pandora's eyes grew wide. "How do the surfers manage not to get hurt?"

"A good bodysurfer knows exactly when the wave will break. If he dips his shoulder, he can slide across the wave ahead of the break, or he can extend one arm."

"Yes, yes," she said in her melodious way. "I watched today down at your beach. You just take a somersault and dive under the wave."

"It isn't so much a straight somersault as it is a roll onto your back, and then you are on your way out again. The whole idea is to stay ahead of the white water. If you are about to fall over the brink, or if you get caught in the turbulence, you tuck yourself into a ball, and let it pass."

"It must be so exciting to get that good at it!" Pandora exclaimed. "How can you know what you are doing when you are totally immersed in water?"

Gregor laughed. "You can lift your head for a few seconds when you start to plane on your chest," he explained.

"But—"she began with a gesture of protest. "It looks so dangerous! Isn't it less so on a surfboard?"

"Actually, it is," Gregor agreed. "More kids hurt their spines body surfing than if they used a board."

"Which do you like to do better?" she asked.

Gregor pursed his lips. "Oh, I like to use my board."

"You certainly were the ultimate when I watched you."

He shook his head. "No," he said, stretching his arm out before him in a slow curve. "The ultimate is to ride in the tube and to come out the open end before you wipe out." He saw the puzzled look on her face and explained, "The wave makes a tube as it spills over. It has to be a big wave to give a surfer the space he needs."

"Have you ever done it, Gig?" she asked curiously, her eyes wide with wonder. A wistful look crossed Gregor's face. "Yes. Twice."

"Then you have accomplished the ultimate," Pandora said admiringly.

"Not yet! *I want to ride in a tube in the sunset and come out to a sea of gold,*" Gregor said with determination.

Again she looked at him curiously. Then she whistled softly. "I have never known such a perfectionist. There seems to be nothing that you don't do well. Besides all that, you are quite a chef. I must ask you for the recipe for those abalone appetizers rolled in bacon."

Gregor laughed and shrugged his shoulders. "Just ask me anything."

"Tell me more about optic conditioning," she answered promptly.

They were nearing the patio. Gregor sighed and was slow to reply. "It's quite complicated. Are you sure you want to hear more? Wouldn't you rather hear about my recipe for raisin cordial, or how the Village is going to crack open some day at the San Clemente Fault?" The cleft in his chin grew deep as he smiled at her. "I know what to tell you about. I'll tell you about this cute chick I just met and all the sleep I lost over her last night."

Pandora's lashes fluttered as she answered discreetly, "Perhaps another time, but I am really interested in hearing about the brain waves. Please?" She pushed straying strands of pale hair behind her ear as she prepared to listen.

Gregor only rubbed his chin thoughtfully and stared at her.

"S'il vous plaît," she pleaded in her most beguiling manner.

Stirred by some impulse that wavered strangely and then eluded him completely, he continued to scrutinize the small figure beside him. "Okay, okay," he agreed.

He took her by the hand and they began to walk again. "There is so much to it that there is no quick explanation, but I'll put it simply. Let's say that no matter how verbal you are and how well you can think, it is still impossible to communicate precisely what your brain might be doing with information being stored or used. Also, let's say that because you are an individual, your brain is unique. Got that much?"

She nodded her head promptly. "The information is subjective. Reactions are unique. I understand!" Pandora replied.

The intensity of her response diverted his thought. He slowed his step and stared at her, a wisp of a woman with a face of a wide-eyed child, yet with the unlimited capacity of a strong mind ready to rush into the unknown. The strange feeling prodded him again and then dissolved, unborn. "Well, I—" He took up his stride again. "Are you sure?"

The pouting expression spread. "Yes, yes," she insisted in her singsong way. "Please go on. Please."

Gregor drew his long fingers through his sun-bleached hair. "Okay! Let's see, how far did we get last time?"

Pointing with one forefinger to the same on her other hand, Pandora enumerated. "We established that there is electrical activity in the brain as it deals with information." She smiled and pointed to the next finger. "This electrical activity is called a brain wave and is measured by a machine devised by scientists." She touched the next finger. "These waves are named according to their lengths and intensity, alpha, beta and theta, the first being the longest wave on the machine." Proudly, she placed her hands on her hips as she blocked his passage. With a saucy tilt of her head, she asked, "Now, am I a good student?"

He shook his head at her audacity and nodded affirmation almost in the same gesture. "Yes," he mumbled, "you sure as hell play with a full deck."

Her brows lifted. *"Pardonnez-moi?"*

Thoughts passed with lightning quickness through his mind. Good God, Morghann...what in the hell is wrong with you tonight...talking out here about phenomenology and scientific stuff instead of getting this dish into the sack like I would any other girl...only she isn't any other girl and...damn...I can't figure it out...this time it isn't winning the bet with Roy that's important....

She was pulling on his sleeve and Gregor hurried to answer. "Oh, yes! Yes, the alpha waves are the longest on the EEG recording. Like I said, they are present when thoughts are pleasant. Would you believe that a person can be trained to produce pure alpha waves? They have devised a filter to separate the waves further still."

"Incredible!" Pandora stared at him curiously.

"Not really," Gregor replied. "For example, these waves operate just like the voltage on your transistor radio. Then there is a way to hook this energy to mechanical gadgets like electric lights."

"How fascinating!"

"Remember my telling you that my brain waves were used to operate an electric train?"

Pandora sucked in her breath. "Incredible!" she repeated. "That seems to forecast things for the future, doesn't it?"

"Yeah," Gregor agreed. "Kids are going to run their toys with EEG power, and they'll operate their Christmas-tree lights with brain waves!"

She laughed. "Toys for the year 2000!" They were walking slowly now, and Pandora was silent for a moment. Then she added, "All this makes one wonder how complex the human brain really is and how much more untapped potential it has. Even the best scientists do not begin to understand its power and limits. It frightens me to think of it."

Gregor shot an inquiring glance at her. "Well, don't worry because there won't be that much progress in our lifetime. It would take ten centuries of intensive breeding and training to create a real super-brained kind of man."

"*Vraiment!*" Pandora exclaimed. "Really," she repeated. "We should have begun with Babylonians and the early Greeks and Romans. They were so advanced even then."

"Yeah, and the Chinese and Cleopatra, they weren't so dumb. The trouble was that they jailed or executed any really advanced philosopher who came out with anything too drastic, anything that contradicted Church doctrine or current philosophies. Look at Socrates and Anaxagoras."

Pandora eyed him thoughtfully. "If we had started way back then, perhaps we might have a real genius or two around now to guide us. I agree. But, Gig, the genes lie dormant somewhere, even perhaps in you and me. Who can tell?"

"My scientist friend, the one who started all this experimenting, may be starting a new era." Gregor pretended to outline giant letters in the sky. "Mankind comes into his own in the century of *The Brain!* Maybe I'll help him with his new machines. He'll need a few more subjects to test!"

Pandora sighed as they neared the apartment. "If only I could stay longer."

Panicked thoughts plied Gregor's conscience...anything to keep her here...I can't let her go...I'll kill that Roy McClouder if he sneaked in again and put those crazy sheets on my bed again...even that date he got for me got mad and left...can't blame her...some of the things he does are gross...God, but that knothead has no class...I'd better check the sheets...she can't leave...Morghann, do something...this is different...do something...anything....

They were mounting the stairs to his place. "What do you mean? You can't leave yet! Sure, you can stay longer. I won't let you go!" He kept insisting, but she only frowned and went on, lips pressed tight.

They hesitated in front of the fireplace. She was looking about for her sweater. "Gig," she said softly, and he thrilled to hear it from her lips. "Gig, I have a seven o'clock flight in the morning. I have stayed too long already, but I can sleep on the plane."

He tried to swallow. His throat muscles tightened into knots. "You just can't go, Pandora! We've only just met. Cancel the flight! Please don't leave me! Please!"

Her wide eyes grew sad as they searched his face. "I have a job with the Council of Churches in Rome. I must be there, Gig."

"But one more day!" Gregor protested. "Can't you stay one more day?"

"It is impossible to change my plans," she announced with finality.

Gregor's hands trembled as he placed them gently on her shoulders. "Oh, my God, I can't lose you. When you finish in Rome, will you come back?"

"Perhaps, but I made a promise to help with some work in Vietnam."

"But it's becoming dangerous to be there! That's no place for a girl like you."

Her dark eyes kindled. "It's only a possibility. I sympathize with these people.

There are many ways I can help them."

Gregor cleared his throat and frowned. "There is another man, isn't there?" His hands dropped from her shoulders.

She shook her head. "There are men, but my work doesn't allow making a home for a man."

"Then..." Gregor's brows arched. "...there isn't anyone else in particular?"

Pandora shook her head. *"Pas un seul."* Then she repeated quickly, "No, nobody in particular. It matters?"

"Well, it hasn't ever mattered before, but—"

"But it matters now?"

"Yes! Yes, it does!" He replaced his hands on her shoulders, letting his fingers bite into her flesh. "Yes, it matters now. I want you to come back to me! Don't leave me like this. I want to see you again. Promise me!"

Her full lips parted as though to speak, but no words came. The facets of light in her eyes melted and mixed, and moisture welled. "Gig," she said hesitatingly, "my work in Rome will take only about three months."

"Then you *will* come? Promise me!"

She stared as he drew her to him. Long lashes lay on her velvet cheek as she lifted her face to his. An inexplicable exhilaration flowed through him as their lips met and he felt the surrender in her body, so complete that the next moment left a memory he would keep a lifetime. Panic struck him when she pulled herself away, insisting that she must leave.

Gregor took her to the airport that morning. When her plane passed from sight, a maddening feeling of abandonment closed over him. Scenes flashed before his eyes and sounds came to his ears. Rain fell on a deserted beach. A lone gull cried in a darkening sky. An unopened letter fell into a consuming fire.

Suddenly, he was a boy again, holding the hand of the new girl in his second-grade classroom as they played indoors on a rainy day. He felt the softness of her hand, the silkiness of her yellow hair as it brushed against his face, the wild beating in his heart, and the difference that the day made. Then, shortly afterward, she left. Gregor remembered the rock that he threw that day at the boy in the fountain in his grandfather's garden. The stone broke part of the dolphin's tail, and Gregor remembered the remorse that he felt as he stood over the irreparable fragments.

From inside him, a feeling of emptiness welled as he strode from the airport ramp. Desperately, he tried to concentrate on his plans to film whales in the bay in Baja where the mammals wintered.

Pandora's initial stream of letters became a trickle as weeks passed during which Gregor and Roy prepared to go to Mexico. When they finally left, no mail could follow. For a while, the task of setting up camp and preparing their equipment was occupying and demanding. Gradually, however, thoughts of Pandora began to haunt Gregor. He found himself moody and irritable as memories paraded through his mind ever more persistent and vivid.

The bay was isolated except for an anchored research vessel and Roy's small camp nestled among the sand dunes. Terns and snowy egrets flew overhead, piercing the stillness with their cries. Sandpipers scurried along just out of reach of the gentle surf like living lace edging the scallops of foam.

The whales were suspicious at first and hard to sight. Finally, the dozen killer whales tormenting the pod of grays left. The huge mammals became more trusting. Gradually, they became accustomed to the rafts and swimmers who, in the meantime, filmed the bottlenose dolphins that approached, unafraid and playful. However, Gregor kept eyeing a particular whale with a baby calf clinging to its back. Repeatedly, he tried to approach it.

Roy shook his head. "Don't try it," he warned. "That young one must be newborn or it would be swimming more by itself."

"Yeah, I know," Gregor said. "They can't swim very well until their flukes harden. How old do you think it is?"

Roy shook his head. "Hard to tell, but I do know that thirty ton hunk of blubber can get damned nervous if you get too close. Gray whales guard their calves carefully. They don't trust us. One of them could upset the whole boat. When you really think about it, we don't have any right to invade their breeding grounds. Those babies are intelligent. Really can't blame them for disliking people. Maybe they have learned instinctively that men murder them."

"But they are protected from commercial hunting since the 1946 International Agreement."

"That's not so long ago and maybe the herd has an elder in it who remembers the whaling ships and teaches his flock to stay away from people. Remember, your friendship now may mean death to the mammal next year."

"How is that?"

"There are still some people who are allowed to kill grays, like the Alaskans who can't do without the whale products. If the whale overcomes her fear of you, you are setting her up. She doesn't know the bad guys from the good guys. You cozy up to her here. Next trip around the Pacific, she gets a steel barb shot into her chest because she thought you were so nice to swim with."

Rubbing his chin, Gregor stared at the calm surface of the bay. "A close shot of the pair of them would be priceless, Roy! I'd give my right arm to get a shot like that. It's never been done!"

With a shake of his head, Roy repeated, "Too risky. Let them do it with the zoom lens from on board some ship. Forget the baby whale. Our job is the underwater mating shots."

"Yeah, but—"

"Yeah, but! Yeah, but! If she sounds while you're filming her," Roy said with a jerk of his thumb toward the whale, "and she slaps you with the ten foot fluke, you'll be no damned good to me down here! I saw a guy get almost killed that way once. Hurt his spine, broke his shoulder and scraped the skin off him like he was rubbed through a potato grater. Now, don't try to be a brave asshole, okay?"

Gregor shrugged. "Okay! Don't sweat it! I'll go take pictures of garden snails if that's what you want."

With one side of his mouth pulled into a twitch, Roy stood with hands on his hips. "Look, buddy," he said in a softened tone, "these mating shots are really important to us. Can't afford to have you hurt."

Gregor helped Roy finish the shots that were on the agenda. Having free time

34

now, he was lured to follow the mother whale. For the next several days, he succeeded in swimming a somewhat parallel course, always getting closer. Three days later, Roy was at the bottom of the bay with Gregor filming background scenes and fill-in shots when the whale with its young one came close and promised to surface. Camera in hand, Gregor swam alongside followed by his irate partner.

Possibly because she encountered the raft overhead, the whale suddenly became apprehensive. She veered quickly, leaving Gregor under her tail as she surfaced and sounded. The untold pounds of fluke lifted into the air and descended with shattering force. About to surface, Gregor saw her shadow and looked up in time to see the huge thing fall on him. He was caught in a maelstrom of compression and foam. He wallowed for a moment, thoroughly stunned. Frightened and furious, Roy pulled him to the surface, then dove to find the camera.

Gregor was fortunate to suffer no more than a backache and painful lacerations over his body from the abrasive parasites that clung to the whale's skin. Evening found him sprawled on his cot, recovering from the experience. His thoughts drifted from the events of the afternoon to memories of Pandora. His eyes closed and he murmured her name softly. "Pandora, come to me. *Reviens à moi. Reviens à moi.* Come to me!"

He remembered the moment on the beach when, dripping wet, he took her into his arms and kissed her. He could remember the taste of the salt, the ecstacy in his limbs, the sound of her voice. It came back to him now.

"It matters?" she was whispering again.

"It has never mattered before," he said in return.

Her voice echoed and wavered. *"It matters now?"*

"Yes! Yes! I want you to come to me now!" he pleaded.

Her voice faded and came again. *"Then tell me what I'm wearing."*

"You want me to tell you what you are wearing?" he asked.

"Yes, tell me!" Her voice trailed. *"Dis-moi. Dis-moi. Come to me!"*

His hand lifted slowly. "I can almost feel you. Where are you?" he murmured.

"Right here. Ici! Ici! Come to me! Answer me!" she implored.

"Yes, yes! I see moonlight and a gardenia in your hair. You walk like a queen." Gregor reached out to touch her naked body but her image disappeared.

He opened his eyes and sat up. His chest heaved with a deep sigh. After peering carefully about, he shook his head to clear his mind. Then he rubbed his face with both hands and lay back again, grimacing with pain from the deep gouges in his limbs. He fell into a half-sleep, waking intermittently because of his discomfort.

A voice startled him. Roy was standing by his cot, his gaunt frame bent over him in an anxious manner. "Gig, I've got to talk to you," Roy began. "You almost got yourself killed today. You realize that, don't you?"

"Yeah," Gregor answered, easing himself into a sitting position again. "But wait till you see the film. You'll have one hell of a sequence."

Roy placed both hands on his hips and glared at Gregor. "If we can salvage it! Now look here, Gig. You work as though you are not entirely with it. Didn't you see the signals? You weren't supposed to get so damned near that baby whale. Why didn't you follow the plan? What the hell is the matter with you?"

"Nothing," Gregor replied casually. "Nothing is the matter with me. I just wanted a couple more feet of that shot. You guys probably scared the big whale with your signals. That's why she veered and slapped her tail and went under."

Roy grimaced and ran his fingers through his unkempt red hair. "Look, Gig, you know better than anybody else that this whole operation depends on split-second timing. You almost lost that whole sequence today, plus camera, plus the housing, plus transmitters. By damn, you're gonna watch the signals like everybody else! You wouldn't be worth shit if there was some real emergency! You know it. Your mind isn't on your work. Now, what's eating you?"

Gregor fingered his forehead and scowled. "Nothing. Nothing's eating me."

Roy's laugh was short and his smile came from one side of his mouth. "You forget, I know you like a book. Something's wrong. It's that girl, isn't it? Isn't it?"

Gregor's face flushed with anger. "Now, look, Roy, it's none of your damned—"

"Oh, yes it is!" Roy snapped. "You haven't been the same since you met her. Now, dammit, she's been on your mind long enough. Usually you sack 'em, and it's over and you're on your way to the next. What went wrong this time?"

Gregor hesitated. "She's different."

"What the hell do you mean, she's different?" Roy bellowed. "In bed, you can't tell who you're screwing. It's all the same."

Gregor's face flushed slightly. "It didn't—uh—happen that way."

"God Almighty! You had two nights with her. Don't tell me that." Roy laughed uproariously. "How come you never paid off on that bet?"

Suddenly, Gregor was resentful of Roy's intrusion, of the big hulk hovering over him, of the eyes of steel and the twitching mustache. "Well, with girls like her, you don't! No use explaining because you wouldn't understand. Just get off my back. Okay?"

"Like hell I will, old buddy. You'll get your mind back on your work or else you'll get your ass kicked from here to Los Angeles," Roy shouted. "You forget that bitch, hear me?"

Gregor reddened with anger. "Look Roy, if you want me to quit, just say so."

With that, Roy left, cursing. Gregor lay back again and slept fitfully, dreaming of when he sat on the beach with his chin cupped in his hands as he talked to the elements. *"My ecstatic perfection,"* the sea was saying once again, *"is when I have thrown my last poignant caress upon the sand and all my water is on the shore. Like me, you are waiting for a place in time—"* And Gregor thought, that's impossible, what does that mean? Then the wind said again, *"...the seconds will fuse and you will conquer the hours."* And the sky added, *"...the earth will fall away leaving nothing but you; indeed, you will be it."* In his dream, his dolphins came and Gregor watched the earth below him fade away slowly until he drifted in the sky, mounted on the back of a dolphin without a tail — or was it a whale?

The next month passed without further incident. The film was finished and Gregor returned from Mexico. There were no letters from Pandora. Although the pain of wanting her had lessened somewhat, he remained moody and refused to go with Roy on the usual forays. Neither Roy's fury nor his compassion, the little that Roy was able to express, helped Gregor to ease his misery.

One Friday evening in August, he returned from Los Angeles late. He found the door unlocked. A travel case lay on the sofa. The scent of heliotrope came to his nostrils. There were footsteps in the kitchen. He took a step forward. His heart leaped like a river plunging into a gorge below, the roar sounding in his ears and the crest of it about to carry him over the brink. Pandora stood there smiling at him!

He gathered her into his arms and in the time that followed it was difficult for him to remember the things they said or whether they talked at all. He knew only that their lips met again and again.

"Gig," she finally said, and once more he thrilled to her saying his name. "Gig, let me explain why—"

"It doesn't matter now," he whispered, and he kissed her again. Finally, he held her at arm's length. "Let me look at you," he said. "Do you realize it's been almost a year? A year, Pandora!"

She nodded. "I tried to break away many times, Gig. There was always some part of the world where I was needed or someone or something to delay me."

A frown clouded Gregor's face. "The man you told me about? He stood in your way?"

The trace of a smile on her lips teased him. "Yes, and then, no."

His grip on her shoulders loosened somewhat. "Well, is he the man who is so in love with you?" Gregor asked gruffly.

"That may be, Gig, but I am here with you," she replied quickly. "I am here with you. Nothing else is important. Don't you see?"

"You're right. Nothing else matters as long as we are together again. Just don't ever leave me again like that!" His hand trembled as he stroked her cheek and held her close once more.

After an interim, she drew back. "Gig," she said excitedly, "I've been waiting so long for a walk on the beach with you—and a barbecue—and surfing—and one of your Margaritas. Nobody seems to make them just like you do."

Gregor smiled. "Come on," he said as he led her into the kitchen. "Let's do just that. We'll make up for lost time. Another Santa Ana wind started up this morning. The beach will be super-great."

"It was lovely this afternoon," Pandora said.

Gregor suddenly realized that her blue beach tunic covered her swim suit and that she had been waiting for him all day. "Just when did you get here?" he asked.

"Yesterday, *mon amour*. I came yesterday afternoon. I remembered where you hid the spare key."

Soft points of light kindled and melted in her large eyes as she looked into his face. "I wanted to surprise you," she admitted. "Am I finally really here, Gig? Really? I have a strange feeling as though I have just awakened from a dream."

The warmth of the desert wind persisted into the night. They walked in the surf, sat on the still-warm sand and walked again. Each spoke of the events of the months of separation.

"...and I wanted to tell you that I did some translation in England for the people who are foremost in the science of optic conditioning." Pandora was saying.

"It's being called viseo interspect bionics now, you know," Gregor interrupted. "VIB for short."

"Oh, yes, yes!" she answered. "However, from this science, we went on to another aspect of metaphysics. Really revolutionary! I became quite involved with their experiments," Pandora retorted with excitement.

"You didn't write anything in your letters. You could have told me so I could have known what kept you."

She shook her head slowly while her eyes became wide and mysterious. "I volunteered as a subject for one of the experiments. It was quite confidential. I could not even tell anyone where I was. It was quite involved and revolutionary. It could not be explained in a letter. Should I teach you what I learned?"

Gregor chuckled at the thought. He closed his eyes and lay back on the sand obviously in deep thought. "My God, what'll they think of next?"

"You haven't said yes," Pandora reminded him. She drew her knees toward her chest and wrapped her arms around them, allowing her toes to tap little grooves in the sand as she waited for him to answer. However, Gregor only folded his arms over his chest and was silent. She was quite aware that although he did not say yes, he did not say no. Then, with a plan in the recess of her mind, she was asking him about his recipe for guacamole dip and cheese fondue, and about all the new shops in the Village, and why so many of the hills were sheared of their chaparral. Finally, she tried to suppress a yawn.

"You're tired," Gregor said with obvious concern.

"I'm fairly exhausted, Gig. No wonder, just look at the time. It takes me two days to adjust to the change when I travel such distances." She stood and began to dust the sand from her clothes. "I didn't mean to stay so late."

Gregor had also jumped to his feet. "You can't leave again, just like that! You stayed here last night. You can stay again!" He tried to impede her progress up the stairs.

"But now you are home," she said. "It wouldn't look right for me to—"

"But you can have the place!" Gregor protested. "Good God! How can anyone be so strait-laced! Okay! Okay! I sleep on the hammock on the patio down below a lot of the time. I like the sound of the surf. You can have the whole place. Just don't go!" He followed her into the living room. "Stay here, now. I'll just get a blanket in case it cools off during the night." He disappeared for a minute and returned with a cover tucked under one arm. With the other, he pressed her to him once again and kissed her long and tenderly. Drawing away ever so slightly, he stared at her for a brief moment, then turned suddenly and made his way down the stairs.

Depositing his frame on the hammock, he found it not as inviting as he remembered. He dozed and tossed and dozed again, restless and empty. Finally he got up and stretched his arms wide over his head, allowing his blanket to fall from his naked limbs.

It came as a shock to him that she was standing there in the shadow of the wall, clad in a shimmer of sheer material that she held securely with her forearm. Gregor reached toward her, but she drew back. His warm body tingled in the night air as he waited. Neither spoke. For an interim, the only sound to be heard was the rustle of the sea. His own breath seemed to be stuck in his throat. Finally, she took a step toward him and her voice broke the stillness.

"I fell asleep and woke with the feeling that you were beside me," Pandora whispered.

"I have been," Gregor replied quickly.

"Then why are you here?" she asked, advancing another step.

Gregor stared at her. The silence weighted the air like concrete and again it was hard to draw his breath. "It's hard to explain," he finally answered.

She, too, waited before she spoke again. "Gig, you puzzle me. I remember what Roy told me about all the women in your life. Dozens and dozens, he told me."

Gregor drew one hand over his eyes and leaned against the wall. "A hundred if there was one, but all I wanted from any of them was one night. Roy and I had a...ah, ah—"

"I know. He told me. You made bets with each other over your, uh, conquests. If one of them fell in love with you, you broke it up in a hurry, he said."

"Damn him anyway! Roy shouldn't have told you."

"Gig," Pandora interrupted, "are you going to let Roy win the bet on me?"

Gregor beat his fist gently against the wall. "All the betting stopped when I met you. I won't let Roy so much as breathe your name, let alone *bet* on you. Damn it all, I don't know how to say this to you. My mind is a blank. I've never said *I love you* to any woman!"

Pandora said quietly, "Oh—then it is clear." She hesitated and wrapped her robe about her more securely. "Then it is that you are already afraid that I will fall in love with you."

"No, no! That's not it at all! It's the other way around. I'm afraid you won't. I don't want to touch you until I know that there is no one else in your life because I couldn't face it if there was. Don't you see? Don't you see?" he muttered distractedly as he stepped forward and put his hands gently on her shoulders.

Her arms stole around his waist. *"Mais je t'aime!"* she whispered as he continued to talk.

Agitated by the need to commit himself, he did not hear her. "How can I ask you so soon? But I've got to know that you love me as much as I love you." He stroked the silky head that lay pressed against his shoulder. "I have to know!"

"Listen to me," Pandora implored. *"Je t'aime!* I do love you. *Je t'aime!"*

Gregor's breath caught in his throat. He stared at her upturned face for a few seconds before he cradled her in his arms. For some time, they stood like statues in the moonlight, immobile but impassioned. They stood until Gregor reached to ease the gown from her shoulders. It floated to the ground. Still, she stood motionless. Her hair was a waterfall of shimmering silk that drifted over her shoulders and the hollow of her breasts.

A shudder ran through him. His cover had fallen to the sand and he lowered himself onto it, stretching his body at full length. With closed eyes, he waited. He was aware of his own breathing. Sounds of the ocean filled his ears as each foamy crest crashed in thunder. The breeze carried a fine spray that made his warm body tingle. The firm sand beneath him still imprisoned the heat of the day. He waited, listening for her breath.

Suddenly, she touched him. Gregor's body tensed. He drew her close, aware of the softness of her body, marveling at her eagerness, wondering over her abandon. Soon he wondered over nothing as everything around him dissolved and disappeared. The sand was gone; the entire beach melted away. The ocean became soundless; the wind was still. The earth fell away altogether leaving their two bodies floating in space, passing by wandering asteroids and sleepy stars.

One of these ethereal spheres sent its emerald dust swirling about the passing bodies, bathing them in a mustard-gold haze, binding them into one being now, one submerged in the other, undulating as they pierced thin sheets of ice, compelled by an overwhelming force. Suddenly, they seemed to be wrapped in a tight airless bubble, the walls of which were closing in on them. For a panicked moment, they fought for breath, grimacing in pain, lips drawn open in agony until a single motion exploded them into specks of burning ashes. Slowly, slowly, the cooling particles sought each other and became whole again in the mysterious mustard glow of the emerald star.

Gently, Gregor drifted to the surface of the faceted emerald sphere. Clasping Pandora tightly to his side, he was imprisoned by mountainous spokes of the colossal gem. Blinding lights shot from one solid hill of precious stone, across a jagged translucent plain of hard emerald material to the glistening spears on the far side. Roughly faceted and cutting-sharp, the smoother planes reflected a series of Gregor's image, all but one. In one translucent rock sat a star-soul, the residuum of a man who once lived but now waited out eternity in the cool prisms of the sphere. Sensitive to Gregor's exquisite passion, the prisoner of the emerald star awoke and spoke to Gregor in bursts of lightning.

"Who are you?" he asked. "What forceful distraction passes close to me and calls me from my sleep?"

Gregor held Pandora more closely and stared in awe at the being in the prism. "We were only passing," he said.

"Only passing?" the star-soul asked. "What great power of transference have you that rouses me from my bed of emerald dust to remind me of the ecstasy, just like yours, that was mine eons ago when I had the form of a man, just like you, a mortal. Are you a mortal?"

"Yes. We were only passing," Gregor repeated as he retreated a step.

The wavering image from the transparent rock spit little lightning bolts as he commanded Gregor to halt. "Wait where you are," he ordered. "Such pinnacle of passion is not for mortals! It is reserved for this state of beatitude in which I exist. Surely you know that you are stealing from your guerdon in eternity! You steal and so will I steal. I will take a spark of your soul so I can reverse time. Come closer. Come!" His naked death-gray form advanced and he reached to touch Gregor's chest.

Frightened, Gregor tried to avoid him but an invisible wall bound him to the spot. Still clinging to Pandora, he watched in awe as the fingers touched him. Thereupon, the form of the star-soul became gradually distinct. His huge body took on flesh tones. Blood seemed to throb in his muscled torso. Color came to his hair. His lips became pink. A robust glow appeared in his cheeks.

"Ahh," he sighed. "The centuries melt—no, no, not back so far that I was just a single cell compelled to fuse with another like me. Rather, stop here in a time when existence was sensuous and my body was like yours. Let me remember how it was with her at my side, eager and pleading with me to touch every soft fold of her. How my blood churned when I placed myself in her body and lost my being in sweet agony to some fusion of us in the intense state that has become the seventh color. Come to me once again so that I may have another eon of memories. Come!" He pointed to Pandora.

An invisible force held Gregor as the image pulled Pandora away from him. She struggled as the giant clasped her to him. His body trembled and his pleasure-filled penis pulsed as his mouth sought her lips. They fell to their knees.

Gregor tried to struggle. "No, no!" he shouted. "She is not for you! You can't do that! She is mine! Mine! Do you hear me?"

"Then we shall be one," the star-soul replied drawing a ring of fire around Gregor.

Gregor extricated himself from the circle of fire, and groped about in the dense vapor it produced until he stumbled over Pandora's prostrate body. He lifted her and immediately seemed to be adrift. Slowly fading away, he could hear the droning tones of the man behind on the star. "Go or you will never return...return... return...turn."

Slowly, the earth took its place under Gregor's body. The hard sand was suddenly there beneath it. The wind and cool spray brushed his skin. Quickly, he reached to find Pandora safe in his arms.

Pandora announced her plans to spend the summer in the Village. However, she said that she had to leave again in the fall. "I have to go to New York for five weeks and then to another important job until mid-December."

Gregor argued with her. "But you promised you would marry me!"

"Yes, but not until these commitments are met. You wouldn't like it if I married you, only to leave you for half a year. In February, I must go to South America, and again in May and June. Then I'll be free. Then I can make promises to you. Please understand. *Tu dois comprendre!*"

Gregor could not dissuade her. Several days later, when he found her packing her hats and gloves in a traveling case, he asked in alarm, "What are you doing?"

She looked up from her packing. Her round child-like eyes crinkled at the corners as she smiled at him. Luxurious lashes fluttered on her cheeks. "Don't be angry. Don't be angry. I found a little cottage. I must have my own place until next summer. Anyway, I'm putting away my hats because they make me look like a tourist. Wait until you see my place! The last tenant sold me a china cabinet that she couldn't take with her. It once belonged to a famous Villager, a famous actress. Oh, Gig, you have no idea how excited I am. I'm going to furnish my place with antiques."

Gregor frowned. "When did you go house-hunting? And why didn't you ask me to help?"

"I knew you wouldn't let me if I told you. Don't be upset, Gig. I talked to the lady who was moving. She comes to the beach every day. She was there while you surfed yesterday. Her cottage was just two blocks from the beach. Will you take me to some of the estate sales? Vanessa said she would take me to the antique shops. And the bazaar at St. James."

"When did you see Vanessa?"

"I walked down past the rocks to her house."

"Hmmm." Gregor bent to help her with her packing. "I can see that you are going to be native in no time."

"Gig, several people have asked me to speak at luncheons when they found that I had done my work in Rome."

"Great! You have a lot to offer, and you speak well. You'll be a hit. I'd go just to look at you." He twined her hair in his finger.

"Someone asked me to a meeting of an open-space group this afternoon."

"Oh, brother! I'll be afraid to leave you on the beach alone any more. This afternoon? Not a chance. We are going to take my ski boat down to the Shores. I launch it on that sandy strip next to the Beach Club when the surf is calm. Today is a great day for it. Hardly a ripple. I want to show you where the other beaches are, from Moonlight on down to Mission Beach and the kelp beds. Remember that map you saw at the Aquarium? I'll show you where the fault is, and the sea valleys. Then you can see why the waves break as they do."

"You seem to know the floor of the ocean as though it was your own back yard."

"It is," Gregor agreed. "I wish you would learn to surf. Then I wouldn't have to leave you on the beach."

"I wish I could." Pandora sighed as she snapped the case shut. "It's all I can do to paddle out there with you on a board."

"It isn't all that hard," he said. "Gee whiz! You spend most of the time sitting on your board waiting for a good wave. Then you paddle forward when it lifts you. You stay in the forward motion, sliding down on it all the time ahead of the breaking tip. Actually, bodysurfing is less complicated."

"You make it sound so easy, Gig."

"It is, once you get the hang of it. You'll learn quick enough."

She shook her head. "No, I'd better not. I'll just swim with you." Her eyes flickered pensively. *"Non, je n'oserais pas,"* she repeated.

"You are afraid of breaking your leg again, aren't you?"

"Oh, yes, yes. Did I tell you that it snapped again when I was away? I was driving in Switzerland. I had forgotten my brace. Do you know there is a little village there that reminds me of yours? It is a quaint place by a lake. They are fighting some of the same problems that you have here. They have no place for parking, their lake is being polluted, and foreign developers want to build several highrise hotels to make it a tourist attraction. They asked me to help with interpreting. I'm afraid that I became involved because of a friend of mine who lived there. They asked me to give a talk, and I did."

"What did you tell them?"

Pandora laughed. "I sided with the group who wanted the townspeople to offer an attractive price for the land to make a park. There were lots of reasons why this was not easy to do, the expense for one. I argued that their town was doomed unless they did, and the curse would be worse than the one that befell Teufelhausen, although the doom that came to them kept it quaint at least."

"What was the curse?"

"It was doomed to sink into the ground for ninety-nine years. On that last remaining day, it came to life for a single day of carousing, then it sank into the ground again for another ninety-nine years." She stepped aside, motioning as though the earth had opened beside her to receive the little town.

"That might be the only solution here, too." Gregor pursed his lips, musing over the idea. "Either way, the Village will lose its identity unless some good planning is done."

"And some restrictions are passed," added Pandora. "Oh, yes, yes! Since I was here last, several areas have been laid naked. All that I see is ton after ton of concrete replacing the green of the land, which is bad enough, but when layer after layer of concrete goes up into the sky, beware."

"Personally," Gregor offered, "I'd rather see the curse of Teufelhausen placed on the Village." He had found their bathing suits, and he tossed hers over to her. "Take something warm in case the fog comes in."

"You feel strongly about your town, don't you?" she asked.

"Lots of young people do. The city tried to put a rest facility at Wind'n'Sea. The kids didn't want the beach spoiled. They fought and won."

"Strangers to the heartbeat of the Village should listen to its pulse."

"That's it! A six-month Village residency requirement for city lawmakers, and a book on orientation for new residents!" He handed her a scarf. "For your hair. The wind is coming up."

The next day, Pandora went to her small cottage. Gregor spent the morning helping her put it in order. In the afternoon, while she lined the kitchen shelves, he went surfing. Before he left, he asked, "Would you like to go to the Belgian Restaurant for dinner?"

"Tomorrow night, please," she begged. "When I finish here, I'll be tired. I'll make hamburgers here so I can work until it's done. Then we can go back to your place, and—"

He interrupted her. "Martinis! You haven't tried my Morghann Martinis."

"Groovy. Hope the swells are good. See you later." She waved him off.

Later, on Gregor's patio, they started a fire in the pit, but the desert wind had passed, and the air was cool. Fog stole in from over the water. They retreated to the living room where Gregor stretched himself on his back on the sofa. He reached to pull her over to him, her head nestled on his chest, her hair spread like a skein of spun gold over both of them.

She lay quietly. A deep sigh passed through her body. "Getting an apartment in order can be tiring," she said. "It is going to be charming. You'll see when I'm finished."

Gregor lay sprawled limply, relaxed and thoughtful. "You would never guess the number of times I imagined you here with me."

A minute passed before she answered. "Maybe I was." Then she added in her sing-song way, "Yes, yes."

Gregor raised his head slightly. "You mean that, don't you?"

She paused again. "When I went to India, I met a swami. I want to tell you about it because—"

This time, Gregor raised himself slightly on his elbow. "You went to India?" He let himself drop back to the sofa. "Whew! You really get around. You are too much! No wonder I didn't get letters."

"Before I went, I had already been through a lot of training."

"Yes, I know," he interrupted, "the work on telepathic information. You told me about that the other day, but you didn't mention going to India. Cripes! You could have been here with me all that time."

"But, Gig, I was. Don't you believe me?"

Gregor's hand passed over his brow. "You really mean it, don't you. Are you trying to tell me that you have perfected the ability to send your mind wherever you wish?"

"Yes, that is what I am trying to tell you."

"Astral travel. We talked about it when you first came here. Whew! I knew that you had a mind above normal, but this is extraordinary."

"Well, what is normal, anyway? No one really knows what the brain is capable of doing because nobody had the tools to measure the brain. Normal is a word-substitute for a good measuring stick that charts mind potential. Now that there are tools with which to measure, normal begins to take on another meaning. Now, normal becomes like what we thought was the paranormal."

"Well, just because nobody has called it by name or charted it doesn't mean that the mind hasn't had these potentials as long as man has been on the planet."

"The science of optic conditioning is as old as Zen."

"And yoga. And it's called VIB now, not optic conditioning," he reminded her.

She swung her feet to the floor, coming to a sitting position on the edge of the sofa. "My swami said that Western culture is like two kids in love who think it has never happened to anyone else before." She stopped to stare at him. "Did I ever tell you that I like your dimples when you smile?"

Rubbing his cheeks and frowning, Gregor protested, "For crying out loud! Don't call them that. Men don't have dimples, Pandora! Call them depressions or muscle adhesions or clefts, or anything else. This is a scar from a spear gun." He sat up and pointed to a spot on his jaw. "Do you know what? You are really something else! You really don't get tired of all this scientific garble, do you?"

She shook her head. "No, as a matter of fact, I started to tell you that I am convinced that astral travel exists."

"You think it is a real thing?"

"Well, don't you find that a good part of what we call reality is simply whatever is agreed upon? What is agreed upon depends upon what the culture is at the time, the point in time, the current philosophies, and so on. Everyone hears so much about facing reality, and yet no one knows where reality lies. That is what confuses young people so much. Many of the things that are agreed upon as truth are really not so. The situation creates false awareness. One of the first things in VIB training is awareness of what is real."

Gregor nodded. "I think that what you are saying is that we are living in an age of materialism, and that when we pass over this, we'll make headway in developing the potential of the mind."

"You *do* believe this, don't you?" Pandora asked earnestly.

"Yes, I do! But, of course, not everyone has this potential or maybe I should say that some people have a great deal more than others. History proves that."

"Gig, do you know that you have such potential? Do you realize that?"

Gregor sighed, allowing thoughts of his grandfather to flash through his mind. He heard the words once again...some exceptional talent...his teacher said he could be advanced a grade...you know what I want for him...I want him to be a normal fun-loving kid...not some genius....

Gregor sank back on the sofa. "Hmmm," he murmured. "Hmmm."

"You didn't answer me," Pandora reminded him.

"Well, yes, I guess I realized it," he admitted.

"I'm sure that is why we knew that we were made for each other from the beginning."

He was up on his elbow again. "You knew this from the beginning?"

"Yes, yes." she smiled and tilted her head to one side.

He pulled on a lock of her hair. "How could you leave me guessing? It was torture. Why didn't you let me know?"

"*Tu savais, tu savais*. You knew," she said quietly.

"But I didn't!"

"Think for a minute. You must have sensed it. You said you couldn't get yourself to be with another girl."

"That is true! I couldn't!"

"That's one proof. Now think really hard. Weren't there times when you could sense that I was close to you?"

Gregor rubbed his cheek. "Now that I think of it, yeah, yeah! There was this one night, maybe more." Suddenly he was alert. "Say! You may be right! When I was in Mexico, there was one time!" His eyes narrowed as he concentrated. "Yeah! It all makes sense now!"

"Yes?" she replied anxiously.

"Remember I told you once to walk naked if you felt frustrated over your leg?"

"Oh, yes! I did. When I was alone at my aunt's villa. One evening I put a gardenia in my hair and—"

"—walked in the moonlight." He paused to laugh softly. "I know. I saw you."

Her face lit with a radiant smile. "You see, it works! Nothing can separate us. We can be together even if we're not together."

Gregor shook his head vigorously. "Look, I want you here with me, soul and body! This other business—it's a great game, but I don't want any more separations, and I mean it"

"*Très bien*. After New York and South America, no more."

"Promise?"

"I promise." She kissed him lightly on the forehead.

"Never again. Now, swear it," he insisted.

"I swear it! I'll never leave you. After I come back from South America, I promise that I'll always be where you are."

Gregor heaved a sigh, sank to the sofa on his back once again, easing her body over his. Down on the patio, the embers sputtered and blackened in the fog.

Gregor was content to have Pandora at his side the entire summer. He was happy to see her become known in the Village. She received requests to speak at dinners, not only about her sojourn in Rome, but about a variety of other subjects on which she was knowledgeable, ranging from art and architecture of the Mediterranean to city planning and antiques. She enjoyed speaking about her African safari, the origin of languages, and international politics the world over, particularly in South Vietnam where her political sympathy lay. She spoke gladly in support of the war effort and in Gregor's opinion, she spoke too strongly.

Regarding this notoriety, Gregor was noncommittal, neither pleased nor displeased. He asked only to be with her. However, he was the happiest during the hours she spent with him in his boat on the ocean excursions to the kelp beds to fish, or when he was diving for abalone around the rocks. By the time Pandora left for New York, Gregor had acquainted her with every craig and point; Seal Rock, Alligator Head, the Cave, and all the beaches from Oceanside to the Bay.

He was alone now, ready to begin a new film project that he and Roy had planned. Roy had made no pretense over his relief to find Gregor free again. It was like old times, but not quite.

Very near the end of Pandora's stay in the East, Roy came home one day, his red mustache bristling and his lanky arms flailing about. "Come on, buddy! Let's you and me make the rounds tonight like we used to. I met a couple of wild girls. Stay here in L.A. this weekend and we'll do the town. We hardly use the suite any more!" His mustache twitched as he grinned in his one-sided way.

Gregor shook his head with a certain finality. "Can't," he said.

Roy reared back on his heels. "What the hell do you mean, can't! Cripes Almighty! What's keeping you?"

Gregor touseled his thick hair. "Pandora's due back Monday." He bent over his work again. "I promised to have this film of hers edited so she could give a travelogue for the church."

Raising one wiry brow, Roy blared out, "If it's work you want, there are hundreds of feet we have to cut out of the last reel because of the accident."

"Yeah, yeah, I know. No sweat! I'll get it done," Gregor replied, raising his hands in protest. "This won't take long. I just have to have it ready."

Shaking a finger threateningly at Gregor, Roy continued. "Now let me tell you, old buddy, you're eating your heart out because of some skirt who flits over the globe doing her thing and forgetting you're alive. What's come over you, anyway? She got you hypnotized? Your brain isn't your own any more! Have you forgotten the things we swore when we got our first company boat? We weren't ever going to let a girl split up the company! What's so special about her? I can't count the number of times you've kicked better out of bed!"

His jaw moved nervously as Gregor frowned at his friend. "Look, Roy, I've got to finish this." He pushed his chair backward and braced himself. "What's this thing you got against Pandora, all of a sudden? Why don't you get off my back?"

Roy pressed him all the more. Hands on hips, he towered over Gregor, frowning at him. "When have I ever given you bad advice? Remember all the times you thanked me for saving you from some dame? Well, I'll do it again if I have to! I've seen some great guys fall under some stupid broad's thumb, but I can't see it happen to you!" He drew back a step and exhaled suddenly, obviously relieved to have aired his feelings.

His eyes narrowed and his face reddened somewhat as Gregor shook his head. "Just get off my back, okay? This travelogue is to raise funds for the new school. Pandora promised the Monsignor. Why don't you ask Bill to go with you? Dammit, this thing is gonna be ready on time!"

Roy glared, then threw his hand up in a gesture of surrender. "Pandora! School! Travelogue! Church! What next? Oh, shit!" He slammed the door behind him as he left still muttering, "You wait and see. Like I said, you wait and see."

At this point, Gregor attached little weight to Roy's threat. When Pandora arrived shortly thereafter, he did not mind Roy's going on several diving jobs with another diver.

The holidays had passed much too quickly with Pandora there beside him. Then, in the spring, she left for South America. This was to be the last of her travels, as she had promised. Gregor found some comfort in the thought as he busied himself with filming a short underwater scene for a movie, part of which was being made on the Village beach. Because Roy refused to work with him, Gregor asked David Holliss to help with some of the heavy gear. Often David brought Kelley and Karla with him to watch the truck and the equipment.

On one such day, Gregor approached the truck from the back while Kelley and her sister were busily building an enormous sand castle near the front of the vehicle, not aware that he had come within hearing range of them.

Lustily, Kelley was singing a favorite ditty in perfect pitch, even slipping into ear-catching harmony when Karla joined in a stanza. "Kit's my cat who ate the rat that played all day in the ivy. Kiddle-dee-didee-doo," she sang, slurring the last line with abandon.

In a few brief seconds, a tentacle of ocean foam stole up to seize the castle, sending the elaborate drawbridge crashing into a memory.

"Oh, kiddle-dee-didee!" Kelley exploded angrily. "All that work!"

She stared disgustedly at her damaged sculpture, reaching to begin the repair, but Karla suddenly demolished the remainder with two motions of her feet.

"Karla!" Kelley screamed. "You ding-a-ling! All that work!" She dived to tackle her protesting sister, and when Gregor peeked to see, he was splattered with a handful of wet sand meant for Karla.

"Gosh! Let's do something else," Karla pleaded loudly. "Let's plan our shell project."

"Well, okay," Kelley conceded, dusting herself of sand. "How many shells did you bring back from beyond the pier when you went with David?"

"Not as many as I wanted to get," answered Karla. "I saw Nichole up ahead of me with that boyfriend of hers, what's-his-name."

"Whatja do then?" Kelley asked. "That's no reason to leave."

Karla shrugged her shoulders. "They were having one of their humongous fights and I didn't want them to know I heard them."

"What didja hear? Anything good?"

"Oo-ah, what's-his-name said—"

"His name is Rex," Kelley reminded, emphatically.

"Okay! Okay! Rex told her how much he was in love with her, and she should stop making such an..." Karla stopped, giggled, and pantomimed the next two letters. "...of herself by pining over Gig. Then, Rex grabbed her and kissed her and she slapped him and he slapped her, then they hollered at each other in Spanish, as they always do, until he grabbed her again, kissing her harder than ever."

Kelley sighed. "They are going to kill each other one of these days."

"Fat chance!" came Karla's voice. "You should see how I left them, in each other's arms, kissing passionately, as though they hadn't said a mean word to each other. What a dumb turkey he is!"

"Maybe they should get married and get it over with. He's handsome." Kelley sighed dreamily as she scraped more sand.

"Kelley, do you like Nichole?" Karla's voice came vaguely. "I mean really like her?"

There was a pause. "Maybe I do and maybe I don't. Nichole hasn't ever bothered me, so I can't make up my mind."

"Well, I made up my mind," Karla announced.

"So?" Kelley scooped and patted designs into the wet sand.

"She is selfish and mean. She doesn't think of anyone but herself. Lisa tells me a lot. Nichole has a nasty temper. I don't think she is good for Rex."

"Oh, turtlepooh! Pandora is selfish and has a nasty temper, but you don't say that she isn't good for Gregor, do you?" Kelley asked.

"Yes, but you still don't want him to marry her, do you? Did you ever notice that Rex looks a little like Gregor? How can Rex be so blond if he is Italian?"

"I don't know. Hand me that shell. I think his mother was a blond Russian countess. David can tell you. Why don't you ask him?" The sound of their voices drifted off as Gregor began to drag heavy gear into the truck.

Satisfied that she would keep her promise not to leave him once she returned from this itinerary, Gregor suffered through the months until Pandora's belated return.

As usual, they spent the evening of the second day walking on the beach confiding to each other how they had spent the time apart.

"Whew!" Gregor said. "Your little trips always cover half the world! You told me only South America! Why did you end up in England?"

"To do more work on astral projection," Pandora said. "The technique is almost perfect! Gig, this is the greatest scientific breakthrough of the century!"

Gregor stared at her. "Well, are you able to tell about it now?"

"Oh yes!" she replied with a wave of her hand. "It was incredible!" Obviously stirred by her emotion, her voice grew tense and she lapsed into a tongue more familiar to her. *"Mon trésor, j'ai tant de choses à te dire!* You may find it hard to believe. I have learned to travel back in time!"

Gregor scanned her features and chucked her under the chin gently. "Only one direction? Why not forward, too?" He laughed, teasing her with his lightheartedness.

"It frightened me," she answered seriously, with a pouting lower lip. "If one is frightened, the process will not function."

With another laugh, Gregor said, "Okay, so you went back to King Henry's court or you discovered the secret of Easter Island, or you helped load Noah's ark, or—I know! You found out what killed the dinosaurs! Not that? You discovered that Cleopatra really took an overdose and it wasn't the snake that did her in!"

They were nearing the wall-enclosed plot of sand under Gregor's porch, but Pandora stopped in her tracks with a worried look on her face. "Gig, I cannot tell you this if you do not believe! I won't say another word unless you are serious. The least you can do is regard my scientific endeavors seriously."

His expression sobered. "By God, you're not kidding! You mean it! You really learned to do this?"

"Mon amour, I could not be more serious. You must listen and you must not doubt." She peered into his face with large eyes that suggested innocence rather than the worldliness that would come from venturing into other civilizations.

Gregor reached to stroke her hair. "Okay, okay," he agreed. "I won't agree not

49

to doubt, but I'll listen," he added quickly. "I'll listen."

When she finished, she suggested that he go with her to the research center in order to see the procedure first hand.

He shook his head. "No way!" he said. "At least, not for a while. Not until I help Roy edit this last movie we made. Maybe we can go after it's done. I promised Roy. Actually, he has a right to be teed off. I have been goofing off this past year. It isn't fair to Roy. I'm going to make it up to him before summer's over. We'll leave for L.A. this week."

The six weeks in Los Angeles passed rapidly. Finally, in August, there was a break in the rigid work load that Roy had outlined. They headed south to spend two weeks in the Village. Even then, it was to retake one short underwater scene in the bay.

They were passing the Farms on the last little stretch into the Village when Pandora mentioned Xionflight again. "It is so complex that it boggles your mind. It is an attempt to understand further the forces of the universe. It explores the relationship between energy, matter, gravity and the curvature of space."

Gregor glanced at her curiously. "You know that I've always held with the theory that there is a world unseen that is superimposed on our world, a world that transcends time. People think it's pure nonsense, so I don't talk about it much."

Pandora grew excited. "But it is so! It is indeed so, a whole new revelation of energy as related to matter."

"Is that what your Xionflight is about?"

"Yes, yes! But Xionflight is still unique in that—" Pandora went on to explain in depth, finally ending by insisting that Gregor go with her to visit the laboratory in England in order to be convinced.

"Okay! Okay! But, look now, Princess, let's forget it for the time being and just lay around and do our favorite things. Brother! I need a rest so bad! Roy is a Simon Legree twice over!"

"But of course!" Pandora agreed wholeheartedly. "We'll do just our favorite things. I have a list already—walk on the beach, take out the boat, abalone dinner, new antique shop, no parties if we can help it."

"Right on! No parties if we can help it. Surfing, Margaritas and just lying around after work. I gotta recharge my batteries."

They were about to turn off Pines Road when Pandora reminded him to stop at the quaint Spanish church several blocks away.

"Why do you want to stop there now?" Gregor asked.

"It has a new painting that I want to see," Pandora answered.

"Oh!" Gregor said abruptly. "Oh! I hoped for a minute that you might be ready to make our wedding plans."

"Soon. Soon, *mon amour*," she promised. Moments later, they knelt briefly under the spreading wings of two angels who held the Madonna's cloak of blue.

At Gregor's apartment, his mail was stacked high. Pandora helped him sort it.

"What shall we do about this invitation to Rosemary's party?" she asked.

"Send regrets," Gregor told her. "I'm going to have to run down to Ensenada for Roy on Thursday."

"And the play at the high school on Friday?" she asked.

"Give the tickets to Kelley. Or David."

"Well, I'll have more time to get my notes organized for my Saturday noon talk at the University," Pandora said. "I hope it isn't this hot on Saturday."

"It's always this hot here in August. And let's stay home Saturday night, too. Okay?" He was pleased as she nodded in agreement.

However, it was not to be that way. The daughters of Night intervened, and the first of the Fates, who had meticulously spun the thread of Gregor's life, now abandoned it to the myopic Lachesis who tangled the string uncaringly before the third sister threatened with her shears. Perhaps she singled him out to make him a puppet for her amusement. No matter how it might have been determined, there was a change in some plan.

Saturday came. In the mid-afternoon, Christopher Holliss called Gregor. "Lad, would you do me a favor? I have a full table of guests at the party at the Club tonight, and Vanessa has one of her incurable headaches. I'd appreciate it so much if you would take care of my responsibility for a section of the floor show and see that everything goes as planned. Bill will explain your part when you get there. Pandora will enjoy the party. The Club doesn't throw a better affair than this one."

If only they hadn't gone—but they did, Gregor in his beachcomber's costume and Pandora in her authentic sarong. Since Christopher had called at the last minute, they had arrived late and were still sipping Mai Tais from coconut halves while most of the revelers had already dined. No sooner had Pandora and Gregor seated themselves than the Polynesian entertainers began to perform on the stage. From the catamaran floating on the pool, the show started with an Island girl's vocal entreaty to the volcano gods.

One such god, carved from mahogany, scowled fiercely from among the palm fronds surrounding the stage. Scorning appeasement, could it have been he who singled out Gregor that night? Did this frowning deity, by chance, decree that one of the revelers should pay a penalty for violating his sacred rituals? Was it, by any chance, he who called the rain?

However, the master of ceremonies had called for holders of certain tickets, and it was not by chance that Gregor had such a ticket because Christopher had planned it that way. Gregor's table companions not only applauded him, but they escorted him bodily to the stage.

"Leave my hat and beads right there, Princess, so nobody will take my place," he had called over his shoulder to Pandora. "I won't leave you for long."

"Not for long, or I will come to find you. I swear it," Pandora answered.

To his friends who were forcing his steps onto the stage, he kept saying, "A dance contest, of all things! Chris should have told me. This is a hell of a way to treat Pandora, getting here so late and then leaving her alone! This better not last very long."

It did, however. The hula contest was followed by a twist and others. As soon as he was able, he pushed his way through the crowd of dancers who quickly flooded the floor. In his anxiety to return to Pandora, he hardly acknowledged friends who blocked his path to congratulate him on his showmanship. All the chairs were empty when he reached his table. Pandora was nowhere in sight.

Swearing softly to himself, wiping perspiration from his brow, he sank into his chair, waited five minutes and allowed recriminations to prick at him...damn...why wasn't I born with two left feet...this is the last time I'll let

51

myself get involved with stuff like this... I'll bet she is mad as a hornet... that time I danced at the benefit... she left in a taxi and I couldn't find her for four days... oh dammit... it's starting to rain....

The waiter who passed mumbled something about Pandora's phone call. "I think it had something to do with India," he said. "You'll have to excuse me, Mr. Morghann. We'll have to move all this inside. We were hardly expecting rain for the *luau!*"

Luau... luau... luau... luau.... The word rang through Gregor's head as though he stood too close to a huge bell. He winced, expecting the sound to bring pain. The sound came, but instead of a bell, it was the wild screech of a horn. His foot shot onto the break pedal. He pulled hard on the steering wheel. Having come within an inch of sideswiping another car, he found himself driving out of a shallow ditch back onto the road. Memories of Pandora's disappearance the week before were dispersed for a few minutes.

Gritting his teeth, his usual composure broken, he took the next off-ramp which led to a coffee shop. Inside the restaurant, however, his thoughts ran on again... Thursday already... five long days and no sign of her... how can she do this when everything was going so well for us... but then Chris keeps reminding me that this is one of her habits... I should try to overlook the few times that her temper shows... but... oh, hell... she could have said something to me at the Club instead of going off like that... good God... I've got to stop thinking about it while I'm driving... I went off the road into that ditch... today reminds me so much of that day we came down together the first time... can't believe it was two years ago but then she was gone so much of that time... I wish I could remember something that would explain this... damn... all those foreign agents in her life and that near-accident at the campus... Nichole hates her... Roy was so pissed off at me... would he dare... no... no... not Roy... this whole thing is crazy and now this Xionflight thing that she's into... it doesn't make sense... steady... steady... if I think this thing over one more time, I'm going to lose my goddamned mind....

He stared at his hand, white and benumbed from his tense grip on the coffee cup which shook, nevertheless, as he guided it to his lips.

Forecast II

The sun was laboring to be seen on the East horizon. In the morning mist, the gnarled pines stood with their twisted trunks leaning toward the sea, stretching like tortured human forms yearning to be free. The figures swayed and seemed to awaken when the wind passed through the pine needles in the mystical aura of near-dawn.

"Eei! Eei!" exclaimed one sleepy form. "Behold, Princess, behold the land!" He pointed across the bay.

Another tree trunk yielded its ghost. She yawned, then drew back in alarm. "The sky has turned to stone! Brother-prince, tell me that it is only a mirage! Tell me that the arroyos and the hills of chaparral are still there. Are my eyes dim from my long sleep?"

His black hair brushed his stocky shoulders as the youth shook his head sadly. "It is no vision. It is truly a monstrous needle of granite rising into the heaven which receives it not!"

A shudder ran through the girl's shoulders. "It frightens me," she whispered. "Jaoko, what age have we entered? Is it too soon?"

"Yes, too soon, my Princess. We must sleep until the dark cloud of acid smothers the orb and the death-rain passes. Then the ice will come and the sea must flood the land to make it clean again."

"Then shall the Sea Indians return?" the girl whispered eagerly. "Shall we come again? Once more, will you be Ruler of Kumeyey?"

"Yes, my Princess, we will return when the air is sweet. Come. We must sleep still awhile. The tremble of the mountain will wake us when the time comes."

The bewitching breeze passed again and their forms hardened into branches.

III

"...some kind of international intrigue..."

uring the week following the luau, Gregor spent countless hours talking to Pandora's friends and relatives, to hospitals, bureaus and agencies, airlines and hotels. By Friday, discouraged and morose, he retraced his steps to Christopher's home. Vanessa met him at the door and drew him anxiously into the living room.

"You look tired," she said compassionately. "I take it that you have no news?"

Gregor shook his head as he made his way to the sofa. "I'm tired, really tired." He sank back into the velvet sofa cushions. Vanessa bent over him to arrange a pillow under his head.

As usual, she wore blue. Gregor tried to remember if he had ever seen her in a red dress. Her dark hair was caught up in a clip and piled high on her head except for two loose curls that masked her ears. "Is there something I can get for you, Gregor? Are you hungry?" she asked in her usual soft tone.

"I could stand a cup of your cinnamon tea," he replied, "and put a shot of brandy in it."

Gregor closed his eyes as her footsteps retreated to the kitchen. Red streaks appeared before him. "Bloodshot," he mumbled. "Got to get some sleep. Can't keep going like this." He fell off to sleep.

When his lids popped open again, he was bathed in the cool shades of blue of Vanessa's room. The large burgundy lamps with the profusion of glass magenta cherries were still there and just as tempting now as they had been many years before. A suggestion of warmth just where it was needed, Gregor thought. I remember how I used to pretend that the big blue chair was my castle...it swallowed me up then...she used to worry that I would tear the velvet but I didn't and I lived through a hundred sieges because the cherries were magic...just pretending to eat one gave me the unearthly power to win every battle....

"Chris should be home early tonight," Vanessa was saying as she approached with a tray.

"That's good," Gregor replied as he eased himself up. "In the meantime, tell me again exactly what Pandora said to you the day I went to Mexico."

"Well, let me see," Vanessa began. "She said she had a chance to do some work in Vietnam if she wanted to. She said you wouldn't let her go."

Gregor glowered. "Hell's fire, no! I wouldn't and that's one thing she can be sure of! It's dangerous over there. Besides, she promised that she would give up her jobs as soon as we were married or at least refuse any job that would keep us apart. She can damn well find work that doesn't send her all over the globe." He held up his hand. "No sugar. Just brandy."

Vanessa looked up. "My girls are coming," she said as strains of a song became louder.

"Kit's my cat who ate the rat that played all day in the ivy." The girls' voices broke into harmony. "Kittle-dee-divee doo, divee doo, divee doo!" With a wild crescendo, Kelley led the way into the room and promptly sat beside Gregor on the sofa.

"Let me do it! Let me do it!" Kelley insisted as her mother reached for the brandy bottle. "I know just how much he likes in his cup." As Kelley measured the brandy, her sister slyly stole her place beside Gregor on the sofa.

Today, the attention lavished on him was especially welcome, from the touch of Karla's warm hand in his to Kelley's adoring gaze as she gave him the cup and sprawled on the carpet at his feet.

"Kelley," Gregor said, "tell me all that you can remember about that day when someone bumped into Pandora's car."

Promptly, Kelley sat cross-legged and alert. "She told the crowd at the luncheon that she was going overseas."

"What else did she tell them? What kind of a luncheon was it?"

"It wasn't so much of a luncheon, really. It was more of a sack lunch during a rally. Pandora was helping an army recruiter talk to the students about joining up. As nearly as I can figure, some people were trying to break up the talks. The recruiter was roughed up. As a matter of fact, Pandora got pushed around. I was scared that she'd get hurt. We bugged out of there as fast as we could."

"Hmm," Gregor said as Vanessa stopped pouring tea. "Why did you keep it a secret from everyone?"

"Because Pandora asked me not to tell, but maybe—" Kelley hesitated and traced lines in the nap of the rug.

"Maybe? Maybe what, Kelley?"

"Maybe you should know the whole story. We were coming down the hill in front of Nichole's house when another car sideswiped us right on the bad curve. I think the two men in the car were the ones who tried to break up the talk at the rally."

Vanessa gasped again. "Good heavens! Imagine that! No one is safe anymore." She turned as Christopher Holliss strode from the hallway and glanced at the grim faces.

"Well," he said, "I can see that something serious is going on. No, no, stay where you are and tell me what's happened." He settled down in his favorite chair as he turned from one taut face to the next. "Vanessa looks as though she has just seen the second rising of Lazarus."

"Chris, your daughter has just told us that some student objected to Pandora's recruiting talk and later tried to run her car off the cliff!" Vanessa explained, obviously appalled at the thought.

"Great Scott! When did that happen?" Christopher asked.

"The day she disappeared," Gregor said. "Kelley says that some students—"

"They didn't really look like students," Kelley interrupted. "They seemed much too old. They looked like hippies, long-haired with humongous beards. Yuk! I was scared!"

Thoughtfully, Gregor stroked his chin. "Was the car damaged?"

Kelley shook her head. "Not really. They caught our bumper and spun us around half a turn so we were aimed back up the hill. We just went back up and took the Grade down, staying with traffic in case we were followed. We weren't, but it still shook us up. You should have seen Pandora handle that car! Like a pro. I haven't had a chance to tell her how much I admire her, but I will when she comes back."

Turning to Christopher, Gregor began, "Do you think it's time to call?" His fingers drummed on the tabletop nervously.

"I seem to remember a bit in the papers about some hot-headed demonstrators who were trying to discourage the recruiting talks. More than likely, Pandora went to Vietnam to spite just such people." Christopher's laugh was short. "Perhaps there was no more to it than that, but then on the other hand—hmm." He hesitated and shrugged.

"Chris, don't you think—"

"Call the phone company once more. Maybe they'll know whether that call came from India." Christopher turned to his daughter. "Why didn't you say something about this near accident, Kelley?"

"Pandora swore her to secrecy," Gregor explained hurriedly. "Don't blame her, Chris."

With a look of relief, Kelley added, "She also asked me not to tell that she had to go to Riverside to get some papers. She could have gone there."

Wide-eyed, Karla bounced on the sofa cushion. "I think that the Viet Cong kidnapped her."

"Don't be so dramatic," Kelley retorted, giving her sister a tug that brought her tumbling to the carpet.

Returning the jostle, Karla fumed. "You're always so smart! If you know so much, why don't you find her?"

"All right, girls!" Christopher interrupted. "It's time for homework. Pick up your books. We want to talk for a bit."

Gregor could hear the girls' voices as they went down the hall. "I think she went to New York to get some of those way-out styles she wears," Karla said loudly.

"But, Karla, it's been a whole week."

"Well, maybe she's getting her knee brace fixed."

"She could be nice enough to tell us where she is."

"Maybe she's just playing games with Greg."

"Huh! That's a rather lethal game to be playing with a man. You don't do that to anyone you love. You wouldn't catch me doing that."

"Ah-ha! I'll bet I know why she's gone!"

"Why, Karla?"

"She's involved in some humongous international intrigue and she's being held as a hostage in some castle tower where she is chained to a bedpost."

"Oh, Karla, stop reading those dime-a-dozen books. Your imagination runs away with you."

As their voices drifted off, Gregor shifted his weight nervously. He exchanged a worried glance with Christoper. "Chris, do you think it's about time to—" he began for the third time.

Christopher interrupted with a lift of his hand. "Let's take things a step at a time, lad. Did you check off that last list?"

"Yes, I did. I don't know what else we can do. Look, Chris, I know that Pandora has a temper and I realize that she's done this before, but I have this gut feeling that something is different this time. It's really bugging me! I really think it's time to—"

"Okay, okay," Christopher said. "Yes, call them now. Don't wait any longer. It's time to call the police."

IV

"...maybe a girl with red hair will marry me...?"

The slender figure of a boy stood across from the elementary school. He looked no older than the oldest of the summer school pupils now being dismissed for the day. His head was covered with a mass of dark curls; his eyes were large and furtive. One hand clutched a paper bag, while the other wiped perspiration from features swarthier than the majority of the children who filed past him. He scanned the stream of youngsters nervously. At last his eyes rested on a red-haired girl chatting with two friends.

Turning almost in the opposite direction, the boy appeared to have found some other object to take his interest.

Just out of hearing, the three girls giggled and talked until one of them said, "Don't look now, Karla, but there is your gardener across the street again. Why don't we stop at Monique's house for a minute so he can't follow you home?"

"He is our gardener's son," Karla corrected. "So what? Sure, he helps his dad. So what?" she repeated.

Karla's friends exchanged glances. "But he's Mexican!" the second girl said.

"Humph! What difference does that make, Monique? You talk to Yermo and Domingo in our class, don't you?" Karla argued.

"We'll tell your sister, Karla," the first girl persisted. "I'll bet your mother wouldn't approve. Would she, Monique?"

"Watch out for that red hair, Kathy," Monique whispered with a sly smile. She nudged Kathy and they broke into a giggle.

Karla's face flushed as her anger flared. She was touchy about her red hair. "Go ahead and tell! I dare you. Boy, oh boy! You don't listen when Miss Cleveland talks about equality, do you? Suppose I tell teacher what happened behind the hedge yesterday!"

Kathy's face clouded. She turned to Monique. "Let's take her off our baseball team."

Her bright hair flew over her shoulders as Karla's chin lifted defiantly. "Billy already asked me to be on his. Who cares what you do!" she retorted loudly as she turned on her heel and started in the direction of the boy across the way. Before she was out of hearing, she heard Monique say, "See what you did, Kathy! Now we don't have a pitcher." Kathy answered her with "Oh, let her go. She thinks she is so smart because she wears a bra already." Their voices faded, but Karla knew that she would be asked to pitch as usual tomorrow.

Karla Holliss was among the more mature students in her class. She knew that she had a way about her that put her in good stead with her teachers and her male peers, a circumstance that made some of the girls jealous. On the other hand, Karla realized that she was a bit chubby, not really overweight, but enough to make her sensitive about it. She also deplored her freckles and her red hair which the wind caught at this moment and blew across her face. She smoothed it back busily as she reached the boy who waited for her.

"Jose?" she ventured somewhat anxiously.

"Hello, Karla," he answered in a low voice, his eyes not really meeting hers.

She folded her arms across her waist as he hesitated. "Well, did you come to walk me to my house, Jose?"

The lad turned abruptly to face her and stood ill at ease.

"I...uh...my father...uh...my father dropped me off here," Jose stammered.

Arms still folded, Karla stared at him for a few seconds. "Jose, if you came to walk with me, say so and we'll go," she said firmly. "If you didn't, say so and I'll catch up with some of the other kids."

Without another word, Jose's stride matched hers as Karla began to walk. Occasionally, she skipped or jogged down a short incline, or balanced nimbly on the length of a brick planter, or threw a pine cone with accuracy at a tree trunk. Her thoughts seemed to be elsewhere rather than on the boy who matched her every step and deed. She felt satisfied that her essay had been the best in the class and she visualized herself someday behind the teacher's desk teaching literature to a sea of faces, one of which was Monique's and one Kathy's. Yermo and Domingo were there. All the rest were duplicates of Jose's sensitive features, soft-eyed and crowned by curls. Suddenly, she was graduating everyone but the two friends who had teased her that day. She, herself, received a best-teacher-of-the-year award and regretfully declined a modeling job and three invitations to a yacht party because of her plans to lobby at the Capitol with a handsome Senator.

She finally slowed her footsteps, somewhat out of breath. "Okay," she said. "Where did we stop last time? Ahh, Hawaii is a new state."

"Alaska is a new state," her companion replied quickly.

"Ah, Richard—" Karla began.

"Wait a minute," Jose reminded her. "It's still my turn." He narrowed his eyes. "Okay. Charles de Gaulle became president of France."

"The Shah of Iran married Farah Diba," Karla snapped back. "Okay. Fidel Castro took over Cuba."

"Vice President Nixon visited Nikita Kr...Kr...whatever his name is." Jose pushed damp curls from his forehead. "Movie. John Wayne in *Chisolm*."

"Doris Day. *Doggie in the Window*," Karla replied promptly. "Song. *You've Got Personality*."

"*Mack the Knife*. I've got a good one for you. Monkeys Able and Baker went up in a rocket. Match that one." Jose chuckled.

"Ah, ah—" Karla began. "I can't think of one, Jose. You win this time. Gee, I'd better hurry. I just remembered that Mom wants to let out, I mean Mom wants to fit my white dress. Come on, I'll race you."

However, Jose eyed Karla's house half way down the block and stood still. "Uh," he said, "I—I—"

Karla returned to where he stood. "What's wrong," she asked. "Forget something?"

Jose cleared his throat, blinked his eyes and shifted his weight to the other foot.

"I asked you a question," Karla prodded.

"Will, uh, will *your* mother mind your walking with, with—" His soft eyes opened wide as he stood undecided.

Karla sighed impatiently. "A Mexican? Is that what you are trying to say?"

The boy straightened himself proudly. "My grandfather was born in Spain."

"Well, think of it this way," Karla said quickly as she placed her hands on her hips, "Will your mother mind if you walk with an American?"

"Oh, no!" he assured her and smiled broadly. Then he followed on her heel as she ran to her front door.

"See ya," she called over her shoulder as she disappeared into the house without another thought for Jose.

The same was not true of the wiry, sweet-faced teenager with the mass of curly, black locks. He stood entranced for a moment, deep in thought...if I work hard enough...maybe someday I can save money to go to college...and be as important as anybody...and maybe a girl with red hair will marry me...if I work hard enough....

He drew his grass clippers from his paper bag and began to work as though his life depended on it.

V

"...leave the surf clean for the seventy scene..."

The daily fervor of the community was always inspiring to Gregor. On one particular morning, it was even more so than usual. The zeal everywhere was electrifying. The infectious ardor was reflected in the faces of the Villagers who thronged the avenue to watch teenagers paint storefront windows in preparation for Halloween. The same ardor rang in the comments about their efforts and in the judging of the best talent. It was even in the puffs of a resolute wind which chose the avenue as its stage that day.

Filling windbreakers like sails at sea, twisting ladies' scarves and small girls' long hair into whirlwind spirals, the breeze blew in prankish gusts. Unchallenged, it imparted its frenzy to all who passed and spoke in its own way to anyone who paused to listen.

Gregor was particularly aware of the message in the wind's whining. "Hurry! Hurry!" it was whispering. "Do not be still. Borrow my passion. Never hesitate. Lethargy has no place in your heartbeat on this day, just as it has no place in my caress. Quiescence is for aging mountains and for ancient pines. It is for the timeless glaciers and for the souls of heroes. This day is not for them. Today is for those of you who can feel my passion and my fury. I must be heard because to still myself is death to me. The sails at sea must strain and groan. It is my finish if trees do not sigh or if the ocean mist does not drift to cover the sleeping village in the night. My survival is the singing of my song. Listen to it. Hear my melody. Listen for a moment and let me touch the strings that make your own music. Let your blood pulse with my passion, because today is made for gladness. Hear me. Hear me—"

Gregor was among those who felt the magic in the air as he marked scores on his chart. He had been asked by the Town Council to be one of those who judged the paintings. Evaluating the drawings was not a simple task. The avenue had become alive with glowering sprites, ugly gnomes and creatures from outer space.

Comments from bystanders flowed freely. "Look at the detail," they were saying. "Some of these kids relieve a lot of frustrations doing this. Get a load of that bomb scene over there. Lots of talent here. Paintings are good this year, don't you think so?"

"Yeah. Neat. Lots of suppressed feelings are showing. You can read what the kids are thinking. It's an outlet for some of them who can't say it any other way. Just look at that one across the street!"

"Say, do you remember the red devil riding a surf board through a tube that ran all the way across Stevenson's windows? Won grand prize."

"Wish the Town Council would sponsor another contest for Christmas. That would really dress up the Village for the holidays. We wouldn't need wreaths on the lamp posts."

"Wouldn't work," another bystander ventured.

"Why not?"

"Well, the merchants don't want their displays hidden, for one reason."

"There's more?"

"Yeah. The Village has become—"

Suddenly, Gregor's attention was taken by a young woman who waved and approached at a brisk pace. "Hi, Nicki," Gregor called out as she got close.

Nichole Vincett had a way of charming only those she wished to impress. She was domineering and seemed to care little for the feelings of others. This trait made many people discount her loveliness even though she was a beautiful woman. She had the figure of a model and her skin was flawless. There was always a slight blush on her high cheekbones. A nose less aquiline would have robbed her features of strength. She frequently lifted her chin in a confident manner and tossed her head so that her glossy hair cascaded over her shoulder. Her assertiveness and fire drove some to dislike her but attracted others. When she was angry or excited, her black eyes flashed as they did now when she confronted Gregor.

Nichole's voice was low and had a purring quality. "What's this I hear about your going to the Orient, Gig?" she asked as if he should not be leaving.

"That's right, Nicki. I'm going," Gregor answered calmly.

"You didn't even come to say goodbye! I thought you would come to bring my shell book back to me."

"I tried to stop the other day, Nicki, but they were putting in those underground utilities. They wouldn't let me through."

Nichole frowned all the more. "Cars can pass now. You can come."

Gregor's brows lifted slightly. "I can't possibly make it. I'm leaving this afternoon."

She stamped her small foot. "You promised."

Gregor pointed to a blond man across the street. "Is that Rex over there? Seems like he is looking for you, Nicki."

Nichole glared at him, turned on her heel and left rapidly to join Rex. Gregor watched her go, then made his way to the pancake breakfast where David and Karla waited for him.

"Whew! That was a job," he said. "There were so many good paintings, it made it hard to choose. Are you getting some ideas for next year, Karla?"

"Can't wait till I enter the contest next year!" Karla sighed. She rubbed her stomach. "Um, yum, smell those sausages and coffee! My tummy's growling. Where is Kelley? She should be here by now."

Gregor glanced at his watch. "Maybe we ought to go ahead. Whaddaya say, Dave?"

"Let's," David replied. "The line gets too long after twelve. Kelley will find us. Anyway, the *Up With People Chorus* is just starting and I want to hear them sing that song I wrote for them." He turned to follow Gregor into the breakfast line. A quizzical expression passed over his face as the chorus sang the second song. It had a pointed message.

"Don't dirty the beaches with litter,
Tin cans and bottles and glitter!
Leave the sand and surf clean
For the seventy scene
For every living critter."

"Well, did they change the words?" Gregor asked when they finished.

David nodded. "Yeah. I knew they would. This is the way it should have been." David began to sing softly.

"Don't crud up the beaches with litter,
Bottles and blankets and glitter!
All those people who care,
Leave no effluent there,
So the water won't taste bitter!"

He hummed as he pretended to end the song with guitar chords.

Karla pressed her lips together primly. "Oh, David!" she exclaimed disapprovingly. "That's terrible." She sighed loudly. "You could write such good love songs if you tried."

David shrugged his shoulders. A smug grin stole over his face. "Gotta tell it like it is, Sis. Shock people or they won't pay attention. Never mind, you'll hear all your gooey love songs as soon as Billy's band comes on after the chorus. He plays all the Beatles tunes."

The band was already playing by the time Kelley came. With her eyes sparkling and her face radiant, she hurried over, clapping her hands to the rhythm.

"Oh, I thought we'd never get done!" Kelley stopped behind Gregor's chair and wound her arms loosely around his shoulders. "We put too much water in the paint and then ran out of starch, then some unregistered friend tried to help us and almost got us disqualified! Gig, did you ever paint a picture?"

"I sure did!" Gregor assured her with a vigorous nod of his head.

David grinned and arched one eyebrow. "I helped him. We painted the whole length of the store with this giant wave and Gregor would have kept painting around the corner onto the next window if we hadn't stopped him, the wave was so long," David was saying. "And this monster of a red devil was riding the wave, right in the middle of it, so true that you could almost feel yourself in there with him, except that..." David paused and lifted one brow in a roguish manner. He glanced at his younger sister as she ate her sausage and he winked at Gregor. "...except that," he repeated, "all these black guts hanging out of his stomach took all the space."

Karla stopped eating and scowled at her brother. "David! You stop that, now! You know Gregor didn't paint any—Gregor, he's teasing me again, isn't he?"

David continued his narration even more loudly over her protests and Kelley's laughter. "Won grand prize! Everybody talked about it. It stirred such a ruckus that the restaurants decided to capitalize on it, so they served black sausages with orange pancakes. Grand prize! Imagine!"

When Karla put her fork down, Kelley snatched a sausage from her plate. "You shouldn't be eating all those anyway if you are trying to lose weight," she said.

"Huh!" Karla retorted, sourly. "If the judges see you, they'll pin a first prize ribbon on you, with all that paint you got over yourself. I can't tell what color your shirt used to be and you'll never get that awful red paint out of your hair."

"We'll be twins," Kelley quipped, giving her sister a patronizing pat on the head.

Karla gritted her teeth all the more. "What's in your painting, anyway? The structure of hydrogen molecules? It's time for Halloween, not a chemistry lesson!"

Kelley's nose wrinkled as she winced. "Ugh! If it's that bad, I'll go eat worms. They are purple puff-ball pussy cats holding hands in an enchanted stylized tree. My painting is pure pretty nonsense. It stands for peace and love and caring for others."

"Huh! You're such a dreamer, Kelley. You're always—"

While the girls argued, Gregor turned to David. "Do you think this poster paint contest would work at Christmas time? I heard someone talk about it."

David swallowed a mouthful of pancake. "Oh, yeah, it would be great if the merchants allowed it."

"You couldn't use a religious theme, though," Gregor said.

"Why not?" chimed both girls.

Gregor shook his head. "The Village has become polyglot."

"What's polyglot?" Karla asked.

"There are all kinds of people here now, Karla. It's not like it used to be. Christmas represents just one of the religions of the earth."

"Oh, I get it," Karla exclaimed. "It's like it is on our school pageant. We had a Chinese song and a Hebrew song and an Indian chant. Well, we could paint a Confucius-type person on a sleigh ride."

"Or a Buddha character opening his annual box of Christmas ties," David suggested with a grin.

"Now you're getting ridiculous," Kelley interrupted. "Be serious, you guys. It's not a joke."

Gregor sighed and pulled Kelley's sleeve. "Come on," he said, "I'll show you where to get your Crêpes Suzette."

Jauntily, Kelley pranced around his chair. "And the Eggs Florentine and shirred oysters! And I must have a silver fizz, of course. Karla, tell the butler to hold the Vienna coffee till later."

With disdain, Karla thrust something into her hand. "Here's your ticket. Get in line for pancakes." She got up to follow Gregor.

With mock hauteur and a dramatic toss of her head, Kelley waved the ticket in the air. Loudly, she recited a line from her French lesson.

Gregor laughed. "Are you sure that you want to do that now?"

Kelley giggled as she tugged on his sleeve. "What did I say?"

"You said 'row the galley, come what may'."

"*Tant mieux. Tant mieux.* It will be all the more spectacular without any water and without a crew," Kelley said as she danced about making rowing motions with her hands. "I'm getting an A in French. Did I tell you, Gig?" she added.

"You don't call me that very much any more," Gregor said.

"Yeah," Karla chimed in, "because Pandora calls you that. That's why."

With a lift of his dark brow, Gregor responded quicky, "Well, that's great that you're getting an A in your French class, Kelley."

Wryly, Karla watched her sister convert her rowing gestures into a version of the popular twist. All too aware that she did not possess Kelley's spontaneity, she said sourly, "Well, you can be sure she wouldn't get an A in rowing!"

Kelley's eyes sparkled mischievously. "My boat just capsized. This dance is called the swim." After a few more steps, she stood still. "Say, this line is hardly moving. What's going on over there?" She wiggled through the crowd to get a closer look.

Returning promptly, she appeared puzzled. "That chef is showing a bunch of teenagers how to strain syrup through a sieve!"

"He isn't a chef," Gregor said. "He sings opera and has the talent to entertain on stage."

"Gee, Gregor, you know more movie stars!"

"He isn't a movie star, Kelley. Would you believe he is one of the best doctors in the Village?"

"You mean I'm going to have my pancakes made by the best doctor in the community?" Kelley scratched her head. "Gee, that couldn't happen anywhere else but here!"

At that moment, one of the teenagers snatched the sieve from the doctor's hand and went off into the crowd shouting.

"What was that all about?" someone asked.

"Oh," came the reply, "some kid lost her contact lens in the syrup bottle."

The approach of the Haunted Evening was celebrated by the community with costumed street dances, school carnivals, pumpkin carving contests, decorated bicycles and the usual bonfire at the Recreation Center. A scarecrow clown charmed young shoppers at the pharmacy. In witches' costumes, waitresses served a Village specialty, pumpkin mousse pie. Tellers in banks came to work in masquerade. Even meter maids wore costumes. Many housewives became Cinderellas or Raggedy Anns as they went on their errands. There was an award for the best costume seen on the avenue on Friday.

Unique in its spirit, this festive Halloween week in the Village offered a challenge to the holidays to come. Even the elements would not settle for mediocrity. A brilliant display of color brushed the sky every evening. An orange cheddar moon glowed behind the familiar white structure on the top of Mount Soledad and the shadow of it cast a blessing on the rooftops below.

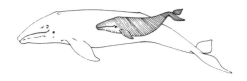

VI

"...half-a-dream hamlet..."

After breakfast, Gregor caught his flight to Los Angeles. Aboard the plane a pert stewardess in a chic orange uniform finished the usual safety cautions "...observe the fasten-seat-belt-sign and bring your seats to the upright position for takeoff."

The aircraft now aloft, Gregor's thoughts drifted again to the woman who came into and out of his life at will. His preoccupation with this became an annoyance. Hell's fire, he told himself, think of something else...the window painting this morning...that spitfire Kelley...she and David could almost be twins...of course, his face is leaner with a rugged look and his hair curls more...but the lift of the brows and the thick lashes are the same...almost the same glow in the eyes...Kelley's have that elfish twinkle...maybe it's something coming from inside...her spirit...her passion for everything...Karla's right...she's a dreamer...she sees the best in everything...some man will find it easy to fall in love with her...she's the personification of the Village...that's what she is to me...enchanting and inspiring and sweet...I love that little town...I always get a thrill out of this view of the bay down there...there's the red-tiled roof of the high school and I can almost make out the parking lot by the church where we ate this morning...the fairways look so green and this view shows you why our streets wind in such crazy patterns to get around those deep barrancas...we are so lucky to have any open space at all...there's the smooth water over the kelp beds...not much surf today...offshore breeze...not really anything so different in the stretch of beach down there and yet there is...the row of palms at the Shores makes you think there was a plan and yet there wasn't...the cross on the hill...now you see it...now it's gone...a half-a-dream place...a funny little half-a-dream hamlet perched on a shelf that hangs over the surf where nobody seems to get any older....

The plane assumed its rightful course. Patches of cloud obscured the land. Gregor unbuckled and looked up just in time to glimpse the back of another hostess as she passed to the front of the plane. There was something about her, the roundness of her cheek and the coil of braided baby-yellow hair, that prompted Gregor to gasp and rise in his seat. The seat tray clattered and his beverage splattered over the passenger next to him. His hostess came quickly.

"Can I help you, sir? Is something wrong?" she asked when she saw his startled look.

Gregor gestured wildly, "That girl—the stewardess who just went into the galley—

who is she?"

"That's Candy Botsford. She works in the tail section."

The blonde stewardess reappeared at that moment. Gregor's face fell and he sank back into his seat with a grunt.

His hostess hesitated. "Are you all right? Would you like some hot coffee?"

"Thank you, no. I'm fine, thank you. I thought I knew that girl, but I don't. Thank you. Nothing else." He waved her away, pushed the seat release and sat back with his eyes closed, forcing himself to think of the preparations for Halloween in the Village, the Beatles tunes, the taste of maple syrup, hot coffee, hobgoblins on the store windows....

He fell asleep almost instantly and dreamed.

In his dream, he found himself wandering at night straining to see the paintings. Suddenly, an unusual thing happened. The forms came to life and followed Gregor down the street to the library steps where another group of misshapen creatures without phylum had already opened a conclave.

On the top step of the library entry, one of these ghouls, a creature with a huge rodent's head and the body and wings of a vulture, seemed to preside over the gathering. The beating of his enormous wings fanned the assembly.

"The session will come to order!" he called out with a choppy accent. His beady eyes glared and his long rat's whiskers twitched.

The next to speak had the head of a barracuda. "Good. Let's do everything in reverse. I move that we adjourn. What are we doing here anyway?"

"We meet to review the prophecies," the rodent-headed creature replied. "Those of you who are not ghosts of Villagers who have sinned against the land may leave if they like. Those who are cursed for violating the land must stay to analyze the prophecies again. Let us come to order!" With this, he flapped his vulture wings again with such force that the other spectators cowered. Gregor retreated to an entryway.

Only the fish-headed monster stood upright. Oddly enough, he had the body of a rodent and a vulture's tail. Gregor stared at the figures. Damn, he thought, my eyes must be playing tricks on me!

The upright creature gurgled and burped but finally made intelligent sounds. "By what right do you speak first?" he demanded.

The rat hissed loudly. "Do you forget? I am in the gorist group. Our sins are the lightest. My sin is the lightest of these whose crime was the least. That makes me your Lord, your Diamio. Do you forget why we are here?"

A cry arose from the assembly. "Yes! Yes! Tell us. We forget!"

"Idiots!" the leader hissed. In a loud voice, he continued. "When our curse was put upon us, the spirit took a vulture from the sky, a rat from the land and a barracuda from the sea. He minced them into three parts with his sword of burning fire. He allotted us the parts as befitted the crime. We, the gorists, who fell unknowingly into our errors, received the head of the wary rat, the mighty wings of the bird and the strong barracuda's tail. You, the zilderogs, who bear the curse in the double degree, were given the stupid fish-head, and the rat's body. All of us must suffer according to how we defiled the land. Now, the court will convene."

"What about us?" croaked another creature as it slithered across the sidewalk. "You made no mention of us."

Comon 86

The Lord Gorist turned his head to one side as though the thing were offensive to him. "Ugh! You useless rat-tailed goomas are beyond mentioning."

"Why? Why?" the gooma croaked. "Because we got the body of the fish?"

"Because you sinned the most and got the useless parts, yes! Now, are there any more issues?"

With a rustle of wings, another gorist arose. "Lord High Gorist," he began, "I am among those gorists who do penance by sweeping the rooftops nightly with our strong wings and raking the beaches with our serrated tails. We are contrite. When will our curse end?"

"Splendid!" the leader squealed. His wings flailed again with such force that the whole assembly bent to the ground. "At this rate, we shall be mighty eagles in less than a century, free to grace the lofty mountain. The court is recessed"

"No! No! There is another issue!" the zilderog insisted.

"Come to the point, Fish-head! Quickly!" demanded the old gorist.

The zilderog burped and sputtered. "We do not have your capabilities. We know our rights. Therefore, we demand to share in your absolutions, those credits already earned. We demand it in the name of brotherhood. It won't add much time to your century."

At that, all the gorists beat their wings and squealed, "No! No! The penance we earned cannot be transferred. The others must earn their shares!"

The creature with the barracuda's head inched forward and was joined by others who had the same fish head. "We will possess what you possess! Move aside!"

The assembly leader fought them with his wings. "You know the proper procedure. Your intent must pass through crystal weight to test it. It won't pass. You will only corrupt the land further. You don't care about the Village!"

"What difference does it make?" the zilderog screamed. "The Village is doomed anyway! Doomed anyway! Doomed anyway!"

At this, the gorist sank his vulture's claw into the zilderog. "No! We will save the Village! You cannot have our absolution!"

The troublemaker's disdainful laughter echoed around the building. "Absolution, indeed! Don't be so stupid. You are only an apparition with a curse on you. There is no such thing as absolution for an apparition with no more soul. It is all a delusion. Just a cruel delusion! A hoax! Step aside and let me tell you what is really going to happen."

The other gorists tried to group behind their chief, screeching, "You agreed to abide by the Chronicle. You all agreed!"

Fur and feathers flew while voices from the fringe of the group moaned, "Doomed! Doomed anyway! Doomed!"

The dissenting zilderog laughed wildly. "We are stronger than you. All the goomas have joined us. We outnumber you. See! See!" He pointed to the conger-like forms behind him, several of which slid over to him, squawked like vultures, fouled the cement steps and promptly fell asleep.

This brought convulsive laughter from the gorists. Even Gregor laughed loudly at which the creatures grew still and stared at him. The rat-faced leader rasped, "You! You there! What was your sin against the land?" He pointed his clawed wing at Gregor.

"Me? I haven't done anything," Gregor answered as he drew back from the

69

group. "Oh, maybe I was over my quota on abs sometimes and I didn't always throw back the shorts. Otherwise I haven't destroyed anything in the Village! You can read my record any time."

"That's it!" the gorists began to mutter. "Read the records. Where is the Chronicle? Review the words of the Kumeyey! Review the Chronicle. Read! Read!"

The zilderogs scoffed at the idea. "Nobody here reads. What a stupid suggestion."

However, the presiding figure shouted over the din, "You over there, you will read for us." Pointing at Gregor, he hissed to his followers, "Take the book to him."

Gregor took the huge volumn hesitatingly and began to turn the pages but the writing was broken, inconsistent and sometimes meaningless. However, the smelly phantoms pressed around him shouting, "Read! Read!" Panic-stricken, Gregor pieced the writings together.

"...and after the virgin hollow of the Sea Indians is taken from them and filled with yellow death, the bowl of the bay will rest until they come who live in great ostentation and who will rob the sea and denude the land. It shall come to pass that the table of purity will be infringed upon by the extinctables. It is written that they will make the air to burn and the ground to thunder until the mountain will crumble and spill over, covering the Village to the Sea. It is also written that five hundred years shall pass before the Indians return once more to the hollow in the shadows of the twisted pine where they—"

"As it is written! As it is written!" the gorists shouted. "There is no mention of the forfeiture of our penance! We will follow the Chronicle."

The belligerent zilderog spokesman spat on the ground and raised himself on the back of a gooma. "Kill! Kill!" he shouted. "The time has come! Now! Kill now!"

From every crevice, his followers appeared. A skirmish began. Shrieks and moans filled the night air. In no time, the sidewalks were covered with feathers and entrails. Some of the monsters crept away, maimed and oozing. A stench arose from the battlefield. The night meant for revelry had been interrupted. All the happier elves and goblins stifled their laughter and stole back to their window panes, leaving Gregor standing alone holding the Chronicle. Only one elf remained at his elbow, whispering, "It's time...in a few minutes...in a few minutes...it's time—"

There was a tap on his shoulder. "It's time to fasten your seat belt, sir."

Gregor opened his eyes and sat forward. The stewardess was leaning over him.

"We'll be landing in a few minutes. It's time to fasten your seat belt," she repeated, "and bring your seat to a forward position."

The aircraft taxied to a halt. While other passengers hurried from the plane, Gregor stood for a full minute intently watching the hostess with the yellow hair. Then he disembarked and followed the crowd down the passageway to the escalators where a record mass of noisy travelers stood jammed and impatient.

One by one, the moving stairway carried a group of uniformed boys who whistled and shouted to classmates overhead. After them came a woman with a screaming child in her arms. Then the escalator lifted from the crowd a figure with pale, sunny hair that fluttered slightly in the updraft. Once again, the posture and the shape of a slightly inclined head could have been Pandora's.

Every fiber in Gregor's frame tightened. His body shook. He drew his hand across his eyes. "Oh, God! I—I can't stand another disappointment!" he said aloud, but nevertheless he elbowed his way to the side of the stair just in time to see her features fully. This time there was no mistaking the Grecian nose, the petulant lip, the round child's eyes, and the full cheek. They belonged to one person, the person of Pandora Lion.

The shout that came from Gregor's throat startled the people about him. He screamed her name. He dove through the mass of humanity, pushing, tearing at those in his way, almost clawing a path through a living wall.

"Stop that woman!" he entreated of the persons above him on the stair when they would not let him pass. "Stop that blonde girl! Pandora! Don't let her get away! Pandora! Wait for me! Oh, God, don't let her get away! Can't she hear me?"

He scrambled off the escalator, pressing past the irritated man in front of him. The staring of the throng and the comments he provoked meant nothing to him. He ran wildly in one direction, then another, calling her name, but she was gone.

He quickly tipped the baggage clerk to have her paged. He telephoned his friend, Sergeant Gray, to come to his aid. With the help of station masters, the search was spread. Taxi drivers were alerted. Two flights were detained for passenger identification. However, even with the help of special squads, no trace was found of Pandora.

It was late in the evening when the search was called off. Gregor agreed with the sergeant that nothing more could be done, and his voice quavered as he spoke. "Bill, I don't understand how a thing like this can happen," he said. "She was right there." He pointed at the spot for the tenth time.

Bill put his hand on Gregor's arm. "Gig, I want to check one more thing. I'll be just one minute. Wait for me in the coffee shop."

Gregor waited in a booth, too tired to drink the coffee he ordered. When his friend returned, Gregor kept repeating, "I can't understand why she couldn't hear me."

The sergeant stroked his chin. "Well," he answered, "the woman's child was screaming and the lobby was filled with noisy boys. That's reason enough."

Both of Gregor's fists came down hard on the table. "Even so, I don't see how a thing like this can happen!"

"Gig, have you considered that this, ah—" The sergeant hesitated.

Gregor eyed the officer sharply. "Considered what, Bill?"

"...that this girl might have been a close double?"

With a set of his jaw, Gregor surveyed his companion. "Bill, how many years did we room together? How long have you known me?" His gray eyes glared as Bill shook his head. "You know I couldn't make a mistake like that."

Thoughtfully, Bill stirred his coffee. "Remember that you're under a helluva strain right now. That might make a difference."

"Well, dammit, yes, I'm under a strain. Nobody will ever know how this is tearing out my goddamned insides! But there isn't a chance in the world of my mistaking someone else for Pandora. Neither could you. You have been with us often enough. There's nobody else like her. Admit it. Could you take somebody else for her?"

"It's not likely, but still, uh, we've got to think of everything."

The fists came down again. "As sure as I'm breathing, Bill, I tell you, I saw her. I swear it! She talked to the lady with the crying child. You know damned well that even you would recognize her anywhere."

The sergeant placed a reassuring hand on Gregor's shoulder. "Steady, old buddy. Steady."

The strange gray eyes closed briefly as Gregor wiped his damp forehead. The image of the blonde stewardess flashed across his mind. "Damn it all, if I hadn't...if I hadn't lingered on the plane—"

Wearily, Bill interrupted. "Drink your coffee. We both need to get some rest tonight. We'll do a follow-up tomorrow."

With a sigh, Gregor rose. "Bill, if I hadn't lingered on that plane, if I had left one minute earlier, I would have...my God...I would have been standing right behind her on that escalator!"

VII

"...to be a bird when I come back to earth..."

esert breezes descended upon the little garden town. The Village unfolded like the wing of a new butterfly. The beaches filled quickly. Shoppers packed the markets. Lines of laughing bicyclers wound their way through serpentine routes. Gardeners shaped the earth. Foxes and squirrels hid in the cool barrancas while thousands of tennis balls flew in the sun.

Kelley Holliss was dancing around the patio table where she and the family had finished a late breakfast. "A beach picnic! Oh, Mom, what a neat idea!" she was saying, with a clap of her hands. "We haven't been to a beach picnic in a long time. We can look for more shells, Karla. David says the tide is really low this morning."

"Let's build a castle, like we used to," Karla chimed in. "A really big one!"

"I'll make some sandwiches, Mom. Karla can make the lemonade," Kelley said as she balanced a plastic plate on her head and slithered into the kitchen without a spill. With her sister's help, she prepared the picnic lunch, chatting and humming Beatles tunes, and only half-listening to her parents' conversation as Vanessa cleared the patio table.

"...and my Uncle Jonathan said that's the name that the Indians gave to the beach. Long Beach. It really is a long one. Why would anyone want to change the name?" Vanessa was saying.

"The real estate people probably changed the name to give it more class." Christopher clicked his tongue. "It's a shame that they ever found it, but then we wouldn't be here, would we?"

"Uncle Jonathan says it was so beautiful before they started to cut the lots and build," Vanessa said.

Christopher laughed curtly. "Well, San Diego would be out a lot of taxes if they hadn't. You'd think, though, that the City would look more kindly on the Village and its requests. We need some long-range planning if we want to keep its charm."

"Hmm," Vanessa said. "Gregor thinks the feud with the City will never end."

"Speaking of Gregor," Christopher interjected, "I wish we could help him more."

In the kitchen, meanwhile, Kelley was busily fattening the sandwiches. "Do you want onions on yours, Karla?" she asked.

"What's on it?" Karla wanted to know. "I thought the Navy was helping Gregor," she added in the same breath. "I heard Mom say so the other day."

Kelley sighed as she wiped her hands. "Mustard, mayonnaise, lettuce, ham, cheese, pickles, olives, egg salad, chutney, sunflower—"

"No onions!" Karla interrupted.

"About Gig," Kelley added, "the Navy is supposedly letting him use some of their facilities while he is looking for Pandora. Didn't you hear Dad tell about the film he's doing on underwater demolition for the Armed Services?" She inhaled suddenly. "I almost forgot the bean sprouts!"

Karla pushed a stray lock of her red hair behind her ear. "Bean sprouts?"

"Yup. Bean sprouts. Oh, yes, and spinach. I almost forgot. I saw the recipe in *Sunset*."

"Oh, yuk! Look Sis, I'll make my own peanut butter and jam sandwich," Karla said with a wry expression, and as she set about doing it, she continued to speak of Gregor. "I wish he'd come home. He promised to show me how to hunt for abalone. Gee whiz, Sis, how can Pandora make us all worry like this? Poor Gig!"

Seemingly oblivious to the question, Kelley sang loudly. "I never promised you a life of ease, tum de tum tum tum—" Then she tilted her head to one side. "Who's worried about her? I'm not worried."

Karla stopped working and frowned at her sister. "Kelley! You don't want her to come back, do you? Well, look who's in love with Gig!" She licked the jam off one finger. "But how can you be in love with your own cousin?"

"He isn't my cousin, idiot! He'd have to be Mom's nephew to be a cousin. He's more like a cousin's cousin, or some such thing. Stop eating the peanut butter and call Mom. We're ready to go."

Kelley snapped her fingers and hummed another lively tune as they drove toward the red-tiled roof of the Beach Club. Suddenly, she pointed to a house painter perched high on one of the three domes which crowned a turreted structure to the left. "Look," she exclaimed. "Someone is painting the Taj domes brown."

Karla stifled a giggle. "The owner was probably embarrassed by all the jokes."

"What jokes?" Kelley asked.

"Oh, Kelley, you know!" Karla's eyes sparkled with mischief.

"No, stupid, I don't know. What jokes?" Kelley kept humming her tune.

"The kids joke about the domes looking like a lady's boobs!" The giggle burst forth.

The humming stopped and Kelley raised her eyebrows. "But Karla, *three* of them? Now there are simply three brown boobs instead of three white boobs."

"Maybe the paint is special for heat conservation," their father suggested. "One thing is certain, though. Nobody can criticize any more that the Village isn't integrated!"

The day wore on. The castle they built that afternoon outshone any structure that had ever risen in defiance of a rising tide. The turrets of Camelot could not have had more charm.

While the girls carved towers and bridges and parapets, Vanessa and Christopher walked, hand in hand, in the surf. "...and she keeps us in stitches sometimes with her antics. Nothing seems to bother her. Where did she get that habit of wrinkling her nose when she doesn't like something? My, she has grown up so fast!" Vanessa was saying.

Christopher nodded in agreement. "And pretty," he added. "She has soulful eyes like yours. Just give her a few more years."

"Karla, too, Chris. Right now, she's going through an awkward stage, and she's so sensitive about her red hair. But just wait till it darkens like my cousin Jonna's did. Hers was beautiful! Karla will lose that chubby look as soon as I put her on a diet. She'll start stretching up soon, too. With her green eyes, she'll be just as pretty as Kelley some day. And she is such a practical person, Chris. She wants to change everything to her liking. What's more, she does it!"

There was a pause. Finally, Christopher said, "Apparently, I see the girls in a different light, Van."

Vanessa stopped walking. "How do you mean, Chris?"

"Kelley is the practical one of the two," Christopher answered.

Vanessa appeared amused. "Why do you say that?"

"Kelley is the practical one because she takes the world as it is. Maybe that is the wiser way to live!" Taking Vanessa's hand again, he guided her back over the beach to where the girls had finally tired of their activity.

"Mom! Mom! Can we go to find more shells?" Kelley begged. "There are just hundreds of them past the pier at Black's Beach. Can we go? Can we?"

"It's up to your father," Vanessa answered. "We won't stay too much longer. The air is getting chilly." She reached for a windbreaker.

Christopher folded his arms across his chest as he watched his daughters prance about him. "Okay, you can go. It's perfectly safe. The only people who use the beach are the few residents from the Farms and skin divers occasionally. Go get your shells and come right back. Your mother and I will meet you by the surfing area."

Kelley brushed the strands of glossy hair from her face. Thick lashes blinked to keep sand from her eyes. Her pretty face, sprinkled with a few fading freckles, was alight with eagerness. The laugh that sprang from her throat was not really a laugh but a bubble of zeal, inexplicably infectious. She danced around her castle once again, then was gone, her lithe limbs carrying a body mature for her fourteen years.

Heedless of her sister's calls behind her, she skimmed the sand and reached for the white gull that flew low above her, wishing all the while that she could be the free creature that rode the wind, wild and without care. She called to the bird, a cry that sprang from something untamed inside her, and her heart beat madly when the bird answered.

"Bird! Bird!" she called out to it. "Listen to me! I want to be like you someday when I come back to earth, belonging only to the breeze and the waves. But what do I want now, bird? What do I really want? I want to live in this glorious place, just as it is, like father said, just as it is because it is packed with pure happiness. Look, bird! Can you feel it, too? Pure happiness, packed all around us, lovely and free, free to take and I want to take it all!"

VIII

regor's next job was the filming of an underwater demolition team as they cleared a sunken barge from the channel at the mouth of a bay. Finding the task more complex than anticipated, Gregor sent for Roy to help him finish.

On the last day of filming, the sun was strong and the water had become calm. In the late afternoon, the last scene was finished. Roy signaled to Gregor to retrieve the remaining marker and to follow him to the surface. Gregor replied with a nod as he traced a line across his throat with his forefinger.

In the years that they had worked together, they had invented an underwater language far more complex than the ordinary set of signals used by divers. *Running low on air*, Gregor was now signaling. *I'm hungry and tired, and I think that large bass blurred the explosion scene. There he is, still curious and not a bit afraid.*

Roy pointed to Gregor's tank of air. *Just get that marker and get the hell up,* Roy signaled.

Gregor nodded. *I'll be right behind you.* He got the marker and started after his partner. As he swam, he noticed that the ship overhead had drifted closer to a rock ledge that held a pretty cove. It's singular beauty made Gregor pause.

Long shafts of afternoon sun shimmered between undulating shadows and threw an iridescence onto the pink anemones that clustered on the rocks. Thick clumps of delicate grasses rose from the sandy shelf and shifted in a lazy fashion. Wavering glints of light deluded the eye. Gregor became so enraptured with the tranquility of the scene that the sound of his own air bubbles became a resented intrusion. Peaceful...peaceful....

Remember the little cove that Pandora found that day we went diving together..same as this one...what was it she said...how did she put it...a sort of universal simultaneousness as though we were the embryo of the world...the rhythm gave her a womb-like feeling...a feeling of being a body within a body...it feels like time has shifted back to that day...Pandora floating with the grass...oh God...is it real...is she really here...that's her hair in that patch of sunlight...Pandora... Pandora...come here...I gotta catch her....

The marker dropped from Gregor's hand and settled on the sandy floor of the cove. His desire to return to the surface was forgotten. Thoughts became muddied as his body struggled for air. Only one resolve remained: to reach Pandora as she floated behind the thick grasses and kelp. With a weak gesture, he managed to encircle her waist, but in the next instant, he convulsed with pain.

In the meantime, Roy reached the boat and handed the camera over the gunwales.

"Where's Gig?" someone asked.

Roy looked down into the depths and hesitated. In a few seconds, he removed his mouthpiece and said, "He should be right behind me. Can anyone see him?"

"Nothing," came the answer.

"He was getting low on air," Roy said with a note of alarm. "I'll go back down."

"Yeah, you'd better. That small shark we saw yesterday came back with a couple of buddies late this afternoon."

Roy motioned for another diver to follow him. "Bring a couple more shark sticks," he ordered. Then he dived below the surface with two more divers not far behind him.

They saw the marker on the floor of the cove and then found Gregor who was struggling feebly for the last of his air. Embedded in his forearm were the vise-like teeth of a monstrous Moray eel. The water was muddying with Gregor's blood.

The eel had backed most of its thick body into a crevice and around an angle of rock. It refused to be dislodged by Roy's tugging. The other diver held a shark stick in readiness. Roy shook his head. "Too close," he signaled as he pointed to the diver's knife and reached for his own. The two of them plunged their blades into the creature's side. With another quick movement, Roy sliced its head off clean. With Gregor free, they left the cove behind quickly.

Slowly, they eased him to the surface, constantly keeping in their line of vision the young sharks that swam in ever-tightening circles as a trail of blood marked Gregor's ascent.

"...the pot-bellied statue...Hot Curl..."

hristopher had not expected to find his wife home when he came from the office on this day in early December. As he entered, he could see that she had been resting on the sofa. An upswept Gibson-girl coiffure crowned her head and straying curls hung softly over her neck. Her eyes kindled as she looked up at him thoughtfully. The velour shift she wore was a blend of blue and gray that wrapped her in cool elegance. Her voice was melodic as usual, but with a note of weariness. "Oh! How nice that you are home early, Chris!"

"I expected you'd be gone," he remarked in a surprised tone. "Didn't you say you had to take Karla somewhere?"

"Oh, David took her, Chris."

He looked at her more closely. "Are you feeling well, dear?"

"I felt a little dizzy all afternoon."

"Couldn't Karla have gone another time?"

"Not really, Chris. As president of her drama class, she is taking quite a bit of responsibility in the staging of a new book for the program in two weeks. She was not about to miss this appointment. If she did, the Grinch would really steal Christmas! When she makes up her mind, nobody can change it. But then, you can't blame her. How often does a girl get a chance to meet a real author?"

Christopher seated himself, reached for a cigarette, and asked, "Well, where is Kelley? One of the girls should be here helping you."

"Kelley fixed a casserole and put it in the oven before she went out to get signatures."

Christopher sighed again. "Vanessa, I want you to make another appointment to see the doctor."

"I don't really feel that bad, Chris, but I will go." *...don't alarm him...he worries so much....*

"Good." Christopher put the cigarette away unlit. "I've been wanting to open my new bottle of Scotch. We'll drink a toast to a good holiday season." *...she doesn't look well...she doesn't like to complain...I'd be nothing without her...nothing...I love her so much....*

"I'm so glad the Junior High was completed in time for Karla to attend," Vanessa continued as Christopher mixed the drinks. "Did you see her name in the *Village Light* with the honor students?" *...how well I remember the first day we met at the university...I loved him that day and ever since...he has the face of a strong man* *and the stride of a king...that's what I thought...it hasn't changed....*

"What is Kelley getting signatures for?" Christopher asked. ...*Kelley is so much like her...musical and artistic and in love with the world...neither thinks anyone can do any wrong....*

"You remember the pot-bellied statue the surfers made with cement and wire? The police won't let the kids keep it on the beach unless they stabilize it in a sizeable concrete foundation. She belongs to the Surf Club, you know. She is helping to pass a petition." ...*he always had such style...he will never lose that...he will never lose that Commander-in-Chief air...his old uniforms still fit...he always looked so handsome in them....*

"Oh, yes. I remember now. The kids named the statue *Hot Curl* and christened him the patron saint of their beach. It made last week's paper, now that I think of it." ...*a saint...that's what she is...I could curb my temper a bit for Vanessa's sake...I wonder how she stands it at times....*

"Did you read about the high-rise that someone is starting near the Country Club? I heard Mr. Burke say that it will ruin the view from hundreds of lower Muirlands homes. Christopher, there isn't enough land there for a fifteen-story building." ...*I admire a man with a strong will...no one ever finds him wrong...but I know how to make him bend when it's important....*

Christopher came over with two glasses. "Do you know where the seventeenth green is?" ...*she still has the best pair of legs of any woman I know....*

"Of course, I know where it is." ...*after all these years...how do you tell a man how much you still love him....*

"Well, it isn't there any more. They started digging today." ...*we'll get away for a weekend...why is it I don't tell her these things....*

Vanessa sipped her cocktail and when she looked up at her husband again, her eyes were moist. "Christopher, remember how wonderful I thought you were when I first met you? You are even more wonderful now, and I love you more."

He placed his glass on a table, then did the same with hers. Seating himself on a footstool, he took both of her hands in his. "Van, let's get away to my uncle's cabin this weekend. No, no, not with the kids. Just the two of us. Someone can stay with the kids. Let's just think about us for once."

"But, Chris, you forgot the Candlelight Ball is this weekend."

His shaggy brows arched and a twinkle lit his eyes. He patted her hand. "Ha! Just today Jack Millord asked me to get him a reservation. He can go to the dance, but you and I are going to walk the winter's forest paths hand in hand and in love again."

Rex Martyne lived in the Millords' guest house, and when Mr. Millord was suddenly called to Chicago, Rex was the recipient of the ticket to the Ball. Of course, he asked Nichole to go with him.

The Candlelight Ball, designed to raise funds for the local hospital, had always been held at the Country Club. However, the Club's facilities had become inadequate for the expanded patronage of the Ball. This year the committee decided to try something new when they accepted the invitation to use a famous Village home for the site of the affair.

A tortuous drive led up to the enormous house at the top of the hill. On the evening of the dance, a solid line of cars wound to the top, bumper to bumper. The normal drive of five minutes took an hour. In the entry, guests were serenaded by a costumed chorus. Huge canopies had been stretched over patios and gardens. Portable dance floors were filled when Nichole and Rex arrived, and spirits were already buoyant except for one woman crying in the center of a group in the entry.

"What's her trouble?" Rex asked Nichole.

"She is the chairman of the committee," Nichole told him. "I overheard them talking. She is broken up because after all the planning to make everything go well, it had to go and rain!"

Rain, it did! The Deities of Wind and Storm, who had so niggardly denied the parched hill for nine months, decided to bless the resplendent affair with their most abundant deluge.

However, the guests were not daunted, least of all Nichole and Rex. They made their way to the center bar where gaiety soared and where they drew immediate attention.

Rex was well aware that his blue, brocaded jacket was a departure from convention, and that his dark skin and head of blond curls drew the glances of many guests. Aware also of the photographers present, he paraded Nichole about.

Nichole obliged. In a clinging white dress, low at the neckline and simply cut to enhance a perfect figure, Nichole stepped proudly. Her black hair was done in a high coiffure except for raven ringlets that hung here and there over a pretty neck. Her cheeks glowed and her black eyes sparkled. She was radiant and enchanting. Rex, already so much in love with her, was breathless.

"Do you know that you are the most beautiful woman here?" he asked.

Nichole laughed. "I used to hear people say that about Pandora."

"Nonsense!" Rex exploded. "Did you count the number of times you've been photographed this evening? Pandora never caused a stir like that. You are by far the most exquisite! Her face is much too round, like a naive child's. It has none of the character that yours does. Her features are passive. Yours have strength."

With a warm smile, she kissed him lightly. "Waltz me around again with one of your groovy waltz steps. No one can do it as you can."

The music changed to a medley. Rex sighed. "Nichole," he began, "I —" His hand pressed against his vest pocket.

"Yes?"

"I still have the ring. If only you would forget Gig! Don't you see? We would be so good for each other."

She surprised him with the sudden pressure of her hips against his at the same time that her arms stole around him. Pleased with her response, Rex held her tightly. "You belong to me, Nicki. If I can't have you, I don't want anyone. We are alike, you and I. It's time you realized it. Will you take the ring?"

Nichole opened her mouth to explain to him that she had only been startled by a cold raindrop which had slipped between two canopies and dropped down her low-backed dress. But, rather than words, a dozen thoughts came when she saw the anxious expression on his face...it has been a nice evening...no point in hurting him now...don't spoil it for him...just pretend it's Gig...Rex is almost as handsome except that his face is thinner and his nose is more aquiline...he is rather nice to have around when Gig is in Los Angeles...he's been flying up there so often...wonder how soon he'll be back....

"Nicki, did you hear me?"

"Oh, the music is divine, Gi.... Isn't it great, Rex?"

"Nicki, the ring! Answer me!"

"We'll talk about it tomorrow, Rex. Right now, all I want to do is dance and dance and dance!"

X

"...it might be Pandora...has amnesia"

fter classes, Karla and her seventh-grade classmate, Mary, were finishing a science report on the reasons birds were becoming scarce on the beaches. Karla had permission to work with her friend after school on Wednesdays at Mary's beach home in the Shores. They often walked down to where they could watch the surfers.

On one such Wednesday, someone called Karla's name. It was Jose, taller now, with tight curls still framing his aesthetic face and a bright smile showing very white teeth. Karla left a sentence unfinished as she stared at the slim figure in patched surfer swim trunks.

Coming to a halt beside Karla, Jose blinked and grinned broadly. "Surprised?" he asked.

"Well, yes!" Karla answered. "You are the last person I expected to see here on the beach." She stared as sea water dripped from his wet hair to a muscled chest that tapered to a trim waist. "What brings you here?"

He pointed to a house just beyond them. "I help my father for about an hour at that house every Wednesday, and then I come here to swim." He shifted his feet as though he felt unsure of himself. "How about you?"

Leaving his question unanswered, Karla asked, "Do you surf?"

"When I can borrow a board," he answered shyly with a quick glance at Karla's friend. "Do the two of you come often?"

"Oh," Karla responded quickly. "Mary, this is Jose. Mary is working with me on a science project."

"Hi," Mary said curtly without a change of expression. Then she turned to Karla. "I'll be late for my guitar lesson. Come on, we'd better get back to the house." She turned to leave, expecting Karla to follow.

"Yeah, it is getting late," Karla agreed. She took a step and hesitated. "You go on, Mary," she called after her friend. "Tell your Mom that she doesn't have to take me home. I can walk. The exercise is good for me." Then she turned again to the lad who stood taller and prouder and grinned more broadly.

"Oh, we can take you home," he volunteered quickly. "I haven't seen you in such a long time."

Karla nodded. "Not since your dad changed to doing brickwork. Aren't you gardening either?"

"No," Jose replied with a shake of his head. "I help my father with the digging on his jobs, but I'm trying to get work as a handyman for doctors' suites in a new medical building. I know a couple of the doctors."

Karla eyed him with a new interest. "That's a step from gardening. You won't have much spare time with all your jobs."

"Oh, if I work fast, I'll still find time," Jose said as he tipped his head and shook it to drain water from his ear. His shyness melted as he drew himself to full height again. "Guess what I did yesterday!"

Karla put her finger on her forehead as though it would help her predict. "Ahh, you got some abalone?"

Jose's eyes gleamed. "Guess again."

"Ahh, you beat the tides walking from Del Mar?"

"Nope! Better than that. I jumped off the Clam!" he announced proudly.

Karla scrutinized him with added curiosity. "But, uh, that's dangerous, Jose!" Her eyes opened wide. "My brother says it's twenty-five feet from the top of the rock into shallow water. If you don't catch the wave right, uh—" She hesitated and pressed her lips together.

Jose laughed, obviously pleased with her concern. "When you realize what depends on it, you just make dead sure that you catch the wave right. I did it five times."

"That takes a bit of courage. Whew! Dad won't let us do it."

For a few seconds, Jose stood digging his toe into the sand. Then he said, "Want to walk up as far as the flag?"

"Just up to the flag? Yeah, I guess that's okay. Want to play our game of *match-what-I-say?*"

"Sure! I'll start. Ahh, song. *King of the Road.*"

In step with his long strides, Karla answered, "*I Never Promised You a Rose Garden.* Movie. *My Fair Lady.*"

"*Sound of Music,*" Jose answered promptly. "Ahh, famous astronaut—"

The game ended when Karla could not name a prime minister of any foreign country, and she conceded victory to Jose once again.

They walked a few steps during which time Jose cleared his throat several times. "They are planning to make the Cove into an underwater park," he said. He paused, but no reply came. "What is your report about?" he asked.

"We want to find out why the sea birds are getting scarce here, the sandpipers and the pelicans, even the gulls. There used to be a lot more birds," Karla explained. "And nobody does anything about it."

"Oh, neat! What have you found so far?" Jose asked, full of interest.

"Not much. We are going to talk with a man at the Oceanography pier tomorrow. We know that the birds' breeding places in the cliffs have been destroyed, and their food is getting scarce."

He guided her around a heap of seaweed. "And pollution," added Jose quickly. "Check out what pollution does to them. Pelicans in particular."

"What happens to them?" Karla asked.

"We pour chemical wastes into the ocean. Like DDT for example. The fish get the chemicals, the birds eat the fish, and the chemicals make their eggshells soft. The eggs can't hatch."

"Really?" Karla frowned. "What a pity that people have to crud up the land and the ocean so that other things can't live! Poor creatures. Think of how happy the birds must have been before people came. It doesn't seem right, does it?" Karla stopped to study her companion for an instant. "How did you learn so much, Jose?"

Again, he smiled broadly. "I read a lot, talk to people, keep my ears open. Come on, I'll race you back."

Later, when Jose helped Karla from his father's car, she repeated her favorite parting. "See ya, Jose."

"When?" he asked anxiously.

The red hair shifted, catching glints of sunlight as she tilted her head. "Oh, you'll see me around," she said casually.

On entering the house, Karla found the family already at dinner. "I'm sorry I'm late, Mom," she called into the dining room.

"Get out of your jeans, Karla. We expect you to dress nicely when dinner is served in the dining room. Don't be long. Dinner is almost cold," her father's voice echoed in the hall.

Karla changed, returned and slid into the blue velvet-upholstered chair at the heavy mahogany table. She heaped her plate as conversation at the table continued without interruption. Karla pressed her lips together as she thought...they could stop and say hi to me or something...ask about my report...something....

However, her father was occupied with Village problems. "I talked with Mr. Corr's wife today. The landowners whose lots touch on the upper Nautilus development are in a rage about being assessed for it because it will only benefit the developers."

Karla's thoughts drifted off...the baby quail that I saw there yesterday...where will they go if they scrape the hills...and the family of foxes...oh...why don't they talk about something else...they don't even know I'm here....

The telephone rang loudly. David went to answer it. In the dining room, Father was still talking. "It's such a pity that the Village has to grow so fast. I drove my regular route past the university today only to find that the cut-off to Miramar was blocked because of the second building they started."

Karla's mother nodded. "That's the way it goes, always more building. True, every family that comes here would like to be the last, just like the fellow who climbs into an overcrowded life raft from a sinking ship. But people will keep chopping away at those hills until—"

Suddenly, a loud shout came from the kitchen. "Dad! Gregor's partner is on the phone," David called. "Something is wrong with Gregor."

When Christopher arose and left, Karla seized the opportunity to have her mother's attention. "Mom, you should see the new bikini swimsuit that Mary purchased at Scott's store. Can I get one? They are so darling! Please, Mom? Can you persuade Dad? If you let Kelley get one, can I have one, too?" she coaxed.

"My, my, you girls are growing up so fast!" her mother exclaimed.

With a patronizing air, Kelley said, "You'd have to take off ten more pounds before you'd look good in one, Karla."

"Well, all right, I will!" Karla agreed. "Then can I, Mom?"

"We will see," her mother replied. "I can't promise what your father's reaction will be. I haven't yet told him that the school sent Kelley home because her skirt was too short."

"Oh, those rules at school are so dumb," Kelley exploded. "Do you know what—"

As her sister talked, Karla imagined herself tall and slim in a scanty bikini, the envy of all her friends, the winner of successive beauty contests. Now she was on a movie set. Those girls who had teased her about her red hair were now asking her for her pardon and her autograph. Her leading man was pleading with her for a date. Her own father stood at the side of the set in awe of her accomplishment.

Vanessa was rambling on about how a lot of the townspeople still begrudged the university all that prime land when Karla finally mounted the steps to claim her Oscar award for best actress of the year. "...but," Mother was saying, "maybe the undergraduate college will be in session by the time Karla is ready to attend."

Heavens, Karla thought, for once they are thinking of me! However, she forgot about herself promptly as her father and brother returned frowning and grim.

Karla broke the awkward silence. "I guess that Gregor didn't find any trace of Pandora," she said. "I can tell by the look on Dad's face."

Christopher shook his head. "Not a trace! He came back so depressed that he isolated himself on the company cruiser out in the channel. Wouldn't let anyone get near him."

Kelley made clicking noises with her tongue. "I just knew he'd go to pieces if he didn't find her. Good grief! How can she be so heartless?"

"Poor Gregor," Mother was saying. "Maybe you'd better talk to him, Chris."

"I certainly would if I could," Father answered. "But Roy said that he took off for Europe to photograph castles!"

"Castles? That's funny," Karla said. "That isn't his bag. I just can't fancy Gregor taking pictures of castles!"

"Yeah, that just isn't his bag," Kelley repeated. "Something is weird. Why didn't he stop to see us?"

"And why won't he talk to anyone?" David asked. "Gregor is ill, isn't he, Dad?"

Christopher raised his eyebrows. "Something isn't right," he said. "Well, you help Mother with the dishes and get to your homework. Nothing we can do about Gregor until we can find him."

Later in the evening, Christopher and Vanessa sat in the living room alone. Lowering her knitting onto her lap, Vanessa said pensively, "Karla was counting so much on Gregor's taking her to surf this summer. She is disappointed, poor dear."

Without glancing up from his paper, Christopher replied, "The beach here below our house is all the beach that our girls need. Have you noticed some of the sloppy characters that are beginning to go to the long beach? Real beach rats! I don't want my girls to be near them. Karla can wait until Gregor gets back in September."

"Chris," Vanessa said reflectively, "doesn't—"

"Yes? Doesn't what?"

"Doesn't Gregor's behavior seem strange to you?"

Christopher folded his paper. "Yes, it does. I get the impression from what Roy said that Gregor thinks he saw Pandora several times."

Surprise flickered in Vanessa's eyes. "He saw her? How could that be? You said he has gone off to Europe depressed over not finding her."

"Roy says that Gregor thinks he saw her a few times but he was never close enough to catch her. She seems to evade him." Christopher waved his hands in the air. "Don't ask me to explain. She disappears or something."

"Disappears? How?" Vanessa's corkscrew curls bobbed as she leaned forward.

Christopher fingered his package of cigarettes, finally passing them by for the pipe that stood in a mahogany rack. "Roy doesn't know any more than that. We can only guess. I figure Pandora has a double or maybe several. Or possibly he sees her somewhere he can't follow. I have even considered that it might actually be Pandora and she has amnesia." He filled his pipe and lit it.

An enlightened expression crossed Vanessa's face. "Chris, do you remember that letter that Pandora received from Russia? She said she had no idea who the man was. I had the feeling the man knew her. Could she have a recurrent loss of memory? She could be living two lives, slipping from one to the other."

Christopher puffed on his pipe and blew the smoke ceiling-ward. "Does it occur to you that she could be living two lives *without* any loss of memory? I keep remembering things that she said like—"

They talked on into the evening.

XI

"...metaphysics and ontology..."

Summer in the Village passed too quickly for everyone. The grunion ran as usual. A warm current passed the coast for one more season, leaving the surf unusually warm for bathers. There was a heavy rain one day in July, unseasonal and welcome because the hills were parched again. The moisture brought heavy ripples of frothy pink bloom to the oleander. Flashy jacaranda flowered with purple passion.

There was much concern about the Vietnam war. University enrollments filled to capacity as young men began to worry about the draft. Enrollment meant exemption.

The Holliss family had almost completed a brick barbecue to the side of their patio. They were trying it out one evening.

"I'd like to put a sea shell mural across the front of the barbecue," Vanessa was saying.

Christopher agreed. "That would really give it class." He stopped his work to stare down toward the beach. "That looks like Karla down there. She really travels. Look at her run."

"All the exercise will make her a 'lean machine.' She is on a diet." Vanessa chatted until Karla came bounding across the patio.

"Mom! Mom! I saw him!" she shouted. "Gregor is home! This time I'm sure because I saw him." She stopped for breath. "I told you I'd be the first to know it when he came home, didn't I?"

Vanessa smoothed her daughter's hair. "Good heavens, child! You must have run all the way home. You are soaking wet. Now, where did you see Gregor?"

"On his balcony, Mom. I saw his light hair. There's no mistaking that. It's easy to pick him out anywhere. I could have gone back to talk to him, but Mary was in a hurry to get to her lesson. I'm sure it was Greg."

In no time, Christopher was knocking at Gregor's door. He was vastly relieved when the door opened. "Lad," Christopher kept saying, "we're glad to see you home."

Gregor smiled broadly. "It feels good to be home. Sit over here. My things are all over the place. Haven't had a chance to put them away. What a nice surprise to find that they finished paving all of the Shores Drive."

"Well, can't have you coming home to mud roads and one-way streets, now can we? Here, let me give you a hand." Christopher helped to pile boxes in the corner of the kitchen and take bags into the bedroom. "It looks as though you mean to stay for a while."

"Need to rest a bit. Traveling can be exhausting."

"How did the film turn out?"

"Just great. Better than I had hoped it would. You'll have to see it. I meant to call you to let you know I was here. How did you find out?"

They talked for an hour, about the war in Vietnam, about Gregor's travels, about inflation, the trend toward small cars and the boat show in Los Angeles. They discussed Styrofoam, the newest material in the manufacture of surfboards, and the daring feats of the men who met the challenge of the Bonzai Pipeline.

Several times, Christopher tried to direct the conversation to Gregor's well-being, but Gregor turned the talk to something else each time. In his discussion, there was no mention of his search for Pandora.

Finally, Christopher asked boldly, "Gregor, lad, Roy said you were having some trouble. Want to talk about it?"

Gregor rubbed his eyes. "Really, Chris, I'm fine, fine as a guy can be under the circumstances. There isn't anything to talk about." He hesitated as the telephone began to ring. "Help yourself to coffee in the kitchen while I get this call, Chris."

Christopher poured the coffee and seated himself again at the small bar that separated the kitchenette from the dining room. On one side was a brass foot rail. The stools were upholstered with black leather. Christopher examined them closely, thinking all the while that his probing was unwelcome. He was thinking...this lad wants to be left alone...I can't make him talk if he doesn't want to...he looks okay...he has that same cool...that confident stance of his...like a lion king in his own jungle...that's what it makes me think of...too cool...keeps things to himself...that's the whole trouble...even though he knows why I'm here...but I might as well go home and try another time....

Christopher was putting out his cigarette when Gregor returned. "Great pair of pistols, Gregor," he said as he prepared to rise. "French, aren't they?"

"From Normandy."

"Did Pandora give them to you?" Christopher asked.

Gregor recoiled as though he had been struck. The color drained from his face. He appeared to speak, but no words came.

Leaning forward, Christopher cleared his throat several times. Not accustomed to playing tender roles, he fumbled for words, and finally placed his hand on Gregor's shoulder. "Come, lad, if there is trouble inside you, it is not good to keep it there. Better let it come out. You know that you can talk to me."

Gregor's voice came, muffled and halting. "I...I can't even...even bear to hear her name, Chris. It hurts me to hear it, and I can't bear to say it. Yes, yes, she gave me the pistols, the night before we went to the luau." He stared at the framed firearms.

Shifting his weight nervously, Christopher hesitated again. Then he spoke rapidly. "Look, laddie, I taught you to walk, and to swim, and to ride a bicycle, remember? I would like you to feel that you can talk to me!"

Vaguely, Gregor could not remember when Christopher had last called him "laddie," but he did remember that it had always been with an affectionate tone at a rare moment, some occasion that called for compassion, a virtue that came up short in measurement among the facets of Christopher's character. It was this tenderness in a man whom Gregor knew to be blunt and unsparing that opened the way for him. He frowned and began to talk.

"Chris, I can't take it any more. I don't know what's happening to me," Gregor confessed. "I think I must be going out of my mind with worry. It just doesn't make any sense!"

"You're referring to seeing Pandora?"

Gregor's eyes widened. "You know about it?"

Christopher took his cigarette from the ashtray and tapped it a few times. "Roy told me," he explained. "He was not very explicit. He didn't say where or how. He seemed to be confused."

With a blunt laugh, Gregor said, "Huh! That's likely to be because I'm confused! As to where and how, Chris, the first time was at the airport in Los Angeles. She was gone before I could get through the crowd. Then, I saw her in Italy, once in France and once in a crowd in a cathedral. I was taking photographs."

Gregor reached for a folder and began to thumb through its contents. "Pandora was such an authority on Gothic architecture that I became interested. Whatever I didn't learn from her, I researched on my own. My photos are really good. The University of Milan asked me to give a series of lectures. I wish Pandora could have done the commentary for my film. Ya know, Chris, I had a double purpose when I went to photograph old churches. I thought that Pandora might be at one of them because she lectured sometimes and took groups on tours. She was so good. No notes. Talked off the top of her head." Gregor stopped thumbing and drew a photograph from the folder. "Look, Chris. Look at this picture. It's an enlarged shot of a crowd in front of a cathedral. Look!"

Christopher stared at the face in the rear of the photo. When he looked again at Gregor's troubled eyes, he struggled to hold back the rampant thought in his own mind. "Hmm," he mumbled. "Uh, strange. Strange."

"You're thinking that she might have a double, right?" Gregor asked.

"Uh-huh. What do you think?"

"That doesn't explain my seeing her on the cruiser," Gregor said, leaning forward tensely. "Or when I was on the floor of the ocean."

Christopher swallowed and stared. "Well—well, that will take a bit of thought."

Gregor fingered the photograph nervously for a few seconds. "Look, Chris, I can tell you this because you understand about my work in the field of extrasensory perception. If anyone else heard about this, he'd think I was out of my mind, but I expect you to understand." He paused and leveled his glance at Christopher.

"As long as you don't get into metaphysics and ontology, I'll do my damnedest!"

"Okay, then. I think that Pandora is being detained somewhere. I'm going to look for her in Mexico next. I believe she is trying to get a message to me. I'm just not receiving it right. I can't figure what I'm doing wrong, but I feel I'm getting close and I'm just going to keep on looking for her."

"Why do you pick Mexico?" Christopher asked, without a change of expression.

"Well," Gregor answered, "you know the way they impound cars down there, and sometimes put Americans in jail."

"Pandora in a Mexican jail! Not likely!" Christopher chuckled. "Why would you even think of that?"

"Oh," Gregor replied, thoughtfully, "she did more than just interpretation for the heads of state. She was into the political scene. I mean really involved in some way. It worries me."

"Very well, then. You want to look for her in Mexico."

Gregor shrugged his shoulders. "It's only a hunch, but when you don't have answers, you have to rely on hunches."

"None of the agencies were able to help you?" Christopher asked.

Gregor shook his head. "Everyone has tried. Nobody can find a trace. Chris, it's maddening! It's eating my blasted guts out! Ya wanna know what I did when I was diving for the Navy? I let my air run out! They came down to get me! That's the closest I've ever come to getting the bends. Imagine me, the best diver on the coast doing a dumb thing like that!"

"Well, don't be too harsh on—" Christopher began just as the telephone rang again. As Gregor went to answer it, Christopher updated his judgment...no real cause to worry...certainly has a right to be confused about the whole thing...nobody will believe this ESP story of his...should I suggest that he see a psychologist...they won't believe him...do I believe him...Good God...I don't know what to think...well...otherwise he looks fine and trim...his macho image hasn't changed....

Gregor returned to the barstool. "They found my lost bag at the airport. Want to ride down with me to get it?"

Of course Christopher went, but strangely enough, they spoke of other things. As much as Christopher may have wanted to, he found no way to turn the talk to Pandora's disappearance. However, he did have the opportunity to suggest that Gregor might allow David to stay at his apartment for a few weeks.

"David is finishing his research on the red tide and he's trying to write a paper," Christopher explained. "He complains that he can't study at our house because the girls quarrel. You might like some good company."

XII

"...huddled against the body of his friend..."

Autumn didn't seem to come to the Village, because summer lingered on and on. Actually, there was considerably more sunshine than in June. The temperature of the ocean dropped a few degrees, but the beaches remained inviting. Surfers caught their waves as usual; divers waited for the lobster season to start. The grunion had stopped running; the yellow-tail season ended. The sun set farther south on the horizon. Other than that, the most significant change on the beaches, particularly Wind'n'Sea, was the shifting of the sands to the south end, leaving jagged rocks naked and cold.

Although there was no dramatic heralding of winter months to come, there were these changes and a few more. Ornamental maples and birches lost their leaves, but poinsettias rapidly thrust their stalks upward, reaching to the heavens like flares about to burst in crimson tidings. Pyracanthus berries began to show in bright clumps. Everything waited to be its best just as soon as the first heavy rain fell, but instead of rain, the desert wind passed once again.

David Holliss had moved into Gregor's place. The two of them surfed or swam almost every morning and jogged in the late afternoons. Evenings generally found David gathering material for a detailed report for his class in oceanography. The warmth of the water had encouraged an unusual number of red tides on the bay at the Shores. David had chosen this as his area of interest.

On this particular evening, the two of them had finished a casserole of lasagne, and David was preparing to go to the library.

"I can't seem to find my last set of notes," he complained.

"Sorry, old man," Gregor apologized, "but I read them and left them over there on my magazine. They have certainly done a lot of new research on red tide since I did my thesis on the subject. They know about everything there is to know."

"Just about everything, except what makes the plankton gather in patches. Nobody seems to figure that out." David looked out over the bay. "This is the first year we have had such a steady run of red tide so late in the fall."

"It has been so hot. That is a factor, but I think this one is about done. The water was colder this morning, remember? There is a water movement out of the bay. That always breaks it up."

"The other theory says that the zooplankton eat the phytoplankton. Here is the last page of my notes. The blooms are decimated by the grazing of the Polykikos and Noctiluca. That's one of the species that shows phosphorescence. Man, it's really something to see that phosphorescence at night! A friend of mine said he saw footsteps glow in the sand several times."

"Want me to watch for you tonight?"

"Will you? Should be lots of people out walking tonight. Well, I'll be back about ten. See ya."

As he drove up the hill to the library, one of the two buildings that graced the young campus, David found himself reflecting on the several weeks he had spent at Gregor's hideaway...wish this were a permanent arrangement...I get so much more studying done...Karla is so noisy...and Dad can't see how many beers I drink...but I really can study better...Gig is planning to go back to his outfit in another week or so...wish he didn't have to go...wish *I* could surf like he does...that guy is something else...wonder if Dad would let me have an apartment...would be nice...Dad is always breathing down my back...miss Mom's food...nice to be my own boss...just look at that fog bank hanging way out there over the ocean...I'll bet our warm weather is shot...Kim said she'd be waiting at the library...paving this grade made such an improvement...I wonder how we ever managed on that road before...an overwide cowpath...that's what it was...oh...that looked like Nichole's car I just passed...too bad she discovered that Gig was back in the Village...there is one hell of a difficult woman...ah...I got here early enough and there is my favorite parking place waiting for me....

David finished his work and finally closed his book, making his way to the car, whistling as he went. Already he could see that the bank of fog had moved in from over the water, just as though some monstrous giant had pulled a spongy blanket over the Village for the night, stealthily, with no sound or warning.

Still whistling, David inched his way down the hill as the fog grew thicker. He parked his car and groped his way down the stairs to Gregor's door.

"I'm back!" he called out. "Made it through that fog alive!" He entered the kitchenette, plugged in the coffeepot, still whistling his tune. "You got that balcony door open for any reason, Gig? It's cold in here!" David strode to the half-open door of the balcony and flung it shut. He re-entered the kitchen and poured milk into his cup before filling it with hot coffee. Then he searched the cupboard. "Gregor, where did you put the cookies?" Suddenly, David stopped to listen. "Hey, Gig!" Next he made a thorough search of the house. Gregor was not there.

"So, what is so funny about that?" David reasoned. "Can't the guy step out for a while? The cookies are in the cannister, remember? And your coffee is getting cold."

He sat on the sofa, humming as he devoured his snack. He sniffed the air. "Nichole's perfume! She was here, just as I suspected. Maybe they went somewhere in her car, because I'm sure that was Gregor's car up there in the drive. Better go up and check."

David groped his way to the drive and back to the apartment. He started to dial Nichole's number when his glance fell on the balcony door which had been open on his return. David flung it open once more. Thick fog pressed against the building, obscuring everything, the balcony rail, even his hand. Unasked and unwelcome, it billowed into the room, ghostly and chilling. David stepped into the room, thrusting the door shut. In several strides, he reached the wooden steps that led to the sandy area below the balcony. Guided by the wall that protected the patio, he stepped forward and tripped over Gregor's body.

"Gregor! God dammit to hell! What happened?" David bent over his friend and swore again. Carefully he passed his hand over Gregor's frame.

"My back. Can't move," Gregor moaned. "Get some help." Then he was still again.

In a frenzy, David massaged his friend's arms. "Don't move, Gig. Hear me? I'll bring a blanket and call Dad to bring help. Hear me?"

He could feel Gregor trying to lift himself on one elbow, and David lent support as he bent low to hear his friend's mumbled words.

"She is...out...out there. See? Go...get her...please! Can't you see?" Then his body went limp again. David tore his own light sweater from his body, covered Gregor, and stumbled twice in his hurry to scale the stairs.

When he telephoned his father, he stammered out his news. "Dad, I think it's a break somewhere in his hip or back, and I don't want to move him. Get an ambulance, okay? I'll keep him warm. Hurry!"

On the beach once again, David began to shiver despite his heavy jacket. He sat close to Gregor, trying to keep his friend warm with heavy covers.

The moments that passed seemed unending. He had never felt so alone. The whole world seemed to have disappeared and what was left was a dismal spot of sand on which he sat huddled against the body of his friend. Panic was difficult to control. He longed for the sound of a voice, but there was only the hissing of the backwash as the water retreated under the oncoming surge. Faintly, the sound of a siren mingled with the sound of the foam as it was sucked back into the sea.

He bent low over Gregor's head. "It won't be long now, old boy," he said, and his own voice startled him. Then from above there was a light penetrating the fog, and the sound of men descending the staircase.

At the hospital, a stucco structure of two stories, Gregor had been given one of the private corner rooms with a view of the ocean. His physician suspected an injury to the spine and had put Gregor into traction. This is the way Christopher Holliss found him when he visited.

Gregor flashed a weak smile as he felt his friend's hand on his shoulder.

"Well, well, lad, you don't believe in giving us a dull moment, do you? Say, now, they gave you a nice room. Better enjoy the view because I understand the new building on the mesa is ready and they will move all of you within the week, if you are here that long."

Wryly, Gregor surveyed the apparatus slung over his bed. "Looks as though my chances of that are good, wouldn't you say?"

For a moment, Christopher stood with lips pursed, features taut. The wrinkles in his forehead appeared a little deeper, his hair a bit grayer at the temple, or perhaps it was the blue in his Glen plaid jacket that made it appear so. The even features of his broad face seemed slightly flushed. Impressive features, Gregor was thinking...tie always tied with that perfect Windsor knot...slacks always creased razor-sharp...his roughcut hair always styled...the tone of his voice, commanding....

"I was here to see you yesterday," he said. "You weren't in any condition to explain anything yesterday. Can you tell me what happened to you lad?"

Gregor shrugged his shoulders. "Chris, I'll try, but it's so hazy in my mind that—"

Christopher looked at his watch. "Gregor, I have only five minutes right now. I have to be back at the office. Now, try, lad. Level with me. Did it happen again?"

"I—I—guess so, Chris." Gregor surveyed the disarray on his bed.

"David said that Nichole came to see you."

"Yes, she can't get along with Rex. We argued. She has a stubborn streak."

Christopher hesitated. "If you say so. Very well. Can you tell me what happened then?"

"I felt hot and sweaty. I went out to the balcony to cool off."

"Have you any idea what time it was then?"

"No."

"Had the fog rolled in?"

"I—I—don't remember the fog."

Christopher patted Gregor's shoulder, nodded his head reflectively, and then walked to the window where he stroked his chin in further thought. Turning about, he stood again by Gregor's bedside. "How do you think this happened, lad? Did you faint and fall over the rail or trip down the steps to the beach?"

"Chris, I just can't believe I passed out and fell. The steps are more likely. Yeah. Yeah. I was in a hurry to get—to get—" He drew his hand alongside his jaw, then looked sharply at Christopher. "What day is this? How long have I been here?"

"Two days. You were delirious yesterday. You said a lot of weird things."

"What, Chris? What did I say?" Gregor asked, anxiously.

With a lift of his brows, Christopher said, "Whew! You must have been having some wild dreams, lad. In your travels, did you visit in Africa or Egypt?"

An urgency crept into Gregor's voice. "Chris, tell me what I said! It's important." He tried to ease himself onto one elbow.

"Now, now, don't get upset," Christopher replied, quickly. As he pressed Gregor back to his pillow, he added, "You were saying something about formulas and flight patterns and Hindu girls in a sheik's tent, and savages and..." Christopher hesitated.

"...and what, Chris?" Gregor asked.

Christopher stroked his chin. "Well, you said something about experimental flight, something that sounded like Xion. You mentioned it several times. You gave us quite a fright, you know. You were comatose for a short while. Van and I were here most of the day yesterday. Something kept disrupting the encephalograph reading and your EKG also. Your doctor said, uh—" Christopher placed his hand gently on Gregor's arm. "Is there something you aren't telling me, lad?"

Gregor let his head sink back onto his bed. "Yes, Chris, I guess there is something."

Nodding his head in thought, Christopher stood for a moment in silence. Then he looked at his watch. "I'll be back tonight. We'll talk tonight—that is, if you want to talk. I'll be late at the office if I don't go now. See you tonight." With another pat on Gregor's arm, he turned and left the room.

It was almost past visiting hours when Christopher returned that night. "Sorry I'm so late. Had a lot to do," Christopher explained apologetically. "You're looking better. Feeling okay?"

Gregor replied with a grunt. "As well as I can under the circumstances. This is a hell-of-a-thing to happen to a surfer, worse than having a three-week flat. But—" He picked up a magazine and pointed to a page. "—I'm not the only one. Look what happened to this guy who surfed the Pipeline in Hawaii last month."

For several minutes the conversation probed the dangers of surfing the Pipeline and the men who dared do it. Then there was a pause in the talk and Gregor said suddenly, "Chris, I promised to level with you. There is more to this thing with Pandora. First of all, though, I've got to know that you understand some of the principles of projection into time and some of the capabilities required to do it. Do you think you understand?"

"Ahh, well, yes, I think so. Not in depth, of course," Christopher answered. "But back off for a minute, now. You know the limits of my mind. Right now, you are stretching that limit. Let me just make sure. Gregor, are you certain that this is not happening in your imagination, or in a dream, or in your sleep?"

Gregor's mouth dropped open. Then he shook his head. "Chris! How well do you know me? This is not good unless you believe me! You have always known that I have rare ability. You and my grandfather both knew it. Remember? Right now, anyone who is too much ahead of normal isn't given credibility, but mark my word, someday, everybody will have this gift of mind. Pandora has it. That's why we were attracted to each other. We could both do out-of-the-ordinary things with our minds. We developed a way to communicate with each other when we were separated. The first time it really worked for me was when I was in Mexico with Roy doing that whale scene. I actually saw her at her aunt's villa wearing the locket I gave her for her birthday. She confirmed it later. That started it all, I guess. The next time, she was driving in Switzerland and broke her leg again. I knew it had happened without her telling me. From there, we just got deeper and deeper into the field of time travel. Finally, she joined some group in England which was really into it. I mean, really! She got me involved. Look here." Gregor turned his head and pointed to a place behind his ear. "Put your finger there. There's a little ridge."

Christopher did as he was told. "There is a little bump."

"Under the skin is a tiny gadget that provides the electrical impulse and guides an energy stream. Let me explain it this way so that—"

Christopher raised his hands in protest. "Whoa! You're getting into the field of metaphysics and ontology, again...a little out of my line. I don't deny that this can happen, but you have to give me time to grasp the concept before you get into the technology of it. Tell me why there is no publicity about this research."

"It's not approved yet, medically, legally, you name it. She called it Xionflight. It's so unorthodox, it's done on the sly."

With a nod of his head, Christopher sat in deep thought. "Did it work for you?"

"I think so, but I didn't have time to practice, really. We set up the lab for it for just a short while. It takes time and at least two people to be safe. She was a pro."

"Hmm. If she is trying to...to appear to you, Gregor, what would be her reason? That is, why should she do it that way? Why doesn't she drive home or take a plane?"

Gregor closed his eyes and ran his fingers through his sunbleached hair. "Oh, Chris, I wish there was some easy answer. It's too much for me. That's why I'm telling you. Damned if I know why she doesn't just drive my car back or take a plane or something. Or telephone! Or send a telegram!"

"There, there, my boy! We'll get to the bottom of this in time. This will all seem funny when she turns up and you find that she has been playing games with you," Christopher said, giving Gregor a pat on the shoulder.

"Do you feel that's what she is doing?" Gregor asked quickly.

"Yes. Unless your story about Xionflight proves me wrong," Christopher replied as he glanced at his watch. "I'm sorry I came so late."

Gregor drew in a deep breath. "Okay. Okay. In a nutshell, Chris, Pandora was so hepped up on this time flight that she wanted to show me how it was done. She had the little sensor put behind my ear and then—"

Christopher began to laugh. "That must be the reason the encephalogram machine broke. The heart monitor on the patient next to you malfunctioned, things were buzzing, telephones ringing for no reason, doctors were in an uproar, electrical engineers came running in, and I've never seen so much confusion in the place."

"Do you think they suspect, Chris?" Gregor asked hastily. "It's important to me to keep this confidential. Promise me you will."

"Don't worry. They decided it was all due to a brown-out in the building," Christopher assured him.

"I was afraid my doctor would ask a lot of questions, but he didn't," Gregor added with a sigh of relief. "He seemed concerned with just my back."

"You've got damage in the lumbar area. That's enough to be concerned about. He doesn't care about your worry over Pandora." Christopher hesitated, shifted his position in the uncomfortable hospital chair, then added, "That would be a psychiatrist's concern."

"A head-shrink!" Gregor grimaced. "Chris, don't tell me that you don't believe my story!"

"Not so! Not so!" Christopher said quickly. Leaning forward in his chair, he added, forcibly, "Mother of God! Who am I to say you aren't right? No, lad, I don't doubt you. I believe, as you do, that we are still mental neophytes on the earth. I foresee an age in which things will happen that we can't envision. Pandora could be ahead of the rest of us. But you didn't finish telling me what she taught you."

"She got some apparatus from England and had some made here. She primed me mentally. Not everyone can do it. Then she tried me out."

Christopher leaned over closer. "Did it work?"

They were interrupted at that moment by a pretty nurse who clicked her tongue, glanced at her watch and said, "Visiting hours are over, Mr. Morghann." She smiled sweetly as she added, "I'll bring your medications in a few moments." With that, she disappeared, leaving Christopher gaping at the door.

"Is that...uh, that isn't the special nurse I ordered for you this morning, is it?" he asked, turning to Gregor.

"I was a bit groggy during the day, Chris. I didn't ask too many questions. But I think she did say you ordered a special nurse. Your taste isn't slipping, Chris."

Holding up his hand in protest, Christopher said, "It was all by phone. I liked her voice. She certainly has class, too." He whistled softly.

"Yeah? Well, she gives orders like a Chief on a Navy destroyer. Be prepared to be thrown out," Gregor advised.

"We'll finish our talk tomorrow. I want you to tell me everything that happened. I'll do what I can to help, but you must realize that I have a limit and that you should really talk to someone who is more knowledgeable."

"The head-shrink again! Chris, you know he won't believe me. He's a doctor, not a metaphysicist! I need a metaphysicist!"

Christopher's toe tapped a rhythm on the floor. "Suppose I find one who is a little of both?"

Gregor gritted his teeth. "No! No!"

Again Christopher hesitated. "Suppose through his efforts, whatever they may be, you find your little lost lady. You shouldn't spare any effort. Just suppose—" He stopped as he watched Gregor's expression change.

"Okay. Okay, Chris. You win. I'll talk to him," Gregor agreed.

XIII

"...fog circled the tall evergreen..."

avid Holliss looked back over his shoulder as he sat waiting on the front porch, his guitar in his hands. As he strummed, he sang with an ear-catching overtone. He knew that his vocal talents were good, and he often wondered why he had turned away professional opportunities.

> "There was a fish in the sea
> Who yodeled much better than me.
> He yodeled so loud,
> Enchanted a crowd,
> His show is now on TV.
> Pity me! Oh...pity...me...ee!

> "There was a girl in distress.
> A poodle tore at her dress.
> I called off the mutt.
> She got away, but
> The dog bit me! What a mess!
> Pity me! Oh...pity...me...ee!"

Again David stopped his song to look over his shoulder. At the sound of his father's voice in the driveway, he put away the guitar and walked to where his father stood by the car. It was already the second week of December but the day was sunny and warm.

Christopher's voice pierced the still air. "Here are the keys, David. You drive," he said as he wiped his brow and tossed his key to his son. "Doesn't seem much like Christmas when it's warm as this, does it?"

David seated himself in the driver's seat. "You forget, Dad, that we have never spent a winter in the snow, only a day or so skiing."

Christopher looked at his watch. "Where is Karla?" he fretted. "If we don't get started, the Pearl Street area will be closed off." He started toward the house just as his daughter bounded out. "Karla, why can't you be on time sometime?" he asked. "You've had the whole morning to get ready."

David watched as his sister's smile faded and she asked, "But where is Mom?"

"She went to lunch with Aunt Joyce," David answered quickly in a low voice in an attempt to avoid further delay. "She will meet us there. Come on,

98

get in."

However, his father continued sourly. "We won't be able to park anywhere near Girard Street. If I can be on time with all the things I have to do, it seems that Karla could be on time, at least once."

Out of the corner of his eye, David could see his sister's downcast face. He turned to her. "This idea of having the parade in the afternoon instead of the evening is not bad," he said in an attempt to divert the subject. "Not bad. The little kids will be able to see more." Near the parade's assembly point, he pointed out a group of sleek palominos. "See them, Sis? Over there."

However, Karla's face did not brighten. She gave her brother a furtive glance, then turned to watch the horses until they were out of sight.

David stopped the car and sang out cheerfully, "Okay, all of you get out here and go find a good viewing spot. I'll find a parking place and meet you at the big bank at the corner."

As he continued alone, David's feeling of compassion for his young sister persisted. Thoughts, otherwise unexpressed, occupied his mind...Karla's insecure...that's why she eats all the time...she'll be cute some day when she loses weight and her freckles and when her hair darkens...it must be tough to have such a pretty older sister...if only she had been a boy...then it wouldn't have mattered...I can't understand why Dad is so rough on her...maybe it's because she looks like Mom's brother...Dad hated his guts but it's hardly Karla's fault that she got those genes...store that in your memory box, David Holliss, and when the time comes, love your kids no matter what they look like...or don't have any...the homelier, the more love they'll get...after all, the beauty that's inside is what counts and not the color of your hair or the shape of your nose...who tells us what is beautiful these days...Hollywood...that's who...Americans judge by what Hollywood throws on the screen...I'll bet that some European painter like Vermeer would have preferred Karla as a model rather than a stereotype like Kelley...there they are now...they hardly look like sisters....

As David joined the family, electricians were making frantic last-minute adjustments on the huge, wrought-iron Eiffel Tower–like structure that straddled the intersection and was to be illuminated at night for this season's special emphasis on Christmas in the Village.

The sounds of a bagpipe band drifted from the distance. David's foot kept time on the sidewalk. "Hey, this is great, this idea of having the parade in the daytime. Why didn't someone think of this sooner, Dad?"

"Well," his father answered, "the merchants grumbled about losing business during shopping hours, but they are cooperating nicely this year."

"But, gee, Dad, look at the people here today! It's gotta double business, not slow it down."

Christopher shrugged. "Some of the merchants are unhappy about closing off the last block to traffic the last two shopping days."

"The whole block?"

"The short one, from the library down. There will be a little red barn in the street with a lamb and a goat, ducks and chickens for the kids to see."

David whistled. "It could happen only here in this Village!" He turned to Karla. "Are you coming to see that, Sis?"

"Oh, yes!" The pink face brightened and red pigtails bobbed. "Mary and I have been given half a day to take care of the animals."

"How did you manage that?"

"We both got an A on our Christmas essays." Karla stole a glance at her father who was occupied with greeting a passing friend. "Look, look," she whispered. "There is Jose in that Explorer Unit coming up behind the motorcycles. Doesn't he look great? I'm so proud of him!" She stopped as she felt Kelley's scrutiny.

"Karla, you don't have a crush on him, do you?" Kelley asked with a frown.

Her smile faded as Karla rubbed the curb nervously with her shoe. "Well, I don't know if you'd call it that. He asked me to meet him when they break up the parade."

Placing her hands on her hips, Kelley looked stern. "Karla, you are only in the eighth grade. Don't let Dad hear that. David, tell her that Jose is too old for her. Why, he's older than I am!"

"Well, ahh," David began.

"What difference does that make?" Karla protested as she turned to her brother for support. "David, he is such a good person. He has manners. He doesn't smoke. If someone in the family would just understand. David, can't you make the family under—"

"Shh," David whispered. "Dad's coming back. Change the subject. With the war going on there aren't as many bands. Did you notice? It isn't the same without all the bands."

Christopher gestured as he approached. "Come on, we're going to get Mother at the coffee shop. She sent a message. The weather has gotten too chilly for her to join us here."

The sunlight of the morning had given way to patches of mist as the parade ended with the lighting of the stately holiday tree at the end of the avenue. Threads of fog encircled the tall evergreen as though the silver garlands were not enough. The crowd scurried for shelter. Shops all along the streets began to fill. David and Christopher turned to go to the coffee shop, but Karla blocked their way.

"You forgot something, Dad," she said. "We didn't get our candy bars."

"Yes," Kelley added, "you always get us chocolate, Dad, remember?"

"Here," Christopher said as he reached for change. "Meet us in ten minutes at the coffee shop."

Karla appeared worried. "That doesn't give us enough time, Dad."

Christopher glowered at his daughter, "I want you to understand, Karla, that you are to stay away from Jose. You stay with your sister. There will be none of this meeting him after the parade. Jose is much too old for you."

David watched as his sister's pink face flushed to a deeper shade. He could sense her indignation under her struggle to remain respectful, but she blurted out, "And he is Mexican. Isn't that what you really mean to say, Dad?"

David heard his father clear his throat in an ominous way. He placed his hand gently on Christopher's arm. "Dad, the Rexall Drug has moved to the old Bank of America building at the end of the street. The girls will need more than ten minutes unless they run all the way."

"Oh," Christopher grunted, meanwhile fumbling with his jacket. "Very well."

David turned to Kelley. "To the store for candy and right back, okay?"

When the girls were gone, he turned to his father. "You are kinda rough on Karla, aren't you, Dad?"

"Karla must understand that we will not permit any romance with a gardener's son, Mexican or not, and especially if he is. She must be made to understand what this does to us. Why should she be permitted to do something that is painful to your mother? There are lots of nice boys to know."

"Maybe we should let it ride and just see how it goes. It might dry up and blow away all by itself."

His father stopped, drew his pipe from a pocket, lit it and dismissed the subject with, "I will not allow my child to follow some course that will offer her about five percent chance for happiness. It's as simple as that. Leave it to me. I've lived longer than you have." They were walking briskly again when Christopher continued the conversation. "Gregor has me quite worried. I don't know what to think of these visions he talks about. He has me convinced that some unusual phenomenon is occurring. It's just incredible. He has me totally bewildered."

"Didn't he promise to see a psychiatrist?"

"Oh, yes, he is seeing one."

David laughed. "I'll bet that Gregor will have him totally bewildered, too!"

XIV

"...she just materialized out of thin air..."

It was evening two days later when a tall, thin man tapped gently on Gregor's door. "I got hung up today. Sorry I'm late," he said as he removed his jacket.

"That's all right, Dr. Quest. The nurse told me you would be late. It doesn't matter to me. I'm not going anywhere, except if they move us to the new building out on the mesa," Gregor answered.

The thin man stroked his chin, then placed both hands on his hips. His shoulders hunched slightly, emphasizing more than usual an angular frame from which clothes appeared to hang suspended. The length of his face was lessened by a shaggy head of hair, thick and unruly. A smile came easily to the doctor's lips and a warmth radiated from his eyes when he spoke. "Well, that might be within the week. They have to move whether half the Village likes it or not."

"Didn't I read that the group opposing the move has taken the dispute all the way to the Attorney General?"

"Yes, but I believe that the whole decision depended on whether the mesa out there can still be called part of the Village, and since there is no established boundary line, I think the issue will be a close one."

Gregor shook his head. "I have never seen the townspeople so divided in opinion."

"Well, you won't believe this, but our neighbor won't talk to us because she knew how much we favored the move."

"I guess you psychiatrists practice mostly in your offices. You don't have to run out to the hospital as much as other physicians."

Dr. Quest reached into his pocket, drew out a pack of cigarettes and fumbled with the tightly packed contents. "I gather that you feel the hospital shouldn't move?" He lit his cigarette. "You don't mind if I smoke?"

"I don't agree with the group that said that this site could be rebuilt to offer a really first-rate hospital. There isn't enough space. But I also don't agree that the hospital should be out of the Village."

"You don't think it is still in the Village?"

"Doctor, to me the Village starts at Torrey Pines Park and stays west of the highway, but I guess that is just a way of thinking."

The doctor exhaled a puff of smoke. "Feeling better today?"

Gregor struggled to adjust the pillow behind his head. "Yes. They think there might be a slight pelvic fracture, among other things."

"Now then, start from the very beginning. Tell me all that comes to mind."
Dr. Quest helped with the pillow. "Tell me again about what happened the night
when Pandora left the Club."

"Just like I told you before, Doctor, I got involved in the dance contest. Damn!
If I had pretended to have two left feet, I would have been out of it sooner. I should
have thought of that."

"Didn't you say that you were an actor at one time?"

Gregor shook his head. "Oh, no. I acted in bit parts, just a few times years
ago. I'm a natural ham, but I didn't have to be such a show-off that night at the
luau, especially since I knew that it bothered Pandora."

"Your dancing bothered her? Didn't she like dancing?"

"She had some kind of bone deformity in her knee. She was sensitive about
having to favor the other leg. Dancing exhausted her. She wouldn't dance and didn't
want me to either."

"Why?"

"I don't know why. I simply know that it started the only bad quarrel we ever had."

"So you think that she resented your dancing again?"

Sweat gathered on Gregor's brow. His skin tingled. He stifled an urgent desire
to break from his bindings. "Yes, I do. I should never have left her there alone,
and I feel responsible for whatever she has gone and done." His eyes were upon
the physician whose pursed lips emphasized the angular bones of his cheeks.

"What do you think she might have done?"

"She might have gone to Mexico or back to South America. God dammit, I
wish someone could find a trace of her, but not one clue has turned up. Last night
I dreamed that the F.B.I. had found her."

The doctor lifted one eyebrow. "Was Pandora in your dream?"

Gregor closed his eyes tightly and leaned back on his pillow. Questions...
questions...talk...talk...what is the use, Gregor thought.

"Not this one."

"But you have dreamed of her?"

"Yes, of course."

"Do the dreams resemble your visions of her, these times when you say you
have actually seen her?"

"Oh, no, doctor!" Gregor laughed nervously. "By damn, I know when I'm
awake and when I'm not!"

"And these times when you see her, they occur when you are sure you are awake?"

"Yes, I'm sure."

"Very well. Now tell me again some of the places you have seen her."

"Well, lots of places. In Rome, in Italy, the other night on the beach here."

The doctor stroked his chin. "Does it appear to you that she is wherever you
are in the world? Does that make any...does it have any meaning to you?"

Gregor shook his head. "I can't say, Doctor. I do know that she was there as
sure as I am here. Those were not dreams."

"Hmm." The physician paced the room, turning to face his patient again. "But
you have dreamed of her. When you dream, where does she appear to be? Anywhere
in particular?"

I wish this was over, Gregor was thinking. His eyes roamed about the room."

"Well, no and yes. It seems to be some place familiar to me, but I can never make it out. In one dream—"

"Yes, go on."

Gregor sighed. "In one dream, the figure suddenly became my mother. I couldn't seem to reach her either. She seemed angry with me. For punishment, she made me dance until my feet were bleeding."

"Do you dream of your mother often?"

"Never before. Except for a small picture that my grandfather had, I hardly knew what she looked like."

"Does she look like Pandora at all?"

"Not a whole lot. I think she had red hair."

"Could there have been times when she was angry with you?"

"No. None." Gregor sank back to his pillow once more. "Nichole was sure mad the other night. She has one hell of a fiery temper."

Dr. Quest seated himself more comfortably and began to make notes. "Tell me about it."

"In a nutshell, Nichole broke her engagement to another guy because she thinks she is still in love with me. She insisted that Pandora was leading me on, that she had some guy in Russia that she was married to. Man! She made me boil!"

Dr. Quest's eyebrow arched again. "Well, does she have someone in Russia?"

"Of course not!" Gregor said quickly. "Pandora has a twin sister behind the iron curtain. She gets letters from her sister. I don't pry. However, I certainly know better than Nichole about such matters."

"Is that what you quarreled about?"

"Yes. She was furious with me, slammed the door and left."

"Then?"

"I felt dizzy and sweaty. I stepped out on my veranda to get some fresh air."

The doctor leaned forward more attentively. "Was there fog?"

"No. I could see the beach clearly. Some kids passed by. Then I saw Pandora."

"Exactly where? Describe it."

"From the direction of the pier, she, ah, I can't remember—" Gregor passed his hand over his eyes, hoping that the doctor could not see how his hand trembled. "She made footsteps in the sand. I remember that."

"Did she see you? Was she close? Was she smiling? Tell me everything you can recall."

"It seems that she was smiling. See me? She might have, I just don't know. I didn't wait."

"You didn't wait?"

"I can't remember what happened after that. It seems like I must have run to try to meet her, but that's all, Doctor, that's all I remember."

"Until David found you?"

"I don't remember David."

The doctor rubbed his bony nose. Wrapped in thought, he puffed on his cigarette. "When you were alone on your cruiser and she came to you, tell me about that."

"Well, I finished my pizza, had a couple of martinis and remembered that I left a varnish brush on top of the cabin. It wasn't quite dark yet, the sun was just going down. I found the brush and looked down just in time to see her coming from the galley. I hollered at her and started to climb down off the cabin. When I reached the deck, she was gone. It shook me up a bit. I thought I must be going absolutely batty."

"Then what did you do?"

"I finished the pitcher of martinis and fell asleep."

The doctor raised both eyebrows. "How do you explain it? The sun? The martinis?"

"No, Doctor, it wasn't the time of day or the cocktails. She was there, alive and breathing, just as we are here now."

"Did she say anything to you? Anything at all?"

"Nothing, she was there and then she was gone. I searched the boat. You've got to believe me, Doctor." Steady old man, Gregor thought, this is as hard for him as it is for me.

"You're trying to say that she just materialized out of thin air?" Both brows lifted again.

It's coming through to him and I'm not sure I want it to, Gregor thought.

"Doctor," he said, "I know you don't believe it is possible because you have never seen it happen. However, you should be among the first to agree that nothing is impossible. Who measures the power of the human mind to do the extraordinary? It isn't so inconceivable that some persons should have special mental prowess, now is it? Most people don't begin to use their brains. You know that as well as I do. Some of us are just ahead of the times. Men just don't know their potential. Maybe they aren't ready for it, but the time will come. Just think back to when laser beams were something out of a Buck Rogers comic strip two decades ago. ESP once didn't even have a name. There were a lot of special mental powers that nobody knew about, and there are still more to discover. Maybe Pandora has some exceptional gifts, and maybe I have the ability to perceive it. Don't close your mind to these possibilities. No, Dr. Quest, you can't sit there and tell me that Pandora has become a figment of my imagination!" There...I got it out...now he knows, Gregor was thinking as he shifted the weight off his tired elbow and sank back into his pillow, paying no more attention to the physician who sat stroking his chin with one hand until the cigarette that he held in the other burned his finger.

When Gregor looked again, the psychiatrist arose, straightened his tweed coat, and said, "Gregor, I want to consider all that you told me carefully and you do the same. Now, I realize that we haven't scratched the surface, that we haven't even touched on Pandora's mind-flight experiments, but we'll get to it. It may take a few sessions. I'm going to see a friend at a convention in Honolulu next week. He has a degree in medicine and in metaphysics. If you agree, we'll talk to him." He paused and waited. "You do want me to do everything possible to help you locate this girl, don't you?"

Gregor lifted his head and strained forward. *"Hell, yes!* Of course, Doctor! Of course!" He blinked and scrutinized the physician with renewed interest. "Do you really think you can?"

The doctor placed his hand softly on his patient's arm. *"Hell, yes!"* he answered with a jolly laugh. His lanky figure straightened as he prepared to leave. "My office will call you before I come again."

"Anytime, Doctor. I'm not planning to surf the Pipeline this week, so I'll be here," Gregor jested as his visitor disappeared into the hall.

At the nurses' station, Dr. Quest stopped to look at Gregor's chart. He had studied the contents for several moments when Christopher Holliss turned the corner.

"You're working late, my friend," Christopher said.

"You, too, Chris, and I think it's on the same homework assignment."

"You've been to see Gregor, then?" Christopher asked anxiously.

The physician's broad smile turned to a worried expression. "Well, Chris, don't ask me to say anything until we have a few more sessions. At this point, mind you, I'm not considering anything like schizophrenia, or any other psychosis, because of what you told me. At any other time, that is, if all things were normal, I might say it looks like a reactive hysteria, a situational thing that will wear off in time. The trauma of Pandora's leaving is compounded by this spinal injury. I was just checking to see if all the results have come back yet. The neurological findings suggest possible minor damage to the lumbar area. Let me see. T-10 to L-1...no evidence of paralysis so far."

Christopher nodded his head. "That much is encouraging. But you said, uh...all things being normal." He looked questioningly at his friend's face.

Dr. Quest's ready smile returned. With a lift of his scraggy brows, he said, "I was coming to that. Your young friend is certainly an exception. He *could* possibly have some rare mental ability."

"Then you don't question the contacts he describes?" Christopher asked. Again Dr. Quest stroked his chin. "Chris, give me a chance to talk with him a few more times. Everything will be weighed in the final analysis. With your permission, I'm going to ask that friend of mine from U.C.L.A. for a consultation. I'll be seeing him at a meeting in Hawaii in a couple of days. Might even ask him to come down here before we leave."

"I have no idea how long Gregor will have to stay here. Even after he leaves, he'll have to take it easy for a long while, so I understand." Christopher gave his perfectly knotted tie a little twist. "Being laid up like this is pretty hard on him."

The doctor grinned from ear to ear. "That bombshell of a nurse he has makes it a whole lot easier."

"Did you ever see eyes that were greener than hers? Beautiful girl, isn't she? Good nurse, too. Certainly has him in tow, but he won't need a special nurse much longer."

The physician tapped the desk with the folder in his hand. "Might be good to keep her though, Chris, until they get the patients moved to the new hospital."

XV

"...telling me not to fall in love with him..."

ancy Starling was a tall nurse who walked with the poise of a model. She wore her copper-hued hair piled high on her head like the coiffure of a demi-goddess at a Roman festival. Her eyes were deep-set and the tinge of jade in them was shaded by heavy lashes. When she laughed, it was a welcome sound like the bubbling of a running brook. She was flippant and cheerful. Even the doctors agreed that Gregor's recovery was ahead of schedule because of her special touch.

The day before Gregor was to be discharged, David Holliss sat in the hospital room softly singing his newest ditty.

> "A pussycat lived on the ice,
> Set traps in his cellar for mice,
> Wished for a dish,
> And he got his wish
> Without asking Santa Claus twice.

> "The sun began melting the ice
> As he started a chowder with rice.
> His Christmas meal
> Has a novel appeal.
> He caught fish in his mousetraps twice.

> "Have you heard the holiday news
> About pussycat's Christmas blues?
> The long ocean swim
> Was too much for him.
> He won't cook any more stews."

As David stopped strumming, Nancy entered, thermometer in hand. "You sound like Burl Ives," she told David. "You should really—" She stopped as Gregor grabbed a half empty glass and drained its contents. The ice in it rattled. "Oh!" she exclaimed. "You'll register like an Alaskan seal! I'll be back in ten minutes." She returned to the nurses' station where she found Dr. Quest talking with Christopher Holliss over Gregor's charts.

Back in Gregor's room, Karla was complaining loudly. "Greg, you've just got to get well enough to go Christmas caroling with us."

"It won't be any good without you," Kelley added. "We practiced so hard, but it isn't the same without your harmony."

"Hmm," Gregor mumbled. "Hmm. Let me see. Well, maybe we can come up with something. Let me see. This may be the best we can do. Here." He reached for a white gown. "Here, Kelley, put this on. You'll look just like a technician. Push over that wheelchair, David. Karla, you go down to the entrance by the parking lot. Then come right back to let us know if the way is fairly clear." He scanned their bewildered faces. "Now then, my aide will appear to be wheeling me to my waiting car." He grinned and rubbed his hands together. "Instead, we are going to sing down on the boulevard!"

Karla's eyes were wide with wonder. "Won't we get in trouble?"

"Chicken!" Kelley hissed. "Don't you want to have some fun? Come on. Do as he says, you guys."

"Don't worry," Gregor said. "Everything is so confused with half of the hospital already moved, no one will question us. They won't miss me until Ash Wednesday."

Meanwhile, after talking with Dr. Quest at the nurses' station, Nancy made her way back to Gregor's room only to find it empty.

Suddenly strains of holiday music drifted from the sidewalk below the window. Nancy looked out in time to see the quartet rounding the corner.

"Oh, good heavens!" she exclaimed. "My patient! Why would he do a thing like that!" In the hallway, she saw Christopher. "Mr. Holliss! Mr. Holliss! Gregor's out there on the sidewalk singing carols! How can he do this to me?"

Christopher chuckled merrily. "It could be because I sneaked him a double Scotch. It's pretty rough on a guy like him to be cooped up in a hospital this long."

With a shout, Nancy headed down the hall, alerting the orderly and two Pink Ladies, nearly knocking down the janitor as she passed. There seemed to be a sudden surge of hospital staff out to the boulevard and, with much flurry, Gregor's quartet was escorted back to his quarters unconcernedly singing about the little town of Bethlehem.

The elderly receptionist kept repeating, "My goodness, we haven't had so much disruption since the day that Dick Nixon was stung by a stingray and came into the Emergency Room!"

Long after other patients were asleep, Nancy brought a cup of hot chocolate to Gregor as he sat strumming softly on David's guitar.

Gregor looked at her without a change of expression. "Nice of David to leave me his guitar, wasn't it? He practically sleeps with this thing." He gave the instrument a slight rap.

She cocked her head to one side and made a wry face. "You didn't give him much choice. You are a mighty persuasive character."

"Oh, yeah?" His brows arched over his gray eyes. "Hmm. Like my music?"

"Groovy!" she said as she straightened his nightstand. "You certainly are a man of diversified talents! You swim, you sail, you get medals for surfing, you dive, fish, film movies—what else is there? You dance well."

Gregor stopped playing. "Who told you that?"

Nancy plumped the pillow on his bed and straightened the blankets. "Kelley told me. She also said that you were an actor at one time."

"Oh, yeah, that." He played a few chords. "Well, I guess I won't be doing some of those things for awhile, surfing and diving in particular. But don't worry, I'll be busy enough. The University of Hawaii needs someone to teach a class in oceanography. I think I'll do it."

"But I thought you said you were supposed to start a new film."

"That's right. Roy and I are going to do another strip on the sunken ships in the harbor."

"How will you manage that with your back injury?" She sniffed at his water glass and grimaced as she took it to the sink.

"There are lots of ways I can help Roy even though I won't be in shape to hang ten at Makaha right away. Did I tell you that we're designing a cage so we can film in shark-infested waters?" Gregor attempted to reach for his slipper. "Hell's fire! If only I could get out of this brace. I'm going bananas in this thing."

With her hands on her hips, Nancy looked prim. "Mr. Morghann, you are so lucky they didn't put you in a cast. By the way, what's your middle name?"

"Michael."

"Gregor Michael Morghann. I like that. Very strong." She got his slipper for him. "Someone better keep a close watch on you so you don't overdo when you leave here."

He changed his strum and stared at her. "Do you know that you smile with your eyes? You do. They really smile. Green eyes." Still staring, he launched into a version of the song. "I've been thinking of getting someone to look out for me when I leave here. You know what the doctor says. Regular care, strict orders. We have to get a secretary anyway. Teaching will take some of my time. There is too much paperwork. You could do it all. Come with me to Hawaii, Nancy."

Nancy stopped her tidying and blinked. "You don't make snap decisions, do you?"

"Good pay and I'll throw in surfing lessons."

"I can surf a little."

"That won't do in the big water. The waves are tricky over there. I'll show you how to ride in a tube." He hesitated. "I'm glad you're coming. You'll like it."

"I haven't said I would go, Mr. Gregor Michael Morghann."

The lights in his gray eyes melted and changed. "Sure you have."

Held spellbound for an instant, Nancy backed toward the door. "I'll...I'll go get your medications. Do you think you can manage to get them down without a double Scotch?" A strange feeling clung to her as she walked down the hall. "Morghann. Morghann," she whispered. "I like that name. Morghann."

In his natty sport coat, a navy and cerise hound's tooth, Christopher Holliss stood toying with his impeccably tied matching tie as he watched his two friends. Jerome Quest and Ryan Ornski presented a study in contrast. Someone visiting from Mars might look at the two and decide that one was from still a different planet.

Jerome Quest was so tall that he had difficulty placing his long angular limbs comfortably when he seated himself. Often he admitted that he needed a house and furniture especially built for him. An unruly mat of hair heightened his already high forehead. Whereas Jerome's smile came and went quickly, Ryan Ornski smiled continuously and sprinkled his conversation with short chuckles. Dr. Ornski's hair was a slick black and was trying to recede. Two dark eyes peered from a round face. With a slightly richer diet, he could possibly have been as wide as he was high.

Christopher and the two physicians were in Gregor's hospital room. Dr. Ornski had been brought in as a consultant. Having been briefed regarding Gregor's contacts with Pandora, he now suggested that his patient should try to remember, word for word, his talking to her about her newly discovered science.

"Just pretend that this is an exact rerun of what happened that evening," the doctor said. "Tell me, as nearly as you can, everything she said and what you answered. Can you do that? Now then, here you are and here is Pandora."

Gregor glanced at all three faces, grimaced and scratched his neck uncomfortably.

The physicians feigned interest elsewhere. "Just start somewhere," Dr. Ornski said. "It will all fall into place."

"Okay, okay. At first, I kinda joked about her new science. She was upset and refused to say anymore unless I took her seriously, so I told her that I was ready to listen—" Gregor closed his eyes as his mind began to reconstruct the scene.

She had taken his hand, and they had walked to a place in the sand inside the patio enclosure as she talked. "They have named this science metaXiontology. For convenience, we call it Xionflight. The process is being kept secret because it isn't approved yet by the scientific world or the medical community. There is a lot of risk involved until the processes are refined a bit more."

"What sort of risk?"

"Oh, a person might get off course, the equivalent of getting lost, I suppose," Pandora answered.

"Lost? Hah! I think that's funny!"

"You promised to listen seriously. Now, don't laugh," Pandora said with a frown. "This is not something to laugh about."

"Okay! Okay! I'm sorry. I'll listen. Go on."

"This science has to do with the discovery of a fifth force, a completely new dimension. Can you believe this?"

"Sure! Actually, I've always felt that there was a ghost world superimposed on ours, a non-matter existence that transcends time. Most people regard this as nonsense and I never really considered that anyone would try to prove it."

"Gig, our scientists not only tried but they did it! You can very well look surprised because it required completely new thinking about particle physics. The very theory of gravity is challenged. It is so complex that it boggles your mind. Xionflight has explored the relationship between energy, gravity, matter and the curvature of space for the purpose of understanding how the forces of the universe interact. Would you believe that we are side by side with an unseen world? My science enters this world."

"Incredible! Now, that is an accomplishment, proving the existence of a non-matter world!"

"No, no, not completely non-matter! Xionflight is still unique because it is not altogether a non-matter world."

"You'll have to explain."

"Let me try to translate this into a practical language. Try to imagine millions of sensitive spokes emanating from the earth, entwining and mingling. These threads have slightly beaded ends separated like the split ends of lightning. Suppose you have a matching spoke or *Xi* material that is somewhat like having your own frequency. We call it an *On-Q* energy stream, therefore the name *Xionflight*. In some persons this energy lies latent. It is there, untapped. In essence, we have learned to guide the flight. There! That isn't hard to understand, is it?"

"Just how do you generate this flight? Does it require equipment, or machinery or mental preparation?"

Pandora nodded. "All of those, coaching, mental exercise, the pooling of brain energy reserves, some monitoring equipment and a surprisingly small metal unit which is placed surgically at the base of the brain. See, here is mine." She placed her hand on a spot at the base of her neck, then guided his finger to the place. "You may not even feel it because it is so small."

"You are right. I can't feel where it is."

"I have an extra unit. If you want to learn Xionflight, I can teach you. I have many of the formulas memorized. You will learn quickly because you have much potential and some ability already."

"Yeah, but not this new stuff of yours. I'd rather wait until they know for sure what they are doing."

"There is not that much to it, really," she reassured him. "It should be easy for you."

"When you come right down to it, Pandora, we are so damned lucky to be born and on this earth and the time is brief enough. Life span is so short. We should be glad we are here instead of trying to escape. Just stop for a minute now to think of how great this is, living on this planet in this age, sitting here by this wonderful super ocean! I kinda like it here."

"Yes, yes, Gig," Pandora agreed. "Yet, there are those who find no happiness, who want to escape, the oppressed peoples, the sick and the starving, prisoners and criminals, those who find life a struggle."

"Great! Maybe your Xionflight will have a use. Can you visualize a medical clinic where a guy goes and says, 'hey, look, get me out of here. I can't take it anymore and I want to go back to the century when my ancestors hunted buffalo right here in the middle of this airport' (or golf course, whatever it may be) and then he steps into this neat little telephone booth, hooks himself up, presses a button as he shouts 'goodbye, you turkeys, I'm going on the no-recall frequency!' Then poof and it's over."

Pandora burst into a fit of laughter. "Oh, Gig," she said. "You can say the funniest things. But then, perhaps people wouldn't have to go and...and... ju...jum..." She broke again into laughter.

"...and jump off bridges! You're right! Maybe there is a medical use for Xionflight. Maybe a legal use, too. Detectives could go back in time and solve crimes. We could solve the Kennedy assassination beyond a doubt."

She eyed him speculatively. "Didn't you say to me once that your ancestry remains a mystery? Perhaps we could explore that. Simple things. Nothing complicated."

"Say! Yeah, let's do that. That I like! When do we start?"

Tired and stressed by the telling of his story, Gregor rubbed his cheek and paused. Dr. Ornski glanced at his watch. "Are you getting tired?" he asked.

Gregor shrugged his shoulders. "Yeah. Kinda. This isn't the easiest thing for me, you understand."

"Sure. Sure." The physician looked at his watch again. "What do you think, Jerry?" He looked inquiringly at Dr. Quest.

"Oh, another ten minutes. Don't worry, I'll get you to your plane on time." Dr. Quest arose to pour water into Gregor's glass. "If Gregor doesn't mind," he added.

After a swallow of water, Gregor said, "To make it short, Pandora got some stuff from her lab in England and started my indoctrination. At first, she did simple things. Our first attempts were non-conclusive. Then, several were borderline and encouraging. But after one particular try, I was sure I made it."

Gregor closed his eyes again briefly while he placed the scene before him.

"We did it! Princess, we did it! It worked this time! I'm pretty sure that I went back to my classroom in grade school. Miss Thatcher's second grade!"

Pandora looked up from her recording material and blinked her eyes. Long, dark eyelashes brushed the creamy skin of her round cheeks. The tip of a straight, slender nose shadowed the ever-provocative, full lips. Even teeth showed when she smiled. All of the lines of her features were delicately mature and womanly, but Gregor saw, through it all, the face of a beautiful child. He saw it now as she asked, "And why would you go again to Miss Thatcher's class, Gig?"

For a few seconds, Gregor stared at her. Then he stepped over to her and cupped her cheeks in his hands. "Princess, think hard. Did your parents ever bring you to California when you were a little girl?"

A smile brightened her face as she retorted, "Ahah! You fell in love with a girl in your second-grade class. Is that it?"

"She looked just like you, Princess! I swear it. It's uncanny!"

"What happened to her, Gig?" Pandora asked. "Didn't she live here?"

"I don't think so. I seem to remember that she didn't speak very much English and when she left, I was heartbroken. I went home that day and threw a rock at the boy in Grandfather's fountain."

"Did you hit it?" Pandora asked.

"No, but I broke the tail of one of the dolphins. Pandora, think hard, now. Did you ever come to visit in California?"

"No, Gig, I never came to California until I was through with my university studies." She nestled her head on his chest and let his arms steal about her waist. "You must not read what is not there in these tests, Gig. It is so easy to interject and assume, but we must restrict ourselves to fact, even though it may be hard to determine."

"Okay, then, forget the girl. I think I'm getting the hang of it, though. I was really in that classroom. Let's go on with it. Tomorrow, I want to try a longer flight, backwards again." He patted her shoulder, rubbed the small of her back gently, ending with a playful slap on her buttocks. "I gotta do that splicing for Roy or he'll give me more hell. We'll give your Xionflight a couple more tries and then" we better take off for L.A. because it will take about six weeks to put the movie in shape. Come on, surf's up today. I'd like to ride a couple more tubes before we—"

The scene faded from Gregor's mind when Dr. Quest cleared his throat and arose from his chair. "I hate to interrupt you, Gregor, but we'll have to get going to catch that plane. I'll leave it to Dr. Ornski as to when he can see you again. We are both going to a convention in Honolulu, you know. We'll nose around a bit and see if we can find the name of the group Pandora worked with."

"Yes," Dr. Ornski said. "That would be helpful. They might give us a lead. It's too bad that she never revealed the site of the lab or a name. But we'll see what we can do. In the meantime, I'll have to wait till I'm Stateside again to hear the remainder of your story, Gregor, but this will do for a beginning."

"Well, suppose I see you over there in Hawaii. That's my next stop," Gregor said. "I'm getting an early discharge because my nurse is coming with me to make sure that I follow doctor's orders." After a few more words, the physicians were gone.

During all this, Christopher had remained attentive, shifting in his seat occasionally. Now, as the two physicians left, he sat forward, tapping his toe gently on the floor. He shot a quick glance at Gregor, then stared at the ceiling with a thoughtful lift of his brows, finally punctuating his reverie with two decisive nods of his head.

"Will it help if they are able to locate the laboratory in England?" Christopher finally asked.

"Humph! They'll need better luck than I had. I couldn't find it, but I hope they do. Yes, it would clear up a lot of things," Gregor answered.

"Like what?" Christopher asked. He drew a cigarette from a package, balanced it between drawn lips as he struck a match.

"Oh, something wasn't going right with Pandora's technique. I should have been going back into the South where Vanessa's family lived or up into the Sierras where Grandpa Jonathan lived, and not to some forest in Africa with a —"

"Mother of God!" Christopher exclaimed as the lighted match and the cigarette fell to the floor. Quickly, he reached to retrieve both, apologizing meanwhile. "Uh, burned my finger on that damned match. Must have been defective. You'd think that they could make matches that don't explode."

"Oh!" Gregor exclaimed with a look of relief. "I thought I said something wrong for a second."

In the act of brushing ashes from his pant cuff, Christopher shook his head. "No, no. I just have to stop smoking! You were saying about Vanessa and Uncle Jonathan, and what else?"

"Oh, Chris, the whole thing got out of hand and was pretty silly after that. I won't even repeat it. I told Pandora that something wasn't working right and she suggested going to visit her lab. I wish I'd gone."

"Why didn't you?" Christopher asked.

Gregor drew his finger across his throat. "Roy would have fried my gizzard if I hadn't gone to L.A. to finish the film. That was in July. In August, she—" He hesitated and stared at the ceiling. His voice quavered as he finished. "In August, she was gone." He let his eyes close for a few seconds. "I wish I could wake up and find all this is a bad dream and nothing more. Nobody believes me, Chris!"

Christopher put his hand gently on Gregor's shoulder. "I believe you, lad. I believe you!"

Nancy Starling never realized how she had been persuaded so easily to accompany her patient to Hawaii. Perhaps she had felt his hypnotic charm just as other women did. However, she began to pack the evening after he asked her.

Days later, Gregor and Nancy left for San Francisco. From there, they continued on to Honolulu. Roy had preceded them and had already found a rambling house with several separate wings. He had hired a native housekeeper. There was a lanai, complete with fountain and hammock. Off the lanai was the guest suite which was assigned to Nancy.

Her position was as Gregor had outlined, accounting and secretarial services, publicity, management of the household and overseeing his recovery.

Weeks passed rapidly. One afternoon, Roy and Nancy were trying to edit film. They had been working in silence until Roy said, suddenly, "I thought your patient was doing pretty good until this morning."

Nancy nodded in agreement. "He gets upset every time he goes to see that Dr. Ornski. Also, he found the photo of Pandora in the old file. That depressed him. I've got to make sure that there aren't any more of those around."

"Being here agrees with him. He was beginning to be more like his old self," Roy said. He brushed his gaunt features with the sleeve of his shirt. "Until today," he added.

Nancy looked up from her work. "I think he's doing fine. No visions. That's encouraging. Hardly any of those disturbing nightmares. I will admit that he gets awful moody."

"Humph!" Roy took his pipe from an ashtray. "You can say that again!"

"I gather that he wasn't always that way?"

Roy shook his head. "Nope. Not like this." He struck a match and very deliberately lit his pipe. "Do you think it's such a good idea to let him go off by himself when he is so depressed?"

"He said he just wanted to be alone for a few hours. He wanted to walk up to the Queen's Surf. Don't worry. He'll be back in a little while." She continued her work.

Roy puffed on his pipe as he watched her. His dark blue eyes narrowed to slits. "You aren't sorry that you took the job?"

Without looking away from her editing, Nancy replied, "I love it here. You must know that I've grown quite fond of Morghann."

"He gets the biggest boot out of that."

"Out of what?" she asked.

"Your calling him Morghann."

"I do it on purpose," she said, still concentrating on her work.

"Because it's different from what *she* called him?"

"Yes. It's different from what Pandora called him," Nancy answered, testily.

Roy puffed in silence for a few seconds. "Uh...about growing fond of him, you aren't forgetting...uh...that he is still in love with Pandora and expects to find her, are you?"

Nancy looked up from her task. "Roy, are you telling me not to fall in love with him?"

Pipe in hand, his smile coming from one side of his mouth, he answered her defensively. "Face it. Everyone falls in love with him. People can't resist him." Roy's steely eyes shifted. "Right now, what he doesn't need is another girl in love with him. He needs to get hold of himself. Think about it."

Nancy threw her pencil on the table and pressed her lips together. "Don't you think I'm aware of that, Roy? Dr. Quest contacts me every week with advice. We have discussed this very carefully. You can rest assured that I will consider Morghann's recovery in everything I do. I think I can handle it, and I don't need any advice from you."

The wiry brows arched. Otherwise, Roy did not back off. "You know that he is like a young brother to me. We have been very close."

Her voice tense, with green eyes flaring, she retorted acidly, "I keep telling you that I can handle Morghann! I have done the right things so far, haven't I?"

Roy's red head nodded in reluctant agreement. "Oh, yes. Yes. He has grown to depend on you. However, if—"

Her hands banged briskly on the desk. "For God's sake, will you stop telling me! I understand. Morghann couldn't benefit by having another woman in love with him right now! I know! I know! Everyone is in love with the poor guy. Kelley says that Nichole is still in love with him. If you ask me, Kelley is a little star-struck herself. I get the messsage all too well and I don't want to hear any more!" She arose and walked to the window.

Puffing on his pipe, Roy deliberated for some time. Then he said, "I thought Nichole had an engagement ring."

Nancy answered without turning. "It seems she returns it to her boyfriend every time she thinks Morghann is available. Very determined woman."

"I take it that you have met her?" Roy asked.

Nancy giggled. "Oh, yes! Near the end of Morghann's stay in the hospital, she came up every day. Stayed for hours. It got on Morghann's nerves, so I started hiding him down in the therapy room until she got tired of waiting, or got the hint."

Roy stretched, yawned and joined Nancy at the window. "I haven't told Gregor that the diving cage has to be designed differently. It's too heavy, for one thing, and it isn't quite as sharkproof as I'd like it."

Nancy turned to look at Roy. "Does that mean that we have to go back to San Francisco? I like it here!"

"Yep. We'll be going in another month." Roy puffed on his pipe.

"Well, let's make the best of the time we have here. Let's ask Morghann to take us up to the beach at Makaha this afternoon. There's a surfing contest."

"Oh, yes, at the Bonsai Pipeline," Roy answered. "It might be hard for him to just sit and watch."

"Oh, nonsense! He'll be back to surfing soon enough. At least, being there will take his mind off his visit with Dr. Ornski." With that, Nancy began to tidy the workbench.

By this time, Gregor had unfolded to Dr. Ornski the entire story of how he met Pandora, fell in love and then waited for her while she came and went, mysteriously, seemingly without much regard for his feelings.

"But she always came back," Gregor said. "And the last time, she said she wouldn't leave anymore. We were very much in love and she promised that we'd be married that fall, but she disappeared in August. That was two years ago!"

"Very well," Dr. Ornski said. "You knew her two years until she left that night of the luau at the Club. In the two years since, she not only comes to you in over-realistic dreams, but appears to you in visions."

Gregor inclined his head slightly and placed his fingers on his brow. "Please, Doctor! They are not visions! I thought you'd understand by now! She is there, flesh and blood, breathing just as you are! That time at the airport escalator and in Rome, and on the beach last month."

The psychiatrist waited. "And on the cruiser? The other places we can explain somehow, but the cruiser, Gregor, is another matter." He tapped his desk lightly with a pencil. "That was a bit out of the ordinary." He waited again.

With a shrug, Gregor said, "If you are looking for a logical explanation, I don't have one. There isn't any, not a logical one." He sighed with a show of annoyance. "We've gone over and over this! If you don't believe me, you'll—"

The physician lifted both hands in protest. "Understand, please, that this is all a sorting-out process to put everything in perspective. We are setting aside things that might be a coincidence, any trick of the mind or the emotions that might affect our findings. We want to work with the facts that remain. I do believe you, but even for me, with my background of experience, this is extraordinary, so please be patient with my methods," he said, smiling pleasantly.

Patiently, Gregor inhaled a deep breath. "Okay. Okay. Then let's go back to the Xionflight experiment and the first success I had with it, the visit to my second-grade class and seeing that girl who looked like Pandora, but—" He shook his head and stopped.

Dr. Ornski kept smiling while he waited. "You said that Pandora questioned her sister and found later that her sister, the ballerina, had been brought to San Diego at that time for an audition for a children's ballet."

Gregor looked at the physician sharply. "Yes," he answered quickly. "Yes, that's the part that doesn't make any sense to me. I just can't figure that out! Could she have been hiding something? Why should she lie?"

Again the pencil tapped a few beats. "I'm sure she'll have an answer to that when she comes back to you."

Gregor scrutinized the smiling face across the desk. It was a handsome face with lines that were weakened somewhat by its fullness. The perpetual uplift of the lips did not appear as an affectation, but rather a receptiveness. "You think she will?" Gregor asked, anxiously.

"She always has, hasn't she?" the doctor retorted briskly. He leaned forward. "Now, you realize as we discussed last time that your going back to your classroom in school could be done with simple hypnosis."

Gregor waved aside his statement as he interrupted, "Yes, yes! You went through that last time. Recall and age regression under hypnosis. I understand perfectly. I know that physicians use the techniques often. I understand."

"Fine! Fine! Now, going back beyond one's own lifetime into someone else's is a different thing altogether, and I want to determine whether this might have happened. Age regression is the proper tool to use in the attempt to find another vehicle to go beyond one's lifetime."

Gregor blinked and pursed his lips. "Do you think it's possible, Doctor?"

Dr. Ornski shrugged. "With the literature pointing up theories about reincarnation, it begins to fall into the realm of possibility." Again, the pencil tapped on the desk. "Now then, on this subsequent attempt into the past, where did you go?"

It was Gregor's turn to lean forward in his chair. "Somewhere tropical, like on the equator. It was hot and humid. I was in a huge stone house standing next to a dark, sultry Cleopatra-type woman. Everything is so hazy. Then, I think I was riding on some big piece of moving machinery like a...like—"

Dr. Ornski hesitated for a second. "Like a bulldozer or a tractor?" he asked.

Gregor shook his head. "It seemed to have a gun on it."

"A tank?"

"Uh, yes, more like a tank." Gregor wiped perspiration from his wide forehead and pushed back his pale amber locks. "I...uh, uh, yes, like a tank."

The doctor glanced at his watch. "You're getting tired?"

"Yes, tired and confused. I don't want to talk about it anymore today. It depresses me." Gregor arose and turned to look through the window at the palms swaying outside.

The physician arose also. "Of course. Of course. It's been a long session. Don't get discouraged. Think of it this way, that you may be helping us to break into a new horizon."

Gregor turned about with a look of relief on his face. "Do you really think that? That helps. I was beginning to think that everything is just one hell-of-a bad dream. I'm numb from it all. I don't have any feeling anymore."

Dr. Ornski hesitated. "Don't overlook the fact that spinal injuries can do strange things. Nothing that can't go away in time. Why don't you consider finding another nice girl?"

With eyes flaring, Gregor placed his hands on his hips in a resolute gesture. "That's out! No way! You promised, Dr. Ornski, to help me locate Pandora! Remember?"

Smiling all the more, the doctor nodded. "I will. I will," he assured Gregor as he showed him to the door.

XVI

"...no horse's ass would go down on a day like this..."

Their film finished, Gregor and Roy prepared for their return to California. Two weeks later they were in San Francisco directing the finishing stages in the construction of their new aluminum cage. Meanwhile, they planned their new venture.

"There will be a current in the channel and we'll have to tie the lines or the cage will drift badly," Roy was saying.

Gregor nodded in assent. "It will mean a 170-foot dive to get the lines tied. We are going to have problems with decompression, that's for sure."

Roy's mouth twitched. "Well, we can't use the squalosphere until it is secure. You remember the last time we tried to film in a current. You couldn't hold the camera because the surge was so rough. With sharks right up against the cage, you won't be able to stick your arm outside the bars."

As Gregor and Roy pondered over the diving cage in the construction yard of the foundry in San Francisco, another group of people stood in the same dense fog, beneath a steep cliff five hundred miles to the south in Sunday Village. The group included two abalone divers, a lifeguard, a policeman and a few bystanders.

The divers in Sunday Village had found a car on the floor of the sea valley. Although covered with sand and barnacles, it answered the description of Gregor's lost car. It was Karla who brought the story home to her father with an account vivid enough to send Christopher Holliss to the scene. Immediately thereafter, he telephoned Roy in San Francisco.

The tenseness in his voice carried over the distance. "Are you alone?" Christopher asked. "It's important, Roy."

There was a pause. "Just a minute," came the answer. There were footsteps. A door closed. "What's up, Chris?"

"Some divers found a car in some thirty feet of water under the cliff past the pier." Christopher cleared his throat. "I'm certain it's Gregor's car."

Another brief pause followed. "Ah...do they know...uh...is—"

"Right now, nothing more than that," Christopher cut in. "The car is almost covered. We need a couple of good divers and some equipment. Why don't you come down here and we'll see what we can do before we say anything to Gregor."

"Has there been much publicity?"

"I'm trying to keep it to a minimum, but there are rumors going around already."

"What rumors?"

Christopher took a deep, deliberate breath. "Nothing that I like the tone of, but you know how people exaggerate. We'll talk when you get here."

"Pick me up at the airport at eight." The click of the telephone blended with his last consonant.

During the next two days, Roy's helpers huddled near the almost inaccessible ledge overlooking the sea valley. Appearing very much like a crew from the nearby Institute, a small boat with diving equipment bobbed on the surface of the swells. Only some of the observers knew Roy's real mission.

That same day, Roy telephoned Gregor, who was still in San Francisco, to tell him to come to identify the car. Purposefully, he omitted the fact that the remains of the automobile had been searched and already identified.

When Gregor and Nancy arrived in the Village the next morning, a chilling wind pressed a heavy bank of fog against the shore. Grim and sullen, Gregor asked no questions and said very little, except that he demanded to make the dive immediately.

"Weather turned bad," Roy grumbled. "Choppy swell. Increase in turbulence." He smoothed his red hair nervously. "Visibility will be near zero. It was bad enough yesterday. Storm coming. We should wait. Maybe it will pass."

Gregor's face tensed until the scar stood out on his cheek. "I'll go alone," he said gruffly.

Roy's teeth gritted together. "Goddamn!" he growled. "No you won't! *No stupid horse's ass would go down on a day like this*, particularly by himself!"

"Then come with me, because I'm going!" A pallor stole into his features that matched the linen-gray of his hair. The firm set of his lip accentuated the cleft in his chin.

Roy grimaced and answered wryly. "Okay! Okay! Have it your way. There will be three of us with you. You know all the rules. Stick by them."

Aside, out of Gregor's hearing, he reminded the others later, "If he tries any funny stuff, you know what to do."

In a short time, they were on the beach at the site of a slight rip, watching the waves intently. "After this set," Roy said suddenly, and they strained to move the craft through the agitated surf.

Finally, when they were opposite the first cave in the cliffs, Roy gave the signal to throw out the anchor. Then he gave final instructions.

"Make sure your air is on," he reminded. "Is everybody's tank topped?"

"What's this? A lesson in diving 101? Let's get on with it," grumbled the skinny diver from the insurance company. "Everybody tops his tank. Yeah, the air's on."

"I'm not asking! I'm telling you!" Roy snapped. "Now, listen and get this straight. With visibility so rotten, we gotta follow a tight plan. We'll sweep north for fifty yards and if we don't see the car, we'll sweep south on the other side of the ridge and come back to this point. If you get separated, surface right away. Got that?" He spat unceremoniously into the water, stared at the drift for a moment, then said, "Someone better stay with the boat." He pointed to David.

"Oh, damn!" David grumbled. "How long will you be?"

"Look for us in exactly half an hour," Roy answered.

"But we can stay down longer than that easy," the skinny diver interjected.

"I said half an hour!" Roy snapped again. "Now are you gonna dive with us or not?" He watched as the young man nodded his head. "Then spit in your mask and shut up."

The diver complied and rubbed saliva on the inside of his mask. Roy reached to purge his regulator. The others followed suit, held their masks in place and slid backward off the gunwales of the craft into the inky water.

The struggle against the turbulence proved exhausting, but they ultimately located the weed-covered automobile. There was hardly time left to probe the wreck. Roy gave his signal promptly, begrudging Gregor every second he took thereafter. When Gregor ignored the second signal, the trio converged upon him and nudged him roughly to the surface.

Having waited anxiously, David sighed with relief when his companions climbed silently into the craft. The last to come aboard was Gregor, who ripped off his mask and glared with narrowed eyes from one grim face to another.

"All right!" he rasped. "There is something you are hiding from me! Out with it!" His hand shook as he wiped his face.

Roy, too, busied himself with wiping salt water from his wiry features, suddenly conscious that some of the droplets were warm. He reached for a packet, unfolded a cloth and handed it to his friend.

With a frozen face, Gregor stared at the contents, a pendant with an angel's head in gold and a plastic buckle from a knee brace. His numbed features gave way to a look of horror and then pain. A gutteral sound came from his throat that ended in a shout. Then he struggled to dive back into the sea, but Roy had a firm hold on Gregor's arm.

"Easy does it, my friend," Roy said. "You aren't going anywhere."

Gregor continued to struggle. "Let me go! I've got to look for her! Don't you understand?" he shouted.

"Don't you suppose that we've already done that? Nobody found anything, only what I gave you. Now, stop rocking the boat or I'll put you out cold, you dumb turkey!"

Gregor howled all the more. "Don't you see? That means she's still down there! Let me go, damn it! I want to die with her. Let me go!"

"God-dammit-to-hell! Suppose she pushed the car over the cliff?" Roy shouted as the boat pitched and almost capsized.

"Let go! Let me go!" Gregor still insisted.

"You stupid asshole!" Roy shouted again as he struck a light blow to Gregor's head. As Gregor dropped forward, David tied his hands. "Now, hold him down," Roy ordered, "and let's get the hell into shore before this squall gets worse."

The following week was one of a kind that Nancy had never before experienced. She processed telephone calls, sorted papers, paid bills, answered police inquiries, soothed reporters, made Gregor's appointments and settled every other detail that arose. Even Nancy, usually persevering and cheerful in the face of anything, was depressed and exhausted at the close of the week.

After a prolonged discussion with insurance agents, she and Gregor finished a late dinner at Vanessa's house. During the meal, Nancy remained restless and quiet. Shortly thereafter, she addressed her hostess with regrets. "We are both so tired, Mrs. Holliss. Please forgive us for not staying longer. It's best if we run on."

Vanessa agreed wholeheartedly. "Very wise of you." She smoothed the folds of her blue hostess gown. Soft curls dangled from the edges of her upswept coiffure and bobbed against the creamy skin of her cheeks. Her voice was gentle and soothing. "Gregor looks about ready to collapse."

Nancy's green eyes blinked sleepily. "Well, he hasn't had a good night's rest all week." She lowered her tone. "If he has slept at all! Being in that cold water almost every day this past week and not eating or sleeping properly has given him a cold, and I wouldn't be surprised to find he is running a fever. I'll see if he will try a sleeping pill tonight. I'll get our jackets from the bedroom. No, no, don't get up, Mrs. Holliss." She found their wraps and when she returned, her attention was taken by Kelley who had thrown her arms about Gregor as she did very often, but this time in a more coquettish way, less like a child greeting a friend, more like a woman in love.

She drew her hand over her eyes, thinking, *I must be tired... I'll drive home... the wind in my face will keep me awake....*

She took the keys. Before they had gone two blocks, Gregor fell asleep. Nancy drove slowly along the route by the water's edge even though the fog was heavier there. Cold dewdrops flew through the open window striking her face until it tingled. The sounds of the sea came, too. As she stole through enveloping patches of slow—swirling cloud, the churning of the waves came to her, then the roar and again a pause.

Almost mesmerized by the sound, Nancy let thoughts sift slowly through her head. *How unending the pattern is... does it sound the same to Morghann as it does to me... did it sound the same a million years ago... would there be any sound at all if we weren't here to listen... is it because I'm so tired tonight that it sounds like a lullaby... like a song with an overtone of eternity in it... that's it... a melody with a kind of foreverness in it as though it were God's own voice soothing the land... or someone's promise of lasting love... love... love... love....*

The feeling of the need to cry ruffled Nancy's face. She bit her lip and whispered to herself, "How can any woman love a man as much as I love Morghann? How can I begin to tell him? Why doesn't he realize it? Can't he see? He doesn't seem to know I'm alive. I'm just a robot to him! What should I do?"

Arriving at the apartment, she woke Gregor with reluctance. In his bedroom, he pulled off his sweater and shirt, took the sedative that Nancy brought to him, then fell on his bed, refusing to stir any further.

Nancy shrugged her shoulders, covered him, and left him in a sound sleep. In the living room, she sank into the sofa cushions to think of her next day's schedule, but sleep overtook her before a moment passed. A crashing sound awakened her. The room was dark. She jumped to her feet only to trip over the shade of the fallen lamp. She lifted her head to see Gregor opening the doors that led to the small balcony where he began to reach for the wisps of passing fog, stumbling in his attempt to throw one leg over the rail.

His rasping voice sounded through the darkness. "Don't go! Wait! Wait for me!" he begged. "Pandora! Come back! For God's sake, come back out of there! Pandora!" Again, he threw one leg over the rail, seemingly intent on stepping out into space, except that Nancy had seized his arm and was shaking him with all her strength.

"Morghann, wake up! Wake up! Morghann, don't!" Nancy frightened herself with her own screaming, but yet Gregor seemed unaware of her as he continued to lean out over space, all the while imploring Pandora to wait for him. Again, Nancy tugged him back. "You're dreaming! Morghann, wake up! Wake up!" She flailed him and tried to grasp his arm, but he shrugged her off. Her hand dug into the waistband of his slacks. She tugged with all her might, but he placed the fingers of one hand around her throat to ward her off. Nancy gasped for breath as his hold tightened and he leaned further over the rail with a motion that threatened to hurl them both to the concrete below. Sucking for air, she twisted her head just enough to sink her teeth into his arm.

Startled by the pain, Gregor lurched toward her, and Nancy felt them both tumble backwards to the deck where her head hit the wall. She lost consciousness just as Gregor's body fell crosswise over hers.

When she opened her eyes, she lay on the sofa, an ice pack on her head. Gregor bent over her, smoothing her hair away from her temple.

"Are you all right?" he asked anxiously. When she nodded, he added, "Are you sure?" He lifted the ice pack. "You scared the hell out of me," he said as he replaced the ice. "What happened last night?"

Nancy looked about. Dawn was breaking over the ocean. She met his inquiring stare. "I think you must have been delirious, Morghann. Your fever must have shot up. You had a nightmare and almost— Why didn't you tell me you were feeling that bad yesterday? Now I know how you hurt your back months ago. And you almost—"

"Almost what? For God's sake, what did I do?"

She began to tell him of her struggle with him in the night. At one point in her account, she reached over to demonstrate her hold on his waist, but she doubled over in pain, clutching at her ribs.

Gregor caught her in his arms. "What's wrong? Are you hurt?"

Nancy felt her side. "I think my rib is broken."

Remorse hung on his features. "Hell's fire!" he mumbled. "What a damned dumb thing for me to do! I'll get you to a doctor."

"Nothing much one can do for a cracked rib, Morghann, except confirm it and tape it, and rest it." She looked at her watch. "And we can't do anything until daylight, so get me some coffee, okay? I don't want to go to the emergency room."

His gray eyes flickered as he ran his fingers through his flaxen hair. "Coffee's all perked. Omelette is ready to go." He retreated to the kitchen.

Nancy's gaze followed him and she noticed that the shattered lamp was gone, the rug was tidy, and the room appeared as though nothing had happened.

Although Gregor was remorseful during the following week and apologetic when the X-ray revealed Nancy's broken ribs, he was so subject to his own bitter loss that he fell into fits of depression during which he barricaded himself from everyone. Frequent visits to Dr. Quest seemed to help him very little.

Another week passed during which Nancy, her chest bound uncomfortably in tape, needful of a little sympathy herself, lost her patience with Gregor's ill humor and complained to Dr. Quest. "Yesterday, when the weather was so bad all day, he sat around and wouldn't talk to me. I find it difficult to be with someone so morose for so long. He makes me feel that *I'm* to blame for everything."

"He doesn't intend to do that, Nancy. He does blame himself, however, for Pandora's death, and without mercy," Dr. Quest said. "He's just assuming that she killed herself in the crash. He thinks it's his fault."

"Yes, yes, I know that, Doctor. I hear him talk in his sleep sometimes."

"This last week?" the doctor asked. "What does he talk about? Can you tell me? It might be important in his therapy."

The jade-colored eyes opened wide with alarm. "Doctor, he keeps saying that he killed her!"

"At this stage, he is likely to do that. It will take time to dissuade him. Advise me, Nancy, if he needs more appointments."

Nancy paused. "Frankly, Doctor, I don't think Morghann should stay here. He keeps on diving, uh—diving to find her body and there isn't one! It breaks me up to watch him. Then he sits for hours on the cliff staring down at the water. I'm afraid to leave him alone. I'm thinking it might be good to get away from here. I'm thinking that we might go back to Hawaii."

Nancy's deliberations ended several days later when she found that Nichole had begun to make numerous calls daily, each time engaging Gregor in more lengthy conversation.

"We're going back to Honolulu," Nancy announced one day. "I've got my things all packed and I'm starting on yours."

His jaw hung open in surprise. "But the diving cage—"

"They don't need you around in order to finish it. I already checked."

"There is no rush to do the film on sharks. There is a lot of editing to do on the last film and the com—"

"We can edit in Hawaii."

"But your rib isn't healed, Nan—"

"I have a referral in Honolulu."

Gregor stroked his cheek. "I had hoped to spend the holidays here," he countered softly, halfway acknowledging defeat.

She felt compassion for him suddenly, and she did something that she had not allowed herself before. Her arms slipped about him for an instant. "Morghann," she said tenderly. Then she drew back, shook her head and added, "It isn't good for you here with all these memories. I have the plane tickets. Come, I'll help you pack."

Nancy was correct about Gregor. He was considerably more relaxed and talkative as he strolled with her on the warm sand of the Waikiki beach.

"Let's sit down to rest here for a while," Gregor said one evening. "Too much walking isn't good for your broken ribs. Get tired easily, don't you?"

She nodded her head as she allowed him to pull her down on the sand beside him. "Uh-huh, I get tired but it's such fun to keep walking."

He made tracings in the sand. "They better get that door placed right on our cage." He continued to trace. "This is how we drew it."

"Aren't you the least bit hesitant to work with something as dangerous as sharks, Morghann?" she asked.

His eyes flickered with amusement. "They aren't half as bad as we make them out to be. They are very curious. They swim around to make an appraisal of an object first. Then they test it by bumping with their noses. A strong blow will usually drive them off. I'm talking about the smaller ones, of course. If they are really hungry or smell blood, they go into a frenzy, like a pack of wolves scrambling over a scrap of food. Then nobody is safe. That goes for the Great White all of the time; nobody is safe near him."

"Are the Great Whites around here? I don't like the idea, Morghann, your being around the big sharks. You don't have an ounce of fear or respect. I heard Roy telling about it." Her hair showed its reddish glints in the evening light.

Gregor grinned. "I stay near the cage. You can always see one coming. They are never still, you know. They move all the time or they sink."

"Why?" Nancy shifted her position.

"Sharks don't have air bladders. Haven't changed in a million years," Gregor explained.

"How do people know so much about it?" she asked.

"Ah-hah! Because of guys like me that don't have an ounce of respect and go out to make studies of sharks," Gregor answered, pointing suddenly to the sky. "Look! A shooting star!"

"How pretty!" she exclaimed. "It went right toward that bigger star."

"That's Venus, that big star, swinging into the orbit that takes it the closest it ever gets to the earth. I figure that this is the time of the year that the first space ship came to our planet."

Nancy eyed him curiously. "Morghann, you never cease to amaze me. You not only think a space ship came, but you think it came at this time of year! Ah-hah! I get it." She snapped her fingers. "The ship came from Venus during its closest swing toward earth. That is what I like about you. You always have some new theory or some way-out idea."

"It isn't a new theory, not with me." Gregor smiled as he explained. "I wrote a paper about it in the sixth grade. The teacher wouldn't grade my paper because we weren't supposed to be writing fiction. Now that we have started to explore space, maybe she would give me some credit for my composition."

"You mean it, don't you, Morghann? You really think that people came from Venus?"

He nodded his head. "I think they came from somewhere. Venus is a good guess."

"Hmm. Possible, but not very probable, Morghann."

"There are many things that point to the fact that the stage of progress we are entering has been reached before. We aren't unique. As a matter of fact, I think that there have been several civilizations that have exceeded ours on this planet and that they most likely exhausted the resources of several other planets before coming here." Gregor scooped up a shell and flung it leisurely into the surf.

"Whew!" Nancy said. "Some of your ideas put a strain on my thought capacities."

He stood abruptly and reached for her hand, saying, "Don't let me bore you with my rambling. Come on, let's walk a bit more."

"No, no, it isn't boring. It's just that I never entertained such an idea. Doesn't it conflict with the story of creation?"

"Christopher and I used to argue a lot about that," Gregor replied with a laugh. "I finally got him to admit that the creation story applied to the universe and that a day on a slowly rotating planet might actually be a century. So the length of

124

time God took to finish the earth depends on whose clock he was using."

Nancy laughed. "You are saying that God might have taken six centuries to work, and that he put the first man somewhere out there on another sphere. Quite a different interpretation, to say the least, Morghann. Really wild! Do you honestly propose that our ancestors came from a spaceship?"

Gregor nodded. "Partly."

"What do you mean by partly?"

"They might have come, established colonies, and interbred with the best earth specimens that they could find."

"The best they could find?" Nancy asked quizzically. "What do you think they found?"

"It's anybody's guess. There may have been some early ape-man forms and some other animals with compatible chromosomal structures, like the creatures that were the ancestors of the satyrs."

"Satyrs?"

"Yeah. The half-goat characters like Pan in the Greek myths, only I think they really existed. They were recorded in historical documents and literature too often to be a myth. Supposedly, they lived in the region of Asia Minor and Pan was reportedly the offspring of the messenger god, Hermes. They were destined for extinction."

"Why was that?"

"Umm, probably a genetic incompatibility with humans of the age, maybe a singular factor resulting in high fetal mortality. They were huge creatures, wild in nature. Humans were terribly afraid of them because the satyrs ravaged their women who usually died in childbirth."

"Or satyrbirth?"

Gregor laughed and continued. "Because of the enormous size of the fetus, I wouldn't be surprised if some women were delivered surgically in order to save their lives."

Stopping suddenly, Nancy exclaimed, "The beginning of the technique of Caesarean sections! Of course!" She put her hands on her hips. "Morghann, you talk as though you were there. You have a terrific imagination. How in the devil do you know so much?" She stepped away from him and held her hand so as to shield half of his body from her view.

"What are you doing?" he asked curiously.

"Wondering what you'd look like if you were a satyr with horns and big ears," she joked as she started to walk again. "About your theory, Morghann, explain why your spacemen left Venus."

Heavy brows knitted and lifted. "To make it simple, suppose that Venus might have had quantities of an amorphous phosphorus, an allotropic red form that would not burn or even melt in the hottest sun's rays. Then the planet inhabitants produced pollutive gases that turned the red phosphorus into an ordinary phosphorus that caught fire and burned from the heat of the sun during each day. Suppose people had to live underground during the day and come out at night when the fire subsided. The resulting phosphorus poisoning would have deformed bones and led to a lot of other illnesses." He peered at Nancy to determine whether she gave his account any credibility.

"How did you get so smart?" she asked with a flip of her head.

Gregor's gray eyes flickered with amusement. "Well, I graduated from high school at fifteen and had a college degree at eighteen. In the two years after that, I took space engineering and meteorology and some archaeology, oceanography, of course, and some nuclear chemistry."

Nancy stopped to stare at him. "How did you fit all that in with your filming and work with Roy?"

"I had my first underwater camera at age twelve. My grandfather got it for me. I've been working with Roy since I was fourteen...during my off time. If I can find a course on nuclear medicine, it might help me solidify some of my theories."

"Like deformities of space people due to exposure to phosphorus on some other planet?"

"Well, what would you say about it?"

Nancy nodded. "About what you do. Phosphorus poisoning would probably leave deformed legs and faces, maybe accompanied by a degree of gangrene." She sat in the sand to rest again. "Whew! I get tired so easily. Just a short rest and we'll head back." As she settled herself beside him, her inward thoughts ran silently...this ventilating is good for Morghann...he needs to think about things unrelated to the trauma he just went through...keep him talking about anything at all....

"Morghann, I've never heard you discuss something like this in all the time I've worked for you. You are something else!"

An apologetic expression passed over his features. "We'll talk about the surfing contest, the parade, or clothes; you name it."

"No, no, I want you to go on with your story. Now, why didn't your spacemen produce a super race right away?"

Once again, Gregor pondered her question. "They suffered something disruptive, brain-cell damage or some kind of mutation or even oxygen poisoning from an atmosphere that was too rich for them. Survival techniques were forgotten, mentalities degenerated with the dilution of the species, selective breeding schedules were disrupted, and maybe the few that were left decided to look for a better planet."

"What better planet could there be?"

"Well, suppose these people had to live in thinner air up at 14,000 feet, maybe in their space-ship shuttles, so that they could avoid oxygen poisoning because the air was too rich for them. Suppose, now, that the shuttles got crowded and some of them moved down to the earth's crust."

Her copper hair hid one shoulder as she cocked her head to one side. "Oxygen poisoning. Let me see. If my memory serves me right, the result would be weakness, progressive to the point of death, also blindness." She bent forward, suddenly struck with an idea. "The Three Fates were blind. Eros was blind. Maybe your spacemen and the deities living on the top of Mt. Olympus were one and the same, coming down sometimes to consort with humans, producing occasional deformed offspring because of things like protein incompatibilities. After all, their blood might not have had cells like ours, but only oxygen-carrying chemicals. But, if they had problems with blood compatibility, why didn't they transfuse? After all, Morghann, their civilization was advanced enough to know about such things."

"Hmm. Maybe they did transfuse. When you think about it, a half dozen cultures until a few hundred years ago based their rituals on human sacrifice to satisfy their god's demand for blood." He counted on his fingers. "The Druids, the Incas, the Mayans. They removed the heart of the victim while it was still beating. Why? Why did they have to satisfy the god's thirst for blood? Makes you wonder, doesn't it?"

"With each of these creatures requiring five or six pints for every transfusion every five or six weeks, they would have had an active program going on. And who knows," Nancy said with a shrug, "maybe they did heart transplants, too." She laughed again. "To tell you the truth, Morghann, I have never carried on such a *way out* conversation with anyone. Is there anything that you don't think about?"

Gregor eased himself backward so that he lay stretched on the sand. "Oh, well, maybe astrology. I don't like to think that my destiny is under the control of some star. If it is, it's one hell of a messed up star."

In silence, she watched his big chest heave with each breath. "Who told you about the sun-lit side of Venus being made of burning phosphorus all the time?" she asked.

"The Greeks named it Phosphorus. I figured they must have had a reason. That's not my star, though."

"Let's see, aren't you a moonchild?"

"Born right on the cusp, so that I don't really belong anywhere. I've always been alone."

"Oh, Morghann," Nancy chided. "How can you say that? You mix so well with everyone. You're so popular. Your rapport with others is so good."

"That's on the surface," Gregor insisted. "Underneath, I've never really felt close to anyone except Pandora." He breathed deeply and exhaled. "She changed everything, the boy in Grandfather's fountain and what the dolphins kept saying to me."

Nancy bent her head inquiringly. "The dolphins?"

He sighed and his eyes closed. "The dolphins were sculptures in the fountain. You wouldn't understand. I mean that Pandora was the only one who made me feel that I wasn't alone anymore." He sighed again and lay still.

Nancy stared at the outline of the figure before her, at his muscled arms, his lean thigh, and his long legs sprawled in the sand. *Why is it, she thought, that I seem to get so close to him and then suddenly it's like I'm not even in his life... so far away that I can't begin to show him that I love him... his doctor warned me that it's too soon... that he can't handle it emotionally so soon after the trauma....*

For a moment, she watched the pattern of the waves as they inched their way onto the beach and she wondered how long a woman could love a man without his knowing it. She wasn't certain when Gregor fell asleep, but when he moaned and muttered something, she bent over him and realized that he was dreaming.

"Uh, the gr...green star, Pandora," Gregor was mumbling. "It isn't really...really green. Myah, it's burning, uh—" He rolled from side to side as he would if he were struggling to be freed from something. "Pandora, I—I don't want to be alone!"

"Morghann!" Nancy said, grasping him quickly on the arm to stop his motion. "You're dreaming again! Wake up!" she commanded, determined to prevent a recurrence of their experience of two weeks before.

Gregor blinked but did not wake. Instead, he continued to toss from side to side, striking her arm with such force as to make her cry out in pain. She bent over and clutched at her taped ribs as she sucked in her breath. Then her eyes closed and tears ran freely.

The suddenness of his next movement startled her further. He was on his knees with one arm about her shaking body. "Nancy, you're crying! What happened? Did I say something that hurt you?"

Her voice emerged between her sobs. "Oh, Morghann! You talk about being so alone and not having anyone. Can't you see that I'm in love with you? Don't you even know? How can you be so blind?" She arose and started to walk. *There, she thought, I'm glad I got it out and I don't care what his doctor said....*

He had caught her arm and was holding it fast. "Just one minute! You never said a thing!"

She steadied her voice. "How could I? All this time, we thought Pandora would come back to you. You were hardly aware that there was another woman alive. While there was hope, I knew you would be true to her. But now the waiting is over and I can't hide it anymore. Morghann, I'm so in love with you that it hurts. Don't I mean anything to you?" she asked fiercely.

"Don't cry," he pleaded. "I didn't think I had to tell you how much I needed you. You know I couldn't get along without you."

The touch of his hand on her hair was soothing. "Yes, I know that, Morghann, but can you say you love me? I need to hear that."

Gregor seemed reflective for a moment. Then he kissed her briefly on her cheek. "Look, Nancy," he said, "this has been one hell of a week. I'm absolutely wrung! I need rest and time to think. Then we'll talk about it. Okay?"

Nancy wiped her cheek. *Try to understand, she told herself...don't press him...the shock of last week has taken a heavy toll...be patient and wait for him to make the first move....*

She smiled weakly, took his hand, and they retraced their steps down the beach.

XVII

"...a broken bottle came flying through the air..."

The infant year passed its puberty and struggled into early manhood. The earth spiraled around, keeping our fanciful ledge of land at the foot of the lonesome mountain bathed in the warm sun's rays despite the monstrous bank of fog that always lurked offshore ready to swallow the hill.

This sunlight struck Kelley's fingers as she daydreamed on her patio and wrote lines to Gregor. Hours later, Gregor relaxed in the same sunrays on an island set like a jewel in the expanse of the Pacific to the southwest.

On the day that Kelley's epistle reached Gregor, he was lounging lazily as he dreamed of the wave he'd like to catch and how it would tube him until he brought his board out, clean and safe. Nancy had just brought him a drink and Roy sat working on a script, his lanky legs fitting awkwardly under a redwood trestle table. His red mustache seemed to be askew most of the time because of his habit of pulling his lips to one side of his face. Like a layer of pliable leather stretched over bulging bundles of wires, his weathered skin rippled over long, hard muscles. He frowned occasionally at Nancy who came and went with a provocative saunter.

Nancy's slim waist showed beneath a skimpy halter. She did not hesitate to show her good figure. Her short lava-lava displayed her long legs to advantage. She laughed when Roy glared disapprovingly at her, and she hitched her skirt all the higher. Her skin had tanned to a beautiful shade, blending with her copper-colored hair. Eyes the color of jade, an upturned nose, and a small mouth that seemed to peak in the center caused many men to glance twice. Her fingers were tapered, with nails carefully polished. As though nothing had been spared in her creation, she also had a soft voice and a musical laugh.

By this time, Gregor was diving again and also surfing, but not as arduously as before, not ready to brave the guillotine or the dangers of the reef if he wiped out. At this moment, he maneuvered his board skillfully to the end of the tube in his mind's eye, but the tube crumbled suddenly when Nancy touched him on the shoulder and handed him Kelley's letter.

Gregor made no motion to separate his limp frame from the contour of his hammock. "You open it and read it to me," he murmured, pushing the letter away.

Nancy opened the envelope and withdrew the contents. "That child never writes less than ten pages," she complained. She fingered the sheets and began to read aloud. "My dearest Gregor, we all miss you, and I do especially much. Please come back before summer is over. We always have more fun when you are in the Village.

I'm counting on you to help me decide on a campus. Dad says it isn't too early to start looking. Scads of my friends are going to Berkeley, but you have probably read about all the anti-war riots up there and all the pressure on students to become involved. Ha! Can't you picture me, of all people, up there carrying a sign that says something like *down with war in lower Slobovia*, or *legalize marijuana for ailing mynah birds*, or *join society for lawful abortion of purple kangaroos*? I guess I hate groups that agitate unproductively. Do you know what would be perfect? A small campus where I could study art and philosophy, where I could love everybody. Got any ideas? I suppose I could study on our own campus, but Dad is sour on that idea too, because some professor is teaching what the Villagers think is political anarchy. Half of the Village is upset with the university. What a ruckus that raised! It's a very confusing time for teenagers. I'd give anything to be more your age. Then we could....'" At a signal from Gregor, she stopped reading.

"Skip that part," he said. "Is there anything important?"

Nancy scanned several pages. "Hmm. Vanessa's doctor seems to be testing her for some kind of tumor of the brain. Kelley says her mother laughs at the idea and isn't very cooperative."

Gregor stirred in his hammock. "Good grief! Give me the letter." He read for a minute. "Kelley says there is no malignancy but that Chris is out of his mind with worry. I can imagine he is. The two of them have always been so close." He struggled out of the folds of canvas and hemp, still reading as he seated himself beside Nancy.

She had loosened a clip in her hair, quite impervious to Roy's chilly stare as her tresses cascaded over her lightly clad figure. "You dropped a clipping," she said as she reached to retrieve a cut section of newspaper. Nancy read from beneath a photograph. "'...on her eighty-fifth birthday...went for her regular swim in the 54 degree surf near her home...an enthralling female...in the first play that was ever televised...played Shakespearian roles...ethereal...she lent stature and grace...projected strength....'" She handed the paper to Gregor. "That says it all! Did you know her, Morghann?"

He nodded his head. "Really great lady. Only one like her. I did a bit part with her once. Pour me some more of that punch, Nancy. I want to drink a birthday toast to a great lady, one of the people who gave the Village its dignity."

Roy had taken the clipping and was reading the reverse side. "Huh! Here's an unpleasant character who isn't going to lend the Village any dignity," Roy said. "Here's a letter to the editor from a semantics major who damns the establishment and casts unkind aspersions on wealthy Villagers! What gall! By damn! Read this now, and tell me what great thing this dissident bastard is going to leave to posterity!"

Gregor laughed heartily. "Yeah. Mouthy students, we don't need."

Roy nodded. "They should have put that school in La Prisa."

"Better yet, Macumba," Gregor said. "What's the kid's name?"

"It's blurred. Rommey Jag...something or other. Can't make it out." Roy took the clipping to where there was less glare.

However, Gregor had taken the letter again and was ploughing through the pages.

"There was a *love-in* at the Cove Park," the letter went on. "I wasn't there, but my friend said there were all kinds of weird costumes like monk robes, old wedding dresses, Indian getups and so on. The kids wore flowers, made peace signs, sang songs, passed potato chips and carried symbols. I persuaded Dad that there couldn't possibly be anything wrong in going, that it's safe enough for me to go next time they have one."

It was not long before Kelley had her chance to attend a *love-in*. It was Saturday and she had promised to take Karla to the Park. When they arrived, the organizers of another young people's group were already there wearing their costumes of Indian blankets and old saris. Kelley ran all the way to the telephone at the library to ask her father's permission to stay.

"Well," her father said, "you can stay for awhile, but Karla is too young. Walk her home as far as the Casa beach. She can come the rest of the way by herself."

Kelley ushered a disgruntled Karla to the appointed place, promising to take her another time. Then she rushed back to the Park, arriving there only to find the scene had changed in the half an hour that she had been away.

In the interim, the near-by residents, mostly those who lived in the high-rise structure, had become disturbed by the repeated gatherings of the *flower-children*, the noise and the resulting traffic jam. They had complained and a law-enforcement unit had been dispatched to the scene. By the time Kelley arrived, helmeted police were trying to move the stagnant traffic.

Whereas most of the young revelers were innocently enjoying their meeting in the warm sun, a few of their leaders grew extremely resentful of the watchful eyes of the police officers.

Nobody knew who provoked the angry exchanges, but shortly thereafter, some of the leaders of the rally were shouting obscenities at the officers, and empty bottles went hurtling through the air in their direction.

Threading her way through a wall of bodies and a screen of palms, Kelley stopped at the sound of a shrill voice. The voice rang with Nichole's accent. Kelley stretched in her attempt to see the speaker as the conversation came to her ear.

"How can you be so stupid and so nasty," the argument went on, "as to do this to me? Do you think that you fool me for one minute? You know that I can make trouble for you if I want to!"

Mingled streams of Spanish followed, ending in a threat. "How beastly to use my sister to try to hurt me without regard as to whether you are hurting her! I can see that you lose your visa, you know!" Another exchange of Spanish flowed before the voice softened. "You come with me before Father finds what you have been up to."

Kelley strained forward just in time to see Nichole pulling Lisa roughly from Rex's hold. Not knowing whether to help or to retreat, Kelley hesitated just long enough to be caught in a forward press of the angry crowd. It carried her along in the path of *a broken bottle that came flying through the air* from behind her. She felt herself being tackled from behind, and she was aware that she was crashing headlong into the trunk of a tree.

When sensation returned, she felt herself being lifted and carried. Her eyelids fluttered open. She realized that she was leaning against a car parked at the curb. A face became visible. She stared at the soft, large eyes that came into view. Seemingly spellbound by them, her only thoughts were...how beautiful...smiling...the kindest eyes I have ever seen....

Gradually, the remainder of the figure before her came into view. The man who stood candidly beside her in torn, wrinkled clothes was not much taller than she was, but then she noticed that he wore no shoes. As her gaze returned to the heavy lashes that fringed his brown eyes, she was startled by a rich, mellow voice.

"If you tell me where you live, I'll take you home," he said.

Her own voice quavered. "I can't see much of you, only your eyes. You are all covered with beard." She reached up to touch a throbbing spot on her head as she continued to stare at the profusion of luxurious, brown beard. "It's so curly and there's so much—" She stopped, realizing that her hand had come away covered with blood. Her knees sagged and the scene blurred. He grabbed her again with strong arms, but his touch was gentle and strangely comforting. The scent of musk came to her nostrils.

"You have a bad cut on your head. Better let me take you home."

She drew away quickly. "Oh, no, no! My father doesn't like hippies...that is...if he thought—" Suddenly embarrassed, she hesitated, eyeing his shabby attire and the matted beard that was somewhat darker than the mass of curls circling his shoulders.

"My appearance is not important," he protested. "That cut is pretty bad."

"No, I can make it. You don't know my dad. He wouldn't—" Kelley stopped again.

"Okay. Okay." Kelley's rescuer turned and disappeared into the crowd before she thought to ask who he was.

She walked home slowly, regretting her abruptness, impatient with her own fear of her father's strictness, wishing that she had asked his name. All the way home, however, she felt that she was being followed although she caught no sight of him when she looked. It was weeks before she began to forget the soft touch of his body, the musk fragrance, the lights that flickered in his eyes. Meanwhile, her letters to Gregor were filled with mention of her nameless Galahad. "...but no one will take your place, Greg. I'll never forget how you rescued me after the shark!"

Nancy Starling was inwardly relieved over Kelley's preoccupation with her mystery man. She was distressed, however, over her own long wait for Gregor's affections. Finally, she decided that she had given his emotional wounds long enough time to heal.

It was evening. They were walking in silence along the water's edge. Native music drifted from nearby. Nancy sighed and blinked back tears. "It's wonderful being here with you, Morghann," she whispered.

Dreamily, he eased her body to his, her back against his chest, his cheek pressed to her temple, and one arm folded about her waist. His voice was low. "You know I couldn't get along without you."

She cleared her throat, waiting for the pain in it to pass. "I really need to know that, Morghann. I've waited such a long time."

A wistful sigh escaped him. Slowly, pensively, he traced the contours of her breasts with his free hand, allowing it to pass over her thigh and back to her waist.

A complete prisoner to the urgency that passed through her, Nancy trembled, totally impassioned, until it was more than she could bear. She twisted herself to face him, her body pressed to his. "I love you so much that I can hardly breathe," she whispered. She held her face to his and their lips met, but she drew back in a brief moment.

"Morghann!" she stormed, beating his chest with her fists.

He caught her wrists and held them tight. "Hey! What's wrong now?"

"Morghann, let yourself go! Please let yourself come to me! If you love me, Morghann, show me!" Once again, she held her lips to his. Then she turned away, tears streaming down her cheeks. "You, uh...you don't love me, Morghann," she said between sobs. "I can tell. Why? What is it?"

He grasped her shoulders roughly. "Nancy, you won't understand."

"For God's sake, Morghann, I've got to understand! Try me," she insisted.

His voice was no more than a hoarse whisper. "It's as though she was standing here between us."

The long lashes fluttered as Nancy stared in disbelief. "Oh!" she exclaimed. "Oh, my God, you are letting her turn you off! She doesn't want you, but she has it all set so nobody else will get you either! That's just what she'd like, damn her! Morghann, if you let it go that way, you'll have a real—" The green eyes opened wide as his hand clasped over her mouth.

"Don't say anything else," he commanded. "Just don't say anything about Pandora!" He paused. "Look, Nancy, you don't have to stay. You are free to leave if you want to. A girl like you shouldn't be out of circulation. Just tell me what you'd like to do."

Nancy wrapped her arms about his waist while she struggled to compose herself. "You don't understand. I...I—" Her voice broke. "I couldn't tell you this while there was the possibility that Pandora might come back. Now I can tell you. I love you, Morghann—I love you! I love you! You've got to love me, too! I just won't have it any other way!" She stopped as she felt his hand stroking her hair, and she wondered...how will I tell him that his slightest touch excites me...what can I do...where should I start...I know I can make it turn out right....

His hand trembled as he put it on her cheek. "Nancy, don't cry," he implored. "Maybe we can ask Dr. Quest to help. The medical profession is beginning to use biofeedback to treat a lot of anxiety problems and you are familiar with it all."

"No chance," he interrupted. "My heart developed an irregularity. It throws the machine off, and they told me that any more training might encourage the irregularity."

"No matter," she whispered. "There are ways. We'll find them. Just believe that I love you very much and tell yourself that you love me, too, even if it's only half as much as you think you loved her."

He drew away from her and looked out at the water. "That's not easy to do. Nobody can take her place. She is always there."

Bewildered, Nancy shook her head. "I guess I just don't understand unless you explain it to me."

"I've never talked much about it. Maybe I could try."

"It might do us both good. I want you to know that I've never felt like this about anyone else. Men have made love to me, but—"

"But what, Nancy?"

She shrugged her shoulders. "Oh, it was never that good. It was never the kind of loving I dream about. It was never like I wanted it to be. Was it for you, Morghann?"

"Oh, yes!" he admitted eagerly. "Oh God, yes! Words won't even begin to tell. Every time, it—was like the world had stopped moving. Funny, but now that I think of it, each time was like there had never been anything like it before. So excruciatingly wonderful as to give you the feeling that you had caught the whole secret of life in the palm of your hand and you owned its power. It still mystifies me. There was a difference."

"Had you ever been in love before?" Nancy asked.

"Oh, hell, I slept with dozens of women. But Pandora! She was something else! We knew it from the first—that we had something that was really different. Huh! She had me scared! You won't believe this, Nancy, but I was afraid to touch her at first for fear I was dreaming, that she wasn't real, that she'd disappear in a puff of smoke. Let me try to explain."

He talked on as though she had opened a dam, a gate that held the flood of his feelings. She could feel the look of wonder that stole across her face. Thoughts sped around in her mind...it's good for him to open up like this...he needs to ventilate...if he would just get it all out....

When Gregor finally paused and looked away, Nancy sighed and pondered, "Morghann, have you ever wished that you could feel exactly what another person was feeling, I mean, just as though you were that person?"

He thought for a few seconds. "You mean past the degree of empathy?"

She nodded. "To the extent of being that person as far as the physical world permits. I think you could make me respond to that degree. Do you understand what I mean? Could it happen?"

Gregor leaned against the trunk of a palm and closed his eyes. "Yes, I think it happens. You can make it happen. We made it happen when we made love."

"Tell me what you mean."

"Well, just at the moment when, uh—. It's hard for me to talk about it."

She held her breath for fear he would not continue. Finally, she asked, "Are you trying to say in the orgasmic state?" She could feel him nod his head.

"At the height of it," he continued. "That is, if your timing is exact, this transfer can occur as though the two of you have been fused at the cord level, just as if you disconnected your brains and actually became like one being."

Nancy sucked in her breath. "A brain bypass! Morghann, you have a terrific imagination."

"It isn't exactly my imagination," he insisted. "I knew some doctors in Chicago. One of them was an authority on sexology and related fields. I used to go to hear his lectures. He said that, outside of the state of dying, the function of the brain is never reduced to such a minimum as in the state of orgasm. He described it as a kind of momentary decerebration. I think he is right."

Nancy was spellbound. "Do you think this happens to everyone?"

Gregor rubbed his finger over his cheek. "No." He shook his head. "I spent nights with dozens of girls. When the real thing came, I knew the difference." He sighed and paused again, lost in thought.

The voice within Nancy gave a warning...take care...it isn't easy for him to talk like this...he is allowing me to share and now I can look inside because the perfect shell around him is gone...but take care that you don't violate this permission to enter the sanctity of his inner self....

Indeed, Nancy had been permitted to enter a small space within him, a small clearing, soft, white and exquisitely tender. She waited here, a bit unsure, afraid to touch the walls of the sacred inner temple for fear they would reverse themselves and the door would clang shut.

She touched his cheek gently. "Morghann, I'm beginning to understand."

He pressed his lips into a thin line. "I didn't mean to say so much."

"It's much better that you do. You can't keep it all inside you. That is part of your trouble." She stroked his hair gently. "With your strong will, everything will be right again. I want you to love me."

A look of anguish crossed his face. "No!" he cried out, pushing her away roughly. "No! I let myself love Pandora and look what it did to her! I'm a jinx! I'm not good for any girl! If I hadn't fallen in love with Pandora, she'd be alive! Do you hear me! Alive! Alive!" His agitation mounted as he clenched his fists and pounded on the tree trunk. "I killed her! Killed her!" he continued hysterically.

Nancy watched for just a few seconds. Stepping up to him, she slapped him on the cheek. She heard his sharp intake of breath as his head jerked backward. Then he held his hand over his jaw and stared at her.

For Nancy, the gates of the temple had closed. She had dared to stir within the sacred place and had violated something holy. She had been pitched out rudely. Now, she stood before the shrine of the man she loved even more strongly when he left her beating at the closed gates.

"Why did you do that?" Gregor asked.

"I'm sorry, Morghann," she said softly. "You were hysterical. That was to make you come out of it." She waited while he rubbed his cheek. "Don't ever do that again, Morghann. Not you. Not a guy like you. Don't ever feel sorry for yourself." She waited again. "Are you forgetting that we aren't even sure of what happened to Pandora? You are *assuming* that she went down with your car. If nobody knows for sure, how can you say you killed her? Hah! Suppose she shows up and says that she's been testing out her telepathy experiments? Now, now, don't get mad at me," she begged as Gregor pursed his lips and began to turn away. "Someone has to tell you these things. I'm sorry, Morghann. I know she has hurt you very much, but you can't go on nursing that hurt. You have to let it pass off. As soon as you do, it will be all right for us." She smoothed the welt on his face. "I love you, Morghann, and I won't leave you as long as you need me. It will be all right. You'll see."

She pulled him down onto the sand. They lay there a long time watching the red shadows in the clouds fade to a warm gray. Finally, Nancy slept, her dreams reflecting fulfillment, her mantle of hair falling like a spun-copper blanket over the muscles of his bare shoulders.

A month after that Roy was bitten by a shark that got into the cage. It was a gray shark about four feet long, and Gregor killed it promptly, but not before it left gashes on Roy's leg and shoulder, and deep scratches on Gregor's forearm. Fortunately, they had enough footage of film and could stop at that point. They decided to ship the cage back to the designer for still another modification while Roy had skin grafts done. Gregor stayed with Roy in Los Angeles for a week. Nancy went ahead to stock the apartment in Sunday Village.

At the end of her week there, Nancy called Dr. Quest.

"We will be here for a few months, Doctor," she said. "Roy's grafts will take a long time."

In the office, the physician's lanky body leaned back in his office chair.

"There has been no report from either of you for months. Am I to assume that everything is going well, then?"

"Not like it should be. I think Morghann needs more treatment. I'm calling to make his appointments."

"What has happened?" the psychiatrist asked.

Nancy's voice was hardly audible. "Well, for one thing, we are planning to be married."

"Splendid!" the doctor exclaimed. "Then I assume there has been some progress."

"I wish I could decide! Well, some. Less dreams. Not many visions. However, Morghann's guilt feelings are ruining his life. I can't make him get over his notion that he is responsible for Pandora's accident. Maybe you can talk him out of it. It seems—" the voice faltered.

The doctor brought his chair forward. "Yes? Nancy, are you there?"

There was a pause. "Yes," came a squeaky answer.

"Are you crying?" The physician waited anxiously.

"Yes—yes, I'm, uh, uh, I'm crying," she admitted. "We've called the wedding off twice. I don't know what to do!" There was the sound of sniffling before her voice came again. "I've just got to talk to you!"

Dr. Quest tapped the desk with his long, bony fingers. "I have a little time free right now, Nancy. You hop into your car and come over now. All right?"

His smile came easily, wrinkling his kindly, lean features. He pointed to a chair and Nancy seated herself, fidgeting all the while with the belt of her flared capris. For a few moments, Nancy talked rapidly, continuously returning to Gregor's feelings of guilt over Pandora.

Dr. Quest brought the fingertips of his two hands together as he leaned back in his chair and listened attentively, occasionally making a quick note on a thick pad.

"Hmm," the physician said finally. "I think that all this can be brought into proper perspective. We have to keep in mind that nobody really knows what happened that night after the party at the Club. All we know is that the car was found."

"That's just it, Doctor!" Nancy interrupted. "Morghann thinks that Pandora drove away recklessly that night because she was angry with him. He keeps saying that if he hadn't been dancing, she wouldn't have been mad, or if he hadn't taken her to the party, she wouldn't have disappeared. Then, he says that if she hadn't met him at all, she'd be alive, that he is a jinx to any girl who falls in love with him. He's afraid to fall in love, to get close to a girl." She sniffed and her voice broke when she tried to continue. "Dr. Quest, please help me convince Morghann that Pandora isn't alive anymore."

The psychiatrist pondered the request for a few seconds. "Why, Nancy? How can I do that if I'm not sure?"

Nancy threw up her hands in a gesture of resignation. "Don't you see? Either way, Morghann is letting his guilt destroy him! Either way! Dr. Quest, I love him and I am sure I can manage Morghann, but *I can't cope with Pandora!* It'll be easier if he thinks that she will never come back. Can't you persuade him?"

The physician made a breathy sound as he drew air through closed teeth. "I'll have to talk to Gregor first. It's been a long time since his last visit. These long absences don't help."

"But Morghann sees Dr. Ornski in Hawaii. Doesn't he continue the treatment?" Nancy asked. "Didn't you refer him?"

"Yes, yes, Dr. Ornski keeps me somewhat updated." He stroked his chin thoughtfully. "Doesn't Gregor tell you about these sessions?"

The jade green eyes opened wide and blinked as she assessed the doctor. She shook her head. "No, no he doesn't. Morghann gets to feeling lower than a snake's belly after those visits and doesn't talk. I don't probe. I thought Dr. Ornski was taking your place."

Dr. Quest shrugged his shoulders. "Well, he is into something different from my treatment."

"Different?" The green eyes widened again.

"Well, yes. He thinks that finding Pandora's experimental group in England will lead to 'a clue.' "

"A clue?"

"Oh," the doctor answered matter-of-factly, "he thinks that Pandora may have had Gregor under hypnosis and that she might have simply used imagery and age regression mechanisms, but we think there's something more."

"Recall and regression are as old as the human race."

Dr. Quest held up his hand in protest. "Let me finish, now. I said that Pandora might have done that. However, Dr. Ornski and I both think that there is something strange going on. No doubt parapsychology is playing a significant role in his verbalizations. There are repeated indications of psychic phenomena and some definite kind of telepathy, like his Xionflight. There are—"

Nancy appeared surprised. "His what?"

The physician hesitated. "He didn't tell you about Xionflight?"

Nancy's brows knitted. She shook her head. "No, he didn't. What is it?"

"Hmm. That's strange. Maybe...maybe you'd better hear it from him, Nancy."

"Should I bring up the subject?"

Dr. Quest's middle finger tapped a light rhythm that ended with a terminal slap. "Better wait. I must talk to Gregor first, and I may check with Dr. Ornski. Suppose we get together again after that." He glanced quickly at his watch.

Nancy sighed loudly and nodded. "I do have an idea, though, in the meantime."

"Yes?" The shaggy brows lifted, followed by the usual quick smile. Dr. Quest watched as Nancy took a pencil to make a quick sketch on a pad of paper.

As she leaned over the desk, her thick, copper hair trailed over the polished mahogany. She toyed with the ornate belt which she hardly needed to hold up the tight hip-huggers. She explained her drawing briefly and prepared to go, but Dr. Quest's thoughts were elsewhere as she talked. What a striking girl, he was thinking...prettier than the last one...he might do himself a favor to forget Pandora...weird woman, really...but then....

Nancy had gathered her purse. His own reflections were still uppermost in his mind as he said goodbye and watched her leave. He wrinkled his forehead as he sighed and seated himself again to begin his telephoning.

Nancy arrived at the apartment just as a car pulled away from the curb. She fumed as it dawned on her that it was Nichole's car. She made her way down the steps to find David smiling at her from the landing.

"You had another visitor here a minute ago," David said.

"Humph! Yes, I saw her leaving. She probably thinks that Morghann is back. She doesn't waste any time, does she?"

David followed her into the living room. "She says that she and Rex called it off, again."

"What, again?"

"Yep. The ring goes back and forth like the Coronado ferry."

"Damn!" Nancy said. "Well, she doesn't have to come here!"

"She says she gets so mad at Rex that she could kill him. She says she has to talk to someone. I think she really hates the guy. I believe her. Rex is off his rocker to keep chasing her."

Nancy deliberated. "It could be that he loves her very much, although I don't see why."

"Uh-uh. The way I see it, he wants her only because she is hard to get. I know some of the other girls he chums around with. Where do you keep the cookies?"

Nancy pointed to the refrigerator. "In there. What do you mean to say, that she is hard to get? Seems that she is always available around here!"

"You've heard of people who always want something just out of their reach. Well, I think Rex chased Nicki because she is always just out of his reach, and that she likes Gregor only because he is out of her reach. If Rex could get Nicki, then he'd be off chasing some other chick who was hard to get. Like I said, he's off his rocker. It's a good thing they split." David threw a cookie into his mouth, sank into Gregor's chair, and closed his eyes. "Boy, am I tired! I just walked the beach from Del Mar."

"I didn't know that you could walk it all the way. Don't the cliffs stop you?" Nancy asked.

"Not if you know the tides."

"What were you doing in Del Mar?"

"Visiting Kimberly Weldin, only her name isn't Weldin anymore. She met this really handsome bit actor after the races, and she married the bum a couple of months ago. Now it's very clear that he married her for her money, which he is using up in a hell of a hurry. He dates other starlets and even brings them home with him. Overnight, yet! The bum!" David reached for Gregor's new guitar, examined it carefully and then began to strum.

Nancy's voice came from the kitchen. "David, how did you get involved in a problem like that?"

"Oh, I dated her long before she met this crum-bum. You have to know Kim. She is the nicest person you could hope to know. She was always such good company. Lots of personality. But she isn't a knockout, no competition for the kids on the movie sets. Marrying some guy who is good-looking is just an ego-builder to her. But then, maybe she really loves him." He stopped playing and took another cookie. "I can't decide. I wish I could decide." He examined the delicacy speculatively before popping it into his mouth.

"She can divorce him if she wants to."

Thoughtfully, David nodded his head, chewed and swallowed. "Yeah, that's what she should do, but she thinks she can stabilize the marriage by having a baby. What a dumb thing!"

Nancy came to the doorway where she stood scrutinizing him as he searched the cookie wrapper. "David," she said in a low voice, "my advice is not to get involved."

"Yeah, yeah. I know what you mean," David answered with a shrug of his shoulders. "Got any more? I'm hungry." Smugly, he tossed the crumpled wrapper across the room into a waste basket, wiped his hand on his blue tank top, and continued to strum the guitar. "Wanna hear my latest?" he asked.

"Bubba-loo, bubba-li, bubba-lee," David sang with abandon, ending in a difficult falsetto note.

> "There was a flea in a tree,
> Who talked all day with a bee.
> 'If I knew how to fly instead of to jump,
> I wouldn't be living on some dog's rump!'
> Bubba-loo, bubba-li, bubba-lee."

Smiling and nodding her approval, Nancy leaned against the doorjamb and waited for the next verse. "More," she demanded.

However, David changed the tempo of his strum and sat in thought. "Here's one that I've been working on." He picked a few more chords. "You know the way the city likes to tax Sunday Village because they feel that everyone here is filthy rich?"

Nancy laughed. "Yes, go on."

"And the Council seems to treat the Villagers with a bit of prejudice?"

"I'm waiting."

Lustily, David sang to a familiar tune.
> "Diego Mio, Our Dear Pater,
> Don't let high rise kill our view!
> Stand beside us and guide us.
> Consider us, for we love you."

Stilling his guitar, he recited the next lines.
> "City council, quite contrary,
> How does your garden grow?
> With banks and bells and cockle shells
> And Villagers all in a row?"

Again came the following in fine voice.
> "The City likes to veto
> Each time we have a thought
> To keep our town three stories high,
> But permits can be bought."

Again, the recitation.
> "A-tix-it, a-tax-it,
> Pamper it, don't ax it.
> We took our plans to city desk,
> And by the way, they lost it!"

Nancy clapped loudly. "Really clever, Davie, but better watch out. You'll have the council down on you."

"How else will we make them hear us? You haven't been here long enough, Nancy. You don't know this town. One has to be a developer to get heard. They find it very easy to ignore five hundred signatures from us plain people. As the affluent, or, in my language, the *rilthy fitch*, we aren't in favor downtown."

"Well, David, the political game is a special philosophy. It must be understood. I dare say they like your taxes, though."

Immediately, David strummed on the strings. "Rub a dub dub, rub a dub dub, three tax collectors in a leaky tub. They can't swim. Blub, blub, blub."

Nancy laughed. "How do you think of that stuff?"

"Oh, it's easy. I have lots more," David answered. "Here's one. Black's Beach cliff is falling down. The nudies frown, falling down."

Nancy clapped again. "Okay, Tommy Tucker!" she said with a laugh. "You deserve your supper." She opened the freezer and withdrew another pack of cookies.

XVIII

"...try not to get stuck in yesterday..."

At the end of the school year, Kelley heard of an opportunity to get work for the summer months.

"Can I? Can I, Dad? It would be so much fun. I know two kids who are going. Do you think I could go?" Kelley coaxed.

Her father chuckled. "A job in Hawaii? You'd use every penny you earned to pay for fare back and forth. No, Kelley, it's not very practical."

Kelley wrinkled her nose with a little twist, her habit when things displeased her. In a moment, she smiled again. "How about next year? I was thinking of applying for a scholarship there at the university, anyway."

Her father looked up from his paper. "Hmm. That might work out nicely. I hadn't thought that you'd want to go so far away from home, but we'll see. Actually, the months fly by so fast, we'd better make some plans soon."

The months did pass quickly. June came with its foggy overcast that stayed on through mid-July. Kelley found herself not really training for the swim competition this year. Nevertheless, she swam daily, sometimes with Gregor and Nancy, or with David or Karla.

Always, she came racing home, splashing through the surf, calling to a low-flying seagull, stopping on her favorite cliff below her home, out of breath and giddy, ready for the challenge of whatever tomorrow would bring.

On one such afternoon, she reached the patio in time to hear the telephone ring, but when she entered the house it had become silent. In another moment it rang again. Kelley grabbed it. "Hello," she sang out. "Did you just now call?"

"Yes," a deep voice answered. "Had that timed just right. Figured it would take you just that long to get to your pad."

Kelley blinked her eyes and cocked her head sideways. "Who is this?"

The mellow voice replied, "Suppose I say that I'm a football scout and I like the way you tackled that tree. How's your head? Any scar?"

Kelley squealed with delight. "It's you! Finally! I just knew I'd hear from you again. You're the man who belongs to those beautiful eyes. That's what we call you because you didn't even tell me your name."

"Way out," the voice replied. "Mobe. That's a good name."

"Mobe? Is that your name?" Kelley giggled.

"You are the one who said so. *Man owning beautiful eyes.* M-o-b-e. Way out."

Kelley laughed again. "I guess Mobe will do until you tell me your name. To answer your question, the scar hardly shows and this is my chance to thank you for rescuing me. You can't even tell where the cut was."

"So I noticed," the voice continued.

"How can you...that is...you mean that you've been that close to...now, wait a minute. I haven't been near any more hippie crowds. Uh, I mean...but maybe you aren't always with a hippie gang?"

"Maybe not."

"Thank goodness. In the Village, hippies are rated lower than a snake's belly. If you aren't...then again if you are—" Suddenly embarrassed, Kelley hesitated.

"I dig. You don't have to explain," he said quickly. "Who is the guy you are with at the beach all the time?"

"Uh, how do you know who I'm with? Goodness me! What do you do, spy on me?"

The voice laughed. "No, I watch you surf with the big guy, the one who stays out of the white water. Not your brother. I saw your brother once. I recognize him. But the blond guy. Boyfriend?"

"Oh, you mean Gregor." Kelley sighed. "I should be that lucky," she mumbled.

"Watcha say?"

"He's engaged to the girl with auburn hair."

"Not your sister? He is a little too old."

"Good grief! What is there that you don't know about us? Mobe, who are you anyway?" Kelley asked.

The voice melted into a low chuckle. "Actually, just a guy who is always too busy with something else to walk up and say hello again. So tonight I got time. I got no one to rap with tonight. I thought maybe we could rap a bit."

"Not up here," Kelley hurried to say. "My father wouldn't...that is to say...he is so strict!"

"No sweat. I dig," the voice broke in quickly. There was an awkward pause. "Just thought I'd call."

"Oh, no, no, don't go! I really want to see you!" Kelley pressed the receiver closer to her ear. "Actually you've been on my mind. I couldn't forget you, Mobe. Really. I couldn't forget your eyes."

"Oh, way out!" Mobe seemed to be pleased.

"And I do want to see you on the beach. How is it that I have missed seeing you down there?"

"My hair is shorter. Wore my shades. What time will you be there?"

"About three tomorrow, but...but—"

"Afraid of what your father might say?" Mobe asked.

"No. I'm just not sure I'll know which one you are."

A mellow laugh came over the line. "No sweat. I know you. See you at three."

Kelley was humming as she walked briskly to the surfer's beach the next afternoon. Arriving there, she reached for her comb to brush the tangles from her hair. Someone tapped her shoulder from behind. She whirled about to face a lightly bearded, spectacled figure whose head was all but hidden by a knitted cap. The man removed his dark glasses and smiled.

Kelley stared for a few seconds. Then she giggled. "No wonder I didn't see you around, Mobe. Your beard is so much shorter, but I still can't see what you look like."

Very white, even teeth showed as he grinned, but his laugh was more in his eyes that seemed to kindle and glow. The expression on his face was kind and his tone was soft as he asked, "Want to walk up the beach for a way?" He held out his hand.

Kelley hesitated, surveying the somewhat stocky man dressed in cutoff jeans and faded tank shirt. Her first tendency was to draw back, but the soft expression about his eyes caught her and her reticence dissolved like snow on a campfire. She took his hand and they started to walk, chatting about anything that came to mind.

The sun almost touched the horizon when they returned to the surfer's beach. "My mom will be looking for me soon," Kelley said. "I guess I'd better head home. Come on, I'll show you my hideaway ledge in the cliff below our house."

"What do you hide away from?" he asked curiously as he followed her.

Kelley's hand arched in a sweeping motion. "Oh, all the worthless things about life, maybe. I don't really know. Maybe the ugliness and meanness in people." His questioning glance made her hesitate. "I don't like to admit that creation is less than perfect. People should be no less perfect than the environment they are given to exist in. Don't you ever try to equate the two?"

His heavy brows arched. "Whew!" he said. "We were talking about bottom fishing and houseplants a minute ago. Well, yes I try to equate the two, probably in a different way than you do. How do you do it?"

A twinkle crept into Kelley's eyes. "I *try not to get stuck in yesterday* or last week!" She laughed as she watched the puzzled look on her friend's face.

"Come again?" Mobe came to a standstill.

"It takes explaining. I have a philosophy."

"Aa—ll right! I'm all ears."

For a second or two, Kelley deliberated. Then she stopped to draw a diagram in the sand. "Look. Pretend that each day is a frame of screening and each person has to pass through today's screen to get to the next day. Now, here is the row of screens and here are the people passing through. Only the person who keeps himself pure or free of abrasive qualities can sift through. If a person harbors hate or jealousy or meanness, it solidifies in the screen and the person gets stuck in yesterday." Her features wrinkled in a frown. "That isn't too hard to understand, is it, Mobe?"

He scratched his head as he bent over her diagram. "Fa-r out!" he said. "These cats who get...uh...stuck in yesterday, aren't they like...uh...not quite alive?"

Kelley smiled. "Exactly right, Mobe! If a guy cheats or lies, for instance, a part of him is sick and dies."

Mobe deliberated. "I dig. Like maybe his substance becomes inert? Something like that?"

"Yes! Yes! You do understand!" she exclaimed excitedly as she jumped to her feet and pulled him to his.

"Huh!" he said. "Then almost everybody would be stuck in December or maybe 1961!"

"Oh, I have that figured out," Kelley said. "If a person gets rid of his shortcoming, he unsolidifies and bounces through the screens until he reaches today."

"But how does all this help you to equate rotten people to a good world?" Mobe asked.

They continued to walk as Kelley answered, "Oh, maybe by widening my understanding of human error. I have to think about that a little more. How would you go about it?"

Mobe shook his head vigorously. "Certainly not the way you would. You use fantasy. I have to do something constructive to keep the rotten people from taking over. The world isn't going to go right unless we do something about it."

"What do you do about it?" Kelley asked.

Mobe continued to shake his head. "Kelley, no amount of deep understanding is going to bring about the changes in the establishment that need to be made. Be realistic. You can't dream away mistakes."

"You haven't answered my questions, Mobe. What do you do about it?"

"I organize demonstrations, sometimes even riots, to show the rotten people that we don't like the way they are running the establishment."

Kelley's face clouded over. "Mobe, I don't like riots and people who organize them."

He shrugged his shoulders. "When a guy sees society go to the dogs, he has to do something about it in his own way."

"But it isn't going to the dogs! It isn't!" Kelley insisted. "It just depends on your viewpoint. There is a good side and a bad side to everything. If we simply take the positive elements and amplify them, we will survive. Don't you see what I mean? If we emphasize the constructive, it eliminates the negative—that idea. Riots are not constructive. They are a backward step, defacing to society, like a worm in a nice apple."

Mobe tossed his head back and laughed loudly. "Far out! That's what the world is to you, a beautiful apple, a rosy place to be happy in! Isn't that right?"

They had reached Kelley's rock by this time. A deep frown clouded her features as she seated herself, her arms hugging her knees. "That's my way," she announced curtly.

He knelt beside her and his arm slipped gently about her shoulders. "We won't talk about it any more if it upsets you," he said softly.

Kelley shook her head. "Oh, no, no! That won't do. We have to communicate, that is if we want to get to know each other. I've got to know what you think about things, Mobe. I want to be able to talk to you about anything."

"Right on!" he answered. "See you here tomorrow, same time." He stood abruptly and strode off.

He was lying on the ledge when Kelley came the next afternoon. As he moved to sit up, his cap caught on an edge of stone, exposing a tell-tale tuft of hair on top of his head, ringed by a shorter length that was obviously growing in after a recent severe shaving.

"Oh, my God!" Kelley gasped. "You joined a cult or something?"

Hastily, he replaced the cap. "I try everything just to know what it's all about. Once is enough. My hair is growing in fast."

Down below them, a passing couple waved and called out. "Hi, Rommey! How ya doin', Rom!"

Kelley watched the figures continue on their way. Then she turned to her capped friend. "So your name is Rommey."

"Yes," he admitted. He grinned broadly. "Rommey Jaggart."

"Rommey," she repeated. "I like that, but you'll always be Mobe to me, too."

She took his hand. "Come .on. Let's walk all the way to the Cove today."

Conversation came easily. Kelley learned that he had no particular job, that he lived in a small studio with a friend. He seemed to be enrolled in several classes taught by a professor who was labeled by the community as an anarchist. One class appeared to offer instruction in organizing against the forces of law. However, his answers to Kelley's questions about himself were evasive and brief, always shifting to something light and general.

Finally, they were back again at their meeting place. Kelley stood staring at him, swinging her beach bag back and forth, head cocked to one side.

"What's wrong?" Rommey asked. "I can tell by the look on your face that something puzzles you."

"Oh, Mobe...Rommey—" She stamped her foot. "You really confuse me! I feel I really am talking to two different people!"

He fingered his cap. "It's the...uh...you don't dig my hair and all that?"

"Not exactly. It's just that one minute we both seem to agree that nature is wonderful and humanity is good. I seem to understand you."

Rommey shook his head and threw a quick glance heavenward. "Kelley," he said, heaving a sigh, "you are a Pollyana. That's what you are."

The beach bag stopped swinging. "What's that?"

"Never mind," Rommey replied. "Just tell me what this other guy in me is like."

She took a deep breath as though the wind had suddenly chilled her. "Just a little ugly. It scares me," she admitted. Then, seeing the wounded expression on his face, she added, "I'm sorry, Rom."

He bit his lip. "Far-rr out! Really far out! You're afraid of me?"

Her hand touched his forearm gently. "No, Rommey. Not really. Only until I see the light in your eyes."

Rommey's smile widened slowly. "And then?"

"And then I know I like you very much."

With his hands on her shoulders, he pulled her to him and kissed her on the lips lightly. In the same gesture, he spun around and started down the path.

"See you tomorrow," she called after him, but he neither answered nor turned around. In a brief moment, he was out of sight.

"You are late, dear," Vanessa said when Kelley entered the kitchen.

"Oh, I saw Nichole and Rex on the beach," Kelley replied casually.

Vanessa looked up from her work. "You mean to say that they are talking to each other again? Well, isn't that nice?"

Kelley nodded absentmindedly. Disturbing thoughts about Rommey ran through her mind, and suddenly she was anxious to be with him again. However, she could not find him anywhere the next day, or the next, or the next. Not even Gregor's homecoming diverted her feeling of loss.

XIX

"...Rex sprang...nursing a bitten arm..."

The Rough-Water Swim was only a few weeks away when Nichole and Rex began to talk to each other again. Shortly after Lisa, Nichole's sister, left for a vacation, Rex was surprised to receive a call.

"This is Nicki, Rex. I need that diving mask you borrowed, the one that doesn't cloud so much. Remember? You helped me get it at Ginder's store."

"Oh, yeah, yeah!" came his surprised answer. "That one. I remember. I let Sal use it. It's a tad worn. Should I get you a new one?"

"Well, the store is out of them and I need that mask for some special dives, so why don't you get it to me?"

"Bring it to you? Oh, sure, sure! I'll be at your house right away!"

"No, no. Bring it to the beach, same place we always dive."

They met and went diving together that day. This went on steadily for two weeks. Rex was happy, hopeful that her attention would prove meaningful. However, he began to have doubts as to Nichole's real purpose and he grew bewildered. Just a few days before Lisa was due to return, his suspicions of her sincerity began to torture him.

...if only I knew whether this is one of her games again, Rex kept saying to himself, if only I could outguess her...damn...she knows that she can have me eating out of her hand if she looks at me twice...what that woman does to me...horny is hardly the word...she hasn't talked to me for months...why the sudden change...hell... is she still in love with that screwed-up bastard Morghann...do I want her any way...yeah...yeah...any way I can get her...Rex, you stupid fug-head...find out why she is toying around with you....

Finally, the torment was too much. "Nicki, why this sudden change of heart?" he blurted out. "Have you given up on the knuckle-head Morghann?"

Nichole fingered her diving mask, then threw her wet, black hair over her shoulder with a nonchalant gesture. "Get this straight, Rex," she began. "Now that he is getting married, I'd be a fool to waste any time on him, now wouldn't I?"

Rex chewed his lip. "But, he—"

"Maybe I don't love him anymore!" she snapped. "Maybe I've come to my senses."

The frown faded from Rex's narrow face. "Are you sure, Nicki?"

"Uh-huh," she replied with a careless shrug.

Like a boxer winning a bout in the ring, Rex jabbed at the air. "You know how pissed off I get when I think of Morghann? I get so mad that I could kill the fuggin showoff for letting you hang around all these years like a bitch in heat, like all the other women who lick his boots! He hypnotizes every girl he looks at! You know that, don't you?"

"Then you still love me, Rex?"

Her question took him by surprise. With an intake of breath, he clutched her shoulders. "You know damned well I do!" he shouted. His yellow curls tumbled over his forehead as he gave her a shake. "What kind of a question is that? Yes, Nicki, I love you!"

Nichole stamped her foot and yanked herself free of his hold. "Then why are you playing around with Lisa?" she screamed at him.

Rex brushed his thick curls off his temple. "But, uh—I haven't seen your sister in weeks. I—"

"Sure, sure! She's been gone. And what will you tell her when she gets back?"

He avoided her eyes and kicked the sand with his toe. *Damn...damn, something inside was saying to him, she reads me like a book...always a step ahead of me...maybe I shouldn't have fooled around with Lisa...what will I say now....*

"Uh, look, Nicki, I admit I did it to make you jealous. I'm sorry. I'll explain it all to Lisa when she gets back. I'm sorry."

"Sorry? You cad! Sorry isn't enough! I suspected that you were just playing with her to get even with me! Don't you think of anyone's feelings but your own? The poor kid thinks she's in love with you, even asked me about taking the pill and all this because you want to get even with me. You beast!" While she berated him in Spanish, her fists came down on his face so suddenly that he fell backward in the sand, dragging her with him. They tumbled over and over until *Rex sprang to his feet nursing a bitten arm.*

"Why, you bit me!" he thundered. "You little bitch, you bit me!"

Through tears, Nichole continued to rail at him. "How could you do this? How could you?"

He studied her for a moment. Then his voice became gentle. "Please, Nicki, please believe me. If you realized how much I love you, you'd know how I nearly go out of my mind when I see you with Morghann. You won't even give me a chance and I go crazy when I think that he is touching you." Rex paused and tried to put his arm around her waist, but she spit at him and drove him off with handfuls of wet sand which he dodged, laughing all the while. Out of breath, he finally knelt a short distance away. "Nicki, can't you see that we're made for each other?" he pleaded. "Only marry me and I swear I'll make you happy." His hand trembled as he brushed sand from his eyes. A trickle of blood crossed his arm and dripped from his elbow.

"Oh! Oh!" Nichole exclaimed as she stared at the red streak. "Your arm, Rex! I didn't mean to bite that hard. Really, I didn't." Snatching a scarf from her beachbag, she ran to wet it at the water's edge.

He watched her as she tended his arm. Finally, he said, "You know you love me, too. You know it. Nicki, marry me."

"Well, we'll have to talk about it, Rex. If you will stop drinking so much, there might be a chance. And absolutely no more drugs, understand?" Nichole glared at him as he nodded his head. "You know that's what turns me off, don't you? Are you willing to make some changes?"

Rex grimaced and sighed. "You know I'll do anything. Anything!" He tried to put his arm around her, but she elbowed him away.

"You prove it to me, Rex," she said as she reached for her sweater. "It's getting cold. Let's get out of the wind."

"I'll prove it to you. You'll see, Nicki. I'll prove it!" Rex repeated, closing his fists nervously. "Just promise me that Morghann is out of your life for good. Now promise me."

She grunted as the sweater came down over her head. Her full breasts lifted as she stretched her arms into the sleeves. The hem of the bulky knit fell over a tiny waist, then to the smooth line of her thigh.

As he watched, Rex stood transfixed. His dark skin glistened with perspiration. Like Gregor's, his nose was very slightly aquiline, his features just a bit more rugged. Even though there were no clefts in his cheek when he smiled, he could have passed as Gregor's brother. He was shorter than his rival and he had none of Gregor's calm and deliberate manner. Instead, he was impulsive, quick and sometimes violent.

At this moment, doubt still tormented him. His thoughts spun like a record *...damn...why do I feel this crazy way about her...I can't live without her...no other girl will do...she is made for me...we are alike...can't she see that...damn...I'll have her if it's the last thing I do...the last thing I do....*

He made no attempt to forestall the emotion that welled inside him. Without shame, he drew her to him. "Nicki, you make me feel so horny."

"For goodness sake, Rex! People are watching," she said as she elbowed him away again. "Anyway, we have a lot of talking to do first. A lot."

"All right. All right," he grumbled. "Have it your way." Snatching up her swim fins, he followed her across the beach.

XX

"...a time barrier broken..."

The winter months passed rapidly for Kelley during her senior year, inasmuch as she was involved in scores of activities. She was secretary of her class; she sang with the chorus; she helped to illustrate the year book; the drama club and her sorority activities filled her after-school hours. Besides that, the vice principal asked her to replace another member of the student committee for the prom.

As the plans for the affair progressed, Kelley's friends asked repeatedly, "Who are you taking to the dance?" When she shrugged her shoulders, they made suggestions. "How about that muscle builder with the beard who rapped with you so much on the beach last September? He was so—oooo neat! You know which one, that Rodney guy."

Kelley laughed. "Rommey," she corrected. "No guy like him would go around without a groovy name." She sighed and her eyes grew wistful. "I wish I knew where he was. He just disappeared from sight."

Vanessa nagged her. "We have to start looking for a dress soon. Why don't you ask Don? He asked you out so much last year."

"Mom!" Kelley squealed. "He goes steady!"

"Oh," her mother said. "Well, didn't I hear Karla say that the Corey boy wanted to ask you to go?"

"Uh, well, yes."

Vanessa made a chiding noise with her tongue. "You know what your Dad is always telling you about passing up one date for another. You'll hurt the boy's feelings."

To her mother's consternation, Kelley quickly confessed, "Oh, I told him that I had another date."

Two days later, the statement became truth. Kelley had been peering through the glass doors of the patio at the glistening moonpath on the ocean's surface when a figure appeared out of the dark. A man carrying a poncho stood smiling broadly in the shadows. Kelley opened the sliding door, not believing what she saw.

"Rommey!" she exclaimed. "Rom...mey!" She stepped out to touch his arm. "I can hardly believe it! Come in, Rom."

With a smile that kindled his features, Rommey stood there in a frayed shirt and cut-off jeans, barefooted. "How ya doin'?" he asked. Then he turned in the direction of the voice that rang from the living room.

"Who is there, Kelley?" came Christopher's loud inquiry.

Kelley clasped and unclasped her hands nervously. "Well, uh, come in and say hello to my folks," she said to her visitor.

The glow on his face persisted as he stepped in and looked about cautiously. "But your old man, remember?" he reminded her. However, Kelley took his hand and led him to the living room.

"This is Rommey Jaggart," she announced hesitatingly to her parents.

There was the rustle of Christopher's paper. "Mrs. Holliss doesn't generally allow bare feet on her carpeting," he said, staring at the figure of their guest.

The smile on Rommey's lips survived. "Oh, no sweat!" he assured them. "I have shoes. Some pad you have here!"

Still wringing her hands, Kelley interrupted. "Dad, Rommey is the one who rescued me from the flying bottle at the love-in. Remember?"

"Oh," her father said, appearing none the more pleased with their unkempt visitor. Throwing a quick glance at his wife, he turned again to reading his paper.

Vanessa herded the two into the kitchen in an attempt to rescue the situation. "I'll bet that Rommey would like some of the cookies we made, Kelley. How timely that we should have baked tonight! They are still warm."

"Far out," Rommey said, walking straight to the platter of date bars. "I don't often get homemade cookies." He reached for a generous handful. "I really dig cookies and milk. Man, what a kitchen!"

Kelley and Vanessa collided in their haste to get a glass for Rommey. Then they both giggled as they fumbled in the cupboard, and when they returned, Rommey was drinking contentedly from the bottle of milk which he had taken from the refrigerator. He wiped his lips on the shoulder of his shirt. "Man, what a pad!" he remarked again as he took two more date bars.

Watching him intently as he devoured them, Kelley thought he must be starved. "Can I get you a sandwich, Rommey?" she asked.

He shook his head, swallowed, and asked, "Where can we rap a little, you and me?"

Kelley turned to her mother. "We won't be gone long. I'll show him how to get to my rock ledge from here."

"Oh, cool!" Rommey said as he prepared to follow her. "Really cool!"

The hand on her watch swept the minutes away as Kelley listened and laughed at Rommey's stories. As he rambled on, she found herself staring at him and wondering...*what does the rest of his face look like...he has such a nice nose...his eyes almost talk and he laughs so easily...such a smooth voice...I feel so comfortable with him...as though I know him really well but I don't and Dad is upset because he is such a hippie...and Dad is going to give me a bad time about it but Rom isn't bad...under all that hippie talk and dress is something that is good...it's got to be that way...I won't let myself think any other way....*

"What'cha doing at school?" Rommey was asking her.

"Oh, nothing exciting like the things you do. I would only bore you if I told you."

"Try me," he replied.

Kelley mentioned a few of her activities, finally confiding her appointment to the prom committee. "After the formal," she explained, "we are going to the bowling alley, the same as last year."

150

"Ho!" Rommey exclaimed. "That's not what we did after my prom!"

Kelley felt her nose wrinkle as it did when she was nervous. "Well, that's what we are going to do," she announced boldly. "Want to go with me?"

Rommey chuckled loudly. "I may not be able to hack that formal stuff, but the last part sounds more like my bag." He held his palm down and swiveled it at the wrist. "Maybe I can hack that. Maybe."

Rommey caused quite a stir at the prom, and after that evening, he became a frequent visitor at Kelley's home. He remembered to wear thongs for the sake of Vanessa's carpets. He even trimmed his beard a little, which provided Christopher with a shred of comfort for the reason that unkempt beards and long hair were strongly associated by him with the element that rioted and engaged in disruptive demonstrations. However, Christopher made an obvious attempt to be civil to his daughter's friend. This was fine at first until his point of view clashed sharply with Rommey's theories during several discussions regarding the establishment.

Then, several of Rommey's writings appeared in the village newspaper as letters to the editor, writings in which he took a stand against wealthy people who represented the establishment. When he touched upon the local scene, he might as well have set off a bomb in the Holliss household. It came to light that Rommey bragged about his part in staging riots, that he called enforcing officers by vile epithets, and that he had helped a group to deny an army recruiter access to the campus.

After that, Christopher became so agitated at the mention of Rommey's name that Vanessa found it difficult to calm him.

"Just consider that I work my damned butt off to pay taxes to support an educational system that encourages rabble like him to spit in my face!" Christopher shouted. "That is one hell of a way to thank a guy for saving this democracy for the likes of him! When this shrapnel wound in my back hurts, I could kill that bastard and a couple more like him!" Christopher raged over and over again.

Vanessa wrung her hands. "Chris, please!" She began to cry softly. "You will have us both sick from worry."

"I *am* sick!" Christopher shouted all the louder. "It makes me so sick that I'm going to vomit!"

After one more confrontation, Christopher made it clear that Rommey was no longer welcome in the Holliss home. It was with a heavy heart that he watched his daughter's tears and listened to her steadfast defense of her friend.

However, his concern was of a deeper nature when Vanessa confided to him her fear that Kelley was meeting Rommey at his studio. He winced and muttered, "As much as I hate to admit this, I guess I'll be glad to see her leave for college in Honolulu. Maybe the choice is a good one after all."

Vanessa sighed. "I don't like to see her go to school so far away, but at least it will break up their friendship." She paused. "Of course, if you let her take that waitress job in Waikiki, she would be leaving in two weeks, Chris."

Christopher frowned and pressed his lips together. "Very well, we'll let her go." He threw up his hands in a gesture of defeat. "Anything. Anything to break up this romance which isn't going to do anything but hurt her. We can't let it go on."

Vanessa's soft voice rose slightly. "Chris, you *must* forbid her to go to his studio." She blinked to hold back tears. "It might have been better if he were allowed to come here."

He looked at her sharply. Christopher took pride in never being beaten and never being wrong. He was not in the habit of coming to his own defense, but now he ran his fingers guardedly through his thick hair.

"Maybe I was wrong telling her that she couldn't bring Rommey here, but I did and I can't very well reverse it now." He reached for a cigarette and lit it, inhaling hungrily. "Now, if I try to stop her from going there too, well, I'll just lose all rapport with her." He laughed nervously. "That's just too high a price to pay to prove myself right." He went on to deliberate at length. "Karla knows of only one time when she actually went to his studio. They meet on the beach. I just can't bear down on her unreasonably, Vanessa." His heavy brows lifted. "Maybe she will find some nice lads to date at school. After all, we will have to be patient for only two more weeks." He winced as the cigarette ash dropped on his slippered foot. Brushing his ankle quickly, he shouted, "God almighty! My father didn't have this much trouble raising five kids!"

Perhaps Kelley's conversation with Rommey several days later would have made her father feel a little less anxious had he heard its content.

On finding Rommey gone from his studio, Kelley left her paperback on his doorstep with a note that read, "I'll be in the surf. Bring my novel. Don't lose my marker."

Rommey found the book when he returned and carried it to a rocky ledge where he seated himself for a moment to watch Kelley splashing in the surf below him. The sheet of paper that marked her place fell from the slim volume and Rommey stooped to retrieve it, glancing briefly at the page of Kelley's writing. It was obviously a class assignment. The first line caught his attention. He scanned the page, then started at the beginning again. Silently at first, and then aloud, he read on.

"It was a strange combination of sounds like the rustle of big wings or the ping of a *time barrier being broken*; I couldn't tell. In the darkness on the cliff where I stood, I had just prayed an impassioned prayer for peace in the world and now I swung about to see what caused the noises. As I struggled to focus through my tears, a shudder shook me because facing me were a dozen or so towering forms, gray-robed with grotesque faces hardly discernible in the shadows. Too frightened to run, I trembled and stared at the shimmering figures whose sagging mouths dripped phosphorescent saliva."

Rommey stopped reading, scratched his temple and narrowed his eyes as he tried to imagine the scene with weird specters who dripped glistening drool over the figure of a trembling teenager. He continued to read Kelley's pages, occasionally acting out the part of the phantoms.

"*What world is this?*" the first ghost groaned as he pointed a bony finger over the land. His tissue-like cloak crackled in a gust of wind.

"Who are you?" I whispered hoarsely, crouching on one knee in fright.

"*What world is this?*" the second apparition rasped. "*What globe are we upon?*"

"This is the Earth," I replied, shielding my eyes from their glow. "Surely, you know that you are on the Earth, our Earth. Where else? Who are you, anyway?"

"We are the sages of the living past come to revisit the green planet that we left to you, but surely this cannot be the same! We left you a fruited plain that stretched from sea to shining sea, bathed in the holy light of freedom." The distorted face of the speaker moved in eerie slow motion. *"What have you done to our green globe?"*

"What—have—you—done—done—done—done?" the other ghosts growled in jangled unison.

"It's a different place, I agree. Your guarantee of freedom's holy light shining over waves of golden grain seems to have run out. Maybe we missed some of the rules in the fine print somewhere. Someone should have told us not to cut down forests and dam up rivers and use our waterways as sewers for waste. We wiped out the buffalo a long time ago. Now the fish are dying off, birds are robbed of their sanctuaries, and even whales are becoming extinct. Soon there won't be any seals left because herds are being clubbed to death for their furs. Should I go on?" I paused to draw a breath.

The sound of their wail rose and mingled with the wind that whistled through the trees overhead. Their mammoth tears splashed at my feet as they chanted, *"Clouds of gases over cities of concrete. The green globe is dying—dying—dying. What more? What more?"*

Their sadness gave me courage. "Well, you may as well hear it all. We have racial strife, unemployment, and people who are hungry. Yet, we subsidize the farmer so he will plow his crops under."

"Destroy the bounty of the fields! Unheard of!" Bewildered, they looked from one to another.

Less afraid, I stood to address the foremost of the group. "You've probably never heard of welfare either, or the national debt, or the underground, or organized crime."

"Why did you do this? We were blessed, bountiful and with peace and goodwill! You don't deserve to occupy the earth!" The apparition lifted his bony hand as if to strike me and I fell to my knees again in fear.

"Not me! Not me! Don't blame me," I pleaded. "Don't even blame my generation! Accuse those before us who let it happen. I understand how you feel. Nobody can blame you for being upset. But what should we do? Our civilization is going to pot, I agree."

The ghost kneeled and bent low to confront me. *"Pot! Pot! Pot! What does that mean?"* Like sad men crying in their sleep, the others repeated the question.

Feeling less timid and filled somewhat with compassion, I stood again to face my visitor. "Well, I only meant it as an expression, but since you ask me, I should remind you that your holy light doesn't seem to affect the men who peddle illegal drugs that threaten to ruin our minds and kill."

"Would you mock our eternal blessing?" they asked, somewhat aghast

154

at my daring.

"Oh, no, not at all! I just wish that your blessed neon had more impact, like some therapeutic effect, perhaps, on our social diseases which seem worse now even in the face of our medical miracles. You want to know the problems my generation faces? Just read the headlines. Did you ever hear of abortion as we do it now? Or resistance when faced with fighting for your country? Or euthanasia? Or murderers going free? No? Well, just stick around a while longer."

The glowing saliva dripped heavily as they moaned. As though a million men were crying somewhere in the sky, the sound grew. *"You curse the land! You violate the covenant with nature! You court your own doom!"* The specters began to march around me in a tightening circle, pointing bony fingers into my face.

"I didn't do it! Don't blame me," I pleaded, shielding my head with my arms, thinking that this breath would be my last as their hot drool fell on my neck.

"You are killing the planet! You poison the air! Even now, you die from the gases. You foul the waters! You destroy earth's verdure and its animals! Surely, you can smell death coming. Insects will inherit the land. Have you no men with wisdom among you? Pray for wisdom! Pray to see the way! Pray while you work and while you learn!" the voices admonished.

"We can't! We legislated against it," I explained. Then, with a lift of my head, I added hurriedly, "But it's okay at football games!"

The figures looked askance at one another, then at me again. *"Only the loftiest, concentrated and unselfish efforts of the wisest among you on the entire globe can save it. Enough with the dribble of fools! Fools cannot see a hundred years ahead!"*

"Well, we have world councils, but there's always so much politics! A hundred years, you say? Huh! Politicians think only in four year periods to the next election. Everyone has his own special interest. There aren't many lofty unselfish efforts and very few really wise men pulling together. We'll probably be blown off the face of the earth before the gases get to us."

One apparition sighed, *"Is there no hope? Is our visit to you for naught?"*

I dared to stand to face them as they gathered into a group again. "What can I do? What can I possibly do to help you? Tell me. I'll try."

The sounds coming from the company grew less discordant. One of them stepped forward. *"Yes! Yes! You will try! You will try and you will succeed. Tell your peers that we charge them with the task of saving this celestial body. They will work hand in hand as your fathers have not done. Tell them that, in them, there is greatness, that mankind is unique and can expand beyond itself. You will see a hundred, even a thousand years ahead, with ultimate wisdom and one purpose."*

Their tears had bathed their faces somewhat of the drool, thereby exposing rather noble features. A sudden rush of excitement filled me. "Sure! Sure! I'll tell a hundred of my peers and they'll tell thousands more until millions of us hold hands like the Olympiads do around and around the world!"

The apparition stared at me. *"Yes, yes, I can see that all of you together will save the green planet. You will not listen alone to your own heartbeat which is gone too soon. You will listen, rather, to the heartbeat of the earth. Greatness will flow from your fingertips and the rivers will run sweet and clear."*

Strangely, the faint sound of magnificent music drifted from far away. I turned my head to find its source. For a moment I searched the beach and the sky. When I looked again for my ghostly companions, I found myself alone in a flurry of crackling leaves and I wasn't really sure whether it was the wind that made the rustling sound in the eucalyptus above the bank. I was sure, however, that I would give the message to a hundred people so they could pass it to thousands more.

As I left the grove, I murmured, "maybe even millions."

Rommey finished reading, lowered the paper and swore. "Damn all my guts anyway! I have the rotten luck to find another one. I can't let this happen to me again, not after Connie. I'll have to fade again, I guess." As he jammed the paper back into the book, there was a sound behind him, a hard intake of breath as though someone had stifled a sob. He jerked his head around to face Kelley who stood there holding back tears.

"Rom, you weren't, uh, weren't supposed to read—read that," Kelley managed to say. "It was for speech class. Now you'll think I'm really square with all that patriotic stuff, and I, uh, as much as called you a coward for dodging the draft. I heard you say that you won't come to see me anymore now."

Through all this, Rommey stood pursing his lips and scowling. Suddenly, he thrust the volume into Kelley's hand with an angry gesture. She fully expected him to turn and leave. Instead, he folded his arms about her. "I think that your paper is really *right on*," he said softly.

Kelley pulled back to look into his face. "You do? Why, I thought you'd be offended. You're not mad?"

Rommey's eyes danced with soft prisms. "No, I'm not mad. Uh, you're a great poet. Yeah, yeah, it's really right on."

She jostled him gently. "You're just telling me that, Rom."

"No, I really mean it. You're a poet. Man, but you make the pencil scream." He nodded his head. "It's good."

"But, I thought you were against everything, Rom, God and law and soldiers and death penalties. You make everyone think that you favor abortion and legalizing drugs and all that stuff that you dissidents—" She was suddenly embarrassed. "There I go again, hurting your feelings." She held her hand over her mouth.

However, Rommey laughed loudly. Placing his hands on her hips, he stared at her thoughtfully. "Actually—" he began and hesitated "Actually, the things I want for the human race are probably the same as what you want in the long run. We just go about it differently. Ya gotta admit that we feel the same way about things like dirty election politics and pollution. Lots of others. Right?"

Kelley shrugged her shoulders. "Yes, I understand that, but—"

"What you don't understand," Rommey interrupted, "is that I gotta do my own thing my own way and I'm hanging tough."

Kelley's face wrinkled with a frown. "You are unreal, Rommey," she said as she scrutinized his matted beard and the kind eyes hidden by the shock of curly hair. She was all the more aware of the proud stance of his stocky, muscled body. As she peered at him through narrowed eyes, he became like a statue of iron surrounded by an invisible wall. "I can't decide if you are one person," she said.

"Fade in again?" he asked as he turned his ear.

"Well, you really have me wondering. You are like—like two people put together."

"Hey! Hey! What do you mean?" He shifted his weight in his macho manner.

Kelley tilted her head to one side. "Rom, sometimes you turn me off altogether, and then you come back sweet and mysterious—and tender," she added with a smile.

Again, Rommey laughed without reserve. Then he put one arm around her and whispered, "You are a cool little cat yourself."

Suddenly, she was comfortable with him once more. The sand was soft under her feet as they ran in the surf with no thought of tomorrow. Inflated with her dreams and her own visions of life, Kelley's balloon righted itself once again, carrying her rosy gondola far above realities.

Two weeks later, Kelley was packing to leave for her job in Waikiki. She was excited and anxious to go, yet she was hesitant. "I'll miss Gregor's wedding," she kept saying. "I was hoping to be a bridesmaid."

Her mother comforted her. "I don't think it will be a big affair, just a ceremony at home with a few friends. Gregor wants it that way."

Still, Kelley pouted. "Yes, but I didn't want to miss it. Gregor said that you could bring me along to that big wedding shower that Mrs. Rentzler is giving. Nancy didn't ask me, but Gregor did."

Her mother looked up from packing one of Kelley's cases. "That was nice of Gregor. Now, don't forget to get your silk muumuu from the dry cleaner, the blue one that Pandora gave you, and remember that you wanted to get your guitar fixed and—"

On the day of Kelley's departure, her father drove her to the airport in Los Angeles since there was no local direct flight to Hawaii. On route, traffic grew heavy and Kelley became absorbed in reflection... *I can't believe that the year has gone so fast and I am really leaving... Rom and I had so much fun together and I'll miss him... and Gregor, too... after what he's been through he deserves to be happy and Nancy better make him happy... Karla will be so grown up in another year and she had better stop seeing Jose if she doesn't want to get thrown out of the house... and I'm going to miss Mom... I'm going to cry....*

Her father's voice broke her reverie. "Kelley, are you all right?"

"Oh, I guess I was feeling bad because Greg didn't say goodbye to me."

"I forgot to tell you. He's in L.A. and will be at the gate to see you off."

When it was time to board the plane, Kelley walked up the ramp with a sparkle in her eye and a bounce in her step.

XXI

"...no magic word for him..."

ancy had just returned to Gregor's place to tell him that, after much vacillation, she had chosen a simple bridal bouquet for the ceremony that was to take place soon. Humming a tune, she walked airily into the kitchen to place a flower in a vase.

Through the open doors, she could see the outline of a seated figure on the cantilevered porch. "Morghann," she called, "Come see the rose I selected to use in my bouquet. It is my favorite variety; hard to get, though." Holding the vase, she stepped toward the dining room and came face to face with Nichole. She stopped so suddenly that the flower and container slid from her hand. "Oh!" she said. "Oh!" She trembled as she retrieved the rose. Then, standing her full height, eyes blazing, she confronted Gregor's visitor.

"What can you possibly be doing here, Nichole?"

With a lofty expression of unconcern, Nichole pointed to a small package. "I brought Gig a little wedding gift."

"Well, you might have let him know that you were coming."

Nichole allowed a malicious twinkle to light her eyes. "He is usually here at this time."

Nancy appeared vexed. "How would you know that? Are you here often?"

"Whenever I need to talk to him."

"Humph! Did Morghann tell you to come over whenever you feel you need someone to talk to? That's hard to believe."

Nichole held her head high. Haughtily, she answered, "Believe whatever you like. You forget that we are good friends...of long standing. As good friends often do, we would go out of our way for each other." She made a move toward the door.

"Uh, wait, Nichole." Nancy lifted her hand as though to place it on the other's arm. "Would you go out of your way to help him now? There is something you could do for him," she said with hesitation.

"I have to be going. Lisa is waiting in the car," Nichole answered flatly.

"Then let me come right to the point. It is necessary to find any kind of evidence to prove that Pandora didn't drive her car off the road deliberately, that it was an accident. It would help if someone could remember skid marks on the road or in the weeds, as though she had tried to stop the car. Anything. You were one of the two persons who passed by there the following morning."

"Huh! What good would that do? Proving it was an accident will not bring

Pandora back."

"You are right. It won't bring Pandora back, Nichole, but it will bring Morghann back."

"I don't understand."

"Morghann has a problem because he feels responsible for Pandora's death. It would help him if someone could persuade him that the whole thing was an accident."

"And you think that I have some magic word to say so he can be happy with you?" Nichole laughed a single loud laugh.

"If you think so much of him, you would want him to be happy!"

Nichole shrugged her shoulders. "I have *no magic word for him*. I don't know what the problem is."

Nancy's face flushed. She hesitated. "Due to his guilt complex, he has a..." Another pause. "...a dread of women—of a sort," she continued. "Surely, you know about it!"

Again, Nichole's eyes flickered with mischief. "No, I don't. I guess I don't bring it out in him." With a toss of her shoulders, she turned, and giving no further thought to the tears she had brought to Nancy Starling's eyes, walked through the doorway, colliding as she did so with her sister who had been standing just outside.

Lisa was silent until Nichole stopped the car in their drive. As they walked to the door, she said hotly, "You could have told Nancy about all that gravel that the truck spilled over the street where Pandora's car went off the cliff. Remember how our car spun on it?"

"Lisa, there wasn't any gravel on the street that morning."

"Sure, because the hard downpour during the night washed it all down to Mack's house. You didn't have to hurt her feelings like you did. She has that party to go to tonight, and I can imagine how I'd feel at a party after having someone say what you did! You don't have to be so nasty."

Taking her sister by the shoulders, Nichole shook her so that her head jerked. "Lisa, I'm warning you. Don't eavesdrop on my conversations again. And if you say anything about it to anyone, I'll tell your mother about your chasing after Rex on the beach yesterday. Dad would restrict you for months if he knew. How can you be so stupid anyway? Can't you understand that you are just a toy to him? You know that he is in love with me. What possible chance do you have?"

Lisa glared at her sister before she too broke into tears and ran into the house.

159

XXII

"...communing in the fog with her ghost..."

The Rentzler home was perched on a cliff near a section of the Farms, just a short distance from Nichole's house. From the patio, the view of the ocean was magnificent. The last glint of sunlight was fading behind the rim of fog that hung out over the water. Nancy Starling's wedding shower had provided a brilliant evening for the guests who brought good wishes. Clad in a halter gown of copper-metallic cloth, Nancy appeared radiant as she and Mrs. Rentzler said goodbye to their well-wishers. Roy hovered nearby still speculating with an oceanographer on the value of further space travel.

"It has been a perfect evening for a party," the oceanographer said to Nancy as he finally approached her in the front entry. "The fog held off just long enough."

Nancy glanced anxiously at Roy. "Fog? There wasn't any ten minutes ago."

"Rolled in suddenly like it was shot out of guns in layers," Roy said. "Spooky. Really weird."

"Excuse me," Nancy said to her hostess. "I think I'll go find Morghann. He hasn't come back with my coffee."

A quick search through the house left Nancy worried. She drew Roy aside. "Roy, I can't find Morghann anywhere. He went to get me more coffee."

"His car is here," Roy said. "You don't suppose he'd get tired enough to fall asleep somewhere?"

"He wouldn't dare! On an evening like this? I'd never forgive him and he knows it." Suddenly her face blanched. She grabbed Roy's arm. "Roy, you don't suppose—"

"What?"

Nancy shuddered. "You don't suppose—oh, he wouldn't!"

"You are white as a ghost, my dear. What is it he might have done?"

"The cliff! The cliff! It is so close by." Her voice was almost a hoarse whisper. "I know he goes there sometimes. You don't suppose—"

"Oh, that stupid asshole!" Roy blurted out. "I thought he was all over that shi...nonsense."

"Good Lord! Look, Roy, I'll stay here. If he is there, just bring him back as fast as you can."

Roy looked about. "There are still enough people here. Nobody will miss him for another ten minutes. Don't let on." He patted her on the shoulder and left.

Ten minutes later, Roy walked in with Gregor pretending that they had made the rounds of the orchid gardens in the lath house. When Gregor and Nancy left

160

the Rentzler home shortly thereafter, the tears in Nancy's eyes appeared to be out of appreciation for the lovely evening.

The few moments it took to get to Gregor's driveway were filled with tense silence. Nancy got out of the car hurriedly, stepped over to her own car which was left parked there, and started the motor intending to leave him without a word.

"For God's sake, Nancy," Greogor's voice boomed through the fog. "I'm sorry. If you're mad at me, at least talk to me and say so. I'm really sorry." He reached into her car and withdrew the keys. Nancy elbowed past him and began to walk to the street, but the fog was so thick that she could hardly find the curb. She stumbled and fell to her knees. Strong arms scooped her up despite her struggling and kicking. She was deposited on the sofa, wild and sputtering while he kept saying, "You are going to talk to me whether you want to or not, damn it!"

Still kicking, trying to tear herself out of his strong grip, she said over and over again, "What kind of a man are you? Our wedding is a few days off and you are out there still nursing your memories of her! How do you suppose that makes me feel? Can't you understand that there isn't a chance for us until you forget Pandora? You are such a fool! Can't you understand? And I thought you loved me!" She broke into hysterical tears.

He attempted to put his arm about her, but she fought him off and slapped her hands over her ears when he repeated, "I do love you, Nancy. I do, I do!"

"The hell you do, Gregor Morghann! If you love me so much, what are you doing out there *communing in the fog with her ghost* during our wedding shower? How stupid can I be, to think that we could make a go of it together?"

"Look, maybe I couldn't stand all those women fawning over me. They made me feel as though I was an exhibit. You knew that I didn't want a lot of people making a fuss."

"That's a lie, Morghann! Your rapport with ladies is excellent. You just can't hide the truth that easily. You actually think that she is still out there trying to talk to you. Admit it! But you know that she is dead. Dead, Morghann! And gone! And you will never forget her. Why can't you face it? You are letting her destroy you. Can't you see?"

She watched him as he closed his eyes. His teeth were clenched. His lips barely moved. "How can you do this to me? I just needed a little more time."

While he mumbled this over and over, Nancy thought how could I be so blind...what hold did he have on me...why did I hang on....

"Time!" she mocked. The green eyes flashed. "Time to look in every shadow for Pandora's ghost? You are not in love with me, Morghann, or with any woman. You will always be in love with the memory of her. Other people suffer losses and they survive. They manage to forget in time. But you! You are letting it destroy you so that you are hardly a man any more!"

She saw his face grow white. "Please, Nancy, don't—"

She showed no mercy. "I need a *man* to love me!" she screamed, and when he tried to touch her again, she slapped his cheek with all her might, turned and left the room.

Forecast III

Rain fell silently on the pine trees. The two Indian ghosts sat on a stout limb watching strong gusts of wind whip the raindrops against a concrete wall.

The girl laughed softly. "Look, Jaoko. See how oddly these strangers live. They make webs like spiders on the land. Like bees on a comb, they dwell in their cells. When we were here, the land belonged to everyone, open to roam and to cherish, shared with the fox and coyote, and the quail and pelican."

"Hush," her companion answered. "They will be here until their undoing. Then they will pass as others have done. Maya, too, once flourished and is no more. Hush and watch the raindrops caress the earth."

XXIII

"...Vanessa's crying didn't come to him..."

Christopher Holliss entered his hallway, still concentrating on the broadcast he had just heard on his car radio. Volume on the big board was fifteen million shares, 800 stocks up and 176 declined, market was up 3½ points on the Dow averages.

The sound of Vanessa's *crying didn't come to him* immediately. When it did, he followed the sobs to the kitchen where Vanessa stood with a letter in her hand. He wiped her eyes and took her in his arms.

"A letter from Kelley?" he asked. When she nodded, he led her to the sofa, seated himself beside her and began to read the letter aloud.

"These people here are so natural and sincere," the letter read. "It is hard to put it into words, and it is so different from home. My classes are great. You'd be surprised at the number of things that there are to do here. Kimo is so nice to me. He has already shown me the whole island, and he wants me to visit his family's main home on the Big Island soon."

Christopher lowered the letter. "Van, who the devil is Kimo?"

"Kimo is the...the—" She wiped her cheeks. "Kimo is the student in her drama class who showed her around Honolulu the first week. The one whose family owns the plantation."

"Oh! Well, I guess she has to make friends," Christopher added quickly.

"Yes, but it's all she writes about, hardly anything about her classes, everything about Kimo, nothing about the other boys she met who were from Los Angeles. Kimo takes her out in his catamaran, on overnight jaunts around the island, and...goodness knows what else."

"Is that what is upsetting you? Great guns, at least she has forgotten Rommey, hasn't she?" He was surprised when the question brought fresh tears to his wife's eyes.

"That is just it! As though that hippie wasn't bad enough...now...now... she...oh, Chris! Now it's a step worse. Now it's...it's...not even a boy with her own background!"

Christopher patted his wife's arm. "Vanessa, it's not like you to be upset so quickly over these things. Just because he is befriending her doesn't mean that she is falling in love. You shouldn't let it worry you."

"But I do. I do. Chris, do you think we would have allowed Kelley to go so far from home if we hadn't been so anxious to separate her from Rommey?"

"Oh, I can't say, really. Maybe, but maybe not. It doesn't help to think about it. Now, why don't you stop worrying? Let's think about us for a bit. Look, I found a nursery that carries forget-me-nots and asters and pink larkspur. I promised to plant that window box by the kitchen. We'll do it tomorrow. You keep saying how you remember your grandmother's flowers. Did I ever tell you what I remember most in my grandmother's garden when I was small? The peonies. Clumps after clumps of waxy, lush blossoms, pink and profuse, or snow white. And I remember the dogwood in the Spring, and tulips and forsythia."

Christopher could feel his wife surveying him curiously. "Why, Chris, you've never talked a lot about flowers. All these years you've had me thinking you didn't know a rose from a geranium." She leaned forward as though to rise, but he pulled her back, kissed her cheek lightly and asked if she felt better. "Yes," she answered. "Tomorrow, I'll write Kelley and try to straighten her out."

Vanessa wrote letter after letter to her daughter. However, in response to the admonitions in her mother's notes, Kelley continued to pen airy volumes about the charm of the island people, her intrigue with the land itself and its customs, climate and color. It might have been simply that she was in love with the island and in conveying this, she included pages about Kimo.

"Kimo is the Hawaiian name for James," she wrote to her parents. "I know Mom has always liked that name. You have never met anyone like him. He is something else! He treats me as though I were a princess. The fellows back home just don't stack up once you've known someone like Kimo. And, Mom, his family is just as nice. Dad, you should see their home. Did I say home? It is more like three homes in one. The main building is on a hill overlooking pineapple groves. The servants have a separate house, and there is a bunch of little guest houses. Everything is around a huge central patio. They gave me one of the guest houses. A maid turned down my bedcovers every evening and brought me a whole pineapple every morning, with the centers cut out and skewered. The sweetest pineapple I've ever tasted! Then, breakfast on the patio before Kimo took me to surf."

The epistles followed, one after another, until she wrote in one of them, "I wouldn't mind living permanently in Hawaii."

"Good grief!" Christopher complained. "It seems that we are putting forth a goodly sum so that she can improve her surfing, watch volcanoes and tour the islands." No sooner had he spoken, however, than he regretted his remark, because Vanessa began to cry again.

"Chris, I—want—want Kelly to—come home. Now. Right away."

Christopher was silent. She gets upset so easily, he thought. She hasn't been herself...she used to take everything so calmly...it would be a pity to interrupt Kelley's studies.... "Van, I didn't mean to put it just that way. I'm sure Kelley is studying hard, too. Things are going along all right. It's probably that nothing looks good to you when you are not feeling well."

At this, Vanessa grew quite agitated. "I'm *not* feeling well, and things are *not* going right. How can you say anything is going right? I have tried to rear my children with proper ideals, and what is happening? My only son runs around with a married woman!"

"David is running around with a woman who is married?" Christopher's voice tensed.

"I told you that Kimberly was married," Vanessa replied reproachfully.

"Well, I didn't realize he was involved with—"

"Chris, you've got to give our children stronger guidelines. And Karla, encouraging the gardener's son! How can you let her do it?"

"I thought we put a stop to—"

"And now, now, Kelley and a Polynesian boy! Chris, it's too much!" Vanessa began sobbing. Christopher attempted to comfort her, but she continued to cry. "You must—must—promise me, Chris, that—you'll straighten them out—if anything...." There was a pause. "...if anything happens to me," she finished abruptly.

Christopher felt his body jump. He was startled. It was the first admission on her part that her health might be in jeopardy despite the reassurances of her doctors. "I'll straighten them out! Vanessa, nothing is going to happen to you!" He found that he was almost shouting, his composure shaken, his mind in turmoil. His wife's premonitions frightened him. The doctor's assurances had suddenly become weightless. He struggled to gain control of himself. "It's this thing with Kelley that bothers you most, isn't it?" He drew a deep breath. Then, he patted her hand and said softly, "Maybe I can call her tomorrow."

She tore herself away. "I don't want to talk about it any more," she said.

Christopher took her gently about the waist. "Look, darling, we'll walk on the beach for a bit. That always relaxes us. We'll talk about something else. Get a sweater. It might be cool."

Without another word, Vanessa disappeared into the hallway. Christopher took up the paper, sat in his chair and tried to sweep his mind clean of problems. Suddenly he looked up, realizing that half an hour had passed. He hurried to the bedroom to find Vanessa fast asleep. A quick flurry of hot tears came to his eyes as he covered her shoulders. Then he made his way alone to the flat rock below his home, thinking all the while... *it's just not like Vanessa...just not like her...something is wrong...maybe we'll get that scan done...not wait...if anything happened to Vanessa...Mother of God...don't let me say that...or even think that...I'd simply go to pieces without her...call the doctor tomorrow again...if only she wouldn't worry so much...little things bother her...she used to take everything so calmly...not that these problems with the kids are little...David could have any girl he wanted...what is he using for brains...Karla...dammit...I'll beat that girl's backside if I have to...but Vanessa worries most about Kelley...shall I call her home...I'd never forgive her if Vanessa's health suffered on her account...damn...no matter how much you try to do the right things for your kids...they bring you nothing but heartbreak...heartbreak....*

When he returned to the house, he reached for a cigarette but his hand shook so much that he put it down.

166

XXIV

"...Riptide! Riptide!..."

As soon as Nichole heard of Nancy's leaving, she began to visit Gregor on pretense of borrowing his reference books, or his diving gear, or to body surf with him in the early morning. Gregor tolerated her company, which served to fill an interim, for he had again become somewhat of a recluse, declining to pursue his usual gregarious activities. Perhaps he was even content to have someone familiar with him. However, Nancy Starling's name was never mentioned.

Nichole armed herself with explanations for Rex in case he should register objections to her meetings with Gregor. For the time being, he appeared unaware of them. Then, one Sunday morning at the Vincett home as she and Rex were getting her diving gear to go skin-diving, Nichole heard her father say, "Isn't this a picture of the girl that Gregor was supposed to marry?" He held up the Los Angeles Times.

"Where?" Nichole looked at the photograph of a bride. "*Prominent Los Angeles Physician Marries*." The words left her heart beating wildly. The picture was that of Nancy Starling.

Aware of Rex staring at her, Nichole feigned composure. "Well, it's a nice picture," she said nonchalantly. "Come on, Rex, or we'll miss the tide."

It was evening of the same day when she was finally alone. She tore the photograph from the page, stuffed it into her beach bag and headed for Gregor's place. When she arrived, she didn't blurt out the news. Instead, she brewed coffee for him as they talked.

"You make good coffee, Nicki," he said when she served it.

Nichole smiled. "I'd like to make it for you everyday."

"Sure, Nicki. Anytime."

"That's not what I mean." She toyed with her own cup. "I mean...well...Gig, would I have a chance with you if Nancy didn't come back?" It piqued her when Gregor laughed and chucked her under the chin.

"What about Rex? What would you do with the two of us? Rex will never let you go. He would shoot himself...or me." He laughed again.

She felt her eyes flare. "Gig," she began, stamping one foot. "Be serious for a minute. I've got to know."

"I would like to think that Nancy will get over whatever is bothering her and that we will go on with our plans."

"Well, face it and suppose she doesn't come." Suddenly, she felt like an animal stalking him, and her blood raced with excitement at the thought of the possible outcome. Unconsciously, she touched her beach bag.

"Nicki, I suspect—okay—out with it. You forget how well I can read your mind. You have heard something about Nancy. Out with it." He reached into the beach bag, drew out the page of newspaper, read it, and swore softly. He crumpled the paper, threw it violently across the room, groaned loudly and deposited himself on his back on the sofa. Nichole stood thoroughly frightened for a moment as she watched him. His face was drained of color; his breathing was so shallow that she looked for the movement of his chest. Still trembling, she went to the kitchen to get more coffee.

"Here, Gig, drink this," she urged when she returned. "It's hot. It will help." She placed her hand gently on his to rouse him.

"Huh? What's that?" he mumbled as he swung himself to a sitting position, absently rubbing his face very much like a man only half aware of where he is.

"More coffee, Gig."

"Oh, yes—yes." His eyes met hers. "That's nice of you, Nicki," he said absently as he took the coffee cup. His shoulders sagged and the stance of the lion king was suddenly gone.

Nichole felt pangs of compassion welling inside her. "I didn't know you would take it so hard, Gig. Honestly, I didn't think you were really in love. You haven't even mentioned her name, have you? Nobody has! As for my telling you about it, you would have found out somehow sooner or later."

He patted her hand. "Yeah. It's okay. You're a good friend, Nicki."

She could feel the frown that stole over her face. "That is just the trouble. I'm always a good *friend*. Maybe it hurts being only a friend. Maybe I love you, Gig!"

Gregor stood, paced a few steps, then turned to Nichole. "I guess love isn't for me. It never works out."

Now is your chance, something inside was telling Nichole. *You may never have as good a time to show him.* "Gig, can't it work out for us? What is it that I don't have? Why can't I make it with you?"

He shook his head. "It wouldn't be good for either of us, Nicki. You need a different kind of man, one who worships the ground you walk on and can give you all the loving you need."

She stamped her foot hard as her temper flared. "Damn! Damn! Don't keep telling me that Rex is right for me! You know the kind of trouble he is getting into? He isn't right for me! I don't want to hear it!" She put her hands over her ears.

Gregor took her wrists in his own hands, forcing her to listen. "But he is. You'll straighten him out if you marry him. He can keep you sexually satisfied, and you need that, and besides—"

The suggestion brought burning tears to Nichole's eyes. The man she loved was telling her to go to someone else! It was more than her pride could bear. Suddenly, she beat his chest with clenched fists. "I don't want to hear it! Don't tell me that!" The more that Gregor warded her off, the harder she cried and kicked at his ankles.

"Stop it, Nicki," he begged. "Please stop crying. Stop it, now!" Finally, he took her by the shoulders and shook her. "Dammit, I can stand crying from any woman but you!" Then he put his arms around her and stroked her hair until she was quiet. In the meantime, he continued in a reflective manner, "Dammit, Nicki, I don't want to hurt you, but you've got to believe me. I'd never be good for you. Someone like Rex could give you all the things you should have. His mother has a castle in Europe. He is the only heir."

He paused, almost expecting another outburst, but none came. "A girl like you, Nicki, could have anyone," he continued. "If not Rex, you'll find someone, but it won't work—you and me. Maybe we're too much alike. Are you listening?" No answer came. "Roy has been bugging me to do more work on the Hawaii film. He asked me to consider coming up Tuesday. I've decided to go. Are you listening?" He could feel the nod of her head against his chest. Gently, Gregor added, "I'll have to get my gear together. Tomorrow's my last day here. Want to swim with me in the morning?" He lifted her chin and peered into her eyes.

"I have to take Mom, Dad, and Lisa to the airport about five to catch an early flight." Nichole brushed her wet cheek daintily on Gregor's sweater.

"Well, then. Come here directly from the airport." He looked at his watch. "It's already almost twelve. I have to catch a few hours of sleep, and you'd better do the same, hadn't you?" He kissed her forehead, and took her to her car.

At midnight, he tried to sleep, but disturbing memories blurred his weary mind. Finally, he decided to walk until he was tired.

He headed toward the Beach Club, past the old duck pond that was once to have been a yacht basin, through the circular drive and up to the intersection of Torrey Pines. He went north to the Del Charro Hotel where he stood remembering hours with good friends. The good things...he thought...I'll think of the good times...the happy hours...the abalone diving...my lobster traps in front of Doyle's place...how we cooked some shorts one time right there on the beach and the game warden caught us...I was only fourteen...like the boy in the fountain...the dolphins are still there...I can smell Grandfather's herbs if I try...heliotrope and bay...the palomino that we bought from the stable right over there in that field....

Gregor crossed the road and found the dirt path that led to a small stable and a corral. Horses whinnied softly on hearing someone pass in the night. He turned sharply and started home, allowing more memories to drift in...*how much more life meant to me after she came...how can I go on without her...what will I do...fires of hell...what will I do...I've got to find...something...something...don't let her ruin your life...where's your guts....*

"Hell, Gregor, where's your metal? Get mad!" he told himself aloud. "Don't let her beat you down. It's only a game to be won. Win it, damn it!"

At home, he dozed fitfully. Finally, he flung the covers back and stepped into his swim suit. "I'll swim first," he told himself. "Then I'll be tired enough to sleep for a few hours."

Thickening clouds were scurrying overhead as Gregor felt his way down the dark stairway to the beach. Near the bottom, he gripped the rail, not certain of what he saw. A wave of nausea rose from his insides. He clutched his stomach and looked again with blurred vision. As he leaned closer, the identity of a sweater-clad figure before him became clear.

"Oh, my God!" he moaned. "I can't be dreaming. I'm sure I'm wide awake! This can't happen again. Not tonight!"

"*Alors!* That's not a nice way to greet me," came a small voice with a soft French accent, "when I have taken all this trouble to come to see you! Don't just stand there gaping at me, Gregor Morghann. Say that you are glad to see me."

"Glad to see you?" Gregor laughed aloud. "After all the tricks you've played on me with your stupid Xionflight? What are you trying to do to me? My friends are beginning to think I've lost my mind. Don't torture me if this is just another of your experiments, if you aren't really here."

"But, *mon amour*, I am really here! Why are you angry with me?"

"Because Dr. Ornski says that I am just an accessory to your experiment."

She stamped her foot angrily. "Does it mean nothing that I am here? *Je t'en prie?* I couldn't stay away any longer. Now, put your arms around me. It is cold just standing here." Her hand stole into his.

Suspiciously at first, Gregor touched her hair, then her shoulder and her cheek. Suddenly, he drew her into his arms and held her tightly. "God in heaven, this time it really is you, Pandora! Finally, no dream! No imagining, no tricks. You're in my arms again! Nothing else should really matter, but why did you stage everything? Why didn't you answer me when I saw you on the escalator? And in front of the cathedral? How did you get off my cruiser? Why did you run my car over the cliff?"

"Shh." Pandora's hand stole over his lips. "You have a right to be angry, but I can explain everything in due time. My twin sister arrived on the night of the hurricane. I let her take your car. It was she who pushed the car over the cliff."

"But the locket! They found the gold locket I gave you."

"Well, uh, I had one made just like it for my sister because she was so crazy about it. Don't be so angry. I'm sorry."

"Sorry! Good God!" Gregor gasped. "Okay, okay, come on upstairs. Nothing should really matter except that you are here and all right."

However, Pandora detained him. "Wait, wait. You were just going out for your swim. Come, I will go with you." She pointed to his swim suit. "Now, see that light out there? That is from my friend's yacht. Come on, swim back out there with me."

"You swam in all the way from a yacht!" Gregor exclaimed loudly. "You must be joking."

"No, no, Gig. They brought me almost all the way in their dory. It is anchored out there just beyond the breakers. They are waiting for me. It isn't far. I made it in without any trouble. Come on." She tugged his arm. *"Viens, viens!"*

"But, how did you come in from a boat? You are dressed."

"Oh, see, I have my damp swim suit underneath." She held up a waterproof bag. "See, I used this to keep my things dry."

"Well, leave your things *here*, because you are coming back with me." He snatched the yellow sweater and placed it in a protected spot in the wall. When he looked up, Pandora was already running to the water's edge, calling back to him. He started after her.

"Wait! Pandora! Wait for me. What's your rush? Wait for me!" He splashed through the surf and plunged into the water. In a few minutes he was directly behind where Pandora's even stroke was breaking the surface. For some time, they swam in the direction of a light bobbing on the surface of the water some distance away. It appeared to come from a small craft anchored there.

Suddenly there was a flash of lightning. Cold raindrops came pelting down.

The waves grew rough. Pandora seemed to have difficulty as the waves tossed her about. Gregor looked for the boat. It should be right here, he thought. We have been swimming long enough to be half way to the Cove...we aren't one bit closer...damn it...we are caught in it...she's getting tired...it's a good thing it's getting light enough to see....

He managed to get Pandora's attention. "Riptide! Riptide!" he shouted. "We have to take a course parallel to shore. Follow me. Can you do it?"

She waved him on. "Are you sure?" he called once more. She waved him on again and changed her direction to follow him.

For another minute they swam side by side fighting the current. Then, suddenly, she was not there when he lifted his head to look for her. He dove immediately in the spot where she had been. Again and again he went under to search, screaming her name when he surfaced, succumbing to panic. Pandora had vanished completely, but still he searched until he was exhausted by the struggle against the undertow. A thought entered his mind. The boat! The dory must have picked her up...she must have spotted it...there has got to be a boat...but where is it...fires of hell...it isn't there...it's gone...she's gone...oh no...no...I can't live through this again....

A terrible cry sprung from his lungs, like a howl from a mortally wounded beast. It rang over the surface of the water as a precursor of Gregor's lessening will. He cried out again, "Oh, God! Don't do this to me, Pandora! This can't happen! Not again! I'd rather die than to face it! I don't want to live any more. Let me die! Pandora! Pan-dor-a!"

His efforts grew feeble and he sank below the surface, but by now, he had left the rip current behind. A vigorous wave seized his body and tossed it along on its crest toward the shore.

By this time, Nichole had arrived and was watching him anxiously from his porch. In a few moments she was shoulder-deep in the water at Gregor's side. A lifeguard reporting early, helped to drag his body out of the waves and worked swiftly to assure Gregor's breathing. Gregor uttered a cry, blinked and propped himself weakly on one elbow to scan the surface of the water.

The guard sat back on his heels. "You are doing fine, Gig," he said.

However, Gregor moaned, fell to the sand again and said nothing. Nichole checked his pulse.

"Should I send for an ambulance?" she asked.

"No!" Gregor said.

The guard's voice came reassuringly. "He'll be all right."

"I think I'll call Mr. Holliss, anyway," Nichole insisted.

When she was gone, Gregor opened his eyes again. "I was doing fine until it started to rain," he mumbled.

The guard looked puzzled. "There wasn't any rain, Gig."

Gregor sprang to his feet. "Was there lightning?"

"No. No lightning. Not a drop of rain. There was a rip current though. Not a really bad one. I'm glad I was here early."

"Was there anyone swimming with me?"

"I didn't see anyone." The guard eyed him curiously.

Gregor winced. "Think carefully. Was there a boat out there?" He withstood the younger man's scrutiny and pointed to the horizon.

"There wasn't any boat. I'm sure." There was a pause. "You look pale Gig. Better sit down. Try putting your head between your knees. Do you hurt anywhere?"

"No. No. I just wish you had let me die," Gregor moaned.

"What's that?" the guard questioned sharply.

"Nothing." Gregor brushed his wet hair from his forehead. "I said I want to get dry. It's chilly this morning."

"Are you all right? Can I take you somewhere?" A worried look crossed the lifeguard's face.

"No, thanks. Here comes Nichole. I'm fine now." Gregor stretched his arms over his head. Giving the lifeguard a gentle pat on the shoulder, he added, "Watch that rip today," and sauntered away. As he passed the wall below his place, he searched quickly for some sign of Pandora's yellow sweater.

Christopher Holliss arrived shortly afterward. Nichole decided to go to the market to get ingredients for breakfast. While she was gone, Gregor talked about his plans to return to Hawaii with Roy.

Pursing his lips, Christopher surveyed Gregor for a while. "Rather sudden decision, isn't it?" he asked.

"No, not really. There is nothing to do here right now, and I can keep busy in the islands. I get a lot done over there." Gregor sighed, walked to the window and stared at the beach below. A note of detachment clouded his voice. "I'm working with a pharmaceutical company doing research on natural drugs. They depend on me to find sea plants. I get a lot of them from around Maui. Anyway, I need a change again."

With a heavy frown, Christopher studied the figure by the window. "I get the feeling that something unusual happened last night." He eased his big frame onto his favorite stool at the bar.

"Humph." Gregor laughed sourly and faced his friend. "Yeah, yeah. Something unusual," he admitted.

"I thought so!" Christopher began. "I believe, uh—"

"Would you believe that I ran into *Pandora* at the bottom of the steps last night?" Gregor interrupted. He sat on the stool facing Christopher whose mouth hung open in surprise. "She said she swam in from the dory of her friend's yacht that was anchored further out in the bay."

"She did—did what?" Christopher stammered.

"She said it was her twin sister who drove my car into the ocean," Gregor continued as Christopher stroked his square chin, dumbfounded. "She was in my arms, Chris! I held her this time!" He banged his fist on the bar. "I touched her! She talked to me! She was real!"

Christopher's eyes blinked and bulged. "Where is she? Well, where did she go, then?"

"She said—" Gregor hesitated and passed his hand over his forehead. "She said she had to swim back out to tell them that she found me."

"Didn't you stop her?"

Gregor grimaced and shook his head. "She ran back into the surf while I had my back turned for a second to put her sweater by the wall. I followed her out until the rip current got us. She disappeared and I dived for her until I blacked out."

"Unbelievable!" Christopher's palm came down on the bar with a thump.

"Absolutely unbelievable!"

"You'd better believe, Chris! Come, I'll show you exactly where she stood." Gregor led the way down the steps to the sandy enclosure below. "Here! She stood right here."

"Do you have any proof? Footmarks? Anything?" Christopher began to examine the enclosure.

"She left the sweater, a yellow turtleneck. I threw it over here. She took some other things with her in a plastic bag." He started to probe the sand just as Nichole's footsteps sounded above.

"We'll keep this to ourselves," Christopher whispered.

Gregor nodded. "Except for Dr. Ornski," Gregor said. "I'm going to see him tomorrow." He turned to answer Nichole's call.

Waving him on, Christopher said, "Go on up and pack. I want to stay here a minute to think." When he was alone, he walked about the wall and continued to probe in the sand as Gregor had done.

The fast receding tide left a wide berth down which Christopher went for a short distance. The swells were spaced and gentle except for an occasional big surge. The backwash rippled noisily as it was sucked back into the sea, its force strengthened by the ebbing water. A few yards from Christopher, a bundle of something yellow rolled in the backwash. He ran to the spot where it had disappeared into the surf. His heart beat wildly as the next surge brought it into view again. Without regard for his safety, he stumbled through the surf after the yellow thing, finally falling on his knees to clutch at it. The big surge that followed submerged him totally, spun him like a wheel and began to pull him under. He surfaced, gasped for air and lost his footing again. The next time his head cleared the water, both Gregor and Nichole had him by his arms.

Standing on the sand exhausted and quite shaken, he searched the backwash on pretext of catching his breath. The sweater was gone. As he composed himself, he kept repeating, "As well as I know those waves, I let one catch me. Those swells are tricky." He rested on the patio for a few minutes, then prepared to leave. "Got a full day at the office. Commodities are suddenly selling like hot cakes. And tomorrow—" He stroked his chin thoughtfully. "Look, lad, I have a stop to make in L.A. early tomorrow morning. Suppose we drive up together tonight. There is something I want to talk to you about. Suppose I come for you at nine. We'll have a chance to chat about your natural drug research. I understand there's a lot of emphasis on finding nature's medicines. Any chance of my selling stock in your company? While we're driving tonight, we'll have a good opportunity to talk about things. Also, Van gave me a dozen instructions for you to give Kelley when you get there." He fumbled for his car key. "Gregor," he began, and hesitated.

"Yes?"

"Keep looking for that yellow sweater. *I think I might have seen it.*"

When Christopher was gone and breakfast was over, Gregor turned to Nichole. "I have packing to finish, Nicki. Thanks for all your help."

"I'm a great packer. Best there is! I'll help," she said, firmly.

"You've been up most of the night. G'wan. Go home like a good kid," he ordered, teasing her with a tug of her still-damp, black hair.

Nichole's eyes widened. Wrath gathered on her aristocratic features. "I won't!"

"Now, Nicki! Don't be stubborn."

"I'm staying!" she retorted, hotly.

Gregor laughed and put his hands on his hips. "Nicki, don't be so damned difficult," he argued. "Why don't you bug out? I appreciate all you've done, but there is something important that I have to do."

She shook her head with a gesture that flung her black hair over her shoulders. Her chin lifted defiantly. "You can't make me go! Chris said he doesn't want you to be alone!"

"Chris said what?" He breathed in deeply, then exhaled impatiently. "Okay. Out with it. Why doesn't Chris want you to leave me alone?"

She faced him squarely, her arms akimbo to mimic him. "Why is it that I can never keep anything from you?" She stamped her foot. "We're wasting time. Now, what is it that you must do that is so important?"

Gregor's face clouded. "I have to go out there and dive around for a sweater. We'll work together."

After an hour of fruitless searching, they returned to Gregor's kitchen, tired and cold. An onshore breeze brought with it a light fog. Nichole complained about the sudden chill in the air.

"I have nothing warm with me. I didn't know I'd be staying," she said. "Could I borrow something of yours?"

"Borrow anything you'd like that isn't packed. Here, try the big chest, third drawer down," he directed.

He watched her curiously as she searched through his wardrobe until she found some knitted items that satisfied her, after which they spent the rest of the day packing.

"Nicki," Gregor said, when they finished a late dinner, "you are a hell of a good cook. That was some Reuben sandwich."

Her eyes flickered like those of an artful coquette. "I have been trying to tell you, if you'd just listen to me!"

However, Gregor yawned unceremoniously and stretched his arms. "I'm bushed," he said as he threw a soft pillow onto the floor. "Take my spare key, Nicki, and tidy the kitchen in the morning." He sprawled on the floor, arms flung wide at his sides. "I think I've been walking around sound asleep for the last ten minutes. You've been a big help, Nicki."

From the kitchen, Nichole replied, "Well, you finally admit it! As a matter of fact, you'd be working till dawn if I hadn't helped. I'm tired, too. Neither of us had much sleep last night. Gig, can I ask you something?"

Receiving no response, she peered in at Gregor only to find him asleep. She sighed and seated herself on the sofa from where she watched for awhile and fantasized a life with him. In her mind's eye, she swam with him, snorkled and dived, lay arm in arm with him on the sunsoaked sands, but in her rigid Victorian way (the imprint of her rearing in a convent), she could not indulge herself to fancy the two of them in his bed, delightfully naked. As hard as she tried, the bedroom always faded away and she was left with a man sleeping on the carpet, his handsome face turned slightly to one side, his lips barely parted, and his eyelids twitching because of the dreams and visions that lay underneath. His long body intrigued her, nevertheless, and she sat staring at him for a long time before she, too, dozed off on the sofa.

Noises woke her with a start. The room was in deep shadow except for the light of one lamp. Gregor was stirring and muttering in his sleep. Nichole leaned forward and listened attentively.

"...rr! Look ou-ou-out! My-my-myah! Help me, help me! It's burn-burning! Look ou-out!"

Bewildered, Nichole leaned over as he clasped his arms about himself and twisted from side to side as though his body hurt. "Gregor?" she whispered, touching him gently on the arm. "Are you okay, Gig?"

A sudden flailing of his arms drove her backward out of his reach as his muttering continued "...rr—it's pulling me back! The star! The emerald! Help me! Help me!" His voice rose and trailed off, and his head tossed from side to side in his attempt to evade his nightmare assailant.

Alarmed now, Nichole took his arm and shook him. "Gig! Wake up! Wake up! You're dreaming! Wake up!"

Gregor's eyes fluttered. "Pandora, don't go!" he shouted. "Come back!" His arms shot out to pull Nichole to him and they rolled over and over again on the floor until the bulk of a big chair stopped them. "Don't leave me again!" he murmured as his eyes opened. He raised himself on one elbow. "Where am I?" Then he sat upright. "What the deuce! What happened?" he demanded as he peered into Nichole's startled face.

"You had a—a nightmare, Gig," she answered, still frightened and on the verge of tears. Shaken and breathless, she struggled to arise to the sofa.

Seating himself beside her, Gregor repeated, "A nightmare? Yeah, a nightmare. What did I say this time?"

"You were afraid of something. You rolled back and forth and cried out."

"Oh?" He rubbed the sleep from his eyes. "I did?"

Nichole stared at him curiously and nodded. "You called out a name. Something like My-yah. Does it mean anything?"

"I'm not sure," Gregor replied, uncertainly. Then he added, "Maybe it was an inscription on a chain of beads that I played with when I was small. My grandfather used it to teach me to print."

The black eyes flickered with curiosity. "What were you dreaming?"

Gregor rubbed his cheek again. "Uh—that someone was pulling me backwards— uh—through time or something, can't put it into words. I was going through a fire. It was burning me alive. I can't describe it."

Nichole sat smoothing her black hair. "You also called out for Pandora," she added.

He yawned and stretched, seemingly unimpressed. "Yeah, I probably did. I probably did."

A loud tap on the door startled them. It was Christopher Holliss, punctual as usual and eager to start their drive.

"Come on, lad," Christopher urged. "Fog might get thicker. Starting now will help us beat most of it."

They left Nichole standing in Gregor's drive preparing to drive home in her own car. Her thoughts crowded out one another as she started the motor. He has been in rips before and he has never had any trouble...he knows how to swim out better than anyone...why didn't he...was he upset because of Nancy...I'm

175

so glad she is gone...she never really loved him...not the way that I do...why is it that he won't fall in love with me...I won't push him...I'll get him yet...give me time....

The lights from the car behind her blinded her. She slowed her car and signaled for it to pass, but it did not. She proceeded with her trend of thought. Gregor isn't ready...when he is...I'll be there...maybe I'll visit him in Hawaii...what will I tell Rex...poor Rex...would it matter if I lost him...actually he is nice to have around just in case...if he weren't so...so...so animal...if I could just believe that he wants more than just my body...no, I just won't give in to him...especially while there is a chance with Gig...if it is to be Gig...there must be no one else before him...he has to be the first for me....

She turned away the rear view mirror to prevent being blinded by the headlights of the car tailgating her. Without the mirror in place, she didn't know until she stepped from her car that the other car had pulled into her driveway. Nichole prepared to run, realizing suddenly that her family was gone and that even the maid was out. Fumbling for her key, she made a dash for the front door. A familiar voice rang out behind her. She spun around.

"Rex!" she exclaimed. "Why—you told me that you would be in Santa Barbara this week!"

"Didn't stay." He blinked his eyes and squinted, strangely.

"You had me scared to death, following me up here like that in Mr. Millord's car. I didn't recognize it in the dark." She searched frantically for her key, praying all the while that Rex had not followed her from Gregor's house. When Rex placed his hand on the knob and flung the door open, she looked puzzled. "But, I'm sure I left that door locked. Well, the maid must have come back early." She felt a bit relieved. Rex had a temper when he was angry.

"No, no. Rex climbs the trellis to the balcony. Finds a window open." His speech was clipped and faltering.

He had stepped into the entryway behind her. She turned to face him, her eyes flaring, her face flushed. "Rex! You're high again! You promised you wouldn't. *You promised!* You have no right to break into the house like that. I'm going to tell my father."

"Not home," Rex said. He reached to finger Gregor's shirt which she still wore.

"Well, he will be," she lied. "And you don't want him to see you spaced out like that. You go on home. Call me tomorrow." She pushed him outside and locked the door.

Deaf to his knocking, she added, "Please go home, Rex. I'll call Mr. Millord if you don't. I don't feel like talking." She heard him grumble, then footsteps echoed down the walk. Breathing a sigh of relief, she went to her room, locked the door behind her and stepped into the shower. In a few minutes, she leaned past the curtains to get a towel. Rex was standing in the doorway of the bathroom.

Blood drained from Nichole's face. White with rage, she screamed at him, "You get out of here. I'll call someone!" She snatched the towel to wrap around her.

Rex remained at the doorway, a stupid, gloating expression on his face. "No one home. I know." He stooped to pick up Gregor's clothing. "Want to talk to you, Nicki. Very seriously. Ver-ry seriously. You are supposed to—to belong to *me*."

"I *don't* belong to you," she snapped. "Now, get out of here. You fool, get out."

He recoiled as though she had struck him. An ugly expression crossed his lips. "I said, you belong to me. You are going to marry me. But—" He pointed a wavering finger at her. "But, you have on his clothes, and you are sleeping with Gregor. Now, I don't like that." His lip curled into a mocking smile.

"You were watching! Spying! What a rotten thing to do, Rex. I wasn't sleeping with Gig! Look, Rex, I am not going to marry you. Ever! Get out of here. I never want to see you again!" She took the ring off her finger and threw it at him. It struck him in the face. For a moment, Rex appeared stunned. Then he reeled toward her, seething with indignation.

"Uh—uh," he grunted. "You don't get away with it this time. Giving me all that crap about your virginity! And all this time—" He grabbed for the towel. Nichole tried to dodge past him, but he lunged for her, angrier than ever. He caught her elbow, pulled her into his arms, talking loudly all the while. "Deceitful little tramp. Lie to me, will you? And all the time, sleeping with Gregor. I saw you there. So, I'm not good enough for you. Well, we'll see about that!" He shook her so that she was dizzy.

"Let me go! Rex, you are hurting me!" she screamed. She kicked and scratched him, but he only tightened his grip.

"So, you don't deny it—that he has had you. Well, what is good enough for him, is good enough for me." He pulled away the towel that Nichole still held about her.

Her fury rose to a new pitch as she snatched up a thin robe. "You maniac! How I ever thought that you could make me happy, I'll never know. I hate you! Let me go, Rex! I hate you! You are no man! You are a pig!" She cursed him in her native tongue.

He did not release his hold. Instead, he tried to force her to the floor. "I'll show you whether I am a man!"

Nichole screamed again. "Rex, don't! My family might come home any minute. Rex, you crazy fool, think what you are doing! Rex!" She cursed him again in Spanish as he dragged her to the floor.

Then she sank her teeth into his shoulder with all her strength. She heard him howl in pain and saw him examine the stream of blood from the wound she left. As he pressed on the cut, she reached into a drawer. When Rex looked up at her again she was pointing a small gun in his direction.

Rex growled like a wounded bear. He snatched the end of the bathroom rug upon which Nichole stood, and pulled with sudden force. The rug gave way. Rex tumbled backward, hitting his head on the hard tile floor. When he arose unsteadily on one knee, his head throbbing and his vision blurring, Nichole lay semi-conscious on the floor, her body partly covered with the robe she had snatched seconds before.

In his foggy mind, Rex realized nothing except that her resistance had come to an end. Had his mind been clearer, he might have not cared anyway. He lowered himself, quite unsteadily, to the floor beside her. In a moment, the room undulated as he clung to her limp body.

When Nichole moved her head again, she groaned in pain. She looked about slowly. She was alone. A cold wind whipped through the bedroom. She started to rise, became dizzy, caught hold of the pullman drawer and bent over the sink, wetting her temple where an ugly bruise began to rise in a welt. Trembling and shivering, she wrapped her robe about her and reeled down the hallway to close the outside door against a rush of chilling, damp air. Through the glass panel, she could see that Rex's car was gone. She sighed with relief, locked the doors more securely and returned to her bedroom to look for the gun. It was nowhere in sight. After a fruitless search, Nichole sat on her dressing stool and wept as she had never wept before.

XXV

"...everyone who isn't a stereotype..."

O n a chilly evening early in December, Karla sat at her mother's desk in the Holliss living room reading the letter that she had received from Kelley.

"Listen, Mom. Listen to what Kelley says."

"Kimo is so upset because another high-rise hotel is going up on the beach. He says that the charm of Waikiki is gone; that Hawaiian heritage is being destroyed. I think I understand why he feels the way he does because he has shown me how the islands were before. He took me to a place on the Big Island where his family has a vacation home. The home was by a stream of water. There was a pretty waterfall and a pool below it where we swam around under the splash. Honestly, Karla, they have such a wonderful way of living, so relaxed, so natural and different from our ways stateside. I never knew that life could be so free of stress. I really would like to stay here forever. You wouldn't believe how tan I am!"

Karla studied the letter for a moment. "Dad, were all those high buildings built since you were there in the war?"

Christopher nodded his head in reflection. "Probably, Karla," he answered. "I was there before the harbor was bombed. I got off the ship only once before I was shipped out again. That was a few days before the bombing. I left a few buddies back there in those sunken ships."

"You have never been back, have you, Dad?"

"No." Christopher looked at the paper, stared at the wall, then turned a page. "I try to forget the war. When my back hurts from the shrapnel wound, I try all the harder."

"I can understand why." Again, Karla scanned her letter. "I have to write Kelley about my straight A report card and about Nancy's wedding, too. And about Gregor's getting caught in the riptide. I'll bet that she will be glad to know that he is on his way back to the islands. But, Dad, she says that she wants me to see her tan in the snapshot she sent to you. Did she send you a snapshot?"

Suddenly, Vanessa looked up from her knitting. "Did she send a snapshot, Chris?" She watched him as he turned another page.

"Why, yes. She sent a letter to the office."

Vanessa eyed him reproachfully. "She has always sent her letters here to the house. Why is she sending mail to the office?"

"Well, I don't know, Vanessa. She just wrote to the office, I guess."

"Where is the letter?" Vanessa demanded, somewhat irritated. "What did she write?"

Christopher lowered the paper to his lap. "You know that all she writes about is Kimo. Kimo did this. Kimo did that. Now Kimo has asked her to stay with them over Christmas. I asked her to send her letters to the office because I know it upsets you. By damn! I don't want you to be distraught over Kelley all the time. Isn't it enough that I'm in a turmoil?" His voice rose. "I'm likely to lose my mind if I hear much more about Kimo!"

Still sitting at her mother's desk, Karla chewed on her lip nervously. "Is it because Kimo is Polynesian? Is that why you are both so riled?"

"Never mind," Christopher retorted. "This is not your problem, Karla!"

"But it is, Dad." Karla took a deep breath and gathered courage. "You and Mom close your minds to *everyone who isn't a stereotype* of yourselves. You won't talk to Jose, and he isn't even Polynesian. What's so bad about marrying a Hawaiian? I just don't understand!"

"That is enough!" Christopher glowered at Karla as he slammed the newspaper to the floor. "I've had enough!"

Karla looked at her mother for a shred of support. None came. David, who had been studying in the kitchen, appeared in the doorway. He, too, was silent. Karla ran from the room with tears in her eyes.

David fidgeted with his collar and cleared his throat. "Really, Dad, you shouldn't treat her like a baby. Can't you see that she is trying to talk to you? She wants to understand your reasons. So do I, for that matter. For Pete's sake, times are changing! It's time you got *with it*! Karla is right. Your prejudice shows."

"David! Remember that you're talking to your father!" Vanessa said sharply. "You're out of line."

"I'm sorry, but I'm not, Mom." David stood firm. "Look, Mom, it has to come out sometime. It's time somebody took Karla's side. You wouldn't even know Jose if you saw him, would you? He is a nice kid, good looking, well-mannered and intelligent. He is working to save money for college. Karla could do worse. Would you be happy if she hung around with the crowd that uses dope? I don't think you're being fair to her. If you don't try to understand her, she will start doing things behind your back."

Christopher was livid. "Just let me catch her!" he warned. "And get this straight. My daughters won't marry Hawaiians or Mexicans. And you would do well to straighten out the company you keep! Why can't one of you do something right?" He struck the table with his fist. A ceramic vase toppled to the floor and broke. "Do you understand me?"

"Yes, sir," David said between his teeth. For a second, he scowled at his father, then grabbed his guitar and a book and left to find Kimberly.

XXVI

"...Poseidon rejoiced...despite the hordes of mortals..."

It was en route to the Islands that Gregor's reflections began. The in-flight movie bored him. He sat watching clouds billow below the plane and stretch far away like brush marks on a giant canvas, then evaporate into lonely wisps. His thoughts concentrated for a while on Roy's proposed projects and then skipped to other things wandering unrelated through his mind.

Nancy was gone, but he decided that he wouldn't think of that. Not again. It really didn't matter any more. All these women in love with me, he said to himself, and I don't understand why. Why me? Why me? What's so different about me? I wish I knew more about myself. Grandfather always changed the subject when I asked. My father died in the last war. I got that much out of him. Chris doesn't know a thing. If Vanessa knew anything, she didn't tell. I guess I'll never know. Oh, well, it really makes no difference. Better start thinking of how to pay for the new camera and equipment that we bought. Roy has more reefs to photograph, then the steam vents on the Pacific floor in the fault. That will be a tough one. It'll be cold down there. Gathering more of that moss for Neil's research lab—that's going to be important. He's sure he's onto something big. A cure for cancer, maybe. It'll take him years. He depends on me for the moss. If only it grew closer to home.

At the airport in Honolulu, Gregor hesitated at the foot of the ramp, looked about and breathed deeply. His step was jaunty as he pondered over where to take Kelley to dinner.

Through the meal Gregor listened while Kelley told about her classes, about island hopping in Kimo's plane, about sailing in a catamaran.

"Kimo's, of course," Gregor said.

"Yes, and I saw a real coffee plantation on the Big Island," Kelley continued, "and—"

Gregor laughed as he interrupted. "Kimo's of course!"

Amused by her exuberance and charmed by her spontaneity, he listened while his own thoughts ran on...she is not a little girl anymore...but still impetuous...still full of the devil...little pixie...never still...always in that rosy bubble she wraps about herself...never realized how pretty she was....

"...and it's so neat to have you here. Come on," she was saying. "Let's dance to this song. Please, Greg. It's one of my favorites. I dance to this all the time."

"With Kimo!" they added in unison.

181

However, Gregor made no move toward the dance floor. Instead, he tried to change the subject. "Want to go diving with me tomorrow?"

Kelley's eyes glowed. "You know I do! Where?"

"Oh, here and there around the island. Remember my letter telling you about gathering sea plants for a drug company's research lab?"

"Oh, yes, you wrote me when you were here last time. Are you still doing it?"

"You bet I am. I am not only their main biomedical forager, I am a partner in the venture. I have sent them two thousand plants from the ocean. There's one moss that I can find only around Maui that might yield a cure for some kinds of cancer."

"Don't they know yet if it will?"

"That was only two years ago. It might take ten more."

"Good grief! That long?"

"It's not that easy. First, the compounds have to be found. Then comes the screening that allows testing on human cells. Then we have to find a way to fuse a cancer cell with a cell that secretes antibodies. This particular antibody will then find a specific target such as a cancer cell in the colon or lung or ovary. The researchers have to make certain that only the cancer cells are destroyed, not the healthy tissue. This takes years of testing before it can be made safe for people." Gregor paused, watching the growing look of admiration on his listener's face.

"How do you get to know so much, Greg?"

"It all started when I did my thesis at UCLA. Since then, I've been working with the company in Texas. Researching natural drugs puts them way ahead of the times. I know everything they are doing. I could set up my own lab if I wanted to."

"Why don't you?"

Gregor shrugged. "It takes a lot of capital and I like to do too many other things. Can't get into a rut. Can't give up my diving and photography. That's what it would take. Doing research and running a lab like that takes complete dedication. I'd have to isolate myself somewhere."

Kelley nodded. "But you shouldn't waste all that talent you have!"

Smiling smugly, Gregor said, "I don't. I'm going to give a talk on antibodies at the medical convention here in the Islands."

Kelley glanced toward the band. Touching his arm gently, she said, "They are still playing my song." She paused. "You still have a thing about dancing, don't you? Ever since Pandora left, right?"

Gregor flinched. "Yeah, I guess I still have a thing about it."

With a sigh of impatience, Kelley said softly, "Gregor, listen to me. Make this a new world with just you and me in it tonight. Pandora isn't in it!"

He tensed at the name and reached for his wine glass while a myriad of thoughts flashed through his mind and spoke to him. ...admit it, you like being with her...she's right about Pandora...look at her...she sparkles...it's catching, hard to resist...it's a new start with just the two of us in it....

He reached for her hand. The next moment found them dancing.

"When will I meet this wonder man you mention in every other breath?" Gregor asked.

"Kimo?" Kelley's face glowed at his mention. "Oh, you'll meet him the minute he returns. His family is restructuring their coffee business and he had to go back to the Big Island for the meeting. He is so wonderful! Wait till you meet him."

"Are you pretty fond of him, Kelley?"

"Oh, I love him dearly, but I love everybody, Greg. And I love you, too."

He smiled and held her all the tighter as they danced on through the evening without more thought about the small village, the charmed ledge of land hanging on the brink of the sea where nobody seemed to grow older.

In the meantime, the small Village of Sundays on the California coast enjoyed the usual sunny days of December and a few hard rainfalls that ran quickly to fill the ocean coves. Here, in the caves under the tall cliffs, *Poseidon may well have rejoiced over the cleansing of the land. He may have held his own holiday court despite the hordes of mortals* that encroached upon his kingdom. He could hardly be blamed if he enlisted the aid of the shark to devour those who dared to foul the waters. He may well have stirred storms to beat upon the ugly structures so provokingly built upon the brink of his domain by some despoiling creatures. He may have extended his blessing over the remainder.

It was true that people were ruining Nature's beauty along the Pacific coastline, and this story could be about any hill that shaded a Pacific lagoon and a cozy town.

In fact, someone who reads this story in a hundred years or less may look for the charisma of Sunday Village as he might search for the truth of Camelot and, not finding it, assume that it sank into the waters with the splitting of the fault, or perhaps from the weight of the concrete that was poured out on the little ledge.

However, whether real or imagined, things were happening there. The Christmas season was passing. Brokers and tennis enthusiasts, bankers and clergy, all spared time to crowd the stores. Gift shops, toy shops and restaurants: all were jammed the whole day, and tickets for parking violations were issued liberally. At night, lights blazed and revelry issued from homes that boasted laden tables and golden eggnog.

The Town Council had promised new decorations for the lamp posts on the main streets, but when they were installed, many Villagers were disappointed because they were smaller than the old ones and less striking.

The merchants had voted not to close off the end of the main street because it would deprive shoppers of badly needed parking. The iron towers used the year before proved too costly to install again.

Probably none of these things had any bearing on the slight change of feeling that appeared to be stealing into the heart of the Village function. However, almost beyond their awareness, the townspeople were exposing their paradise to unrest, a kind of morphological diversification, possibly stemming from worry about the national economy and the unpopular Vietnamese war, more certainly from overcrowding in the Village.

Many of the newcomers brought to the area a dilution of direction and resolve. There were many entrepreneurs who did not hesitate to exploit the resources of the community. While the majority of residents registered apathy to these depredations in an attempt to preserve their own peace, a few groups combined forces with intent to fight cancer-type growth with better planning. One such group called Villagers

Incorporated, worked with such dedication as to produce not only approval by those who wished to preserve the Village atmosphere, but bitter disappointment, even angry controversy among some other citizen groups.

Of course, all this was shelved for the holiday season, and feelings of goodwill drifted in like *snow covering the ugly scars of the earth.*

At the home of Christopher Holliss, Christmas celebrations were also not quite the same as usual. David had decided to go to Mexico with a group of friends. Kimberly Weldin was among those going, and this disturbed Vanessa greatly.

Karla received an invitation to spend the vacation with a friend at their family's cabin in Julian, where a record snowfall had turned the mountain crags and tall pines into a fairyland retreat. Karla's excitement was unmatched.

"Oh, Mom," she exclaimed, "there will be sleigh rides and snowball fights and hikes and taffy pulls!" She paused for a breath. "And dances for the kids, snow sculpture contests—oh, just think of it! But I feel so bad about leaving you alone. Really, I do."

Vanessa replied convincingly, "Don't worry about us, dear. We have been looking forward to a week alone."

"Yes," Christopher added, "and we have a party of some sort scheduled for almost every night: Ifida Club's Christmas party on Wednesday, Wright's party Thursday, and the punch fling at Rick's office."

"And the program at Sumner Auditorium, the director's reception at the Club, and Sandy's twelfth-night party. Good grief, Chris, I'm going to need a new dress or two."

"Maybe we can have dinner at the Hotel Del Coronado sometime next week, and we'll ride the ferry one more time. I always loved that old ferry. They will probably discontinue it when the new bridge is built." Christopher stopped to reach for his pipe. "So you see, we will have a very busy week."

Karla's smile melted. "It sounds as though you won't miss me at all!"

Vanessa glanced at her husband anxiously. "Karla, of course we'll miss you!" she insisted. She smoothed her daughter's auburn hair. "Your father is just saying that because he doesn't want you to worry about leaving us alone."

Karla left for the mountains reassured. Christopher caught Vanessa crying softly only once at the foot of the lonesome-appearing Christmas tree. Only after he had distracted her attention to the task of answering holiday notes from old friends did he allow his thoughts to drift...*we should take a trip to some new place...Vanessa and I...what a trim figure...after all these years...Kelley has the same beautiful carriage...Vanessa has been feeling better lately...nothing is wrong...just a part of getting older...but...what would I do without her...look at this week...what would I do... the kids live their own lives...I'd go to pieces...maybe I'll take her to that doctor at the medical school in L.A. for a checkup...I have to go up there sometime in February anyway....*

"Vanessa—"

"Yes, Chris?"

"Let's go window shopping down Prospect and talk about—just things."

Weeks slipped by until it was late January. Waiting for the others of his foursome to appear for their usual Saturday afternoon game, Dr. Quest stood in the pro shop of the Country Club discussing his backswing with Mr. Runyan, the Club's professional.

"With all those contractors' trucks parked out there, how are we going to provide enough parking for the Ace-Deuce-Queen Tournament? I could hardly find a place to park today," Dr. Quest complained.

"They'll be finished by next Thursday, Doctor," Mr. Runyan reassured him. "Have you been in there? The ceiling in the Jewel Room is all done and the bar comes out today. I was just going to see if they are able to get it out in one piece. The new one should be in by tomorrow so that service won't be interrupted very long."

"Great," Dr. Quest said. His lanky form followed Mr. Runyan into the grill. "Then what else is there to be done?"

"Just the carpeting, Doctor. The bar is the last thing before the carpeting is installed."

By this time, they were in the grill where a small crowd began to gather to watch the task of dragging the loosened bar structure away from its lodging of many years. Soon it became apparent that the fixture would have to be split into parts to be removed.

Leaning on his five iron, golf hat in hand, Dr. Quest surveyed the effort. "Kinda hate to see the old bar go," he said.

"Yes, I do, too," someone else agreed. "We've had some hellishly good times around that bar." Slowly, he withdrew his visor from his head and stood with it clasped to his chest as he contemplated the best of the hellish moments. "I feel as though we're losing a friend."

As the tufted leather siding was split, another golfer, and then another bowed his head sadly and placed his cap over his heart in mock mourning.

From the direction of the putting green, another of Dr. Quest's foursome approached. "What the devil is going on?" he demanded, looking from one drawn face to the next. "Looks like an Irish wake yer-r havin'!" Laughter passed through the group.

The first section of the structure was now being eased away from the wall where the telephone had been. A deluge of ball markers, papers, coins and olive pits that had accumulated in the crack over the years fell to the floor just as old Barney the waiter, passed through the room.

"Go ahead, Barney," Mr. Runyan said, pointing to the debris on the floor, "scoop up that change that fell. There's even a dollar bill."

The waiter obliged, sorting out the findings, keys, earrings and a folded note which he opened and read. "Deah Gig," Barney read hesitantly. "I got an important call from India. Too noisy heah. I'm going to the Fahms to take the call." With a shake of his head, Barney stopped reading.

"What's that, Barney?" Dr. Quest stepped forward.

"Mr. Gig sho' nuff didn't get this message. Looks like it's been heah fo' some time." He started to crumple the already tattered paper when Dr. Quest snatched it from his hand.

"I hope this is what I think it is." Jerome Quest scanned the faded note. Then he read aloud, "Too noisy here. I'm going to the Farms to take the call. I'll be back in a jiff. You look great. I love you. Pandora."

Waving the note over his shoulder, Dr. Quest's lean features lit with a broad smile. "Finally!" he exclaimed.

"Someone you know?" asked his partner.

"Chuck, old buddy, this is the one story that is too long to tell. Larry is out there looking for a game. Tell him to take my place today. I have a call to make." Dr. Quest's lanky frame turned to go.

"We can wait. A call only takes a few minutes," Chuck said.

The psychiatrist shook his head. "Not this call! It's to a patient of mine in Hawaii who has waited years for this news, and it may change the guy's life!"

XXVII

"...the gallery heaved like a huge animal laboring..."

avid Holliss returned home from classes at the University late one afternoon to find Karla, head buried in her arms as her body shook with sobs. The salad she had been preparing lay unfinished on a counter top which reflected days of neglect.

"What's wrong, Sis?" David asked. His voice only brought louder sobs from Karla. He placed his hand on her shoulder. "If you are worried about Mom—well, you know that she is only going for those tests because Dad insisted. It isn't actually that she was feeling that bad. She'll be home tomorrow." He surveyed the kitchen. "This place is a mess. It's a good thing that Dad will be late for dinner. Come on, I'll help you."

He was baffled when Karla continued to cry. Seating himself in the chair beside her, he asked, "Karla, what's the matter?"

His sister sat upright. Her voice came between sobs. "I'm going to run away! That's what I'll do! I'll—run—run away!"

David blinked his eyes in mild surprise. "Oh, real cool! Now you're running away. What brought this on?"

Karla ignored his question. She wiped her eyes as she continued, "I just don't care about anything anymore. Nobody here seems to know that I'm alive. Oh, oohooh," she wailed. "Oooh—I just can't stand it anymore." Her body shook.

David patted her copper-red hair gently. "Well," he said, "I thought that maybe you were worried about Mom. Instead, you are fussing because you are expected to do a little work. It wouldn't be so bad around here if you'd put away some of these things. Come on, I'll help."

With tears still streaming from her eyes, Karla returned to finish the tossed salad. "Of course I'm worried about Mom, and I don't mind taking care of things, David, if only—if only—" She faltered, struggling to control her voice.

David looked at her. "If only what?"

"If only they would stop treating me like a baby, David! I can't talk to them, my own father and mother! I can't even mention Jose's name or I'm doing something criminal. And if they knew that I've been seeing him, I—"

David felt his brows lower into a frown. "You've been meeting him?" He watched as the pigtails bobbed up and down. "You haven't told them? Oh, real cool! Man, will you be in trouble!"

"That's just it! David, don't you see? I want them to understand, but I can't

187

even talk to them about it! If Dad would just take a minute to meet Jose. You know, just talk to him, that's all I'd ask. It's so terrible to have to sneak to see him."

"Where do you see him?"

"Down on the beach, mostly." She looked toward the kitchen clock. "As a matter of fact, he is waiting down there for me now. He had something important to tell me, and I don't dare leave now in case Dad walks in the door." Her lip quivered. "David, would you go down to tell him I can't come? Please?"

"Karla, are you out of your mind? Wasting your time on someone who is beneath your class! You ought to have some sense knocked into your head."

Karla's eyes flared anew as she turned to face him. "See? See what I mean? You are as bad as they are! You haven't even tried to get to know him, either! He is a very, very fine person, and he has a straight-A average, and he intends to make something of himself some day. And...and I love him, David. I really do. I love him!"

David lifted his chin and laughed. "Oh, red-hot hail and sharkspit!" he exclaimed briskly. "She is only sixteen and she thinks she is in love." He waved the thought aside. "Karla, at your age, you don't know *anything* about love."

Tears came again to his sister's eyes. "See! There you go! You are poking fun! How can I explain to you that we love each other?" She sank to the floor and sat there, her face bent down into her hands, her frame heaving. "I'll—run—run away," she sobbed.

Speechless for a moment, David dropped to his knees beside her, finally placing his arm about her shaking back. "Oh, far out!" he said. "I didn't realize it was that bad. All right, Sis, dry your eyes and tell me about Jose. I'm ready to listen. Come on now, before Dad gets home. I'll even go down to get Jose's message for you."

Karla's stained face lifted. "He—he is—such a great guy, David. He would do anything for me. Dad keeps telling me to go out with some of the boys in my class, but if he knew what some of them expect from a girl! Well, you know, David. Dad wouldn't push me so much if he knew."

"There must be some nice kids around somewhere, Sis."

"Well, face it, I'm not as pretty as Kelley. All the boys I'd pick seem to be taken. You don't understand. Jose would never do anything to hurt me. He is one of the, uh, few that still think there are some things sacred to marriage. He'd kill me if I touched dope. He is clean and honest. How often do you find a guy like that?"

David nodded his head. "But what about his family? There are bound to be cultural differences and different standards."

"I wouldn't be marrying his family!" Karla snapped.

"Don't be too sure about that." His brown eyes pinned her with a warning glance.

"Well, anyway, his family adores me. I like all of them, too. Just because we live in this big house is no reason to believe that we are any better than they are. Basic values are important. Jose's parents are honest and sincere and they don't pretend. They don't lie or cheat at income tax. That is more than you can say for some of the people who live on our street."

David shook his head. "Now you don't like people?"

Karla made a wry face. "You know what I mean. Take the girls at school. They say that brotherly love is the thing and that racial prejudice is on its way out, but they poke fun at Jose when I'm not around to hear."

"How do you know that?"

She shrugged her shoulders. "I hear about it. They tell me that my hair is pretty and then they make jokes about it when I'm gone."

"Karla, that is nothing to be upset about. Everybody with red hair gets ribbed about it."

"Just wait. Someday, I'll get even." She toyed with her hair, releasing one uneven braid. Thick, silky strands fell over one shoulder.

Seated on the floor beside her, David took her hand in his. "Sis, I wish my psych prof could talk to you."

"What would he say?"

"Probably that you are taking exception to a lot of people and things because you are angry with the way Mom and Dad haven't been understanding. And I think you need to be careful."

"About what?"

"That you aren't using your friendship with Jose to get even, to prove something."

Karla shook her head vehemently, allowing the other braid to fall free, dark and rich over her shoulders. "Oh, no, David! It's not that. Not at all. We really love each other. Jose has the basic values that I want to live with. I'm happy when I'm with him. David, it is getting so late. Would you go down to see if he is still there? There is something he had to tell me."

"All right, I'll go. Better set the table." He helped her to her feet. "I'll give you a hand when I get back."

It wasn't until later that evening that David had a chance to give Jose's message to his sister. When he delivered it, he watched Karla's eyes glisten.

"I caught Jose as he was about to leave," David said. "He wanted to let you know that he got a job at the Tournament at Torrey Pines Golf Course this week. He gave me two passes. I promised to take you."

"Oh, groovy! Can you take me tomorrow? I can get out of class early. We can get home before Dad does. Oh, David, you won't tell on me, will you?"

"Why can't Jose phone you about these things?"

Karla sobered at the thought. "Can you imagine what a furor that would cause if Dad happened to answer the phone?"

"Oh, for crying out loud! Then why don't you call him? Dad will find out about these secret meetings on the beach. Nothing gets by him. I mean nothing!"

"His family doesn't have a phone. They save every cent toward sending him to college."

"College? I thought you said Jose had a job in Alpine doing construction work."

"That's only until he has the money to go to school full time. He works days and takes classes at night now."

David let out a lengthy whistle. "What does he plan to study?"

"Well, his father wants him to study medicine, that is if he doesn't get called by the Army."

"Oh, far out! Medicine? He'll never make it. Do you know how many years that takes? And how much money? He would do better to stay in construction."

"Oh, pooh! Anybody can be anything he wants to be if he really tries. That's all a guy needs. Determination."

"And money! Or a rich uncle," David added.

Again Karla hesitated. "I think he has one—in Spain."

David whistled once more. "Or in China. Well, *rots o' ruck*. Come on, I'll help you stack the dishwasher."

David took Karla to the tournament the next day as he had promised. Then, two days later, he returned alone to watch the finishing rounds. The course was crowded. As he threaded his way through the throngs of spectators, he felt a tap on his shoulder. He looked about, bewildered by the man facing him. Then he grinned broadly.

"By damn! I hardly recognized you," he said. "Your head get caught under a lawnmower, or did you surrender to some barber? First time I've seen you in real shoes, Rommey." He continued to scrutinize Rommey's sport shirt and neat cardigan. "You up here just watching? Tell me what has happened since I turned off my car radio. Last thing I heard, Nicklaus needed a birdie that would have tied him for the lead."

Rommey fell in stride beside David. "He is putting now. If we could just make it over to the other side of this crowd. Come on." He pointed to a row of bleachers. At that moment, an uproar erupted from the stands and the mass of heads undulated, dragon-like, as spectators stood to see past each other. David pointed toward the fifteenth hole. "Right on! It's a tie. Sudden death playoff on the fifteenth. Come on. Let's get a place." He started to walk briskly to where television cameras were already focusing on the carts that were to bring the players into view. A hushed gallery gathered quickly.

David and Rommey stood jammed against the rope that kept the spectators in line. They edged themselves around to the bulge of the slight dog-leg that lent challenge to the hole. Opposite them was a group of lazy eucalyptus trees that guarded the green from anything but a miracle shot.

Toward this grove, the opponent's ball sailed, up and up, a tiny white disc seemingly wanting to float forever, losing itself in the fading sunlight without a voice in its trajectory or a care for its fate. *The whole gallery sighed and heaved again like a huge animal laboring* for its breath as the ball came to rest behind the clump of trees.

"He needs a miracle," David whispered. "Better throw up a prayer for him."

Rommey shook his head. "Not a chance. Can't get through those trees. All Nicklaus has to do is keep his ball to the right side of the fairway and he has an easy shot to the green."

Later, as they walked to the parking area, David found himself wondering again about his friend's neat appearance. "Say, Rom, I thought you hippies detached yourselves from these games of the elite. Where did you learn so much about golf?"

A shrug preceded the complacent smile on Rommey's face. "How's Kelley getting along?" he asked.

David drew from his wallet a photograph of Kelley standing by a waterfall.

"Who's the guy with her?" Rommey asked. "Bit short for her, isn't he?"

"That's Kimo. Guy she met in one of her classes. Has a big plantation, catamaran of his own, plays guitar, sings, has a room full of surfing medals and is graduating in pre-law. Some girl is going to be lucky to get him."

Rommey stroked his chin. "Is she serious about him?"

"There's no telling, but I don't think so," David answered. "If I know Kelley, she has never had a serious thought in her head about anyone."

As the weeks passed by for Kelley, some serious thoughts did filter through her head. Kimo's absence seemed to make little difference to her as long as Gregor and Roy allowed her to go with them on some of their dives and on their weekend jaunts to Makaha. During the week, after Kelley finished her English compositions and psychology reports, they often romped on the beach, playing tag and wrestling in the sand as they had done when they were children back in Sunday Village.

Kelley was determined to make Gregor forget the haunting memory of Pandora. Quite aware that her vigor and spontaneity charmed him, she did not hesitate to throw her arms about him with complete abandon and to shower him with coquettish attention whether Roy was there to stare or not, and particularly if he was.

One late afternoon just before Kelley's finals, they stood alone with arms about each other, exhausted from their capers.

"When's your first final?" Gregor asked.

Staring at the color stealing slowly across a rim of low clouds, she answered with a shake of her head. "Don't want to think about finals right now. I'm watching those beautiful clouds up there change their shapes. They look like crowds of people marching across a void. Did I ever tell you that sunsets make me sad?"

"No, why?"

"Because the *day that was* won't ever come back, and every day I think of all the hours wasted, hours I've had to do something great, something special."

"Haven't we done something special?"

"Oh, yes, it's really special, being with you, Greg, but that's not what I'm talking about. Everyday I want to do something absolutely exquisite or think some great thought or understand a profound truth. Take this island. I feel there is some mystery to understand. It has something to tell us."

Gregor laughed. "You and your fantasies."

"Look, Greg, see up there in the clouds? They are lined up all the way down the beach and over the water, warriors and kings and lovers and—"

Kelley closed her eyes tightly for a second while she motioned with her out-stretched hand. Slowly, a gleaming aureole appeared, a gigantic golden halo in the sky in which moved a thin filament of the unborn who were yet to walk this beach. Under them, an army of those who had already passed this way reviewed their passing once again. Borne lightly by sea mist, row after row of bronze forms came ...lines of tall men, limber children, proud princesses and fierce rulers, sages and goddesses, priests and captains of ships.

The scene faded as Kelley opened her eyes. Closing them again, she imagined men coming from the sea and from the air, all singing. Around one's neck hung a cross of gold. Reflections from it danced in the melting sun, piercing the capsules of the cherubic forms of those yet to come. Their many eyes opened and small voices whispered eagerly, "Is this to be our land?" Then the wail of infants rose over the sound of the surf, and Kelley thought...why should they cry so soon...maybe if we could only talk together now, they could tell us the secrets of the future so we could lock their destiny into time and they wouldn't have to cry....

Gregor's voice startled her. "Should I read your mind?" he asked. Her reverie faded as she looked up at him. "You can't do that, or can you? Are you joking?" she asked.

"Maybe," he answered, laughing softly.

"Hmm," she said. "I just don't know about you, Greg. I think you can."

"No, not really, to be honest. I could only tell you were in deep thought and you were away in one of your fantasies."

"Guess what I was thinking of. Guess, Greg."

Gregor sighed and pursed his lips in thought. "You were wondering about the people who were to come here after us and it made you sad. Why?"

"You are uncanny!" Kelley exclaimed. "I don't put anything past you anymore. Your eyes put me into a trance if I let them. Did I ever tell you that? You've got me believing about the unlimited things that a man can do with his mind."

He chuckled again. "And especially with mine?"

"Especially with yours," she agreed. "And how about yours and mine combined?" she asked. "After all, you worked it out with Pandora, so why not with me?"

"We talked about it a lot. Pandora and I agreed that concentrated group thought could generate power that we know little about for the time being."

"Tell me more. For instance, where does this power go?"

"Maybe it's recycled into a new dimension and superimposed on our physical world."

"Recycled? Sort of a reincarnation, you mean?"

"Yeah. Used again and never lost."

"But Greg, suppose there weren't any people living on the earth to generate this power. Would there be none then?"

"Hmm. How can we depend on people being here forever? No, it can't be dependent, but certainly people's strong creative thoughts would be reinforcing."

"Creative? You mean good thoughts. How about destructive thoughts? What would that do?"

"Okay. Let me explain it this way. We think that an energy-weak force combines with a strong force to hold the nuclei of atoms together—that sort of thing."

"In your theory, half of one and half of the other?"

Gregor shrugged. "Factor unknown. What's your guess?"

"I think—" Kelley tilted her head reflectively. "I think that there has to be more of a positive kind of energy than the other way around, more good than bad."

"Perhaps the balance of the two keeps our planet together."

"Yeah, and if something goes wrong, poof! We disintegrate like a meteor." Kelley giggled, then grew serious again. "Greg, does anyone else think about these things?"

"Sure, but this concept is so way out that it boggles the mind. The more serious men in the field think it's bizarre. Anyway, how can anyone do research on a thing like this? We aren't ready for it. Maybe in another twenty or thirty years."

"Not until 1990!"

"Yeah, but once they do it, they will have unraveled the last fundamental law of the universe."

"Phew! It's mind-boggling, I'll agree." Kelley grimaced. "Just what is it that we are trying to say?"

"Ya want it in a nutshell?"

"In a nutshell, Greg."

"We have been saying that there exists a ghost world, a creative energy mass superimposed on our physical world in proportions incomprehensible to man, yet responsible for his existence."

"And without a name," Kelley added.

"I call it my theory of ubiquitous subsistence." Gregor chuckled. "Roy kids me about that. He calls it my ub-sub formula."

"Hmm. I would—" Kelley began dreamily. "—call it God's Garden."

"Kelley, you're such a dreamer."

"Well, someone deserves credit for this wonderful universe. And you know what, Greg?"

"No, what?"

"Maybe people aren't supposed to know everything of that sort, because as sure as they do, they'll go and destroy it. Maybe we shouldn't probe, just live and be happy."

Gregor gave her waist a little tweak. "You are such an aesthetician! You could never do research."

She squealed over the pressure on her ribs. She felt frail against the strength of his hands. "You know Gregor—" Her voice trailed off.

"What?"

"You know, there has never been anyone I can talk to the way I can talk to you, Gregor. It's so neat to trade ideas."

"Ideas," he repeated. "Ideas, man's most precious commodities, if he can express them."

A sense of contentment passed through her, not something calming but more like a bubble that threatened to burst. She lifted her small hands to either side of his face. "Greg—"

He bent his head a bit closer to hers. "Yes?"

"I like being with you." She was glad he couldn't see her eyes grow misty.

Gregor laughed and rubbed the tip of his nose on hers playfully, Eskimo-like, tightening his arms about her just a little. Then, suddenly, he let one arm drop, stood erect and listened intently to the noise coming from a group of young men standing a short distance away. Kelley listened also. There was the sound of a growing quarrel, profanity and threats.

"Yippies," Gregor said. "Let's go."

"They aren't always that bad, Gregor. Look at Rommey," Kelley argued, but she followed him closely, grasping his hand firmly as they made their way to a lighted walkway.

"Well, these were bad. I saw a knife flash." He walked in silence for a few minutes before he said, "I know what we'll do. I'll show you that little beach that was once the crater of a volcano. It is secluded and great for swimming. Come on."

The drive to the little beach was short. The approach to it was a steep path down the side of a cliff. Once at the water's edge, they stood on a stretch of sand surrounded on three sides by a circle of cliffs, open to the sea only where a small section of the old crater had eroded. Here, the swells mirrored faint moonlight before they rolled onto the shallow beach, but the hollow under the cliff was dark. Kelley looked about slowly before she whispered, "Oh, Gregor, this is the prettiest place on the island." She placed her towel in the shadow of the wall of lava. In the next few seconds she had wriggled out of her bikini.

"What are you doing?" Gregor's voice rang with alarm.

Kelley giggled and answered, "What a chance to swim without a suit." She ran into the surf, calling over her shoulder, "Don't be chicken!"

Lying in the shallow water, she watched him approach. He was reprimanding her. "Get back here and put your suit on, Kelley! Dammit! I promised your father that I'd take care of you." Under his breath, he mumbled, "Good grief, Chris Holliss better not hear about this. God, would he blow his stack!"

"Nobody will know," Kelley persisted. "It's too dark here. Nobody will see me. Don't be chicken." She dived to deeper water when he advanced. When she surfaced with hair shimmering and dripping over her shoulders, she dared him again. "If you don't, I'll never talk to you again," she laughed.

The amphitheater gave her voice an eerie, hollow sound. Gregor passed his hand over his eyes, struggling to keep another image out of his mind, a petite form almost encircled by a cascade of pale hair. Muttering to himself, he left his suit beside Kelley's and followed her into the water.

Side by side, they swam to the opening that let in the sea. When the swells grew choppy, they turned back to where Kelley could touch the bottom with her toes.

Suddenly she called out sharply.

"What happened?" Gregor asked

"Either something bit me or I cut my foot," she answered. She limped to where the water was waist-high and brought her foot above the surface for him to inspect. She closed her eyes and winced as he felt along the sole of her foot. Neither saw the approach of a swell that dragged Kelley off balance and into the water, pulling Gregor with her. Gregor righted himself first and drew her up, both of them coughing and spitting sand.

The pain in her foot was forgotten as he held her close and steady in the onslaught of a still stronger swell. Kelley became conscious only of their bodies pressed together, swaying with the ebb of the sea. She pulled his face towards hers and her lips were on his, fierce, demanding, satisfied when they met a like response.

Minutes passed until Gregor looked suddenly to the top of the cliffs.

"I hear voices," he said. "If they come down here...good God, Kelley, what your old man would do to me if I compromised you in any way!" He took her hand to drag her to where their clothes lay, but the voices had abated. "Get into your suit," he ordered, "and toss me my trunks. They may come back."

As Gregor peered to the clifftop to make certain no one would descend, Kelley seized his trunks, tossing them toward a high ledge, but they came tumbling to the ground. Laughing, she threw them high a second time.

"What are you trying to do? You crazy kid!" he said as she caught his suit only to heave it once again. This time the garment lodged on a projection out of reach and too steep to climb. "Hell's bells, I'll have to go home in my towel."

Kelley watched him as he found his beach towel. A feeling of fury stole over her. She ran to him, snatched the towel also, chiding him all the while. "How can you end it like that? How can you, Gregor? As though it isn't the greatest thing that has happened to me—to both of us? How can you? I won't let you!" Her voice broke. She was ready to cry. "Gregor, don't end it like this!"

He shook her gently. "Come to your senses," he said. "We are on the beach, naked in the moonlight, and, and—" Transfixed by a thought, he let his voice trail off.

She pulled her shoulder from his grasp. "Yes, yes I know! It was that way with her, wasn't it? Is that what you are trying to say? That stupid Pandora again? Is that what is stopping you? It is, isn't it? Oh, I hate her!"

Fighting a memory, he brushed the back of his forearm across his brow. "Damn it, Kelley, don't do this to me," he implored. "Can't you understand?"

"No! No, Gregor, I don't understand! What has that got to do with us, whatever happened before? This is a different time, a different place, and I'm Kelley, not anybody else, Gregor. Whatever happened before has nothing to do with us now. I'm the girl who has been in love with you for years and years and never had a chance until now. This could be the greatest single moment of my life, and—and you—" She felt tears welling.

He put one arm about her shoulder. "You're acting on an impulse, Kelley. I can't let you do something you'll regret tomorrow. I've been wrong for so many girls. How can I explain?"

Kelley buried her head in his shoulder and allowed her tears to flow. "But— Gregor, I love you! I—I—always have. And now even more." Her words coming forcibly through her sobs, she continued, "I thought that—you were beginning to—be really happy with me—and in love with me, too."

He pulled her against him to calm her. "But, I am! I am! I'm happy with you and I love you. But I promised your father. Kelley, I can't let anything turn out wrong for you!"

Her voice softened. "If you love me too, how can this be wrong for us? Dear Gregor, don't take this moment away from me, because it's mine, all mine. It belongs to me, to us. Don't spoil it. Let it be beautiful—let it—"

Their lips met for a brief interval before the two of them sank onto the sand and lay side by side, forgetful of all else for the time. To Kelley, it became a blissful embrace, ecstatic in intensity as she had never dared to imagine and equally agonizing in its unfulfillment. Seconds passed, then a moment, then a moment more.

For Gregor, too, minutes passed unnoticed. As it had done once before, the sound of the sea grew dim in his ears and the earth began to slip away from under him. Now, with her clinging to him, he was floating free in space again. Then, a sharp cry escaped him, a frightened, angry cry that shook him from his fantasy and brought him to the shadows of the crater once again. He had thrown himself from her roughly onto the sand. In the next instant, he was in the surf, feeling himself melt into the waters, all the while moaning, "Let me be! Do you hear? Let me be!" He plunged into the waves, diving under them until he felt his lungs about to burst.

Kelley sprang to her feet when she heard the splash and looked for the sight of his strong stroke breaking the surface. When there was none, she panicked. Screaming his name, she ran to the water's edge. "Gregor! Come back! Come back!" She was shoulder-deep in the waves and still shouting for him when he surfaced beside her.

"Damn you, Gregor!" she shouted at him. "You scared me!"

"Why?" he asked calmly.

"I thought—I thought—well, I don't really know what I thought. I just got scared that you wouldn't come back or something, that you were really angry with me."

"I'm not angry with you, Kelley," he said softly. He cupped her face in his hands and stroked her wet hair gently. "Don't worry. Please. Why should I be angry?"

Kelley struggled to still her quivering lip. "Maybe I know that it still upsets you to have someone try to take Pandora's place." She watched his eyes blink, but he was silent. "I can't help it that I love you so much, Gregor," she added.

"Kelley, I've been happy being here with you. Don't ask me to explain about Pandora. Just believe me when I say that I love you, too."

"Enough to marry me, Greg?"

He nodded. "Enough to marry you, but first we should call your father tomorrow to ask him."

She sighed. "Gregor, you're so logical all the time."

"I have to be, you're such an...aesthete!" He pointed to her suit. "Put it on," he said, "and we'll go home."

She did as he instructed. "Gregor, my towel is bigger than yours if you want to use it," she offered, but when she took the towel to him, she found that he had retrieved his trunks with a long piece of driftwood.

"Let's go," he said. He led the way to the steep exit. Half way up the incline, Kelley stopped to look back. He tugged on her hand. "Come on," he urged.

"I want to remember it," she whispered. A cloud passed and cool moonlight replaced the shadows under the cliffs. "Once the crater was filled with fire and maybe—"

"We'll be coming here again," Gregor said.

Still, Kelley hesitated. "Yes, I suppose so, but I want to remember *tonight*. Tonight is just once, and the hours of tonight won't happen again."

Gregor turned to the sea, nostalgia overcoming him, thoughts of long ago crowding in...*blue velvet...the splash of a fountain...a dolphin leaping high in the air...the shadow it made as Gregor plotted his own destiny at its base...the scent of heliotrope drifting delicately...or was it the plumeria that blossomed at the crest of the cliff....*

He sighed and turned to look at Kelley.

"You're a strange girl," Gregor said after a moment, and drew her again toward where the path wound upward.

XXVIII

"...everything turned to blackness and oblivion..."

aving spent a busy morning putting his affairs in order at the office, Christopher Holliss still sat at his desk at two o'clock in the afternoon, intending to leave directly for Los Angeles to visit Vanessa, who was still in the hospital.

He had had only coffee for breakfast and had not taken time to eat lunch. The wrinkles were deeper in his forehead this afternoon, mirroring his concern and frustration. His face was taut and gray. When the telephone rang, he almost barked a curt hello. He was surprised to hear his daughter's voice ask, "Dad, is that you?"

He allowed his erect shoulders to sag a bit. "Oh, Kelley! You are the last person I expected to hear from today. How are you?"

"Oh, fine, Dad. Nobody answered at the house, so I finally tried your office number."

"Well, I decided to catch up on things this morning," Christopher explained as he looked about the room trying to derive some comfort from his efforts. "Is everything all right with you?"

There was a pause. "Things must be pretty pressing, Dad, if you gave up your Saturday golf. You're never at the office on Saturday."

Christopher leaned back and his body sagged even more. "As a matter of fact, things are pressing. I haven't been in the office all week. Your mother is still in Los Angeles." Nervously, he loosened his tie.

"But Karla's letter said she would be home today. I wanted to talk to her. I thought it was just a routine checkup."

"They want to do one more test. She—she had a seizure of some sort."

"Gee, Dad, don't the doctors know what's wrong?"

"Oh, they are narrowing it down, I guess," Christopher said. "Nothing really specific yet." No point in spreading alarm, he thought, not with Kelley's exams scheduled this week.

"You sound tired, Dad. You're worried, aren't you?"

"Yes, I am. It has been a rough week. I plan to drive to Los Angeles tonight. Tell me how you are. Mom asks all the time. Seems that you are on her mind more than anything else. Are you calling to tell me that exams are over?"

"No, I have two to go." Her voice grew less audible. "I wish Mom was home. I have something to tell you."

Christopher sat upright. "What is it? You're all right, aren't you?"

"Now, Dad, don't get upset. I said that I was fine."

"Look, Kelley, I can tell by the tone of your voice. Is something wrong?" He could feel sweat on his brow. "Out with it."

"No, Dad. Nothing is wrong. I'm just calling to tell you that I am going to get married."

Christopher grasped the edge of his desk to steady himself. "Married? Married? Good God, Kelley!" he shouted. "We have had only one snapshot to see what Kimo looks like! You hardly know the boy! What on earth are you using for brains? We haven't even met the lad."

He heard Kelley clear her throat. "Dad, forgive me for not keeping you abreast of what has been happening here. Really, I'm sorry that this isn't what you want to hear."

"Well, so am I, little girl. We are spending a small fortune to send you to be educated, not to be married!"

A breathy sound came over the line. "Please, don't get upset, Dad. I can't talk to you when you are upset. I am not going to marry Kimo. He is just a good friend."

Christopher found his patience wearing thinner. "Well, for God's sake, Kelley, who is it?"

Another breathy sound. "I'm going to marry Gregor, Dad."

Now it was Christopher's turn to draw a deep breath. "You can't be serious! What are you saying? He has always been like an uncle to you. We will have to consider a lot of things before we let you make that choice. What about the difference in age? What about the emotional shock that he has been trying to get over? And suppose Pandora comes back? No, no! We'll have to discuss this carefully when you come home this summer."

There was a brief pause. "Dad, I am not going to wait until summer! I want to be married as soon as we can get a license. We need you to say it's all right. I want Mom to agree, too."

Christopher came to his feet. Grasping the telephone with one hand and the edge of his desk with the other, his voice rose again. "Good God, Kelley! It's hardly the time to approach her with this!"

"Do you want me to call her myself? I've got to explain this to her. She always understands."

"You will do no such thing!" He was frustrated and shouting, his face reddening with the effort. "You won't get married either! Do you hear me?"

Kelley's voice sounded far away and shaky. "I am going to marry Gregor whether you like it or not, Dad. You know that I've always been in love with him. He feels the same way. I'm sorry, Dad, but it's hard to explain all this over the phone. Maybe Greg can do it better. Just a minute."

"Wait a moment! I haven't finished with you yet, young lady. I won't talk to him until you and I get some things straight. Are you listening? You will wait until you come home. *Then* we will talk about it. We will do everything in due time. Do I make myself clear?" He paused as he heard Kelley begin to cry. "Kelley, listen to me!"

"Dad, I've lis—listened to—to you all my life. All my life, you and Mom have told me what to do and when to do it. I am a person. I can think for myself. I want to live my own life." The sound of breathing came. "I know what is right for me!"

"Look, Kelley, please understand, this must wait. I can't face another problem right now. I am exhausted, haven't slept well in a week. I'm no good at the office. The new housekeeper got sick and left. David is never home. Karla doesn't come home after school, and I can't watch her. The house is unsightly. If I sound grumpy, it's because I'm at my wit's end, not to mention your mother's being ill, and—"

Christopher's discipline gave way. His throat tightened. His voice refused to come. He fumbled for tissue in a drawer and blew his nose loudly. "Kelley," he managed to say in a raspy voice, "I'll call you again tomorrow." He replaced the receiver before his daughter could reply.

The next morning, just after breakfast, Gregor surprised Kelley by appearing at the dormitory. "Couldn't call," he explained. "Your phones are all out."

"Oh, yes, that remodeling has started. Good grief! The phones will be out of order for days, I think. How will I call you if we don't have lines?"

"You won't need to. Roy and I are flying over to Lahaina on Maui today," Gregor explained.

"Today!" Kelley said in dismay. "But we were going to talk to my father again. How soon are you leaving?"

Gregor felt ill at ease as he looked into her upturned face. "As soon as I finish talking to you. Roy is waiting for me at the apartment."

"Oh, Greg! You can't leave right now. Please, don't go," she pleaded.

"I wouldn't, except that we forfeit our down payment if we don't call for the boat we are buying. Also, Roy has to try out some equipment while a certain mechanic is there," Gregor explained.

Kelley's pleading eyes did not leave his, and Gregor's uneasy feeling returned. He took her by the arm and guided her away from the building toward a long path lined with hibiscus. She was saying, "Roy never thinks to consider you, Gregor. When will you get back?"

"Oh, in a couple of days, maybe a week, no more," he assured her.

"As long as you're not leaving because of my father or because of what he said yesterday, I guess it's all right." She picked a hibiscus leaf and began to shred it. "I wish I could go to Maui with you."

"You could go if you didn't have a couple more exams to take. Just what would your dad say if I took you away from finals?"

"You are afraid of him, aren't you?"

"No, but I respect him. He trusts me. You wouldn't think much of me if I broke that trust, would you?"

Angrily, Kelley threw the shredded leaf to the ground. "I don't even want to talk to him again."

"Don't feel like that," Gregor hurried to say. "Your father's decisions are always wise. I can't come between you and your family, Kelley. You wouldn't want to put me in that position either, if you stop to think about it. During the week I'm away, he will have had time to think about it and then I'll call him."

As Gregor went on to explain his plan, he led her to where thick clusters of blossoms hung, vivid and lush, making a canopy over the path. The air was filled

199

with the hum of bees searching for the sweet pollen of the trumpet vine which was climbing heavenward through the thicket so that its huge blossoms might hang free in the sunlight. Jammed in the dense foliage of the hedge, one blossom had trapped a bee, which was signaling his distress with loud buzzing.

Gregor had stooped to kiss Kelley tenderly. "I won't be gone long," he repeated.

"I wish Roy had arranged his plans differently. I don't want you to go, Greg," Kelley answered, still reproachful.

He cupped her face in his hands. "It will give us time to think," he said.

Kelley's big eyes narrowed. "That is what you want? Time to think? You aren't sure you love me, are you?"

Gregor drew his breath slowly. "Please try to understand, Kelley. There are some things that I have to straighten out in my own mind."

"What things, Greg? About Pandora?"

His hands dropped to his side. "Things that you can't help me with, nothing I can explain to you. Just believe me."

"Is it that you aren't sure that you love me?" Kelley asked again wistfully.

He shook his head. "No, no. I love you. I know that." He kissed her again. Then he took her hand to lead her back to the building. "That isn't what I have to decide."

"But you still have to decide something?"

He walked in silence for a moment. "Only my manner of thinking. I have to resolve my way of thinking, not a question of whether I love you, Kelley." He stopped to place his arms around her once more. "I do love you."

Kelley's dark eyes blurred as she answered. "Greg, I've always loved you, for as long as I can remember. I thought there would never be a chance for me. Now that we have found each other, it's not easy for me to let you go. I just—want to be near you."

"Tell you what," Gregor said cheerfully. "Maybe I can arrange for you to join us on Maui. You have to take two more exams, right? I'll call you tomorrow night or the next night to let you know."

"But the telephones! They are putting in a complete new switchboard. We may not have service for a week!"

Gregor reached into his pocket. "Here, here's my key. Stay at my place until you hear from me. Tell you what you can do for me. I packaged that seaweed we found yesterday. They're waiting for it at the lab of the pharmaceutical company. Put it into the mail for me, will you?"

"I'll mail it for you, Greg." She took the key. "Can't I help you pack?"

"All done. We aren't taking much. It's only for a week." He put a white blossom in Kelley's flowing dark hair, kissed her tanned cheek and left her watching his retreating figure.

Some distance away, the trapped bee finally squeezed his way through the petals and began to fly in erratic circles as though he had lost his way.

During the short flight to Maui, Roy toyed with his pipe, wishing that the no-smoking sign would turn off. He finally put his pipe away and turned to Gregor.

"This thing between you and Kelley popped up all of a sudden."

Gregor was slow to answer. He closed a magazine and glanced at his watch. "I think I'll marry her," he said in a low tone. "As soon as we talk to her father."

"Oh." Roy smoothed his shaggy bright hair and was thoughtful as the plane circled the island below. "You are sure that this is the real thing? You are certain that you're in love with her?"

Gregor's heavy brows arched. "Do you think I would be planning a step like this if I weren't?"

Roy sat wrapped in thought. Finally, he answered. "You realize, old buddy, that I can read you like a book. We have been together for a long time. I get the feeling that something is bothering you. It's about marrying Kelley, isn't it?"

Gregor winced and sighed. "Well, dammit, Roy, I'm happy with her. We are right for each other. My God, I wouldn't go this far if I weren't sure of that. But her father was really upset."

"Is that all that is eating at you?" Roy's heavy frown deepened the wrinkles on his already scored features.

Gregor laughed. "Well, no, that isn't all of it. I didn't think that my troubles were showing all that bad, though."

"Look, old buddy, you've been through a hell of a lot of trying situations and I don't want you to get yourself messed up again. If you don't want to talk about it, don't. I didn't mean to pry." Roy smoothed his fuzzy mustache.

"Well," Gregor answered, "maybe—maybe it's a good thing for me to talk about it. Yeah, get it off my chest. I examine my feelings and damned if I'm sure just what I want. I think that I'm in love, but then I'm not sure what love is anymore. Yet that's why Kelley would be good for me, don't you see, Roy? You won't understand this, but I'm not sure I want from another woman the intense love I knew with Pandora. It doesn't seem fair to Pandora, somehow." Gregor shifted his weight in the cramped seat.

Roy, usually deliberate in his response, fairly exploded. "Well! By damn, are you going to be fair to the other girl? Hell, Greg, you speak of Pandora as though she was the first and only woman in your life! She wasn't, you know. Remember Alexa? Remember the girl from Texas I wouldn't let you marry? Remember the blonde model, and Stephanie, and, oh yeah, the actress? Each one was better than the last."

"Well, I didn't know that—" Gregor bit his lip and nodded reflectively.

"Sometimes, you wouldn't know your ass from first base if I didn't tell you." Roy laughed abruptly. "Can you remember all those dames?"

Gregor shook his head. "All before Pandora. She stands alone. Hell, Roy, how can I explain it to you when you've never been in love?"

Roy was silent as he watched the monstrous ocean below lapping the edge of land that rose from its depths and spread itself like a huge emerald in a pool of water. "Maybe I've been in love and maybe I haven't," he said almost inaudibly. His gaze left the window and fell again on Gregor. "Have you talked to Dr. Quest or Dr. Ornski about this?"

With a shrug, Gregor answered, "Yeah, yeah, in a way. What can they tell me? Make sure it's a deep relationship, not a replacement for Pandora? Play the field? What can they say?"

With a skeptical glance, Roy asked, "Where does Kelley fit into that scene?"

"Well, with her, marriage is the only way to go."

Roy laughed. "That doesn't compute with what you just said," he argued.

"Humph! You know what Chris Holliss is like, don't you?" Gregor squirmed in his seat again. "Well, nobody had better play around with his daughter!"

Roy began to gather his belongings. "We'll be landing in a minute," he said. "Want my opinion?"

"Why not?" Gregor replied with a shrug. "You'll give it to me anyhow."

The sound of Roy's voice was drowned by the shrill landing instructions that suddenly poured from the loudspeaker.

That afternoon, Kelley tried to study for her final examination, but her room was hot and the noises from the other students bothered her more than usual. Finally, she threw some things in a handbag, locked her room, and signed out. She designated an address in Maui as the place where she could be found.

She went to Gregor's place, spread her books about her and began to study. The house looked larger without Gregor. The radio did not dispel the emptiness. After some time, she found herself too restless to concentrate.

I'll walk down the beach, Kelley said to herself...a walk before it gets dark...this place is not the same without Gregor here...we've had such happy months and I know we are right for each other...Dad will understand when we explain it to him and I know Mom will because she always does...she will win Dad over because she always does...she has a way and she really runs the family...she'll make everything go right but I wish I could talk to her right now...I shouldn't use Roy's phone...she should be home tomorrow or the next day and I'll call her before I leave for Maui if Roy doesn't spoil our plans...good grief, if only I didn't feel that he has such a hold on Gregor and that he doesn't really want Gregor to get married because it would be harder to drag him off on his ventures...he plans to film reefs all over the world...he gives me the feeling that I wouldn't be welcome...oh damn...why does life have to be so complicated....

She scooped up a piece of driftwood and heaved it into the surf where it bobbed at the mercy of the ebbing tide. After watching it carefully for a few moments, she returned to the house where she stood before Gregor's mirror and addressed the reflection.

"You, Kelley Holliss," she said pointing at her image, trying to frown frightfully at herself, "you can do anything if you really want to do it! Everything is at your fingertips." She pointed all ten fingers at the mirror. At once, wheels spun, imaginary blocks snapped into formation and gears ground. "You are not like that helpless log floating in the surf. You can change the world! Think of it! Don't let it beat you. Ride on top! *Don't get stuck in yesterday!*" She waved her hand again. Cables appeared swinging in space, levers lowered and rose, bubbles filled the whole scene and burst into lightning as she touched each one.

Kelley laughed, found her book, then sank onto the sofa after placing the telephone under the coffee table within her reach. "Now," she directed, "call me, Gregor. Use some of that extra-sensory perception that you have so much of. Call me. That's first. Priority billing. Just call me." She closed her eyes.

While the sky blushed and glowed and darkened to the stars, she slept. Suddenly, she sat on the edge of a clear pool that stretched endlessly before her. Just as quickly, Vanessa stood waist deep in the pool, her clothing still perfectly dry. She smiled at Kelley, wafted her a kiss, turned to walk away, and then stepped onto the upturned edge of a broad knife embedded in the sand at the bottom of the pool. A droplet of blood fell from the wound that the knife inflicted and turned into a gem that sent blinding iridescence through the water.

Kelley screamed. She swung herself to a sitting position on the edge of the sofa where she struggled against something that held her there. "Don't go further!" she screamed again. "The bottom! Watch out for the bottom! It's made of solid knives! Come back! Mother! *Moth...er!*"

To her consternation, her mother smiled gaily at her. "It doesn't hurt anymore. Come sit on my lap. Here are the binoculars to watch the whales spouting. Get your sweater, dear. Winter is coming. Give the beads back to Gig. They are really all he has left. Just keep smiling and you will get through it if anyone will." Her voice faded as she walked away, passing Rommey, who was there struggling to overcome a leaping dolphin twice his size.

Kelley screamed again and fell forward, awakening as she did so to find herself sprawled over the coffee table. Frightened and dizzy, she struggled to her feet. Perspiring profusely and trembling, she was vaguely aware of pain in her ankle as she felt her way to a light switch. The loneliness that filled her was not dispelled by the flood of light in the kitchen. She looked at the clock on the wall. Only ten o'clock...still time for him to call...if I could stay awake...that dream has me so scared...I don't like being here alone....

She took her notes into the bedroom, but her attempt to study did not last long and she was asleep again on the bed in the light of the table lamp. She did not stir until she heard the sound of the doorbell. She hurried to open the door. Kimo smiled at her in the morning light.

"Aloha," he said as he entered. "Your telephone is off the hook," he added as he stooped to retrieve the instrument lying on its side under the coffee table.

"How did you know?" Kelley asked. "I didn't realize. I must have kicked it over when I had a bad dream last night. But how did you know?"

Kimo's handsome face wrinkled again with a warming smile. Except for a broadening of his nose at the nostril, his features were aesthetically fine, almost overpowered by black eyebrows. "Gregor called me when he couldn't get through to you."

Kelley made a little sound deep in her throat. "What did he say?"

"He said to have you at a telephone at dinnertime. I suggested that you would be at our plantation at a party to celebrate the end of finals. The celebration will probably last for several days."

The expression on Kelley's face was blank. "But, but, Gregor said that I could fly over to Lahaina to join him."

Kimo hesitated. "Ah, they aren't coming back directly. He and Roy have signed a contract to do a film, a kind of documentary for a wealthy Samoan family that owns an island somewhere between Samoa and Fiji."

"That must be the man who sold them the boat. Blast him. Gregor promised!"

Kimo seated himself on the sofa. "Well, he said he would call tonight. I'll study while you get ready, and then we'll have breakfast at the cafe before we go to class." When Kelley hesitated, he pointed in the direction of the dressing room. "Scram," he said authoritatively as he flipped open a book.

In fifteen minutes Kelley appeared, her hair moist and dark, her eyes sparkling. "I'm ready," she said, "but I should get some things from my room to take along to your house."

"Got your bikini?" he asked as he arose to face her. "That is all you will need. My sister will lend you closets full of muumuus, like the last time." He drew near to her, placing his hands to the side of her waist, and Kelley reciprocated with arms about his neck.

"That is what I like about your family. It is impossible not to love all of you." She kissed his cheek and drew away, but he pressed her to him again gently.

"Kelley," he said wistfully, "I wish I could be in Gregor's place. You must be able to guess that I have been in love with you and not able to tell you about it."

She put her cheek to his. "I know that we have been more than good friends to each other, Kimo. You are very dear to me, you know that. I figured there was a reason it couldn't go beyond that, something to do with your family. Am I right?"

"My mother and sisters all love you, but my grandmother made me swear to do certain things to preserve our lands. I am engaged to marry the daughter of my cousin. I have no choice in the matter."

"That figures," Kelley said. "Have I met her?"

"No. She is in a finishing school abroad. She is only fifteen."

"Do you have a picture of her?"

He released her and drew a photograph from his wallet.

Kelley stared. "Why, she is absolutely beautiful, like a princess!"

"Our families represent the oldest in the islands." He replaced the picture.

Taking his hand, she said, "You are doing the right thing. But, Kimo, I'm glad you told me that you love me, too. It means a lot to me, and I'll always remember that. Always, Kimo." She gathered her books, locked the door, and they left in Kimo's car.

Later that evening, at Kimo's plantation on the big island of Hawaii, a call came for Kelley. She went to the quiet library to receive the call. It was brief, and afterward she sat by the telephone until Kimo came to find her.

"What happened?" he asked at once.

Unable to trust her voice, Kelley shrugged her shoulders. She finally admitted that the call was from Roy telling her that Gregor had indeed gone with the Samoan gentleman to his island to film a two-week-long celebration.

"Didn't Roy go with him?" Kimo asked.

"Roy said that his ship wasn't quite ready. As soon as he fits some equipment and stocks supplies, he will follow with cameras for the underwater shots. They want pictures of a battleship sunk in their harbor during the war." She blinked to keep back the tears. "They wanted Gregor to go right away to film the activities on land."

Kimo looked thoughtful. "Hmm. If it is an island held by the Japanese during the war, it has to be considerably north of Samoa, maybe the Gilberts."

"What difference does it make where it is? Greg is gone. He was going to come back right away to talk to my father about getting married. Now he is gone. Somehow, I get the feeling that Roy is behind this. He doesn't want his partner to be married. But if only Greg had talked to me first! How can he just go off without even talking to me?"

"He tried to call you last night, Kelley," Kimo reminded her. "I'm sure he'll try again when he reaches another telephone."

Kelley's lip quivered. "I'm sure Roy has something to do with all this. I hate him."

"I wish I could help somehow," Kimo said. Then his face brightened. "I know what we'll do. We'll go up to the hut by the high waterfall for two days. It will make you forget your worries. When we get back, surely there will be some word from Gregor." They packed and went that very day.

On the second day, Kimo's brother joined them at the hut. Kimo spoke quietly with him. Then he came to Kelley. His usually smiling face was grave.

"Kelley," he started. "Ah, did your father give you any idea of how ill your mother was?" He took her hand.

Kelley felt a panic welling up inside. "That dream I had at Greg's place! Mom! Something has happened to my mother!"

Kimo looked graver still. "Your father didn't want to tell you how serious it was until your exams were over. The doctors operated to remove a brain tumor."

"Not Mom," Kelley whispered hoarsely. "Is she—" She stopped and stared into Kimo's grim face. A scream ripped through her throat. "Are you trying to say...she didn't pull through?" She could feel the color drain from her face. Her skin grew clammy. She gaped as Kimo nodded his head. "Not—my mother," she moaned. Her knees began to buckle and she saw Kimo reach to catch her as *everything turned to blackness and oblivion.*

Forecast IV

Lightning flashed in the heaven over the limbs of the gnarled Torrey Pine. A branch stirred and the imprisoned form of the Indian girl came to life. She shook the tree but her companion slumbered on. After wandering alone in the night air, she returned to cry quietly under the tree.

"Jaoko, awaken! Awaken!" she pleaded.

The Indian prince descended to sit beside her. "What sadness fills the night, my Princess?"

"Our foxes! Our foxes, Jaoko!" the girl moaned. "Our beautiful foxes who carried the spirits of the rulers of the Sea People! They are all dead! We nurtured them in the few arroyos that remain, my pet Lobo and all the little ones. Oh, Jaoko, they died in such pain!"

"It is hard to believe! How?"

"Men put powder in food that they ate."

"But why? The barrancas belonged to them long before we came. Dead? All?"

She pointed to the limp body at her feet. "All! Oh, Jaoko, I have little love for those who kill my foxes!"

Jaoko bent to lift the lifeless form. "Sacred animal of our forefathers, come. Live with us."

He murmured words over the small furred thing and then faded into the tree with the fox in his arms.

XXIX

"...my pad is big enough for two..."

One by one, the leaves of the poinsettia dropped leaving the straggling stalks bare. The pyracantha berries withered. A few hard rains in December had soaked the earth enough to encourage fresh growth on the hillside shrubs that thirsted through the long summer months. Iris lifted its tender stalk up from the softened earth and threatened to bloom early if the days remained sunny. Over entire slopes, brilliant magenta and orange blossoms of iceplant began to signal another change of the seasons. Branches of the eucalyptus kept reaching for the heavens and fruit trees swelled with soft, brown buds.

These were all signs that winter had passed, these and the bleakness of the beach at Wind'n'Sea, where the tides had labored fastidiously to deposit much of the sand to the southernmost stretch of the shore, leaving gaping cracks between the jagged rock cliffs. Now the stone ledges stood naked and lonesome, anticipating the shift in the ocean tides that would cover them snugly with warm sand once more.

It was early dawn when Rommey walked at the base of these cliffs, carrying one abalone. The water had become turbulent enough to interrupt his diving. A storm cloud had gathered overhead and raindrops were growing steadily larger.

For a moment, Rommey paused to survey the drenched shore, his spirit daunted not in the least by the deluge. Scowling under the tangle of tight curls which framed his face, his head erect in a position that would match the temper of Poseidon, Rommey might have passed as another ocean god searching for his team of seething sea horses, daring to show himself in this moment when the fury of his passing had driven all mortals from the beach.

All but one, because just then Rommey became conscious of a figure sitting in a bent-over position higher on the ledge and over a way. Rommey's thought flashed backward...*that's how I met Connie...she was sitting here in the rain that morning...huh...Connie...I don't know why I waste a thought on her...but....*

Rommey stopped short and stared. He took a few more long strides and stopped again.

"By damn!" he said. "Either that is Kelley Holliss or I'm King Tut's uncle! That's funny. The semester's started. Why isn't she in school?" Choosing a precarious route up the side of the incline, he reached her side in a few more minutes.

Kelley sat bent forward with her hair trailing in her lap and one hand hiding her face. Rommey dropped his gear, sank to his knees and placed his hand gently on her forehead. "Kelley," he said, but she paid no attention. "Kelley, it's me,

Rommey," he repeated as he drew her hand aside and peered into her eyes. They were red and swollen. Her face was flushed. She made a small gutteral sound and let her head fall to rest on her knees again.

"Kelley, what's wrong?" Rommey demanded. "Are you sick?" He took her hand and rubbed it to give it warmth. "For crying out loud, what are you doing here at this hour, soaking wet and half frozen? You crazy kid!" He reached for her arm. "Come on, I'll take you home."

However, Kelley jerked her arm away, made an angry sound and hugged her knees tightly.

"Poor kid is in shock," Rommey mumbled to himself. Then he bent low and said gently, "Okay. I'll take you to my pad. You can't stay here like this." He lifted her to her feet, sheltered her from the wind, and together they climbed over the path to the street. In a short while, they stopped at a caretaker's cottage connected to a green garage, separated from the house above it by a steep stairwell.

Rommey led her into a small, neat room overcrowded by a couch and bunk beds along with ten or more huge hanging plants. This arrangement allowed no occupant to take more than four steps in one direction.

Kelley glanced about briefly as Rommey lowered her to the couch. Breathing hard from exertion, he eyed her anxiously. "Are you all right?" He felt her forehead. "Kelley, are you all right?" he asked as she looked at him with glazed, listless eyes. He was relieved when she nodded her head and moved obligingly as he eased her out of her thin windbreaker.

"Cold," she whispered. "Tired."

"I'll get some hot coffee. How long have you been out there?"

"Since before daybreak," Kelley mumbled.

Rommey made disapproving noises with his tongue. "Dumb kid! You should know better than to get chilled like this." He snatched a cloth and began to dry her hair.

"I couldn't sleep," Kelley complained.

"No reason to spend half the night in a cold rain! I'll find something of mine for you to put on." He reached toward a chest.

"No!" she shook her head vehemently and lay prone on the couch.

Rommey pondered the situation for a few seconds. Then he pulled something from the chest. "Here, put this on," he ordered. Meeting no response, he added, "If you don't, I will!" He grinned broadly as she snatched the garment from his hand and plodded into the small bathroom to change. Meanwhile, he busied himself in the tiny nook equipped to be a kitchen, whistling as he prepared coffee, but when he turned to give Kelley the steaming cup, she was sleeping soundly on the couch.

Again, Rommey studied the situation. ...*poor kid...she is really wiped out...better let her crash for a while...hmm...cute chick...pretty nose...what a tan she's got...can't see her freckles anymore...and what a bod...man...does she look good on my bed...looks like she needs help with her problems...she'll be hungry....*

Rommey stood smiling over his pan of sausage when Kelley awakened. He poured an omelette as he said, "Well! Good morning! Breakfast in one minute. Feel better?" Unvoiced, the thought ran through his mind again that it was nice to have her awaken on his sofa bed.

Kelley nodded her head. "Better, Rom," she said, but inside her, a voice kept repeating...*I must be in heaven...Rommey's smile and good coffee and sausage...someone who cares...it must be heaven....*

"Well! Well!" Rommey was saying. "How long have you been back in the Village?" *...lucky that I came along on the beach this morning....*

"About ten days—about." She shrugged her shoulders as though it didn't matter. *...why don't you tell him how good it is to see him...but not if you are going to cry some more....*

Rommey poured coffee for her. "Here, come drink your coffee while it's hot." He pointed to a ledge that served as a table. "Does that mean you'll be leaving right away to start classes?" *...that would be my luck as usual...maybe she's not going back....*

Kelley sipped her coffee. Then she toyed with the rim of the cup and sighed loudly. "I'm not going back, Rom." *...I wish I cared...nothing means anything to me anymore....*

"Here, this is an omelette made with my special recipe." He placed a plate by her cup. "Not going back to school? Why not?" *...I'm kinda glad she'll be around but I hate to see her so wiped out...not like her....*

"Oh, I don't want to study. Nothing seems to matter anymore." She shrugged her shoulders again. "Anyway, Dad needs me to help with Karla and the house since, uh, since—" *...I just can't cry anymore....*

Rommey chewed on his lip. "Uh, your brother told me about your mother a couple of weeks ago." He shifted his feet uneasily. "I want to say I'm really sorry, but I'm not good at saying things like that." *...maybe I should keep my big mouth shut....*

"I, uh, I guess—that I understand, Rom." She turned her head away suddenly. "Oh, Rom, I'm so mixed up! I'm not sure I understand anything anymore!" *...don't tell him how bad it is....*

For a second, Rommey frowned. Then a warm smile stole over his face. "I dig," he said. "I dig. Eat your breakfast now. Don't let it get cold or the cheese gets hard." *...get her to change the subject...stupid...change the subject....*

Kelley nibbled at her omelette. "Yum," she said and took several more bites. "It's super, Rom. Didn't realize how hungry I was."

He watched while she devoured the remainder of her breakfast. Then he asked, "Want to walk down to Black's Beach with me? I told some guy I'd be there in a half hour."

She looked up at him and shook her head. Her brows arched and lowered expressively. "Rom, Dad says there are some nude bathers who are using the beach. He says we can't go there anymore."

"Wear dark glasses. Your Dad would never know you've been there."

Kelley still shook her head. "There is nothing he doesn't find out. I'd be looking for a place to live. You don't know my father!"

However, Rommey's eyes seemed to melt with laughter. "Move in with me," he suggested.

"Oh, sure," Kelley answered bitterly. "As it is, he's hardly talking to me. Don't get me to tell how bad it is!"

"Hmm," Rommey said. Then, after a pause, "When is Gregor coming back? David said he asked you to marry him."

As Kelley stared at him, two tears trickled down her cheeks. She wiped them away with an impatient gesture. "He left for the South Seas without telling me, and, and—" Her voice faded.

"What's that? Oh, bummers! Just what you needed!"

"I haven't heard from him since. Nobody seems to know what has happened to him." She stood to reach for a towel to dry her face.

Rommey put his hands gently on Kelley's shoulders. "Poor baby," he said. "You're kinda *stuck in yesterday*, aren't you? Well, don't worry, we'll pull you through."

Then, suddenly, her tear-stained face was on his shoulder, and his arms were tight about her. "Oh, Rommey! You remember!" she said between tears and laughter. "You are such a good friend. I'm so lucky."

"Sure, sure, but you're in love with another guy!" He sighed. "It always happens to me."

Tenderly, softly, she answered him. "You know that I think you are wonderful. Thank goodness that you found me this morning. Look, you go to your meeting and I'll stay just until I clean the kitchen."

Loath to release her from his arms, Rommey moaned, "Why does every nice girl that I meet have to be head over heels in love with some other guy?"

"Maybe I can come tomorrow," Kelley said.

"Yeah, yeah. We'll have a chance to rap a little. I'll fry abalone for you. You come tomorrow." Rommey withdrew his arms, gave her a pat on the shoulder, turned and left the room.

It was not until a week later, however, that Kelley appeared at Rommey's door well after the dinner hour. He needed only to look at her to tell that she was downcast and distraught. She greeted him briefly, threw her sweater on the floor and sprawled face downward on the couch.

Rommey curled up beside her, one arm flung over her back. Three minutes passed before Kelley turned over suddenly, catapulting Rommey roughly to the floor. He laughed at himself and edged back up beside her with such antics that soon she was laughing with him.

"Hey," he said, "I dig that noise!"

She raised up on her elbow, gave him another push that sent him back to the floor. But Rommey was quick to pull her with him as he fell. They wrestled for a few minutes until Kelley conceded the match and lay on the floor giggling.

"Rom," she gasped, "do you know that I got through the day today only because I knew that I could come here to talk to you tonight? I feel so much better already."

Rommey propped himself on his elbow. "It's that bad at home?"

She sat up and smoothed the silky strands of her long hair. "Dad won't talk to me except when he absolutely has to," she confided in a low tone. "It's driving me up the wall, Rom. I can't stand it any longer and I don't know what to do."

Sitting cross-legged, he combed his fingers through his own unkempt beard. "My roommate is gone. My *pad is big enough for two.*"

Without seeming to have heard him, Kelley stood up, still arranging her hair. "I realize that Dad is in a state of shock and very bitter, but I just can't stand to be in the house any—"

"Look out!" Rommey shouted. "Don't knock that plant down! That is my rare insect-eating specimen. Man, is it hard to grow! Eats nothing but insects. I try to fool it with hamburger, but no sir! Nothing but insects. It's hungry right now."

Carefully, she stilled the swaying plant, eyeing it cautiously. "Come on, Rom! You're joshing me."

"No, no!" Rommey replied soberly. "I'm serious. Come for a walk with me. We'll find some moths or gnats. Mosquitoes or spiders are good, too. I'll show you how to feed it."

"Rom, I do believe you *are* serious!"

"Right on!" He smoothed his curly sideburns and reached out toward her.

She took his hand and allowed him to lead her into the night. "When did you get interested in plants?" she asked. "I thought you'd be out organizing demonstrations and stuff like that."

He looked at her reproachfully. "I'm keeping the plants for a friend. These are not ordinary plants. Let me tell you about this one variety. It curls up and makes a squeaky sound when your breath hits it, like it's talking back to you!"

Rommey rambled on giving Kelley no chance to dwell on her troubles. It was late when he walked her home as far as the shadow of her patio, lingering there only until he was certain that she was safely inside.

After that evening, Kelley came more often, and several weeks passed by. Then one evening she came with a letter in her hand.

On seeing it, Rommey smiled. "Good news, I hope," he said.

Kelley sprawled on the couch as usual and made a small, grunting sound. "From Kimo," she explained. "He has friends who travel through those Polynesian islands, and one of them thinks he might know where Gregor went."

Rommey stroked his luxurious beard and appeared perplexed. "How is it that Roy doesn't know where he left Gregor?"

She shrugged her shoulders. "Roy knows where they did the filming, but the Ahkars own several little islands here and there, and they took Gregor to one of their hide-away places. Roy knows less than Kimo does about it." She shook her head despairingly. "I just don't know what to make of it all!"

A heavy frown clouded Rommey's broad features. "The guy must be off his rocker to keep a girl like you waiting!" he exploded.

"The thing that bothers me the most is his not writing me or calling or something!"

Rommey hesitated as he noticed Kelley's lip begin to quiver. Gently, he lifted her chin with his hand. The lights in his eyes faded with sadness. "Why don't you forget him?" he asked softly.

Struggling to keep her control, Kelley stammered, "Rommey, uh, do you—" She bit her lip. "Do you—you think that he has, uh, found another girl?"

Rommey lifted his eyes heavenward. "Oh, far out! Faa—aar out!" He puffed a breath of air. "Look, are you really in love with the guy? I mean, really in love?"

Kelley nodded her head vigorously. "Really!"

He stood for a few seconds in thought. Then he rubbed his hands together briskly. "Salome is hungry," he said with a change in his tone.

She stared at him. "Who?"

"Salome," he repeated briskly, pointing to his plant. "I named my plant Salome. And you won't believe this, but I found a plant that throws a blossom when you waft it with alcohol fumes."

Kelley continued to stare. "An alcoholic plant? Now, you are kidding me again, Mobe." She pretended to step on his foot.

"*Mobe. Mobe.* I like that. You're feeling a little better, aren't you?" He grinned broadly. "But, no, I'm not kidding you. It'll be here tomorrow." Rommey pointed to still another plant. "I call this one my sunny-day umbrella plant."

With a curious toss of her head, she asked, "Why do you call it that?"

"Well, touch it and you'll see."

Kelley fingered one leaf. The leaves and stems began to droop until all of them hung vertically against the main stalk. "Oh, Rom! Oh, no! I've killed it," she moaned.

"No, you haven't. It just folds up when you touch it. Like an umbrella on a sunny day. Isn't that far out?"

"But—but, I've ruined it!"

"Uh-uh. It will recover in a couple of hours. You'll see."

"What makes it do that?" Kelley continued to stare at the wilted plant. "Is it from the heat of my hand?"

"No. You disturbed its plumbing."

"Plumbing?"

"Yes, its water balance. A very slight touch disturbs its water balance."

"But, I hardly—"

"Let me explain. All that supports the leaves and branches of this particular plant is a series of swellings that are a part of a plumbing system of thin walled cells. This finely balanced system gives the plant rigidity or turgor when the distribution is just right. The very slightest stimulus can make the balance go haywire and the plant collapses."

Kelley examined the little tree ruefully. "It does look like a closed parasol. It will get better, won't it, Rom?"

"Yeah, yeah. Don't worry. It becomes turgid again when the plant pushes its protoplasm to the limits of the cell walls and stretches them tight."

With new admiration, Kelley eyed him sharply. "Rommey, you surprise me. You really surprise me! What else do you know?"

"Come on. We'll rap some more as we walk." With a broad grin, Rommey reached for her hand. "We'll watch for the red tide. There's supposed to be one tonight."

She took his hand with renewed confidence as they started for the beach.

XXX

"...stop hating one man...stop loving another..."

Overwhelmed by his loss, Christopher Holliss had become depressed. He was bitter about the changes in his household, irritable when routine did not go smoothly and dismayed when his children did not understand him.

Pain from the stomach ulcer he had developed forced him to come home early one afternoon after a visit to his doctor. He found Karla stealthily closing the patio door as Jose disappeared down the beach stairs.

His eye swept from the clutter on the counters in the kitchen to the beribboned bottle of wine only half hidden behind his daughter. On another day he might have been more subtle, but today his patience was a bubble of water disappearing on a hot pan.

"What is going on here?" he demanded. "Karla, what makes you think that you can disobey me?"

His tone frightened Karla. Her face reddened as she stammered, "Let me explain, Dad. He only—"

"Where is the cleaning lady?" Christopher walked into the living room, kicking the sofa pillows that were on the carpet. "What is this obstacle course you have here? What are you trying to do to me?"

His daughter stumbled in her haste to replace the cushions. "Just a few things are out of place, Dad. We—I was playing miniature golf on the carpet."

The scowl on Christopher's forehead deepened. "Karla, how many times have I warned you not to be seeing Jose? How many times must we go through this? It's bad enough that you're fooling your time away instead of tidying the kitchen." He waved at the mess in the kitchen sink. "We can't just stack the dishes until Carmella comes once a week. You kids have to shoulder a bit of responsibility. Where is Kelley? Where is David?"

"David didn't come home and Kelley is down at Rom—" Involuntarily, her hand went over her mouth.

Christopher glowered. "Good God! Don't tell me that she's seeing that bum again! Well, I'll put an end to that, too. I've had about enough, especially for today. The last straw is Jose's sneaking up here, bringing you wine!"

Snatching the bottle, he poured the contents into the sink.

Karla let out a cry. "Daddy, don't! Please! He made it for me. It's cherry cordial to be put away for a year!" However, the bottle was drained. "Oh, no!" Karla groaned. She turned and fled, slamming the door behind her.

At the sound of another footstep, Christopher's deeply pained eyes swung to Kelley who stood in the doorway. "Daddy, you shouldn't treat Karla like that," she said. "Mom wouldn't have let you be so mean."

Like a wounded bear only aware of pain, Christopher faced his older daughter. His voice was barely audible, carrying a harsh finality that Kelley had never heard from him before.

"Understand this." The words came slowly. "If you meet that filthy, degenerate hippie one more time, you will no longer be welcome in this house."

Kelley's hand trembled as she pushed a strand of hair from her forehead. Time hung heavily as they regarded each other through a haze of pain. Slowly Kelley became aware of the ticking of the kitchen clock.

"Yes," came her murmur. "I understand."

Christopher closed his eyes and turned away with his hand over his aching stomach. When he looked again, she was gone. Conscious only of his own troubles, he surveyed the kitchen. His eye caught his reflection in the mirror that Vanessa had hung in the breakfast nook. He began to loosen his tie, but his eyes came back to the haggard face in the mirror. Beads of perspiration stood on his forehead. His hand shook as he smoothed his graying hair.

"God, Chris! What is happening?" he whispered. His fist banged on the counter and came in contact with the ribbon that had been on Karla's bottle of wine. Christopher read the printing on the small card. *Happy Birthday to Karla.* His jaw sagged and a groan escaped as realization flooded over him. "Good God, what have I done?"

With Jose's card clutched in his hand, he let his chair swallow him. Soft music filled the room. Christopher's head fell back on the headrest. He closed his eyes and tried not to think of the pain gnawing at his insides. Immediately, his mind flooded with reflections...*why does this have to happen to me?...Vanessa...I can't go this alone...why did you leave me?...I can't pull myself together...I forgot Karla's birthday and I picked this afternoon to fight with her...I'll rest for a minute before I go make it up to her and Kelley too...didn't mean to bear down so hard....*

When Chris awoke several hours later, Carmella was there. The table was set for one.

"I warmed your dinner, Mr. Holliss," Carmella said as she fumbled for something in her pocket. "Karla said that Sally is giving a birthday party for her tonight. David is not here. And Kelley—" Carmella shook her head. "Kelley wrote this note for you, and left with a suitcase."

"*Sorry, Dad. I'm leaving,*" the note read.

Christopher tried to cover his consternation. "Uh, Carmella, I'm not very hungry yet. I'll eat a little later. Thanks for coming."

He waited until the door closed behind her. Then he read the note again. He read it aloud. The words echoed in his ears. "*Sorry, Dad. I'm leaving. I'm leaving...I'm leaving.*"

Muttering to himself and swearing softly, Christopher walked slowly through the darkening house. At the bar, he poured Scotch and milk into a glass.

Dropping dejectedly into his chair, he continued to mumble, "Tastes terrible without ice, but it's better for my stomach. Never realized how big and empty this house could be." Christopher concentrated on the liquid in his glass as he waited for the effects of it to numb the chaos in his life.

The glass was almost empty when Christopher was startled by the doorbell. He pulled the entry door open gruffly and stood staring wordlessly at Nichole Vincett.

She looked small and frightened as she said, "Mr. Holliss, I'm having an awful time trying to locate Gregor. Can you help me?"

Christopher's conscience spoke loudly within him—*that makes two of us with problems that can't be solved and I think I need more help than she does.*

"You do remember me, Mr. Holliss?" Nichole asked uncertainly. "I'm Nichole Vincett."

"Oh, yes, yes! Come in, please. I was searching my mind for the latest bits of information we've had about Gregor. Here, here, sit on the sofa. Can I get you a drink? Coffee? Coke?"

"No, no, I don't want to trouble you."

"I was about to mix myself another Scotch. It's no trouble."

Nichole looked at the milk-stained glass. "Some Coke would be fine, thank you."

Gathering his composure as he filled the glasses, Christopher reviewed Gregor's venturings. "—then they bought a new boat in Maui and promised Kelley to come back in a week. Kelley said that she and Gregor were going to get married, but Gregor got a job making a film for some wealthy Samoan family on some remote South Pacific island that nobody can find."

"I understand that Roy has returned."

"Yes, but he can't figure out where the island is because it's hidden so well."

"But he went there once."

"The first time, he was taken there. The location was kept a secret. There are countless small islands and many groups of islands. Gregor seems to have simply faded out of sight. Kelley has been quite upset."

The sudden flash in Nichole's black eyes at the mention of Kelley did not escape Christopher's attention as he handed her a glass. He found himself watching her closely as he eased back into his chair.

She breathed deeply. "I understand that Kelley is back."

"Yes. She's been here since the end of January, just a week after my wife di—" Christopher's voice caught in his throat. He swallowed hard.

There was an awkward pause. "I'm really sorry about Mrs. Holliss. Sorry is always such an empty expression. I know it doesn't help to say it." She hesitated again. "I realize how hard it is to go on alone." Nichole twisted a strand of her black hair and leaned forward as though ready to leave. "Am I keeping you from anything important, Mr. Holliss?"

"Oh, no! You're not keeping me from a thing. It's so nice to hear a cheerful voice in the house." He drew out a handkerchief and blew his nose loudly.

"Could—could I talk to Kelley?"

"Kelley isn't here. Karla isn't either. Her friend is having a birthday party for her tonight."

"Well, when will Kelley be home?"

Christopher looked away, wondering how to avoid the subject. "Kelley has been distant and understandably upset. Gregor's behavior has depressed her terribly." His first impulse not to tell gave way to a second thought. "Now she's run away." He handed Kelley's note to Nichole. "It's partly my fault, I'll admit. I don't know what to do. I haven't really felt well in weeks. I fell asleep in my chair this afternoon and didn't wake up until the evening news came on."

Nichole's hand tightened around her glass. "Then you probably heard about the accident that Rex was in."

"On the evening news? Rex?" Christopher stroked his chin. "Do you mean the wreck in Chula Vista? Oh, yes, one kid got killed. There was dope involved. The driver was injured. Martyne, that was his name."

"That was Rex." Nichole lowered her head and her face seemed drained of color.

Christopher whistled softly. "Drugs. That's bad news. How did he get mixed up in a smuggling operation?"

"Mr. Holliss, I just don't know!" Nichole toyed with her glass again.

"Please, please," Christopher said with a wave of his hand, "call me Chris. Have you seen Rex lately?"

"I haven't seen him in months. He promised me so many times that he wouldn't touch pot again. Now he's in even deeper trouble. He left my gun in his car."

"A gun? You had a gun?"

She nodded. "I travel a lot and drive at night alone. I felt safer with one."

"Well, why was it in Rex's car?"

Her hand drifted unsteadily over her eyes. "I threatened him."

With pursed lips, Christopher hesitated. "You threatened him?"

"Yes. I threatened him with it one night, and—and he—he took it that night."

Christopher leaned forward in his seat. "Are you saying that you threatened him with a gun?" He regretted his question the next instant when Nichole's eyes rolled upward and she slumped forward onto the coffee table. With his heart pounding against his ribcage, he reached to shift her weight back to the sofa. He massaged her hands and sighed with relief when her eyes opened. "I'll get some ice water." He turned away but stopped as she started to cry.

Shouldn't ask too many questions, he thought. She has problems worse than mine...poor kid is really uptight...maybe something hot would be good....

Not certain of what he should do, he hovered over her. "I'll make some coffee," he said, but Nichole shook her head. Uneasily, he settled back in his chair. "I don't mean to pry," he began softly, "but I'm a good listener."

It was then that Nichole poured out the story of how Rex had followed her home from Gregor's place and had broken into her dressing room. She described the scene that had followed the violent argument. She stammered out the story of how Rex had left her unconscious and had taken her gun.

Christopher listened in disbelief until she finished. "Have you told anyone about this?"

She shook her head. "My father would have torn him to shreds! You know how principled my family is. I am too, Mr. Hol—Chris. I was educated by nuns in Spain until I came back to California. I guess I'm not like these young people with no morals." Her hand trembled slightly as she dried the side of her face. "Rex might—might have killed me," she said in a half whisper. Then she looked up and added, "We might have killed each other."

Christopher's arm shot out again as she lowered her head. "Easy now," he said, gently.

She rewarded him with an appreciative glance. "Uh, I'll take that offer of coffee now, Chris."

"How can Gregor help you, Nichole?" he asked as they made their way to the kitchen.

"Promise not to tell anyone?"

"I swear."

"I want him to help me get settled in Hawaii. I'm going there for a couple months." Her voice had grown steady and her composure returned.

"To get away from Rex, possibly?"

"Partly. I think Rex is doing these things to worry me, to get even with me. Maybe he can straighten himself out if I'm not around."

"I doubt that anyone can find Gregor, Nichole."

Nichole's head came up. "I'll find him," she said.

Christopher met her steady gaze as he allowed opinions to form...determined woman...a lady with old-fashioned principles is rare these days...by God...she *will* find Gregor....

"Let us know when you do," he said. "Let Kelley know."

Nichole toyed with her cup for a few seconds before asking, "Uh, does Kelley still think that she is in love with Gregor?"

"I wish I knew. I hope *she* knows. She has always idolized him and I just hope that she knows the difference between that and love."

"Do you know how long I have been in love with him?" Nichole asked. Then she laughed. "I could write an Odyssey." She turned to thumb through pamphlets on Vanessa's bookshelf.

"Well, Kelley is too young to get married. She should finish school. She needs time to know herself better." Christopher shook his head. "Gregor is—is a strange personality. He seems to have a quality that makes women fall in love with him."

Nichole's smile had a bitterness to it. "Yes, I know."

"Feeling a little better?" Christopher asked.

Still feigning interest in the bookshelf, she answered, "I wish I could find a book here on how to *stop hating one man* and how to *stop loving another*." There was a pause as pages turned. Suddenly, Nichole laughed. "Yes, I feel better. You'll probably never know how much you've helped me."

But Christopher did know. As he looked at Nichole, he thought...*she'll never know how long it's been since I've heard someone laugh in this house...we both needed to talk....*

By the time Nichole had turned back from browsing on the bookshelf, the moisture which had welled in Christopher's eyes had been replaced with a calm he hadn't felt in months.

Life was beginning to lose some of its grim outlook for Christopher by the time Easter had come. At least, all was going well at his office. His desk was in perfect order once more, the files were updated and the week had brought several large, new accounts. His ties were new and narrow and he brushed his hand over a crew cut which was stiff after yesterday's visit to the barber.

At the end of the day, he surveyed his office critically before he reached to turn off his lamp. The light fell on Nichole's last letter. Taking up the many pages, he settled back in his chair to scan the contents once again.

"...and from all the information I have, it seems that Roy is in the Delta doing underwater studies of pollution. If I had known, I would have talked to him there first. However, here on Maui, I was able to locate Wayne, the mechanic who helped Roy on his South Seas trip. I must talk to him once more. It is true that Gregor and Roy purchased the sailing vessel from a Samoan gentleman who owns a whole fleet of them. The man's name is Ahkar, but it was his nephew whose yacht docked alongside Roy's ship that first day on Maui. Wayne said that when the Ahkars saw all the camera equipment and determined that Roy and Gregor were photographers, they promptly offered Roy an irresistible sum to do the photography for their festival. It seems that there was a native girl aboard who appeared to be giving the orders and who seemed to be captivated by Gregor, ultimately insisting that he sail with them as security for the advance sum they paid Roy, but Gregor might have gone anyway. According to Wayne, she was the most sensuous and beautiful woman he had ever seen. However, since Wayne has some Samoan blood in his own veins, who can say with what prejudice he judged the degree of her beauty? It seems that Roy caught up with the yacht later somewhere in the Gilbert Islands. From there, they ferried him and Gregor to another island. When they finished their film and were ready to leave, they couldn't find Gregor. Then they got a message telling them to leave without him. Feeling that Gregor might have been detained against his will as a further guarantee, they waited around three more days before leaving. As far as being detained against his will, since Gregor is a man with a strong mind of his own, he could certainly escape if he wanted to. Knowing Gregor as I do, it becomes hard for me to believe that it is this woman who attracts him, or their way of life, or the salary they might offer, and so it remains a mystery. He is not the kind who would forget his obligation to his company, to Roy, to Kelley and most importantly to himself. Then I begin to think that possibly, *Madre de Dios*, he has lost his mind completely! *Amigo precioso....*"

Christopher did not finish the rest of the letter which was written in excellent Spanish. He nodded his head with satisfaction as he replaced the letter in his pocket, withdrawing at the same time the answer he had already penned. His eyes jumped to the paragraph about Gregor.

"...and since you are so determined to find him, please contact Kimo, whose address is enclosed. Kimo has friends throughout the Polynesian chain, and somebody will find a clue soon. I don't understand why you keep your mission so secretive, but my promise to keep your confidence holds. In the meantime, I have advised your family not to worry and that you will return when you can. Keep me informed as to...."

The telephone rang and he replaced the note in his pocket.

"This is Dr. Roper's office calling for Mr. Holliss," a brisk voice said.

"This is Mr. Holliss." Christopher tapped the desk while he waited and allowed his thoughts to drift back to Vanessa, to when they had first met on a blind date at the university, to the night he asked her to wear his pin. The sound from the instrument startled him when it came.

"Hello, Chris! How's the golf these days?"

"Getting out more often. Played yesterday," Christopher answered.

"That's great! How are you hittin' em?"

"Well—ll," Christopher replied hesitatingly, "I didn't hurt myself."

The doctor's laugh came over the line. "Get yourself out there regularly now."

"Oh, I'm starting to play again, Ken. My game's gone to pot. Handicap went up to nine. But you know how it's been at home with Vanessa gone. Lord! Am I beginning to appreciate what wives go through running a household and raising kids! I don't understand what is wrong with young people these days! You give them everything and they expect more, but with no responsibility for anything. It wasn't that way when I grew up."

"It was the same with me, Chris. I got the back of his hand if I didn't say 'yessir' to my father and do what he asked right then."

Christopher chuckled softly. "I didn't even know what it was to get out of line," he confessed.

There was a pause before the doctor continued. "I don't know where the time goes. I suppose David is ready to graduate."

"He would be if he'd stay in school. He skipped a quarter for the Mexican tour."

"And Karla?"

Christopher sighed. "Karla needs a woman's understanding. She was close to her mother. Perhaps I should have had her finish her education at a private school, but it's too late now. And I might as well tell you about Kelley because you'll ask. Kelley packed and left."

"Yes, I know."

"You know? Do you know that she has the gall to be staying with some no-good hippie right here in the Village?" Christopher's laugh was bitter.

"You've tried to find her?"

"Oh, my, yes, but this character moves just as fast as you can locate him. I'm worried sick about Kelley." Christopher gritted his teeth. "Someone better tie my hands when I find that son-of-a-bitch hippie, because I'm going to break his neck!"

"Chris," the voice continued, dropping a tone, "the purpose of my call is to tell you that Kelley came in to see me yesterday."

Christopher froze. "Is she all right?" he managed to ask.

The voice was calm and low. "She came in to—"

"Just tell me if she is all right!" He wiped perspiration from his brow with the back of his hand.

"Now, Chris, if you'll listen to me for a minute, I'll tell you all I know. She came to me for some medication for some abdominal pain she is having."

"Pain? Good Lord, if she is, uh—" He stopped abruptly. "What is causing it?"

"She wouldn't let me examine her," the doctor answered. "She probably would feel more comfortable with someone else. I want your approval before I send her to another office, Chris."

"To whom?"

"Maybe to Bert or to Chuck."

Christopher sucked in his breath. "Obstetricians! Mother of God! She's pregnant!"

"Correction," the doctor's voice came chidingly. "Gynecologists. Please don't jump to conclusions, Chris. It sounded more like a gynecological problem, possibly

219

in combination with a stress reaction. She also mentioned that she hurt her back."

"How? How did she hurt her back?"

"She said she got tossed around badly in a rough surf just before the onset of pains."

"Oh," Christopher said as he transferred the receiver from one sweaty palm to the other. "Oh, very well. Very well, do what you think is best. I'll go along with whatever you recommend."

"Fine. I'll get to it in the morning."

"Did you get her address?"

"No," the voice replied. "She wouldn't leave her phone number either. She prefers to call me."

"How is she otherwise? Is she getting enough to eat?" Christopher asked anxiously.

"She's a little thin. Depressed. A little droopy because her friend had given her sleeping pills and a muscle relaxant, so Kelley said."

"He could be, uh—," Christopher began. "Hmm. He could be giving her drugs. Good God! What next?" He brought his fist down forcefully on his desk.

There was a pause. "I don't think we should assume anything until we have reason to, Chris. I'll follow this up as closely as I can," the doctor's voice came reassuringly.

"Let me know what you find out." Christopher's fingers drummed nervously on the desk.

"Whatever I can. Remember that I have to keep my patient's confidence, too. But if it is anything serious, you'll hear from me. And, in the meantime, take care of yourself, Chris."

Christopher prayed silently. "I appreciate what you've done, old friend," he said.

"Hold it down, now."

"Yeah, yeah, if God gives me strength," Christopher answered. "I'll try, but if you find me behind bars, it will be because I've killed that bastard hippie!"

XXXI

"...the shark incident was a hoax..."

ummer in the Village had all but passed, but not for Karla Holliss. Jose was competing in the Rough-Water Swim, and she was one of the first to arrive at the Cove early on the morning of the event, with a sack lunch to ward off starvation because the starting time was not until two o'clock. However, Karla knew that the available seating would fill quickly and she was determined to see Jose plunge into the surf.

The pink puff of smoke in the sky signaled the beginning of the activities with the descent of sky divers, an added attraction this year. Invisible at times as they drifted through scattered fog layers toward the smoke, the divers finally splashed into the swells.

Karla watched patiently until the advanced divisions finally plowed into the waves. A man behind her kept a running commentary. "Water's cold for this time of year. Swell is getting choppy. Look, it's slowing them down." He was still expounding on the wiles of the currents as the swimmers began to round the buoy and disappear from sight on the second leg of the course. Karla gathered her belongings and started to bicycle to the beach where the race would end. She was out of breath when she arrived, but not half as much as Jose who thrashed through the surf with David not far behind, not in time to win, however.

Accepting consolations, Jose was anxious to know the winner's time and soon the announcement came over the loudspeaker. "Twenty-two minutes, fourteen seconds."

Karla offered comfort. "After all, Jose, he probably trained daily, a lot more than either of you did. Anyway, the two of you looked great."

Jose shook the water from his ears. It was the exact same gesture he had used as a thin teenager. However, Jose now filled out his six-foot height. "Well, I'm glad the sun finally came out bright," he said as he took the towel she handed him. Wrapping it about his lean hips, he pointed to a girl in the center of a crowd. "Say, isn't that the daughter of the man who swam the course alone that year of the shark scare to prove it was safe?"

"Yes," Karla said. "He didn't want them to cancel the event."

David's eyes twinkled. "Karla wouldn't remember that far back. They were still feeding her pablum."

"Did they?" Jose asked.

"They sure did!" David replied, grinning from ear to ear as he dodged the

221

wet towel that his sister threw at him. "She used to like it mixed with bananas."

"Jose means did they cancel the swim, you dummy!" Karla turned to Jose. "They cancelled it. They couldn't take chances. There wasn't much swimming done that summer until people forgot about the man-eating shark being around."

"Oh, drivel!" David said. "There is no such thing as a man-eating shark, I mean a shark that just likes to eat people."

Karla frowned at her brother. "You don't think that the shark ate that diver? The court declared him eaten by a shark."

"No, no," David interjected. "That's not what I'm saying. I mean that sharks don't hunt people. They probably even try to avoid people for all we know. But they do eat anything that smells of blood, and that shark was following the guy who came in with a bleeding leg. Blood makes them go into a frenzy."

"Oh, turtlepooh, David!" Karla argued. "You are making it sound as though that shark ate the guy by mistake."

"Sure, he did," David insisted.

"David, that's dumb!" Karla pursued.

"Well," Jose interrupted, "there are people who say that the whole *shark incident was a hoax*. Just the other day, I heard two guys argue about it." He shook his head once again to clear his ears of water. "It's still a hot issue."

At this, David's features grew sober. "Some guy thinks that *that* shark was a hoax? Well, I can tell you that it wasn't. Man, oh, man! Listen to Kelley's story and you won't think it's a hoax. She just missed being fish food that day. You ask her if it was all a fake. I wish she were here to show you the scar on her leg!"

At the mention of her sister, a wistful expression crossed Karla's face. "I wish Kelley were here, too. This is the first Swim she has missed. It doesn't seem right, her not being here."

David pressed his lips together. "No, it doesn't seem right. I agree, it's not like Kelley. Tomorrow, I'll try again to find her. And," he added as he put his hand gently on her shoulder, "I don't think she has forgotten."

It was true. Kelley had not put them out of her mind. At that moment, she stood by the window of a small room overlooking the course that the swimmers had taken. She was saying to herself...*I feel so trapped...as though something had me in its grip or tied so I can't breathe...trapped by this pain in my side and this loneliness...and not being able to forgive Dad and the world for doing this to me...if I could just figure out how to get free...not to be stuck in yesterday...oh Kelley, what is wrong with you...why aren't you down there skimming over the sand with the birds...just what is wrong....*

In exasperation, she struck the pile of books on the table beside her, sending them tumbling to the floor. Had Gregor been there to see her, he might not have thought that this was the same girl he had watched so often running free and wild at the water's edge. Indeed, she wasn't. Bewildered and depressed by the turn of events that surrounded her in the months since January, Kelley had changed.

At that instant, she heard Rommey's footstep and she bent hurriedly to retrieve the volumes, but instead she clutched her side and cried out in pain as he came in sight.

Gently, he forced her onto the sofa and waited for her breath to come more easily before he spoke.

"I have news for you, little girl," he said with a firm tone. "You are going to a doctor whether you want to or not. When you pass out like you did yesterday, there's gotta be something really bad going on." He was on his knees, bending over her anxiously, and now he raised one knee on which he leaned with his muscled forearm. "You shouldn't be left alone. I worry about you all day long. You're a sick girl and I have to find someone to take care of you."

Kelley's lip quivered. "Whatever you think is best." She patted his arm tenderly. "I shouldn't be a burden to you."

He stroked his thick beard nervously. "Look, I'm no doctor and if anything happens to you...what I'm trying to say is that you aren't any burden. There is just so much I can do. I'm worried."

"I understand," she answered with a sigh. Her glance followed his as he scanned the book-strewn floor. "I got tired of reading all day long. It's so boring when I run out of things to do. Look, I've even written poetry to keep busy." She pointed to some papers lying on the table.

Taking the papers, he scanned a few lines.

Shine, shine, flicker of sun
To tell us our time is near done.
All too soon, men will toil
And fill the earth with sweat and soil.
So climb, climb, cloud in the sky,
And look at the land and cry.

"You are depressed, I can tell. Anyone would be under the circumstances, cooped up like this and feeling rotten. I gotta find a place for you." He stepped over to examine several unpacked boxes in the corner of the room. "Look, I'll finish the unpacking. Don't touch a thing, understand? It was a bad time to be moving."

She watched him as he adjusted an old tarp over the unpacked crates. "Rom, will you tell me something?" she asked.

"Yes," he replied, bending over the fallen books. "What is it?"

"You have me so puzzled. Tell me if—"

"Tell me if what?" He continued to pick up the novels.

Kelley allowed her features to wrinkle with a small twitch that was reminiscent of her younger days. Then she started again. "Tell me why you move around so much." When he seemed to recoil, she continued, "Rom, I'm on to you! You aren't the crummy guy you pretend to be, are you? I think I realized that from the beginning. It's all a front, isn't it?"

The smile in his eyes had disappeared. His face darkened in a glower. "You women!" he exploded. "Can't you ever be happy with things the way they are? I'll never learn!" He banged two books together.

Alarmed, Kelley sat upright. "Let me explain. One of those boxes broke at the bottom. A paper was sticking out in plain sight. Don't be so upset, please."

Rommey frowned. "Why can't women learn to mind their own business? Why do you go poking your noses into a guy's affairs! I just didn't expect that you would start prying and playing detective. Not you, Kelley." He gritted his teeth. "I'll never learn!"

Stunned by the fury of his response, she began again to explain. "I wasn't prying. I was trying to clean this place up a little. I ran out of books to read."

He kicked a book out of his path. "Well, I'll get you some more to read so you'll stay out of my things," he retorted sourly. "I'm going out to work on—" The door banged behind him.

What have I done, she thought dejectedly as she began replaying their conversation in her mind. She became aware of the sounds of Rommey working on his car in the street.

He frowned as she sat down on the sidewalk by the car. "I won't ask any more questions, Rom. Forgive me. I won't say a word to anyone. I promise. Can't we pretend this didn't happen? Please?"

The moment of silence seemed forever to Kelley. When he spoke, his tone was still brusque. "Tomorrow, you are going to a doctor. Understand?"

"All right. All right, as long as it isn't someone in the Village. If someone thought I might be pregnant and that got around the Village, my father would die of shame. You don't know my family."

"I know! Believe me, I know." Rommey looked up from his work. "You *are* sure it isn't a pregnancy?"

Kelley grinned as she shook her head convincingly. Then she chuckled softly. "Dad would think it was your fault," she teased.

He stood upright, still scowling. "Wrong, and not very funny. Get this. I'm not the kind of heel who would screw my friend's girl."

"Oh." Kelley's smile faded.

Rommey's voice softened as he continued. "Now, if she loved me, that would be different."

She touched his shoulder tenderly. "Oh, Rommey," she murmured apologetically.

He ran his fingers through his hair, tumbling the rich curls in all directions. His expression changed. "I've got it! A plan just came to me. Really cool. There is a nurse I know really well in San Francisco. She'll help you. She is engaged to a doctor. Does welfare work and is working on a thesis for a degree. She could use a typist and there is some stuff you could help her with. We'll phone her today and drive up there tomorrow. I have to go up there for something anyway. Why didn't I think of this before?"

They had made their way back into the house and Kelley curled up on the sofa again. "I'm tired, Rom. I'll do whatever you say. I'll go," she told him as he spread a quilt over her. "You're such a neat guy, Mobe."

Rommey looked at her sharply, hoping to find a deeper meaning in her words. Then he turned away with a sigh and went to the telephone.

XXXII

"...go home and forget him..."

The big island of Hawaii was the site of Kimo's coffee plantation. Frequently, his business took him to the islands to the south. Whenever he traveled, he contacted friends who might help in the search for Gregor. This time, he returned with vague information about one of the palaces of the Ahkar family, reportedly the resort in which Gregor was a guest.

Kimo had been forewarned by Christopher Holliss that Nichole would be making inquiries of him. Countless messages on Kimo's desk bore witness to Nichole's untiring attempts. A dozen brief telephone conversations preceded the day when Kimo was finally able to meet her for lunch.

Nichole wasted no time in stating her mission again: to find Gregor wherever he might be. Kimo listened attentively. His richly embroidered white shirt contrasted sharply with his dark skin and hung loosely over a superb physique.

When Nichole finally paused, Kimo asked curiously, "If I may inquire, just how well do you know Gregor?"

Nichole looked down as she smoothed the folds of her bright muumuu. Then her chin came up and the fiery black eyes which met his did not waiver. "I've been in love with him ever since I met him seven years ago. I thought we would be engaged until that girl from Greece came into his life."

Kimo blinked his eyes, but did not move. "Kelley told me about Nancy, but I never heard of the girl from Greece."

Nichole hesitated, reluctant to speak of Pandora. "She went over a cliff into the ocean in a car that wasn't found until much later."

"How terrible for Gregor," came Kimo's soft, low reply.

"Then Nancy took him to Honolulu for about two years. I never seemed to get a chance to show him that we were right for each other, not even after Nancy left him."

"This other girl, ahh—"

"Pandora."

"She meant a lot to Gregor?"

Nichole nodded, "They were to be married. They knew each other two years."

The brown eyes under the massive brows flickered. "Hurt from losing one you love is not easy to heal. It leaves a man bitter."

Nichole shrugged her shoulders. "Sometimes I think he is bitter toward all women, even me."

225

He eyed her curiously. "Why is that?"

She answered with a sigh. "Gregor thought perhaps Pandora was a victim of a plot against her life. And since the cliff she drove off is not far from my house, he makes me feel that I should have done something to prevent what happened. It's crazy. I knew nothing."

"Could you have?" Kimo asked.

Nichole's eyes flashed. "Could I have what?"

"Could you have prevented it?" Kimo repeated quickly.

"Of course not!" Nichole snorted. "It happened during a flash flood in the middle of the night."

Kimo leaned back and flashed a quick smile of apology. "I don't mean to anger you with all these questions, but I need to know how important it is for you to find Gregor. Traveling these islands is not easy."

Nichole's voice gathered intensity. "I *must find* Gregor. I can't eat, I can't sleep. I can't think of anything else. I must find him while he is free of any other woman."

Still contemplating his guest, Kimo asked, "You know about Kelley, of course?"

Her answer was quick and impatient. "If you knew Gregor at all, you'd realize that a Pollyanna schoolgirl like Kelley could never be a good match for him. She lives in such a dream world that she can't face disillusionment of any kind. She thinks she can simply wish away the ugly facts."

Kimo considered this for a moment. "You wouldn't do the same, Nichole?"

Nichole's eyes blazed brighter and color flooded her cheeks. "Judge for yourself how realistic I am. Gregor and I are suited to each other." A hint of a smile crossed her lips. "Aha! You know something I don't. Something unpleasant. Try me. Don't you understand that I love him? I will do anything."

Kimo tapped the table with the knuckles of one hand. Thoughts had been flashing through his head...*she is small for an American woman...delicate... with a nose like mine....she is so determined...and probably passionate...another woman in love with Gregor...what strange charm does he have over women...even I have never left such a trail of broken hearts....*

"Nichole," he began. Then he pressed his lips together.

Nichole leaned forward. "Kimo, I'm going whether you help me or not, so there is no point in holding anything back."

Giving the table a final rap with his fingers, Kimo said, "Yes, perhaps it's better if you know. Gregor is on an isolated island, unapproachable except by air. It's easy for the Ahkars to detain someone there."

Sparks of light seemed to fly from her wide-open eyes. "You mean he's a prisoner there? It's true, then! *Madre mia!* I must go to him!"

It had occurred to Kimo that while Nichole was very determined, she was also selectively blind. "There's more you should know. There's a woman involved." He braced himself for her reaction.

But Nichole's answer was rapid and controlled. "The girl on Mr. Ahkar's yacht? His daughter?"

"Well, yes and no." Kimo shifted uncomfortably in his chair as he reflected that perhaps, after all, Nichole did not know Gregor well. "Do you know anything of the culture of the various Polynesian peoples?"

"Nothing."

"On some of the remote islands, customs have remained unchanged for centuries. Some still have forms of group marriage that you may not understand." He paused. "This woman has taken Gregor into her group."

Nichole drew back as though he had struck her. She sat staring at Kimo's unyielding scrutiny.

"Are you trying to tell me that Gregor has married Mr. Ahkar's daughter?"

Kimo sighed uncomfortably. "It is not that he has married her. Anyone in this group can bring in another who is acceptable to the group."

Nichole's mouth dropped open, and in a rare moment of speechlessness, the color drained from her face. "I...I just can't believe Gregor is married to a flock of women. Impossible!"

"This one woman seems to keep him to herself."

"How can Mr. Ahkar let his daughter do this?"

Kimo cleared his throat. "She isn't his daughter. She is his youngest wife."

Nichole gasped and leaned back again. "What?" A smothered moan escaped her. "I can't believe what you are saying to me!"

He touched her arm gently. "Do you still want to go?"

Very slowly Nichole's eyes opened wide. This time it was Kimo who faced pools of steely iris. Long before it came, he knew what her answer would be. "Yes, I will go free him."

"Very well. I will arrange transportation and provide you a list of friends who will help you." Kimo pushed back his chair and started to rise.

"Kimo?"

"Yes?" he answered half seating himself again.

"Do you have any advice for me?"

"Yes." Kimo smiled with a sadness in his eyes. "But you won't take it."

"What is it?"

He stood to help her from her chair. *"Go home and forget him."*

XXXIII

"...throw the damn tie away..."

In a shabby part of San Francisco, Polly Pellard received her new roommate and, within a week, took Kelley to a specialist.

"Rommey, it's so hot up here," Kelley complained bitterly over the telephone. "The air is so damp! And the bugs are terrible. I'm not ungrateful. I know Polly is doing me a favor, keeping me and taking me to the doctor. She's been so good to me, but I'm dying of the heat and boredom. I don't know how she can live up here."

Rommey chuckled softly. "Polly's finishing some research for a thesis. She'll leave as soon as it's done. You're in good hands. At least, you got to the doctor and that's progress! Now, tell me what the doctor said."

Kelley swung the telephone cord in little circles as she spoke. "He did a pregnancy test first, a frog test that he feels sure will be negative. Of course, it will take a few days to get the result. Then, as soon as I have some X-rays taken, he can tell for sure what the trouble is."

"What does he think it is?"

"He says it could be a rapidly growing cyst."

There was a brief silence. "A cyst? By damn, it's got to be a big cyst!"

"I know. I know. I can't wear any of my clothes. I'm wearing Polly's smocks."

"Good grief! It's a good thing I got you to a doctor." Rommey sounded relieved. "Did he give you something for pain?"

"Yes, after I fainted in his office."

"What causes all the pain?" Rommey inquired impatiently.

"The doctor said that if the cyst twists, it causes pain," Kelley answered. "He may have to operate."

There was silence. "Oh, bummers! Let me talk to Polly."

"She went off somewhere. Won't be back until Saturday morning. She made me promise to stay inside." Kelley wiped perspiration from her forehead. "I won't die of the pain but I may die of the heat."

"Damn! I wish she hadn't left you alone. Suppose you faint."

"Oh, Rom, don't worry. The doctor said that the pain can't kill me and he told me what to do if I feel dizzy. I'll be all right." Kelley's words voiced an assurance she didn't feel.

"*Don't worry*, you tell me!" Rommey mimicked with exasperation. "You might as well tell me not to *breathe*. You may need surgery and I can't be responsible for you, not when it's something this bad. You're going to have to tell your father now!"

Kelley found herself nervously twisting the cord of the telephone. "You may have to help me."

"Keep cool. I took you up there. I'll get you back. I'll come for you Saturday."

"The test results won't be in and the X-rays can't be taken until Monday."

"The X-rays can be done here. The results can be phoned. We shouldn't waste time. I'm driving to Berkeley anyway on Saturday, but if my plans change, Polly can bring you down."

"But, Rommey!"

"No buts!" Rommey's voice came explosively. "Dig me?"

Rebuffed by his tone, she sighed loudly. "Rom, I don't want doctors who know me to be involved."

Over the phone came the sound of a fist banging on wood. "Oh, brother! You are something else! Grow up! You may be facing serious surgery and all you think of is what people are going to say. Now listen and get this straight! When Polly starts for San Diego on Saturday morning, come with her if you haven't heard from me. Dig me?"

"Okay, Rom. Okay."

"Stay inside. I mean, stay *in-side*! Don't go anywhere. It's only for a few more days."

By now, the telephone cord was a mass of twists. "Okay, Rom," Kelley promised. "I won't go anywhere except out on the deck if it gets unbearable in here. You know the way Polly's porch sticks out over the yard of the downstairs apartment? There's a little breeze out there and I go out there sometimes when nobody's in sight, but some rowdy bunch seems to have rented the place below for the week. You know, Rom, one of the group looked so much like Rex. Is that possible?"

"Possible, not likely. Keep me posted."

Kelley sighed. "I guess I can bear this one more day."

"Right on!" Rommey sounded pleased. "Write some more poetry or something."

"I did. There was so much noise downstairs that I wrote half of the night. I'll write a note for Polly so I won't forget at the last minute." Kelley heard a shuffling sound like the opening of a phone booth door. Loath to lose the sound of his voice, Kelley pressed the receiver closer. "Rom! Rom!"

"Yes?"

"You are such a neat guy, Mobe," she said.

There was a pause. "I'll see you, Sugar." The line was suddenly dead and Kelley was left to untwist the long cord.

Outside the booth, Rommey took two steps and stopped, suddenly wide-eyed. "Sugar! I called her Sugar!" he exclaimed. "I haven't called any girl that since I fell so hard for Connie!"

Through the remainder of the day, Rommey was harassed by the trend of his reminiscing...*damn...I really loved that Connie girl...you can bet I won't get trapped like that again...not with a girl who is in love with another guy...thank God I'm not in love with Kelley...once is enough to get hurt like Connie hurt me...why am I doing all this for Kelley...damned if I know because she just isn't my responsibility...I'll just get her back to her father and then I'm through...I don't want to be blamed...I'd*

229

better talk to him after my meeting tonight...he can't be such a bear when his daughter's health is at stake....

That evening, Rommey drove for the first time over the new Ardath cutoff which led almost directly toward the sprawling red-tiled roof that was a landmark along the water's edge. The lush hills where stallions had romped in emerald pastures and chaparral were gone. Now the land was denuded and laid in naked layers. Rommey scanned the expanse of dirt as his thoughts came like a replay...*the Village can't support more traffic and more sewer lines...more telephone poles and more people on the beaches...the whole side of the hill has changed...the Village is beginning to look like anyplace else....*

In another five minutes, he stood at the top of the stair at the Marine Room. As he looked about, his concern for the land was replaced with other memories, painful reflections that refused to be buried. All too vividly, a scene unfolded and Connie was asking him to wait for a few minutes while she made sure no strand of hair was out of place.

He stepped over to where the tiny seahorses stared back at him with beady eyes, just as they had stared that evening. *It was right on this spot*, Rommey was saying to himself, *that she came and kissed me as though nothing was about to happen...and there is the table where we sat when she told me that she loved that jerk more than she loved me...imagine letting me take her to a steak dinner just to tell me that...huh...that she wanted our last evening together to be a nice one...hell and hell all over again...I boil every time I think of it...no wonder I hate women...nothing seems different tonight...not even the music...even the tide was high...like my hopes...the waves were splashing on the window just like they are doing now...wild...really wild...the whole idea was wild...a beautiful rich girl falling for someone like me...how dumb could I be...no...it won't happen again....*

He went outside again and wandered around the building, through the parking lot and on to where seagoers launched their small craft. Even now, the motor of a car whined as wheels spun helplessly in the soft sand. Rommey's attention focused on the driver attempting to pull his half-submerged trailer and its craft from the surf. It was a sight and sound common to this spot on the beach, just as was the laughter and shouting of the passersby who finally helped to move the car on its way.

Rommey watched, still reminiscing. Then he took the path past the old duck pond, refuge for many a small quacking thing that came with an Easter basket and had since grown ungainly and unwanted. Rommey could hear them making soft noises as he walked back toward the buildings.

Again, memories crowded in, and Rommey found himself thinking...*why do I let Connie equal nostalgia...nostalgia is only a word for a feeling...an attempt to recover something lost with time...a subconscious desire not to have lived further than that point in time...an irretrievable sensation...oh hell....*

Rommey shook himself. "Come on, old boy!" he said loudly. "You stopped loving Connie a long time ago. Remember? Better find the guys. They will be here by now. Hope they make it short because I still have to talk to Mr. Holliss tonight."

Rommey was pleased when the meeting turned out to be brief. He proceeded slowly on Torrey Pines Road in a makeshift lane because (much to the Villagers' disgust) the street was torn up for the second time for major repairs. When he came to Girard Avenue, it was a stretch of void, with hardly any traffic in sight as far as the theater. Deserted, the street looked wider and prouder than ever. It could well be arrogant with its five banks, Rommey thought, and subconsciously he took comfort in its still being an early-to-bed village.

At the Holliss house, he was both disappointed and relieved to find no response to his ring. The house was dark. Rommey decided to wait in his car for Mr. Holliss to return.

"I've just got to talk to him tonight," he kept repeating. He settled himself in the seat and closed his eyes with no intention of falling asleep and programmed himself not to think of Connie.

When he opened his eyes, the sky was blackened by rain clouds. Heavy hail began to make a deafening clatter on his car. Rommey tried to look at his watch. Suddenly he realized he had been asleep and the car had become painfully cold.

"Nuts to this," he grumbled. "I'll go home." He turned the ignition key. The starter grumbled, too. After countless attempts, he sat back, angry and cursing. Pulling his coat over his head, he stepped into the hail, lifted the hood of his car and continued to curse.

"I'll have to get some help," he said. Looking about for a lighted house where he might find someone awake, he gathered courage to knock on half a dozen doors.

"Damnation!" he swore when he found he could arouse no response. "Either everybody has been killed by a raid from outer space or I'm imagining things! Goddammit! I'll walk to the station. I'm halfway there anyway."

As he walked, lightning began to flash ever nearer until it struck directly in front of him, hurling his body through the air. He felt himself carried over the houses perched on the cliffs and deposited on the beach in the boiling surf below. Badly bruised and bleeding, he scrambled toward a sandy place between two huge boulders, the only haven in sight. As he struggled against the angry swells, he stumbled over another body. The water receded enough to reveal that it was Connie. With a strength that surprised him, he tugged at her body, tearing it away from the current and dragging it, face down, onto the strip of sand. Keeping a firm hold on her wet hair, he braced himself for the next deluge. It battered him and receded, leaving him clinging breathlessly to a splinter of rock.

Infuriated, he screamed at the oncoming surge of water. "Stop! Damn you anyway! Can't you see what you are doing to her? Enough! Stop!" He made a gesture of command toward the towering crest as if he were blessed with the power of Moses at the Sea. Then he stood amazed because, as it did for Moses, the water obeyed and became gentle.

Quickly, he lifted the limp body at his feet. "Oh, God, it's not Connie at all," he shouted. "It's Kelley! What the devil! Kelley! Kelley, wake up! What's going on here, anyway?"

At the sound of her name, Kelley opened her eyes and smiled faintly. Rommey stroked her wet hair as he repeated, "I do love her. I do love her." He held her close to him and sighed as a feeling of contentment passed through him. "I do," he repeated. "I do. I do. I do."

Now, a towering figure approached. A hand clutched him by his collar, tearing him away from Kelley and throwing him to his knees.

At this instant, Rommey wakened enough from his dream to realize that Mr. Holliss had taken him by his sleeve and was about to administer a blow that would have knocked him senseless except for David's intervention.

David was pleading loudly as he kept a firm grip on his father's arm. "Don't hit him, Dad! Can't you see that he was just sleeping? He isn't drunk! Stop! Don't! Dad, *don't!*" He struggled to block his father's path.

"Just let me get my hands on him! Didn't you hear him admit that he gave her dope? Didn't you hear him say he does when I asked him?" Christopher fumed as he allowed his son to push him away from Rommey. "Talk about heaping insult on injury! Sleeping off his drugs right here in front of my home! Isn't it enough that he compromised your sister? How does he muster enough gall to come here? Let go of my arm, David, because I'm going to pound him to a pulp!"

Half expecting a blow, Rommey shielded his face with his forearm. "Please listen to me, Mr. Holliss," he begged. "I have to talk to you!"

Christopher only struggled to approach him while David stood his ground, calling over his shoulder to Rommey, "It won't do any good now, Rom. Better leave while I try to calm Dad. Drive down as far as the drug store and wait for me. I want to talk to you."

Rommey nodded to David. "Tell him it's about Kelley. It's important." He rubbed his aching jaw and drove off.

Alone in the living room of his home, Christopher listened to the sound of David's car backing in haste from the driveway. He went to the bar, reached for the Scotch, thought better of it and began to talk to himself.

"I've had enough Scotch for one night. I shouldn't have hit him. I should have talked to him. What's wrong with me, anyway? Dammit! My hand's shaking. Drinking on an empty stomach with my ulcer, it's no wonder. I haven't been eating right. Better warm some coffee. I haven't been doing anything right since Vanessa left. She used to bring out the best in me. I need someone. I can't go on this way. Nothing is right. Even the coffee isn't good anymore. I'll walk on the beach for a little way. Maybe it will steady my nerves."

He emptied his cup and left by the patio door. The wooden steps to the beach were getting old and loosened. Shaky, just like me, he thought . . . I must do something about that . . . nothing is the same . . . look at the water . . . ugly . . . black . . . it used to be comforting . . . I can't understand . . . is it my soul . . . .

Christopher leaned against the cold surface of a boulder and buried his head in the crook of his arm. Chilly sweat stood on his forehead, but warm trickles ran down his cheeks. "Vanessa!" he cried out. "Vanessa, I can't make it alone! It's destroying me. Help me. Don't just abandon me like this. I need you. Oh God, I need you!"

In a moment, he rallied himself. "I'll walk," he said. "But my clothes and my shoes?" he muttered, looking down at his attire. "Oh, to hell with them! I don't really care. I'm tired of always doing the right thing. Convention, convention. I hate it. It's strangling me. Loosen my collar. Throw the damn tie away. Look at what I've done to my kids by trying to make them live by my rules. Yes, *throw the damn tie away!*"

Suddenly a wave knocked him to his knees. *Steady, old man,* he thought...*your reflexes aren't so good tonight...you want a solution...not an end...there has to be a solution...Vanessa always told me what to do...she never let on that she was doing it and I never let on that she did...how can I manage alone...what am I to do now....*

He walked on for some time until he came to a house blazing with lights. Strains of loud music came from within. Hmm, Christopher thought...*I must have been walking fast...Jonathan's place already...Jesus Christ...they must have had some brawl to be going strong at this time of night...people all over the place...I hope nobody recognizes me but there I go again...what the hell do I care if someone knows me...I'm so tired from just that walking...I'll just sit here on the sand for a bit...what in God's name...don't tell me they are setting off fireworks at this time of night...I can just hear what people on the hill are saying about that...good Lord...my eyes must be deceiving me or do I see two people over there in the water?...naked and playing in the surf like two bear cubs...those aren't kids because I can see fat rings around his waist...the woman too...now what kind of example is that to set for our young people...no wonder our kids are going to extremes...this just can't be happening...something is wrong with my eyesight...am I seeing the crest of the wave bounding over the rocks...maybe my mind is playing tricks...I must be tired...lie down for a minute...sleep for just a minute...just a minute....*

Christopher slept for no more than five minutes, or possibly ten, because that much time elapsed before the couple in the water started back across the beach to where their towels lay almost next to Christopher's prostrate figure.

During those moments, Christopher drifted off into an interim of fantasy. At any rate, in the years to come, he confessed to himself that it may have been fantasy, but on that day he swore that Vanessa stood there and talked to him as he prayed she should do.

She tapped him on the shoulder and he raised his head, not surprised in the least to see her slender form towering over him. Her blue terry beach robe was slit to the thigh exposing Vanessa's shapely leg. A flimsy scarf lay loose on the dark hair which was piled as usual on the crown of her head. Her wide mouth smiled at him. Still, he was not surprised.

"Look, Vanessa," he said to her, "Just look at this ostentation. Demoralizing, isn't it? And imagine grown, responsible people making love right here on the beach!"

He waited while Vanessa adjusted the scarf over her shoulder. "Love is the substance of God, Christopher," she said slowly, not really meeting his gaze. "The wrong is only in the way you look at it."

Sitting cross-legged at her feet, he leaned forward and stared at her. "Vanessa!" he said sharply. "You were never like that. What has happened to you?"

She knelt beside him, eyeing him compassionately. "I have been where I have seen different things, Christopher. You cannot imagine!" She made a wide motion with one hand. "I have seen masses such as no man can measure, great clouds, not of dread, but of joy and love, expanses that would make a planet, with energies that would move the sun!" Her face alight with expression, she continued. "The sun! Yes, move the sun!" She clasped her hands together. "Take my children to live in the sun, Christopher. Find the sun!"

Christopher could feel his face twitch with bewilderment. "What are you trying to tell me? Why don't you speak plainly? Are you trying to tell me that I should forgive Kelley after what she has done? Are you saying to let Karla bring a Mexican to me for a son-in-law? Humph. I don't know if I can, Vanessa. And what about your son?"

She cupped his face in her hands. They felt velvety cool on his sweaty brow. "Christopher, the gut of love is understanding."

Notes of irritation crept into his tone. "For goodness sake, Vanessa! Don't quote poetry to me at a time like this! Tell me what you want me to do. For God's sake, don't you realize that I need help? How am I to live without love? What am I to do?"

Vanessa arose slowly and stood with one hand on his forehead. "What a pity," she whispered. "Good surrounds us everywhere, but it does not enter man's mind. Chris, if you find a love that is pure, it becomes an homage to...to...." Her voice trailed off.

Again he waited while she stood straight and adjusted the scarf on her shoulder. "To what?" He leaned forward tensely. "To what, Vanessa? Stop talking riddles! You know that I never understood poetry and parables! Just tell me what you mean! Homage to what?"

Her voice sounded far away. "...to the greater essence of ourselves, the *all* in everyone, the tranquil one—" The rest of what she said became inaudible.

He tugged at the scarf. It drifted slowly to the ground. "Are you saying that it would be all right for me to love someone again?"

She smiled at him sadly and stepped away from him, growing dimmer all the while. She mumbled something, only a word or two of which made any sense "...envision...conciliate...the sun, the sun, Chris!"

On his knees now, he reached for her wildly. "Vanessa, don't go," he pleaded. Her image grew transparent. "Vanessa! Come back here!" He lunged forward to grab the hem of her robe but he sprawled full length on his stomach and clutched at what felt like her ankle. Slowly, he became aware that he was lying prostrate at the feet of the couple who had come up from the surf.

The man was speaking. "Gad, is he bombed." He adjusted the towel about his waist before he knelt to address Christopher. "That was some anniversary party the Jonathans gave, wasn't it, pal?" When Christopher did nothing but stare, he turned to his companion. "He is really in bad shape, and the tide is coming up fast. We had better get him into the house."

Christopher left them gaping in surprise when he leaped to his feet and strode rapidly down the beach with a steady step, suddenly becoming aware that he was clutching a flimsy scarf in his hand. He looked back at the woman whose ankle he had clutched, shook his head and held the scarf tighter yet.

<hr />

Dawn was not far off when Christopher entered the patio door of his home, wet, sandy and exhausted. David sprang from the sofa where he had fallen asleep waiting for his father's return.

"Jesus! You sure had me worried, Dad!" David exclaimed. "Where have you been? I combed the streets for you! I drove all over town, called everyone we know! Where did you go?" He tried to ease his father into a chair in the living room.

Christopher resisted. "David, I'm all wet. I'll get Mom's blue chair dirty."

"The devil with the chair, Dad. Are you all right?" He waited until his father nodded. "Go get into something dry. I have hot coffee ready."

When Christopher returned, he let his weight drop into the chair. "I'm sorry to cause you concern. I had to walk things off my mind."

"Well, listen to what I found out, Dad." David proceeded to repeat all that Rommey had told him about Kelley. "So you see, Dad, Rommey hasn't given her any narcotics and she isn't pregnant after all."

"Huh!" Christopher snorted. "I don't think much of your source of information. A tramp like Rommey! Devil take him!"

"Dad, Kelley isn't pregnant. If she is, it isn't Rommey's doing because he hasn't touched her. She has been ill and needs surgery and he is the only one who is trying to help her."

"Likely story!" Christopher stormed. "Christ Almighty, what would you expect him to say after taking my daughter away from home the way he has?"

David raised his voice. "Look, Dad, stop thinking of how much you've been wronged and start thinking of the plain facts. Nobody can tell you anything!" He ran his fingers nervously through his rough-cut hair. "Holy Moses! You have the idea that you and your generation were something special, that loyalty and altruism stopped there. You think the kids of my generation are a bunch of slobs. You think that we don't have any sense of values. Why don't you give us a chance? I'm trying to tell you that Rommey took Kelley to a gynecologist in San Francisco because she wouldn't go to a local doctor. We probably owe Rommey a good bit, and you won't listen. You are still trying to beat the hell out of him while he may be saving Kelley's life!"

Completely surprised by his son's outburst, Christopher rubbed his chin and was silent. Then, his expression softened somewhat. "Very well. Suppose he hasn't misguided your sister. Why is he doing all this?"

"We have all misjudged the guy." David brushed his tumbled brown curls again. "I'm not really sure, but I think he's some kind of special agent. I can't quite figure it out." He watched his father's face as disbelief faded into a look of fatigue.

"I'm tired, David," Christopher admitted. "I can't seem to make my mind work anymore. This night is like none I can remember." He paused and sighed. "Are you saying that Rommey is some kind of agent?"

Now I'm getting through, David thought. "Yes, some kind of government agent."

Christopher's lip twitched. "That would be a switch! What makes you think so?"

"I overheard a phone conversation one time. Rom didn't know I was there. From then on, I just noticed little things."

With a whistle, Christopher exhaled slowly. "I hope you're right, son. I'd owe him quite an apology," he said thoughtfully. "Do you know how to get in touch with him again?"

"He won't tell anyone where he lives, but I know how to get word to him. It takes a day or two for him to answer."

Again, Christopher looked weary. He let his heavy frame sag further into the big chair. His lids fluttered and closed. The square jaw was taut. Heavy brows that peaked over the bridge of his straight nose were raised even higher. Though relatively unscarred by wrinkles, his wide forehead had borders of telltale gray. The brows straightened again as he sighed and opened his eyes.

"Quite a turn of events, I must say. I hope you are right. Send a message to Rommey."

David looked like his father except that his face was narrower. Whereas his father's features were rugged and ruddy, David had his mother's smooth, ivory complexion. He had grown his hair longer and unruly curls tumbled when he nodded as he did now. "Okay. Okay. What about Kelley?"

Christopher arose. "Rommey said he would have her here by Saturday, and we'll get her to the best surgeon in town right away. Now, if I don't get some sleep, I won't make it to the office alive." He turned quickly in the direction of the hall before David could ply him with another question.

XXXIV

"...she had been made a prisoner..."

The castle gate loomed forbiddingly before her. Scowling, carved faces, staring down from dank niches, gave Nichole an uneasy feeling. She was fully aware that she would never have gained access to this point if it had not been for the influence of Mr. Namu, with whom she had made contact according to Kimo's instructions.

Finally, she and Mr. Namu were admitted into the huge garden entry of the Ahkar palace. After another hour's wait, they were told that Mr. Namu should leave and return in four hours for Nichole. Despite Nichole's pleading, Mr. Namu prepared to leave.

"I don't know a word of what they are saying," Nichole argued. "How will I understand? Can't you tell them that I need you? If Gregor is staying at the far end of the bay, as they explained, he is still an hour's journey away. Frankly, I'm frightened. Tell them that I want you to come with me!"

Mr. Namu's attempts to intercede for her were useless. After a few minutes of courteous verbal exchange with the palace attendant, he turned to her quietly. "They have said they do not receive guests and have already made a very special allowance to grant you audience. Under no circumstances will I be allowed to go with you beyond this point. I will return for you at the specified time. You are asked to accompany this man." He pointed to the attendant who wore a purple tunic tied with a magenta sash.

With that, he turned and was gone, leaving her clutching a shoulder bag as she watched him retreat. The attendant motioned for her to follow. Holding her head high, she pointed to her small case which lay on the tiled floor beside her. The man clapped his hands loudly. A young woman in a sarong appeared quickly. Taking the case, she followed them down a long passageway lined with towering tiki carvings. Partly hidden in the foliage of gigantic ferns, the half-human faces glared down upon Nichole. Ponds appeared unexpectedly, fed by trickling waterfalls overgrown with purple bougainvillea. The air became oppressive with the heavy scent of tiare blossoms and damp vegetation.

They walked for some time, passing groups of women who dug roots from the earth, following paths through tropical growth that skirted the main buildings. At one point, they passed through a cave lit with torches and smelling of rotted fern.

Overcome with mounting nausea, Nichole lowered herself shakily on one of the curiously carved benches that were placed at intervals along the path. Her lungs seemed to reject the hot, heavy air. Her forehead was clammy and dripping as she lowered her head over her knees. The attendant appeared concerned as he addressed Nichole in words strange to her. Then he sent the servant girl off in another direction. When the nausea receded and Nichole indicated that she was ready to go on, the man carried her case and proceeded more slowly.

Stepping out from under the dense growth, they came to a pier where a small craft waited, manned by a lavalava-clad native who had been playing a guitar made of a coconut shell. The man waved Nichole to a seat in the clumsy craft where she waited until the girl returned with a glass of milky liquid and some wafer-like bread.

Nichole sipped the coconut concoction and nibbled at the wafer which did little to calm her nausea. When she indicated that she was ready to continue, the boat, bearing all of them, was rowed across a large lagoon that appeared to fill the center of the island, losing itself in winding directions into the jungle, but rimmed by a rise of steep cliff over which came the faint sound of ocean surf.

By the time they reached their landing place, Nichole felt a slight stupor come over her. She followed her guide slowly up a walkway leading to a temple with a long courtyard through its center.

At their intrusion into this shadowy corridor, the air filled with wild chattering, a mixture of shrieking and calling, frightening in its sudden onset and intensity.

Nichole shielded her head, expecting to be attacked by an army of frenzied flying things, but none came. As her eyes adjusted to the dim light, she saw the curious wicker cages that imprisoned the birds. Large and ponderous, they hung in recessed niches between heavily carved arches surrounded by lilies, wild and abundant.

Pondering the possible reasons for caging the frenzied birds, Nichole passed by the cages. The birds screamed louder. Only in one cage were the birds silent. Here, the guide paused just long enough for Nichole to see the still, outstretched wings of a white-feathered dove that lay dead on the floor of its compartment.

Nichole drew a sharp breath and swallowed hard. With a sense of foreboding she hurried on, taking more careful note of their progress as they made their way to the seaward side of the structure. Here, they were approached by a matronly woman who dismissed the man and the girl, placed Nichole's case on an entry table and beckoned her to follow. They passed through a gate which the woman closed behind them. At the top of endless flights of wooden steps, they paused on a veranda overlooking a long stretch of beach. They entered a room that held only a wicker couch and a wash stand with towels. Wetting one of the towels, Nichole sponged her face, then turned to address the matron, but she had disappeared silently down the unending tiers of wood stairs.

After resting for a few moments on the couch, Nichole pinned her damp hair high on the crown of her head. Then she left the hot room in favor of the veranda where she sat on a wicker stool, hoping for a breeze from the ocean. The air remained still and heavy with the musty smell of jungle decay and jasmine blossoms. After an hour passed, Nichole began to chafe.

How does Gregor dare to keep me waiting like this, she thought over and over...surely he knows that I'm here and how unbearably hot it is waiting like this after walking so far...please come...it's been hours...hours...something must be wrong...I know something must be wrong because there is no other way off this terrace, only that gate...I'll go back there where I left my case....

Arriving at the gate, she found it locked. Frightened and frustrated, she shook it and called his name. "Gregor Morghann!" Eerie echoes filled the air. "Gregor! Gregor!" she called. Only then did it occur to her that *she had been made a prisoner.*

Determined to fulfill her mission despite her qualms, she returned to the veranda where she stood staring at the distant stretch of beach. Kimo's words came clearly to her mind. "My advice is, go home and forget him—forget him."

After examining the length of the veranda, she leaned as far as she could to see the ground below. Hmm, she thought, I wonder if I could climb down that vine if I had to...I guess I could but Gregor will come....

Suddenly, she narrowed her eyes and strained to see against the glare. Two distant figures were approaching slowly, strolling ankle deep in the gentle surf. Gradually, it became apparent that one was a woman with black hair. Her companion was a tall man wearing a wide-brimmed hat. Both wore only lavalava cloths about their hips.

As she strained to see more clearly, Nichole's vision was obscured by the swaying fronds of a low palm tree that stood in a grassy oasis in the path of the strolling couple. The girl sat on the grass, drawing her companion with her. The man lay on his back, his upturned face shaded by the brim of his hat, his arms flung out at his side. The girl knelt beside him and began to massage him. When he stirred, she pushed him down gently again, after which she sank to her knees between his outstretched legs and pulled his buttocks into her lap until their thighs crossed. Her ebony hair fell forward over his body as she reached repeatedly to knead his chest and abdomen with a rhythmic stroke.

Nichole stood mesmerized, not wishing to watch but unable to draw her eyes away. Minutes passed, uncounted. Immobilized by the curious drama, she ignored the small warnings that came from within her...run, Nichole, run, they were saying. Instead, she stared, spellbound, as the man's body began to rise and tense to the rhythm of the kneading.

Just as the man pulled his partner's body over his, a cloud threw a shadow over the beach. The fronds of the palm tossed in a sudden breeze, screening the drama from Nichole's view. A quick deluge drenched the porch driving her back under an overhang. Just as suddenly, the rain stopped. The odor of decaying jungle rose sharply. When Nichole looked again, the man and woman were rolling in the surf and laughing like children. The hat fell from the man's head, exposing his light hair. Nichole gasped as she realized that the man was Gregor. All her strength seemed suddenly drained. She grasped the rail to keep herself from fainting.

She was horrified to feel her stomach grow tight with spasm. Leaning over the rail, she retched miserably, again and again. A part of her being had been brutally plucked apart. The veranda had been an amphitheater to a stage. Someone had meant it to be that way. Nichole breathed deeply to regain her composure, but the vapors of rotting vegetation and moldy wood overpowered her.

The girl on the beach was making her way toward the building. Her carriage reminded Nichole of Pandora for a fleeting moment, but no more because Nichole shouldered her purse and stumbled hurriedly down the steps to the locked gate. She rattled it furiously, intending to call out, but it fell open under her hand.

Feeling that she had come from some Alice-in-Wonderland experience, she found her case, then wound her way to the craft tied beside the pier. The pilot held it steady as she stepped in. The servant girl met her on the other side of the lagoon and took her to where Mr. Namu was waiting. He addressed her quietly.

"The Ahkar family has readied a plane to fly to San Francisco with one stop in Hawaii. They asked me to tell you that the plane is at your disposal. Mr. Ahkar's nephew urges that you allow the transportation to be of service to you. He awaits your pleasure."

Nichole sighed wearily. Then she straightened to her full height and replied in an unwavering voice, "Tell Mr. Ahkar that I welcome his kindness. I will go. *Yes, I want to go home.*"

Forecast V

The ghost form of the young Indian searched the cliff impatiently until he saw his companion approaching from below.

"Princess, where have you been through the night?" he asked.

The girl shrugged her shoulders wearily. "Jaoko, prince-master, I went to watch the curious way of the people who crowd this shore. They have a dying place filled with strange white beds. In the same white beds, they are strangely born, not as we were born, listening to the wind in the pine which was the breath of the spirit-god giving new life."

Jaoko paused in thought. "Not always are they born so. Remember, Princess, the man-child who was born in the sea? Remember? He lived when you plucked him from the waters."

"Ah yes! He with the fathomless eyes and the charm of the emerald-god on his spirit. He also waits for the waters to be crystal-clear and the winds to be sweet again."

She sighed as she took his hand and they drifted back to their sepulcher pine tree.

XXXV

"...he reached for the scalpel..."

elley scanned the pages of her writing that lay scattered over the table of Polly's kitchen. She took one page and began to read aloud.

"I'll never know just why I strayed...
Left behind the sand and sea
For a place so damp and grayed,
It killed the spirit that was me.

"Frozen faces, hollow-eyed,
Not like friends I had before,
Surrounded me until I died
And tried to find my loves once more.

"My soul became a whitened gull
Who flew until she found the sand
While breakers whispered in the lull
Or roared upon the sea's command.

"The sweet air bore her circling slow
To find the little surfing shack,
And there was laughter, soft and low
As one by one, her friends came back.

"Everyone was young and strong.
Each with joy that he could bring.
Each found love, each sang his song,
But she who had no song to sing.

"She rides the wind, she flies there still
Above the wandering, restless sea,
A ghostly gull upon the rill
Who is the very soul of me."

Suddenly, Kelley struck a line through the page and threw the pencil down. Tears welled in her eyes. "I hate what I'm writing. I hate it!" she said. With a swift gesture, she sent her papers spilling through the air. Elbows on the table, she propped her chin in her hands. "But it's true. It's true. Gregor is the sea, restless, never finding peace, forever looking for a finality that never comes. And the white sea bird wanting the freedom of the ocean is my soul."

She pushed her chair roughly from the table. "Why do I write this stuff?" A trickle of perspiration found its way down her forehead. "It's hotter than hell in this stupid place," she chafed. "I'll only be here one more day if I can live through it. Good grief! Rommey was right. I want to go home."

She wiped her forehead with a towel, drank some water, then went to search Polly's closet for something cool to wear. She tried on a sleeveless print robe, the length of which made her stumble. She grew accustomed to hoisting the hem an inch or two by thrusting her hands into the pockets.

In the hallway, Kelley passed the note she had placed for Polly by the telephone. "Rommey insists that my surgery be done at home," the note read. "He is coming up for me late Friday night, so if I am not here when you get back on Saturday, I'll be with him. Please bring my big luggage when you come. Rom's car is too small and I am taking only my little zip bag."

Kelley propped the note in a more obvious position. She rearranged the band that held her damp hair high off her neck. Perspiration still dripped from her face. She drank some ice water, then bathed her face in the remainder.

I'll die if I don't get some fresh air, she said to herself. I'll just stand on the landing for a bit...all that noise downstairs...those kids must have come back...really a big gang of them...how can they get so wild...I wish Rommey would call...at least there is a little breeze out here...oh darn...here comes another car full of hippies...that one with the blond hair looks a little like Gregor...he has a dog with him...Rex had a dog like that...could it be...no...I must be imagining things...I better go in before they see me...I promised Rommey....

Kelley retreated before the group reached the walkway below her porch. Inside Polly's living room again, she watched television for a short while. When the programs bored her, she took up her pen again.

Try to make it cheerful, she told herself. Write about favorite things.

She sat in thought for a moment. Then her pencil ran over the page...my prom dress...rain in July...little sea crabs in the tide pools...the sound of the pounding surf and the tingle of the spray...guitars around the picnic fires at the long beach...double poinsettias dripping with December dew and daffodils in January...Kimo's waterfall...the smile in Rommey's eyes...the touch of Greg's hand....

Kelley's lip quivered. Poising the pencil in mid-air, she continued aloud, "...and strawberries fresh from Mom's garden, and singing with her while we made jam and how cozy her blue kitchen always seemed and, and—" Spasm paralyzed her throat as giant sobs shook her frame. Without warning, her pencil struck crazily across the page until the point broke and Kelley hurled it across the room. "Oh, it's no good, no good!" she cried out. "Nothing is the same anymore! I'm just *stuck in yesterday,* and I'll never get free! Everything is gone and I'm so lost!"

She seized the sheet, crumpled it in her hand, and started to cry again just as the telephone rang. Her hand shook when she took up the instrument, and the lump in her throat kept an answer from coming.

Rommey's clear voice kept repeating, "Kelley? Kelley? Are you there? Hello."

"Yes, Rommey, I'm here," she finally managed to say.

"Are you crying? Is something wrong?" Rommey's voice persisted. "Is the pain worse?"

"No. It hurts just like before. Mostly, I'm just lonesome. And scared."

"Is that crowd of longhairs still in the place below you?"

"They just came back, about twice as many of them. And, Rom, they were talking about something they had stolen, seemed like it was from a hospital. I didn't see it but it was heavy and, from the noise it made on the walk, it was metal. This may sound funny, but it seemed that they were going to use it to get high. Does that make any sense?"

Kelley could hear Rommey's sigh of concern. Then his voice came. "Good God! I should never have taken you up there."

"Well, why are you so worried? I won't go near them. A few times, I've stepped out on the landing just for a minute for a breath of fresh air. It is so unbearable in here, you can't imagine."

"If I could get a message to Polly to get back sooner, I would."

"What is it, Rom? Do they have a bomb or something?"

"Not a bomb, but it's possible that some kid stole a tank of nitrous."

Kelley hesitated. "Should I call the police?"

"No. Let me handle it. You keep your door locked."

"It's like a sauna in here," Kelley protested. "It can't possibly get any hotter."

"Just for one more day, Sugarbaby. Now, listen, here's the plan. I should be there to get you late Friday night. If anything detains me, and I'm not there by the time Polly starts out, you go with Polly. The sooner you get home, the better. If you aren't there, I'll know that Polly took you. Got it?"

"I got it," Kelley assured him. "See you soon."

"Just one more day," he answered. "Just stick it out one more day."

If Kelley thought that the weather could not get worse, she was wrong. The next day was even more humid. At six o'clock, she could bear the heat no longer. She stepped down to the stair landing. A light breeze blew in gusts. She removed the nylon band from her damp hair, wiped her forehead and sighed with relief. The wind caught the flimsy nylon and blew it across the alleyway down below her. Kelley hoisted her skirt and hurried after it. The sound of a motor startled her. She snatched the band and tried to dash back to her apartment. Her foot caught in the hem of her smock. She pitched forward onto the fender of the oncoming car. Kelley braced herself as she slid across the hood and brushed the windshield. An intolerable pain seared through her middle as she bounced off the other side.

Later that evening, at the wharf on Bay Street in San Francisco, two tall figures stood relaxed at the entrance of a specialty restaurant. Either one could have been a product of Malibu Beach. Certainly they stood with perfect showmanship, as though they had come directly from the stage of the playhouse, precisely the place that passers-by guessed they were advertising. The taller of the two wore a crown of laurel over his black corkscrew ringlets. His features were passive with a tinge of hauteur. Jet curls also framed his chin and cheeks. Over his white tunic he had draped a striped scarlet and purple toga. His sandals were gold-laced, and in his hand was a sceptre-like staff.

His friend was burlier, with thick Atlas-like legs bulging from gold leather boots that were laced clumsily in the front. The ponderous metal belt which gathered his short black tunic was almost hidden by a purple cloak that he wore draped about his massive shoulders. Jet ringlets also framed his swarthy face.

They made an impressive pair as they leaned idly against the frame of the restaurant entrance. The neon sign above threw a weird light so that passers had to squint to see them. These people either gaped or tittered, neither of which disturbed the composure of the two giants in costume.

At this moment, two well-wined middle-aged couples approached to enter the restaurant. One woman giggled loudly. "My, my! What won't they do these days to get some advertising! Where did they find you two?"

The two costumed men exchanged prankish glances. Then the more kindly of the pair answered, "Pliny sent us."

The woman giggled again. She ignored her husband's tugging on her arm. "Aren't you cute?" she repeated over and over. "You don't look real! I've got to touch you." She weaved her way to where he stood, but his fierce frown discouraged her, and she turned to the other of the pair. "Can I touch you?" she begged.

The burly man took his friend's staff, warding her off with it as he shrank back into the shadow of the building. "If you do, it will be the end of you," he warned. His heavy foreign accent befitted his costume.

The woman laughed. "Oh, those muscles. What's your name, honey?"

"I'm Pluto," the man answered readily, his eyes alight with mischief.

"Sure, baby, sure. I'm Mickey Mouse. And I suppose your friend is Donald Duck." She giggled again.

"No. He is Jupiter."

The woman's husband took her forcibly by the arm. "That's enough! We are already late for our reservation. Bob and Minnie are getting upset."

"I'm coming, honey. Better put out your cigar. It's nauseating." She disappeared inside as her husband went obediently to flip his stub into the gutter.

Pluto whispered to his companion. "Nauseating is the right word. I loathe women like that, that son of a..." He caught his friend's warning glance. "...of a cabbage," he added.

Jupiter shook his head. "Living in your Dark Kingdom as you do addles your brain. You have your neuter wrong and your botany mixed with zoology again."

Pluto shrugged his shoulders. "All right. Have it your way. She is the daughter of a harlot." He laughed heartily, but stopped when he found himself looking into the face of the woman's angry husband.

"Look, Sonny," the little man said. "Don't make fun of my wife." He raised his fist. "I'll smash you no matter how big you are." He squinted as the figures faded further into the shadows of the alcove. Then he followed his wife, mumbling to himself, "I guess that scared them good."

After a while, the two figures emerged again. Jupiter spoke. "You will be our undoing, my brother. You need to be less the cousin of an ass and more the uncle of the sabre-tooth if you wish to insult such women for sport."

"Wrong again, Jupiter. The sabre-tooth was extinct here with the Pliocene."

Jupiter chuckled. "By my father, the swallower of children, you still do have a wit."

Mischief glowed in Pluto's eyes again. "Well, my brother, son of Cronus, author of all good things, although our mission tonight is a sad one, I see no harm in having a little sport with these weak mortals while we wait."

"Remember that the world has changed. There are no longer such divinities as Pallas Athena, although surely there must still be a few noble women."

Pluto scowled fiercely. "Bah! Weaklings! Unprincipled! Immoral! Mercenary! The world would be well rid of them all."

Jupiter sighed and leaned on his staff. "It will happen. When mortals overcrowd the planet, they eventually destroy one another and their world. You may be right. It is time to start a new breed, if any are left to start it this time."

He looked up as the sound of sirens filled the air. An infinite sadness passed over his features. A great sigh rumbled like thunder through his big chest.

Pluto placed his arm comfortingly about his companion's shoulder. "The moment has come," he whispered.

"Yes. The time for sport is done. The moment to redeem Adonis comes once again." He frowned as he watched several patrol cars stop close by the parking lot beside the wharf. Police began to fill the area, centering about one yellow car parked far to the back. Spectators gathered about. An ambulance arrived.

With a composure that appeared to be indifference, the two carnival-costumed figures chose their way carefully through the parking lot to where the doors of the yellow car had been flung wide. The body of a young man, found in the vehicle, had been laid on the wharf while a medic worked to restore his breathing.

Someone was shouting, "Hey, Rom, there is a dog in the front seat here under this newspaper!" The animal stirred, raising her head in a convulsive effort.

The man so addressed lifted a small silkie collie and placed it near the unconscious man. "Damn!" Rommey swore. "He had to bring the dog, too. What else!"

"You know this kid, Rommey?" the first man asked.

"Yeah, I know him," Rommey answered, bending over the dog that lay gasping for air. Then, with the unshaken trust and devotion left in it, the animal struggled to its feet, took two shaky steps to her master's body and fell dead.

People watched with silent concern while a team continued to work over the prostrate figure. After a long interval, a stretcher was brought. As they lifted the unconscious form, the young head lurched back and sideways. A thick mass of wavy, golden hair fell to cover one cheekbone of a handsome face. His lips parted as though he might surprise everyone and speak, but there was only a faint smile. Long, slender fingers fell limp.

To hide the tears on his face, Rommey concerned himself with searching the yellow car. On the seat was a tank labeled in large letters. *Use only with oxygen.* Rommey picked up a stone from the ground and flung it with all his might into the water beyond, swearing under his breath. Then, he sat on the pier and vomited into the bay. "Rex, you stupid son-of-a-bitch!" he moaned. "Why did you have to do this? Why? Why did you close the windows? What a stupid thing to do!"

At this moment Pluto stepped forward. "Come, Jupiter, while he is unattended, let us take him lightly by one lock of lustrous hair, for his soul form will separate and has no weight as yet." He touched the golden head. "I redeem you, Adonis, son of Myrrha."

Jupiter glowered as he interrupted. "For shame, Pluto, to eye this fair child with such avarice for your dark, infernal kingdom. For shame!"

Anger showed in Pluto's dark features. "Avarice, indeed! Do you say that I do not judge him fairly? This boy can be no other than the risen Adonis, beloved of Aphrodite, killed by the boar, and decreed by you, yourself, Jupiter." He paused, cleared his throat, and allowed his voice to rise a little. "...decreed to rise in the springtime. How can he rise in the spring, unless...."

An officer nearby finished writing something on a pad of paper. Without lifting his head he muttered, "Well, this one won't be rising in the spring!" He looked up. "You can bet those gold boots on that!" He bent his head again to continue his notes.

Pluto glanced down at his impressive footwear. "I'd better fade," he whispered. "Juno made these for me, and I wouldn't want to lose this pair." He shrank back into the shadows until he was fairly invisible.

The officer approached. "Okay! You two characters from a Mardi Gras, give me your names. Say, where's your buddy? He couldn't get past me! Devil take it! What is going on?" He searched behind him.

Upon the mention of his name, Pluto's image showed again. "You called?" he asked.

The officer examined his spectacles. "I gotta get new glasses this week," he said as he shook his head. "Now, just where were you two going in those get-ups?"

Jupiter caught the twinkle in his brother's eye. "We were going to the arena for the big game," he explained quickly.

"Oh, smart alecks! I think I'll take you two in. What's your name? You!" He pointed to Pluto. "Where are you from?"

"You wouldn't believe it," Pluto answered.

"Wise guy! Follow me, you two," the officer snarled.

Pluto shrugged his massive shoulders. A malicious smirk crossed his lips. He beckoned for Jupiter to follow him and started after the officer. "Until I give you the signal," he whispered. "Then you know what to do."

Jupiter whispered in return, "But, Pluto, stay your distance! Your slightest touch will bring his demise. Consider that he has not wronged you, in all fairness!"

"Bah!" Pluto exclaimed. "They all offend me, these mortals of the new breed. Mercenary! Immoral! Greedy! They stink! They close the windows on themselves, even as this one did. Did you not hear his own friend say that the thing that he did wrong was to close the windows?" He shifted the position of the ghost form under his arm.

Once again, the look of immeasurable sadness crossed Jupiter's serene face. "Not correct. The only thing he did wrong was to be born so handsomely in a god's image and into this decade."

That same Friday night found an equally strange event surrounding the Village of the smugglers' cove five-hundred miles to the south. The top of Mt. Soledad, usually crowded with people and cars only once a year at the Easter sunrise service, found itself swarming with villagers this evening, as though it were an ant hill for the human race. Among the cars winding their way to the top in a funeral-like procession, was Christopher's station wagon. When the mass of parked vehicles prohibited further progress, Christopher and Karla continued on foot to the towering cross which stood in the center of a wide circle of roadway.

They stumbled in the darkness, following along at a slow pace, until they arrived at the curbing with other small groups, all of whom conversed in hushed tones as they stared at the eerie distant glow.

Whereas chairs were provided for the Easter service that celebrated rebirth and life, now the curbing offered the only seating for a show of death and destruction which appeared on the horizon in a circle around them. A feeling of doom settled over the spectators as they clung to each other for comfort.

Every year, the heat brought fires to the back country, some of them widespread and hard to control, but never had there been three at once. The fire in Mexico, just below the border, was a long rim of hazy glow. The blaze to the east was reported to be spreading rapidly. Already people were speculating on how long it would be before it would reach the settlement if fire control failed.

Karla had seated herself by her father, her transistor radio to her ear. "They are saying that the fire over there behind Clairemont is racing through a valley that's directing the blaze toward the community, Dad. Like a wind tunnel."

"That's probably it over there, that brighter area. See?" Christopher pointed.

"Do you suppose the people are prepared to move out if they have to, Dad?"

"Well, Karla, my guess is that they have methods in reserve to use if they can't stop the fire at a certain point. But I'm only guessing. What do you think?"

Karla did not answer. It had been a long while since Christopher had asked his daughter for her opinion. In the darkness, he could not guess that tears had come to her eyes, but apparently he sensed some need, and he put his arm about her shoulder.

"That's the worst one, though," he continued, pointing to the awesome sight to the north where monstrous outsized tongues of flame leaped skyward, an unchecked inferno spewing smoke over the countryside. Obliterating the sky, the billowing smoke clouds extended as far as the eye could see, fed by intense flames that lighted their passage far out to sea. Pieces of ash blanketed everything, roofs and patios and streets, like gray snowflakes.

"I hung some things on the line today, and I had to bring them in to be washed all over again," Karla complained. "I'll have a new appreciation for the sun if it comes out tomorrow."

Christopher shook his head. "It won't. The smoke is too thick. Everything looked so weird in the gray-green light today. Wouldn't a rain be wonderful?" he speculated.

Someone behind them was speaking in a hushed tone. "It's *so* unreal," the man was saying.

Another voice replied, "Yeah. As though the whole world is going to burn up right under us."

"More like sitting high in hell," a third person observed.

Karla answered her father's question. "A rain would be a blessing." They had risen and were following the crowd to a different vantage point.

248

Christopher Holliss was already praying, beseeching God for a deluge that would soothe the troubled earth and praying for peace for his own troubled mind, because this night's occurrences had brought thoughts of penance long overdue. He tried to remember what Vanessa had said to him in the vision... I have seen masses... such as no man can imagine... not clouds of dread... not clouds of dread....

As Vanessa's words echoed in his ears, Christopher covered his eyes with his hands, dropping back behind Karla for a few moments. "Saints preserve me," he said aloud in a low tone. "I can see her so plainly, even now. Her words were so clear. It couldn't have been a dream that night. She said *find the sun, Christopher. Live in the sun. Love is understanding.*" He opened his eyes. "God forgive me. Show me a better way. Make me deserving." He gazed thoughtfully in the direction of his daughter and hurried to rejoin her.

Karla had her radio to her ear again, and now she was repeating the words of the radio commentator about the number of acres of land already destroyed. "I feel so sorry for the animals that get trapped. Poor things. Jose said yesterday that—" She stopped abruptly, peering at her father in the shadow, afraid of his displeasure.

However, Christopher's answer surprised her.

"Yes, what did Jose say?"

Karla cleared her throat and stammered. "You—you don't like to hear about Jose."

"I don't mind hearing about Jose tonight, Karla. Tell me about him." Christopher could feel Karla draw a deep breath, then she was still.

"Karla? Are you crying?" He could see her body tighten. "Karla?"

After a few seconds, an unsteady voice replied, "I'm sorry, Dad. It's been such a long time since... I don't mean to cry. You have never asked about Jose. You've always exploded when I mention him."

Now it was Christopher's turn to be wordless. He patted her arm. After a while he said, "Why don't we start toward the car, and you tell me about Jose."

As she walked, Karla dried her eyes. "Dad, I've got to tell you the truth. I have been seeing him. We tried to stop seeing each other several—" Her voice broke again. She walked in silence for a minute. "He loves me, Dad. You don't know him. He has changed so much. He's so tall now. He wants to be a doctor."

"A doctor?"

"Yes, Dad. He's always wanted to be a doctor. His family wants him to go to college and medical school. Jose is very intelligent. His mother's uncle in Europe has promised to finance him if he earns enough to put himself through one year of college. That's what he is doing now. He's been doing construction work. Sometimes he is out of town for a month or two on a job."

"Hmm, where is he now, Karla?"

"Up in Gardena, working on a tract development."

"Why haven't you told me all this?"

Karla stopped in her tracks and threw up her hands. "Because you wouldn't listen, Daddy. You never gave him a chance."

"Now I am listening, Karla."

They arrived at their car. As Christopher held open the door, the overhead light showed his daughter's face wet with tears. She leaned her head on his shoulder. His arm went about her protectively.

"Dad, I can't keep from crying. I'm so happy. It didn't seem that this could ever happen."

"Young lady, you've gotten skinny."

"It's about time you noticed." Karla's face brightened.

Christopher had the feeling that it was no longer the smile of his freckled, round-faced teenager, but that of a lovely young lady. "Oh, I've noticed."

"Jose wanted me to take off a few pounds."

"You are getting to look more like your mother."

"Did you notice that my hair is a little darker? It really isn't red now. I don't mind it so much anymore. Jose thinks it's beautiful."

"Your hair has always been beautiful, like your grandmother's. Not many people have such a lustrous head of hair. You know who else has a good head of hair?"

"No, who?"

"Those Vincett girls, both of them, particularly Nichole."

"Oh, yes, I guess so. I like Kelley's hair better."

Christopher talked for a few minutes about Nichole's letters from the islands. As they turned into their driveway, he added, "She wrote that she was coming back after she found Gregor."

Karla turned her head and was staring at something through the car window. "Dad, I think that she found Gregor."

"She did what? Found Gregor, you say?" Christopher turned off the ignition. "What makes you think so?"

"Well, if I'm not mistaken, Daddy, that is Nichole in the car that just drove up to our house. Look." She pointed to Nichole's green Fiat.

Dr. Nickolas Bardo, an emergency room doctor, bent over the figure of the comatose teenager on the hospital bed. He looked up as a nurse approached him.

"This isn't just a head injury. Better call the—" he began.

"Excuse me, Dr. Bardo, but the little boy who swallowed the pin just came in," the nurse said.

The physician eyed the frantic mother of the boy and stepped over to talk to her.

"Bobby's going to be okay," Dr. Bardo assured her. "We're going to get him to X-ray to make sure he really swallowed that pin. You know, he might have spit it out somewhere. If it's there, we'll see exactly where it is and get it out, if that is the only alternative, with a gastroscope. Dr. Clemmens does lots of these. So keep calm and that will help your boy not to be apprehensive. Okay?" Dr. Bardo put a comforting hand on the mother's shoulder to still her sobbing.

"Wil—will this hurt him, Doctor?" the distraught mother stammered.

The physician shook his head. "Not at all, Mrs. Wilson. We do it all the time. You'd be surprised what kids swallow. A closed pin is one of the easiest. We may have to do nothing at all. Now don't worry, and Dr. Clemmens will take charge. I have to go to the operating room with a very critical patient." Dr. Bardo glanced in the direction of the unconscious teenager.

Mrs. Wilson held her child more closely as she followed the doctor's gaze. "Thank you, Doctor. I hope that—that your patient will be okay."

The physician nodded, turned and spoke to the nurse rapidly. "The head injury isn't the cause of the shock. There is a palpable mass in the abdomen. She is comatose, pressure is down, pulse is a hundred, thready and weak. Better call Dr. Lindley quickly. I think he is the gynecologist on call tonight, and even though I'd eliminate the head injury as cause of the shock, better call in a neurosurgeon."

"Dr. Zen is on call tonight," the nurse answered.

"Good. Don't lose any time." He turned away again as another accident patient was wheeled into the room.

By the time Dr. Bardo was able to return to the teenager again, the two specialists were finished with their examinations. The neurosurgeon spoke first.

"You were right, Nick. The head injury is superficial and is not responsible for the shock." He turned to the gynecologist. "It's something in her belly. Looks like it's your problem, Jess."

The gynecologist nodded and bent over Kelley again. "There is obvious intra-abdominal hemorrhage," he said. He stroked his chin, then nodded his head. "Hmm. Could be a tubal pregnancy. Also, with her history of trauma, a ruptured spleen must be considered." He turned to Dr. Bardo. "Nick, don't we have any information on her? It would help if we did."

Dr. Bardo shook his head. "All that we know is that a group was picked up at a pot party over near Ashbury and the police ambulance brought four of them here. None of them knew anything about this one. Two of them are discharged. One girl died of an overdose. There was also a premature infant and nobody could say whether the girl who died was the mother of the infant. That's all we know, other than a name on an envelope in the pocket of the patient's dress. The operator is trying to locate a relative."

The gynecologist reflected for a few seconds. "You said she was in shock when the ambulance picked her up?"

Dr. Bardo nodded with a worried look on his face as he bent over the pressure cuff. "That's right, Doctor."

Dr. Lindley touched his patient's abdomen once more. "The mass could be an involuting uterus, but I doubt it. I have to consider a ruptured ovarian cyst, too." He stood straight again and turned to the neurosurgeon. "I'll take over. Thanks." As Dr. Zen left, he spoke to Dr. Bardo again. "She's bleeding internally, obviously."

The younger physician frowned heavily. "Barely holding her blood pressure, Doctor."

Dr. Lindley eyed the face of the worried emergency room doctor. "Order a central venous line. We've got to open her now."

"Even with this transfusion, she isn't holding her pulse stable, and I've ordered two more units," Dr. Bardo said.

"Better order three," the gynecologist advised. "We'll operate now. She is going to be a touchy one to pull through."

"I've called the anesthesiologist," Dr. Bardo answered.

"Good! We'd better get a general surgeon to assist on the outside possibility it's a ruptured spleen. Get the emergency O.R. crew."

"They're ready," replied Dr. Bardo.

The nurse began to make preparations. "Someone will have to sign the operative permit," she reminded them.

"Dr. Bardo and I will. You can witness," said Dr. Lindley. "Get her ready as soon as you can." He bent to sign the permit, then handed it to Dr. Bardo. "You did well not to lose any time. At best, this won't be an easy one."

The younger physician rubbed his chin. "It makes life easier on us in the E.R. to have back-up by doctors like you and Dr. Zen. Someday, I'll have the confidence and assurance that you have."

"You've got a good start, Nick. Just remember that every tough case is a learning experience. Profit by your successes and mistakes. You know, just last month, I had a case something like this. Couldn't get a history because she was strung out as well as in shock. We knew that she had been in an accident, obvious intraperitoneal hemorrhage and generalized abdominal tenderness. Everything pointed to a ruptured spleen. Right? Wrong! When we got in, we found a left tubal mass—a tubal pregnancy. The massive bleeding, about 2000 c.c., was from a small ruptured artery on the surface of the tube. Took us ten minutes to evacuate the pregnancy and repair the tube. She could have died if she hadn't been brought to the hospital." The gynecologist glanced toward the flurry of activity around the teenage patient. "Oh, it looks like our patient is ready to go to the O.R., Doctor. We'd better get over there."

Kelley was hurriedly transported to the operating room and in ten minutes the emergency crew had the patient ready for anesthesia.

"Has she eaten anything?" asked the anesthesiologist, who had made a quick entry.

"Can't tell. She was picked up by a police ambulance in the middle of the night. Sure hope not. We've got enough trouble without her vomiting or aspirating. She doesn't look like a typical user. I don't smell anything. Did you check for barbiturates?" Dr. Lindley asked.

"Yes, at the same time that we crossmatched, we ran an amphetamine and barbiturate level. That's routine for these kids from the district, but I have a funny feeling about this one," Dr. Bardo said, bending low over his patient.

"Check the lab to see if they have the toxicology results," Dr. Lindley said to the nurse. Then he turned to Dr. Bardo. "What do you mean, you have a funny feeling?"

Dr. Bardo shrugged his shoulders. "She just doesn't seem to belong to that crowd they brought in."

The nurse returned. "Clean as a charter member of the PTA," she said.

"Even that doesn't mean much these days," Dr. Lindley answered.

The anesthesiologist peered anxiously over his mask at the gynecologist. "Her vital signs are deteriorating. Let's go!"

"Keep pushing the blood. She's losing it fast. We can't wait." The gynecologist reached out his hand for the scalpel.

XXXVI

"...Kelley is on the critical list..."

aturday morning dawned to find the Village covered with a layer of powdery ash. Karla dusted it off the telephone as she answered it.

"Karla?" the caller asked.

"Rommey! Oh, Rom, we've been looking all over for you! David told Dad what you said about Kelley and that she went to see a doctor in—"

"Yeah, yeah," the voice interrupted. "Just tell me if she got home."

"No, Rom. Is she supposed to be here?"

"Yeah. She should have been there hours ago with Polly."

"Who is Polly?"

"Polly is the nurse she rooms with who took her to the doctor. I was supposed to be there to get Kelley myself but my car broke down in Marin County and I'm still sitting here in the garage waiting for a part. I've been calling Kelley's number since seven last night. Nobody answered. That means that she and Polly started out last evening and they should be there by now. It shouldn't take this long unless they stopped in Santa Barbara."

"Oh, dear! David said that Kelley needed an operation. You don't suppose that—"

"No, no. If they stopped somewhere, they'd call you. Look, Karla, I gotta rap with your old man. Is he—"

"I'm the only one here, Rom." She stifled a yawn. "I just woke up."

There was a pause and a rustle of paper. "Oh, cool! Well, here, take this number. Call me as soon as Kelley shows."

"Rommey, what is wrong with my sister?"

"She'll tell you all about it. Look, I gotta talk with your father. It's important. Where can I find him?"

"I'm sorry, Rommey. I'm still half asleep. Nichole came to talk with Dad last night and she stayed past three o'clock. When I crashed, they were still talking. Dad had to take some important papers to Los Angeles this morning. I think Nichole went with him. I didn't mean to sleep so late. What time is it, anyway?"

"Almost ten. Did your father say when he'd be back? I gotta explain some things to him."

"Maybe he's up there checking the doctor's office to find Kelley. You know my Dad!"

"Yeah, yeah, do I ever!"

"Hmm. You're a neat person to be doing all this for us. Come clean, Rommey.

You aren't the crum-bum guy you pretend to be, are you? Are you an undercover agent?"

There was a sound of a throat clearing. "That's nobody's business right now. Uh, what did Nichole have to say? Did she find Gregor?"

"She really didn't say. She just talked a lot about traveling."

"Okay, okay, gotta go now. Call me the minute Kelley gets there or when your father arrives."

There was a loud click. With a vigorous puff of breath, Karla blew more dust from the telephone. After she dressed and made the coffee, Karla set about polishing the furniture.

"These ashes!" she complained loudly. "It will be days before we'll be rid of them. Everything is covered with soot. Right now a good rain would be worth a million dollars. Maybe the TV will have the latest news on the fires." She walked to the television set and while the picture struggled across the screen, Karla peered through the windows at the forbidding horizon.

Her thoughts reverted to the days of sunny skies and fresh ocean air. How we take all the good things for granted...never miss them until they are gone...look at that...you would never guess that sometimes we can see way out to Catalina...we shouldn't take it for granted...shouldn't spoil it...that cloud is frightening... depressing...makes you think we're on another planet....

It was true. The ominous, leaden cloud hung over the land and completely hid the sea to the north. The sky to the south was somewhat lighter and even held a promise of blue. Karla set the volume on the radio so that she could hear any news that might begin. Then she went about her dusting, finally seating herself at the telephone. She dialed at intervals and was ultimately rewarded by Jose's cheerful greeting.

"I hope it's all right for me to call you like this," Karla said. "How soon can I see you, Jose? I have the best news!"

"Let me guess what it is. Let's see, uh, you got a high SAT score? You were elected class president?"

"No, no," Karla protested. "I wouldn't call you like this just to tell you those things. Oh, Jose, it's such good news, but I wanted to tell you in person."

"My car is still not running or you know I would come."

"Couldn't Bob drive you down? Tomorrow is Sunday," Karla argued.

"We work, even on Sunday. If I don't, I won't be able to afford parts to fix my car. But this job will be done in one more week."

Impatiently, she fingered strands of her auburn hair. "A week?"

"It will go fast, but don't keep me guessing. I won't be able to concentrate on my work. Is your sister coming home?"

"You must be a mindreader, Jose. We're waiting for her to come today, but that isn't the big news. Jose, you won't believe this! My father finally asked all about you, about you and me! He listened when I told him how wonderful you are. He finally believes that you are going to study medicine!"

"Great! I can't believe this is true!"

"I thought Dad would never change and then all of a sudden, he just asked me all about you. He put his arm around me and just listened. He wants to talk to you, too!"

There was a pause. "I wonder what brought this change of heart?"

"Well, we were up on Mt. Soledad watching the fires. As I sat there, I prayed really hard that Mom would make Dad hear, and maybe she did."

Jose's voice was lower. "Now we can make some plans."

"I can get a job when I graduate," Karla volunteered. "I don't mind helping you get through school. I can take night classes, too."

"We'll see. We'll start planning."

"Dr. Jose Ronrico. It sounds so wonderful. You'll be the greatest doctor. Oh, I'm so happy that I could cry."

No sooner had Karla finished the call than the phone rang again. She answered and began to listen intently. The smile faded from her face. When the conversation was finished, she searched with trembling fingers for Rommey's number. Seconds later, she blurted out the contents of the message she had just taken.

"Rommey! Rommey!" she almost screamed. "Polly just called. She says that Kelley is in General Hospital in San Francisco and that she almost bled to death and they had to operate and—"

"They what? What are you talking about?"

"Polly called me just now," Karla repeated more slowly. "She had just come back from her trip when the hospital called."

"God Almighty! Are you saying Polly wasn't with Kelley last night? And they operated on Kelley? God Almighty!"

"Yes, Rommey," Karla's voice wavered. "And—and—Kelley almost bled to death!"

"Almost bled to death? How, dammit, how?"

"Polly found a note from Kelley saying she was with you and then the hospital called. Kelley has been there all night. Polly says to call her right away and to tell Dad, but Dad's not home, and I don't know what to do!" Karla's voice rose to a panic pitch. "Rommey, what should I do?"

"Karla, listen to me," Rommey's order came authoritatively. "Pull yourself together. You stay by the telephone. I'm going to call Polly and the hospital. Try to locate your father and tell him to head for San Francisco. Have you any idea where he might be?"

Biting her lip, Karla answered nervously, "If he left his meeting, he might be at the cabin. Maybe he took Nichole to see it."

"For Pete's sake! What cabin?" Rommey's voice rose in a shout. "Did you say Nichole is with him?"

"Rommey, don't yell! Dad goes to check my uncle's cabin in Idyllwild every month. Maybe Nichole went along. I'll call up there."

There was a pause. "Karla, do you have any idea what was happening between Nichole and Rex?"

"No, not really. I think she hated him! Why are you asking questions about Nichole at a time like this when Kelley is—"

"Karla!" Rommey's voice cut her off rudely. "I need to know if Nichole would be upset if something happened to Rex."

"Are you trying to tell me that something happened to him?"

There was a brief pause. "Yes. An accident."

"Oh, no! What happened? Is he—"

The answer came slowly. "Freak accident. Yes, he's dead."

255

Karla drew a breath and gripped the receiver. "How awful! Well, look, Rom, I'm not the one to tell Nichole, and neither is Dad. Do you want the number so you can tell her?"

"No time right now. Gotta make a couple more calls, catch a ride, and in five minutes, I'll be on my way to see Kelley. Find your father. I'll keep in touch. The most important thing now is your sister."

"You're in love with her, aren't you, Rommey?"

There was a grunt and a mumble from Rommey. "Look, I gotta catch a plane. I'll think about that when I'm up in the clouds."

"Ha, you may not know it, Rom," came Karla's answer, "but I think you're up there already."

The bell on the telephone disturbed the peace of the tiny chalet nestled on a hillside overlooking a ravine. A fat gray squirrel dropped his acorn on the porch and leaped into an oak tree, scolding angrily. Listening at intervals, he sailed from limb to limb with tremendous agility and showmanship, and soon decided to ignore the bell altogether.

Sheaves of afternoon sun fell through silent pines, highlighting corners of the chalet. The majestic crags of Mount San Jacinto dwarfed the tiny glade.

A car wound its way into this clearing. The sound of voices echoed in the hollow. The fat squirrel sniffed, chattered a last protest, then left for less violated haunts.

Awed by the peacefulness of the scene, Nichole Vincett stood on the porch as Christopher fumbled with the door. When the ponderous door creaked open, she followed him into a large room beamed overhead with heavy timbers. A massive stone fireplace dominated the room. The firepit was as tall as Nichole. As Christopher opened the shutters, Nichole gazed about, charmed with the message that this woodland room communicated to her. She listened as if a hundred knotty mouths of the mottled paneling were signaling in silent pantomime. Her fingers touched the rough fireplace boulders as they stood, crystalline and resolute, saying to her... *stand by us for we are adamantine...congealed for a thousand years and then a thousand more...we will house the sparks that glow here until the secrets of the sun unfold...we will warm you too...rendering you alight within....*

Christopher had been talking all the while as he busied himself about the cabin. "It will take me only fifteen minutes to fix that leak over the window. I'll start the coffee pot. I could build a small fire to take the chill off the room if you'd like. I see that David cut a lot of firewood when he was here. You haven't said a thing, Nichole. Do you like the place?"

"Oh! Oh, yes, I like it. That fireplace is overwhelming," she answered quickly.

"My uncle built it himself. He had quite a talent. This place is built solidly. First time this window has ever leaked." He prodded the window jamb. "This won't take long. We won't have to be here more than a few minutes." His coat was off and he took some tools from a kit.

Inwardly, Nichole was delighted with his unsureness. It made her master of a situation. She stretched her arms. "It feels so good to stand after that long drive. This cabin is so cozy. Your uncle surely chose a secluded site for his hideaway.

Almost lost in these trees. No one could find it."

Christopher paused in his labor, then applied himself with new diligence. "If you think it's not—" He paused again. "That is, if your family would disapprove of your being here, we can leave right away."

Aware of her advantage, Nichole laughed softly. "You forget that it was I who asked you to drive me to Los Angeles to get that matter settled. And don't worry, no one will disapprove. I am older than you think I am, older than your son. By all means, let's light a fire."

While Christopher arranged the kindling, Nichole checked the coffee and continued to explain.

"Everyone thinks I'm younger because I'm still taking classes from time to time, but I already have my master's degree. Took me forever to get it because I had to repeat a lot of my undergraduate work when I came from Spain. Actually, I'm more Gregor's age, so you see I don't have to answer to anyone." She smiled at Christopher's quick scrutiny.

"Very well," he said, turning back to his work. "I'll put it out of my mind. It cools off rapidly here in the late afternoon. The cabin gets none of the afternoon sun. The tall trees throw long shadows."

Nichole sank into a big chair in front of the blaze. She put her head back and closed her eyes. Christopher was using a noisy saw. She let his words run through her thought. Tall trees and long shadows in the afternoon. To her mind came the picture of a palm fluttering in the breeze, throwing lengthy shadows on the two lovers on the mound of turf. For the hundredth time, she saw the motion of their bodies, the sudden fall of rain, the saucy saunter of the brown-skinned twin of Pandora. She could smell the rotting jungle. Again she felt faint and she cried out.

Christopher was bending over her. "You fell asleep," he said. "Are you all right?"

Nichole passed her hand across her perspiring forehead. "I'm fine. Just sleepy because I didn't get to sleep until late last night, and hardly at all the night before. That coffee is what I need. No, let me get it," she insisted when Christopher started toward the kitchen. "I'll pour while you finish your window."

In the kitchen, she tried to rid herself of thoughts of Gregor, but his image remained clearly in her mind. Again, she could see his muscular frame with only a loincloth flung about his hip, the leisurely stride so peculiar to him, the shock of sunbleached hair. Why is it, she asked herself, that this feeling about him won't leave me? Am I still under his spell? No? Then why am I shaking like this? I should hate him for turning me away in favor of that little savage. I hate him all the more when I think that I would have weakened to him as to no other man. Let him have his Pandoras and all the other women who fall under his spell. I will not be one of them. I must find someone else. Look at Chris. He must have been an athlete, a handsome one. He still is. He is masterful. His face shows strength, yet his eyes are kind. His voice is commanding. I like a man to be wild and fierce, but gentle on the surface. Not as wild as Rex. Not that wild.

Christopher had come into the kitchen, had taken his coffee and was talking to her. "...and we used to come up here just to get away from the kids for a day. There is a trail by the little brook. Well, I can tell you about it on the way home."

"Chris, I don't want to go home," she said.

His brown eyes twinkled. "Is it bad at home? A quarrel with your father?"

257

"No. With my stepmother. The minute I got in the house yesterday." She fingered strands of her hair nervously.

"Stepmother?"

"Yes. My father remarried when I was young, shortly after my mother died of pneumonia in Spain. Dad had been teaching there. My stepmother thought it best for me to stay in the convent school near my aunt's home until Dad finished another year of teaching in India. Each year, he said he would send for me, but it didn't happen until he came here to the West Coast."

"Ah-ha! I suspected you had had a quarrel at home before you visited us last evening."

"How could you tell?" Nichole's dark eyes blinked.

"Oh, I have ways," he teased.

She stamped her small foot. "Tell me, Chris."

The creases to the side of his eyes deepened as he smiled. "Your voice takes on just the hint of an accent when you are excited, or perhaps it's just the way you clip your consonants." He added quickly, "It becomes you. It gives you the air of a Spanish contessa. So, Cinderella of Spain, you and your stepmother had an argument."

Nichole hesitated, then she laughed. "Very well, Chris," she said. "My stepmother and I never really understood each other. She was furious because I spent a good bit of my inheritance on my little excursion to find Gregor. It does sound like a fairy tale, doesn't it? Only in reverse. Cinderella spends family fortune traveling across the world in search of lost love."

"Without success," Christopher reminded.

The black eyes blinked again. "Chris, you mentioned that you had to come back here next week to put up the storm windows. Couldn't I stay for the week?"

Christopher reached to pat her hand, but thought better of it. "Well, it would be lonesome here by yourself. But I suppose it's all right. I could ask my neighbor to keep an eye on you." He sighed. "Sooo, Cinderella, come with me and I'll show you how to secure your castle against siege, dragons, drought, squirrels and elves of the woodland. A person can relax up here. You must be tired after your frustrating effort to locate Gregor. It's too bad that you couldn't at least have seen him."

Nichole frowned and pressed her lips together. "Chris, I did see Gregor."

The heavy brows arched again. "But that isn't what you told us last night."

"I'll have to explain."

Christopher's eyes kindled. "Well, well! How was he? Tell me all about it." He pointed to a chair. "Here, sit here and tell me how you located him."

"Kimo knew where he was. His friend, Mr. Namu, took me there."

"Why didn't you mention it last night?"

"There were things not appropriate for Karla's ears."

"What about his hair-brained idea of marrying into a native royal family? Is it true? How did he explain it? What did he say?"

Nichole took a deep beath. Her voice was low. "I didn't talk to him."

"But you just said you did."

"No, I said I *saw* him, but I didn't talk to him."

"Incredible! You saw him, but you did not speak to him? Incredible! You traveled thousands of miles just to look at him? Now, that is a Cinderella story. You must be kidding me."

"No. It's true." She watched his amused expression turn into a frown. She heard him clear his throat. She realized that she was testing him, and derived pleasure from her ability to puncture his composure. She guessed that he could be perturbable and passionate. However, her second thought of how she would cope with it frightened her.

Suddenly, she felt like talking to him. "Chris, it's simply impossible to explain unless I tell the whole story. You won't understand just bits and pieces."

"Okay. Start at the beginning." Christopher settled back in his chair.

Nichole began her story, starting with the briefing that Mr. Namu gave her. "I think that Kimo knew what was happening. He tried to discourage me," Nichole admitted. She described the palace, the cool reception that she received and the weird terrace where she was left to wait. She reached the part of the story in which the couple had seated themselves in the shade of the palms, and had barely begun their erotic lovemaking.

Wide-eyed, Christopher exclaimed, "Good Lord! In plain sight?"

At that moment, the telephone rang. Christopher went to answer it. Nichole paid little attention until his voice rose.

"You aren't serious! Mother of God. Yes! Yes! I'll catch a plane. That's all you know about it? If that's all the information they can give you, I won't bother to call. I'll just get going. No, no, now's not the time for that. Give me the number of the hospital. If there is a wait for a flight, I'll telephone then. Thanks, Rommey. Thanks. I'll get there as fast as I can. Thanks."

Nichole stood anxiously awaiting an explanation. "Bad news?"

Christopher appeared dazed. His face was drained of color. "*Kelley is on the critical list* at a hospital in San Francisco following emergency surgery." His voice grew raspy. He cleared his throat. "I have to leave right away. You'll be all right here. I'll call every day."

She pressed his arm, compassion showing in her eyes. "I wish I could help."

His jaw tensed as he shook his head. "Take care of yourself," he said as he took his jacket. In a moment, he was gone. The big squirrel waited until the sound of the car faded. Then he returned to his place on the porch.

XXXVII

"...the infant was barely alive..."

hristopher Holliss arrived at the hospital in San Francisco in the early evening. With mixed emotions, he made his way to Kelley's room. Rommey was already there. Seeing Christopher, he arose hastily. Christopher ignored him and leaned immediately over his sleeping daughter's bed. Tenderly, he stroked her brow and bit his lip in an effort to control his feelings. Then he looked at Rommey's worried face and their eyes met for a few meaningful seconds. His lips opened to speak, but instead, he blinked rapidly and began to fumble with the button on his coat. Willingly, he sank into the chair that Rommey offered.

"She woke up once while I was here, Mr. Holliss," Rommey broke the silence. "She's still sleeping off the anesthesia."

Christopher eyed the soft-spoken young man's expressive face. Dressed in Levis and a Mexican shirt, sandals and beads, he presented quite a contrast to Christopher whose suit was immaculate despite his tiring trip. Whereas Rommey's head of thick curls defied the touch of a comb, Christopher's short hair was neatly brushed.

"When did you get here?" Christopher asked."

"About noon."

"Have you talked with the doctor?"

Rommey shook his head. "I talked with the nursing supervisor and the doctor who saw Kelley in the emergency room."

"Yes?"

"He said that Kelley was bleeding internally from a cyst that ruptured. She was unconscious when the police ambulance brought her in together with a couple of other kids from a pot party."

"Kelley at a pot party? That's hard to believe!"

"Apparently, a couple of them had taken an overdose and someone called an ambulance. The doctor in the Emergency Room decided that Kelley was not one of the group. I know she wasn't. The doctor would have found out soon enough because they do a toxicology study on all of these cases."

Christopher looked at Rommey sharply. "Hmm. You seem to be well informed about hospital procedures. What makes you sure that Kelley wasn't at the pot party?"

"Because she was rooming with a nurse, a friend of mine who is engaged to a doctor. Polly took Kelley to his office. He had already diagnosed the cyst. We had arranged for her to drive back home for her surgery. I talked to her two days ago. She mentioned that a pretty wild bunch of kids had rented the place below

Polly's apartment. I told her to lock the doors and stay inconspicuous until she and Polly left." Rommey rubbed his damp palms together.

"Then she knew she would need surgery?" Christopher asked.

"Oh, yes!" Rommey assured him. "She was coming home to tell you. I just can't figure out how she ended up with the rowdies."

Christopher shifted his feet and was silent. Suddenly, his eyes grew moist and he stood quickly, made his way into the hallway and paced the length of it. Rommey followed a step behind. After a moment, Christopher turned to Rommey. In a faltering voice, he said, "She could have, have—di—di—"

"She's going to be all right," Rommey interrupted, quickly. "You can talk with the doctor when he makes rounds after dinner. Maybe we'd better find the coffee shop and grab some coffee and a sandwich."

Engulfed in thought, Christopher said very little as they ate. He remembered that a year ago he had felt inclined to tear Rommey limb from limb. Now he felt a growing respect for this long-haired lad with soulful eyes that seemed much too beautiful to be wasted on a man.

Kelley was awake when they returned. She smiled feebly and said, "I stood up and the car came. That's all I remember. I'm so glad to see both—to see both of you." She fell asleep again.

Rommey finally left, but Christopher waited until Dr. Bardo came. The doctor recounted the details of Kelley's arrival and quick surgery. "She's doing fine, Mr. Holliss," Dr. Bardo assured Christopher for the tenth time. "She'll recover quickly from the abdominal surgery. The broken bone in her leg will take longer to heal."

"When did you find that?" Christopher asked.

"When she came to emergency. We could tell from the swelling and the position of her foot that it was a fracture of the leg just above the ankle."

Christopher sighed. "You've been thorough. Thanks. I'm grateful. Now that you have explained everything, I can get some sleep."

"Not quite everything, Mr. Holliss," said Dr. Bardo.

"What else is there, Doctor?"

"The infant they brought along in the same ambulance."

"Infant? You are joking, Dr. Bardo!" Christopher's eyes narrowed.

The physician cleared his throat. "One of the kids in the group said he thought the baby belonged to your daughter. Naturally, we have to follow up," he explained in a kindly voice.

The remark caught Christopher off guard. "Wait just one minute!" he began. "Do you mean to tell me that you are in doubt as to whether your patient delivered a child before she was brought to you? Have you talked to my daughter?"

"Mr. Holliss, I don't mean to upset you. You realize that there is nothing to go on except what one person said. We have to check the story. No one has been able to question your daughter. She hasn't been conscious enough to talk."

"Is it a newborn?" Christopher asked with growing alarm.

"We can't decide exactly." Dr. Bardo rubbed his chin which had begun to suggest tomorrow's whiskers.

"What do you mean, you can't decide?" Christopher demanded.

"*The infant was unconscious, barely alive!* It was dehydrated, had irregular breathing and a collapsed lung. It had to be placed in an intensive care unit."

"Good Lord!" Christopher mumbled. He reached for a pack of cigarettes.

"Would you like to see it?" the physician asked.

"Not so fast, Doctor. We will wait until there is an indication of its parentage."

The following morning found Kelley surprisingly cheerful as she devoured a scant breakfast. She smiled broadly when her father and Dr. Bardo entered together. The conversation was light until the physician introduced the subject of the infant.

Kelley grew thoughtful while her father buttoned his jacket, opened it, and buttoned it again. Kelley frowned, wrinkled her nose, and put her fork down. "Hmm, I seem to remember waking up once that night, and I vaguely remember a noise like a baby crying."

Dr. Bardo's eyebrows arched. "Can you give me any other information? Have you any idea who might have been holding it? Anything?"

"No, I can't. My eyes weren't even open. I was barely conscious." She turned to her breakfast once more. "They make such good scrambled eggs here."

Dr. Bardo watched her for a few seconds. "Is there any help you can give us of any kind? It's important that we find the parent of the child."

"Why don't you ask the kids in the group?" Kelley smiled and took another bite.

"We have. None of them claims the baby. They said to ask you."

Kelley swallowed hard, blinked her eyes and grew thoughtful again. "You aren't even suggesting that it's mine, are you?" She looked from her father to the face of the physician and back again. When Dr. Bardo remained silent, twisting the pen in his pocket, she replaced her fork and pushed the tray away. "Is that what you think? Isn't that rather ridiculous? The doctor who operated couldn't tell that I didn't have a baby? Don't you have things like blood tests, and stuff like that? Ask the doctor that Polly took me to. He'll tell you."

"We did that. Nothing is conclusive."

"Oh, Daddy, you aren't listening to him, are you?" When her father fumbled for a word, she shoved the tray violently so that the dishes went clattering to the floor. "How could you do this to me? I was feeling so good, and you have to go and do this to me." She turned to one side, burying her head in her arms.

Christopher stepped forward and patted her hand gently. "Kelley, don't misunderstand. These are just routine questions. Don't get so upset."

"Well, I am upset," Kelley answered in a faltering voice.

"Look, sweetheart," her father began again.

Kelley's voice was muffled. "If you mention it again, Dad, I won't talk to you."

"Very well, Kelley, I won't." Christopher looked sternly at the doctor.

"Promise!" Kelley demanded. "Promise me!"

"I promise," came the soft reply.

Dr. Bardo placed his hand gently on her arm. "Kelley, let me explain." However, he got no further because Kelley burst into hysterics. He stepped back, signaled to Christopher, and the two men withdrew into the hallway. "It's upsetting her too much. It can wait."

"Too bad that Kelley didn't know more. I had hoped she could supply information that would have ended the whole thing." Christopher continued to talk as they made their way to the lounge. "Don't you have ways of recognizing a newborn? And ways to tell if a uterus has just borne a child? And what about blood types?"

Dr. Bardo sighed. "Let me try to answer your questions one at a time. The baby was so weak and dehydrated that it was difficult to tell. It could have been a week old or premature, although I would guess it wasn't either. Its reaction to light suggests that it was a newborn. That's the most significant sign."

"You'll have to explain that to me."

"Newborn infants have no reaction to light stimuli. This one didn't react to light. To answer your questions further, there are ways to identify a postpartum uterus. After birth, the uterus is not well involuted, and it doesn't become so until about two weeks after birth. In your daughter's case, the uterus was well involuted, but with so much bleeding, our primary objective was control of the blood loss and reversal of her shock."

"What caused such a blood loss? You said that a large ovarian cyst was torn loose, but that doesn't mean much to me."

"The tearing of a cyst is serious enough, but this one tore loose at the pedicle or stalk, which is the base of the ovary. This type of tear bleeds profusely and can be fatal if it isn't stopped immediately. We had to work fast, Mr. Holliss. There wasn't much time for exploration."

Christopher pursed his lips and nodded. "It would seem, then, that thanks are in order for saving my daughter's life." He hesitated. "About the baby, I take my daughter's word for it. Of course, if there is any evidence to the contrary, let me know right away. Otherwise, it is my wish that you do not mention it again to Kelley. When she is home and feeling better, I'll get a chance to talk to her about it. I'll be talking to you and to Dr. Lindley again to arrange for Kelley to go home. Thanks again. I'm grateful for your fine care." Christopher shook the physician's hand, buttoned his coat for the tenth time and strode in the direction of the elevator.

XXXVIII

"...it went out with bobby socks and swing..."

During the next few days, Christopher Holliss had difficulty concentrating on his work. He called Kelley and her doctors daily and arranged for his family physician to continue with her care when she came home.

Christopher also set aside time in his busy schedule to telephone Nichole daily. On his first call to her, after reassuring her about Kelley, he announced, "Now, the special news! Karla and Jose will be engaged by Christmas! I am certain Jose will be accepted at our local campus."

"I hope he makes it through," Nichole answered. "Tuition and living expenses have gone up so much."

"If I am any judge of character, Jose will make it. His uncle has promised to help him. If that doesn't do it, I may arrange something for him. It's funny to think that Karla will be the first to be married and gone."

"You'll miss her, but Kelley will still be with you."

"Oh, yes," Christopher hurried to add, "besides, David is coming home to live until his graduation."

"Where had he been?"

"Hate to admit this, Nichole, but he has been living with Kim in her Del Mar beach house," Christopher explained in a guarded tone.

For a few seconds, no voice came over the line. Then, "I take it they are splitting?"

"Yes. If you ask me, he has just been a convenience to her. She doesn't really love him and nothing much he can do will change it."

"How well I know. That's the way it was with Rex and me. It all ended in my hating him."

"You and Rex were not suited to each other," Christopher began cautiously, debating whether to break the news of the accident in San Francisco, but Nichole's quick answer precluded his saying more for the time being.

"Chris, I never want to see him again."

He cleared his throat. What shall I say, he thought. Say something. Anything. "Ah, you knew that Kim was married to an actor, didn't you? Handsome fellow."

"Yes, I know. I introduced Kim to him. My sister told me that Kim had plastic surgery done on her nose and that she bleached her hair, and that her husband wants her back because she is suddenly a knockout. I'm sorry for David."

"Nichole, every one of us advised him against becoming involved with another man's wife. He wouldn't listen."

264

"Don't be too critical," Nichole's voice pleaded. "More and more young people are doing this experimental thing. Times are changing."

Christopher's foot tapped a nervous beat on the floor. "Well, I can't accept it. My generation was taught an altogether different kind of morality. That was an age when mothers held to the stork myth. They made a *classic* out of the birds and bees approach. Chaperoning was an industry!"

Nichole's chuckle sounded over the line. "Now there are more and more sexologists opening up offices. It's a trend."

Christopher whistled. "Great Scott, but that is a switch! When I was in college, the first experimental course on *marriage* was offered. It was supposed to be sensational. Only seniors could take it. Of course, we were all single because marriage was not permitted for students then. Do you know what we talked about? The importance of abstinence before marriage and fidelity in the married state! And the old double standard." He laughed and was still chuckling as he added, "You don't even know what that was because *it went out with bobby socks and swing.*"

"You forget I was raised in a Catholic country, in a church school taught by nuns who meted out rigid discipline and tough guidelines. But I try not to be too biased or I won't get along with my peers."

"I guess I don't have that problem," Christopher speculated.

"Well, let me ask you a question. Would it be any less wrong for singles to live together if they didn't do it so openly?"

Christopher's foot tapped on the floor again. "Possibly, in that it may be offending to others. But," he reflected, "it bears some thought, I agree, even though it's hard for me to accept."

"At least they are honest," Nichole's voice went on.

"True. True," Christopher admitted, "but the scale still doesn't balance. Someone gets hurt nine times out of ten. Look at David."

The lengthy calls to Idyllwild continued until Karla remarked, "Brother! Wait until Dad gets the phone bill!"

At a beach house near the race track in Del Mar, David Holliss let his trim shoulders slump against a door as he surveyed the results of his morning's efforts. Suddenly, he swore. As if to relieve his frustrations, he placed his hands against the header beam, pushing with force until the frame threatened to separate. He swore again, then turned to finish his packing.

His lean face now sported a neat beard that lent breadth to his features. He reached to push bothersome tufts of hair from his dripping forehead. The muscles in his arms bulged as he carried the last of his packed boxes to the garage. Then he drew from his pocket a small booklet entitled *Times and Tides for the Coast of San Diego.* He consulted his leaflet and climbed the stairs to the porch to get a good view of the direction of the ocean swell. At the landing, he was confronted by a young woman dressed in tight hip-huggers and a revealing pink blouse. Her hair was platinum blonde and smartly done.

David stopped abruptly, glaring at the girl's rounded figure and her little-girl face with its upturned nose. "I thought you said you would be at rehearsal this morning, Kim," David said.

Kim wrung her hands nervously. "I couldn't let you leave without seeing you one more time, Davie," came her unsteady voice.

A look of desperation stole over David's narrow face. "We said goodbye three times! Why go over it again? Look, I was the one who told you to go back to Tony, remember? What more is there to talk about?" He turned and walked back down the flight of stairs into the garage where his guitar lay on a packing box. She followed him. David took the guitar, examined it carefully, then sat on the crate and began to strum.

> "There was a bear in a tree," David sang softly,
> "Who smelled honey quicker than me.
> He found a hive,
> Ate the queen up alive,
> But I got stung by the bee!
> Pity me! Oh...pity...me...ee!"

He stared at Kim as he softened his voice further and finished his song in a lower key.

> "I loved a girl who was blond.
> Of another guy she was fond.
> He promised her fame
> If she'd take his name,
> And I'm a spare fish in a pond!
> Pity me! Oh...pity...me...ee!"

David stopped, felt in his pocket for his booklet and watched Kim as she pressed her lips together in an effort to fight off tears.

In a shaky voice, she finally said, "I feel so terrible. We can't let it end this way."

"What way, Kim?" David gestured questioningly. "There isn't anything to feel terrible about. I haven't said or done one thing to make you feel guilty, have I?"

"That's just it, Davie. You've helped me so much. I owe you so much, and then to tell you it's over, well—"

David shrugged his shoulders. "That's the way it is, Kim. After all, he *is* your husband. I keep telling you that it's great that you are back together again. Beyond that, you'll have to struggle with your own feelings. There's nothing more that I can say." He scanned his booklet again.

Kimberly touched his arm. "You know that I love you, too, Davie."

He withdrew his body from her reach. "Oh, sharkspit!" he said.

"But I do," she repeated."

"Yeah." David laughed bitterly. "Yeah. You love me, but I can't get you a part in a movie the way he can. Don't give me that bull."

Tears came to Kim's eyes. "You are going into the Navy, and I feel it's my fault."

Again, David showed his annoyance. "Kim, I'll explain it again. My draft number is almost up anyway. I'm going to volunteer as soon as I graduate because I think that the Navy will give me the training that I want."

"I may never see you again," she whimpered.

266

"Sure, we can see each other, Kim. Sometime after your baby gets here. Any time you want. You name it."

"But you know how jealous Tony is," she reminded him.

Disgruntled by her remark, David stared at her, then turned to go, calling over his shoulder, "If I don't get started now, I'll miss the low tide."

She started down the steps after him. "Davie, you aren't walking past the rocks. Come back. I'll drive you home."

David turned around, confronting her fiercely. "Can't you understand? Don't string it out! Leave me alone!" His hand trembled as he brushed his hair from his eyes. "I want to walk. I'll come for my things tomorrow when you are gone. Man, oh, man!" His voice rose with exasperation. "Goodbye, Kim!"

He pivoted and headed toward the wet sand. For a moment, the cold surf was almost painful. Little whitecaps danced far out to sea. To the south, the sky held the threat of a storm. Feeling the challenge, he walked swiftly, seized by an overwhelming need to skirt the rocks, to pass the bend.

As the clouds on the horizon thickened, the tempest within him abated.

XXXIX

"...dabble in the brook..."

Despite his good intentions, it was almost two weeks before Christopher was able to return to the small chalet in Idyllwild. When he arrived, the sunlight that stole between the tall pines was warm and relaxing. The problems of home seemed to melt, especially when he saw Nichole, dressed in his old shirt and a pair of Vanessa's jeans which she had found.

"Chris! Chris!" she called out as she ran to meet him. "I have coffee and sandwiches ready." She reached him, out of breath with excitement. Without hesitation, she slipped her arm through his, almost urging him to the porch. "After we snack, I want you to wade in the rapids with me. Do you know, Chris, that I haven't played in a brook since I was a child? I've been dabbling in it all week like I was a kid again. I know every stepping stone, and all the falls and pools. I hope you aren't in a hurry to get back." Nichole's olive skin glowed with excitement.

Indeed, she looks like a child, Christopher thought, especially in that oversized shirt of mine. "Well, well!" he said. "A few weeks here have certainly been good for you. Actually, I'd like to rest a bit. That drive is not the easiest. We don't have to start back for another hour or so." He sniffed the air. "Coffee smells good."

"Everything is better up here. Maybe it's because this weather makes you so hungry. And, oh, does it get cold at night!" She wrapped her arms around her shoulders and shrugged.

By this time, they were inside, and Nichole reached to pour the coffee. Christopher sat down, watching her, thinking...very determined little person...not quite what you would call pretty but attractive...that shirt of mine swallows her. "Oh, the clothes you asked me to bring are in the car."

"Great! I can put on my own shirt and go hiking."

Christopher's eyes grew wistful. "Vanessa used to go hiking down that stream all the time." He shook his head. "It doesn't seem like almost a year ago since we—" He left his sentence unfinished and pretended to stir his coffee. He waved his fingers as though dismissing something. "Forgive me. Vanessa comes to my mind all the time. I can't help talking about her." The lines of his mouth tightened as he looked about the room. A lengthy sigh escaped him. "There are so many reminders." He could feel Nichole's compassionate gaze as he realized, too late, that he had already sugared his coffee once.

"It's all right, Chris. It's good for you to talk it out," she said. "I don't mind."

"These sandwiches are good. Didn't realize how hungry I was." Christopher took an oversized bite.

"You haven't told me how Kelley is," she reminded him.

"We got her home, finally. She is still a pretty sick girl. Jose's mother came up to take care of her for a few days. You'd never guess this. Mrs. Ronrico has red hair. Very nice lady."

When Nichole left to get her clothes from the car, Christopher finished his sandwich. On her return, he surveyed his own attire. "I'm afraid that I'm not dressed to go wading, Nichole. I can't go like this."

She disappeared again. A closed door squeaked, and Nichole came back holding a pair of his golf shorts. "They were in the back closet."

Christopher laughed as he took them. "Very well, we'll *dabble in the brook.* Vanessa used to say..." He paused, then added apologetically, "But there I go again! This place brings back memories." He finished his coffee and rose. "Why don't you wait for me at the end of the path?"

When he caught up with her, she was balancing precariously on a rock in midstream. She waited, then hopped across the stones to the trail on the other side. Little pixie, Christopher thought, she thinks that I can't follow her. "I have some good news," he called as he hurdled the stones two at a time.

"What is it?" she called back over her shoulder.

"We got a postcard from Gregor."

Nichole swung around to face him. "Where is he?"

"We're not sure. The postmark was smeared. The message, too. I think it said that he was on his way back."

"If he comes, I don't want to see him," she said as she turned again and hurried down the trail with Christopher following behind on the narrow path.

"Great guns!" he said. "I thought you'd be happy to hear."

They were side by side in the rapids now. They picked their way cautiously until the brook ran deep and smooth again. His legs were numb with cold. On the trail, they walked briskly, dodging the undergrowth and stepping over logs. Finally, Nichole sat to rest on a fallen trunk.

"Chris, I don't want to see him," she repeated.

He stared at her. Her face was tense: her black eyes were troubled. "I'm sorry I upset you," he said. "I thought I was bringing good news. You don't even want to see him? Is it because of Kelley?"

"No, Chris. You know me better than that. I keep thinking of what happened at the Ahkar palace, and I've made up my mind."

"You know that you didn't finish that story. Was the man on the beach Gregor?"

Nichole nodded. Then she finished describing how she had panicked and fled from the island.

Throwing a stone into the stream, then another, Christopher sat for a while, finally saying, "I still don't understand the whole thing. Who was the girl? How does Gregor fit into the Ahkar family?"

"I know only what Mr. Namu explained to me. He said that many very old customs still prevail among some of these island people. Some are hard to understand. A few of the cultures are morally stricter than ours. However, most of these groups have simple marriage forms, and divorces are easy. Some of them don't marry until they are sexually satisfying to each other."

Christopher aimed a stone at the trunk of a tree and hit it squarely in the middle. "Hmm," he said. "I suspect their divorce rate isn't very high."

"It also makes one aware that our generation isn't doing anything that hasn't already been tried." Nichole let her brows arch and drop.

With a shake of his head, Christopher said, "I still can't understand where Gregor fits into this whole picture. How can he step in and take over someone's wife?"

"I am coming to that. In this group, conjugal fidelity is hardly considered a virtue. Outside the group, it's a different story."

"I see, but how could Gregor be taken in by this family?"

Nichole rose. "Let's walk as we talk. We have time to go as far as the first little fall." She scrambled nimbly down a steep grade.

Christopher followed, trying to be as agile as she. "I'm listening."

"Mr. Namu said that in this group a man inherits his brother's wives when the brother dies. This girl was the wife of Mr. Ahkar's young brother who was killed while shark hunting. Now, Mr. Ahkar was dying and the palace was already somewhat in mourning. Apparently, he was the last of a royal line."

"But you still haven't explained why they brought in someone like Gregor."

"I was told that under certain conditions and especially if the wife is high-born, other men could be brought into the marriage circle," Nichole answered.

"Curious! How do you suppose the others accepted an American?"

"Mr. Namu said that Gregor was somewhat of a prisoner there. The girl kept him to herself and he had no way to get off the island."

"The story gets more incredible!" Christopher pursed his lips and whistled. "Do you think the girl knew you were there?"

"Oh, yes! I'm certain she knew," Nichole answered quickly.

"Unbelievable! Then she more or less planned that scene under the tree?"

Nichole nodded her head. "Uh-huh. If she didn't, someone did!"

"For what possible reason?"

"I can only guess. They have taboos. Maybe I was taboo. Maybe she thought he would go away with me. Maybe it was a progress report on his happiness and his virility."

Christopher eyed her curiously. "Was it a good report?"

She nodded. "It seemed to be."

"But why did you run scared after the trouble it took to get that far?"

"I felt that someone was theatening my life."

"Oh!" Christopher exclaimed. "It frightened you that much?"

The corners of her mouth twitched and she smoothed a strand of hair that fluttered in her eyes. "Everything was weird. I guess I could be wrong, but I was certainly frightened then."

"And that's why you left so quickly?" Christopher persisted.

Nichole hesitated. She kicked at a twig that lay by her foot. "Oh, I left for several reasons. One, well—" She paused again.

Christopher waited. "Yes?"

"Well, have you ever heard Gig expound on the infinite power that the mind can have?"

Chuckling, Christopher replied, "Oh, yes! You can't know Gregor and not have heard of it!"

She kicked the fallen leaves again. "This woman looked so much like Pandora that it frightened me. Just like her except she had black hair. I—I just couldn't stay."

"Hmm. That isn't much like you. It bothered you that much?"

"Yes!"

"Can you tell me why?"

Nichole's eyes flickered. She lifted her chin. "I finally realized that Gregor will *always* be looking for Pandora. He will never love anyone else. Perhaps I'm no judge, but I think that he's psychologically messed up. I wonder how I could have been in love with him for so long."

"Aren't you still?"

They had reached the waterfall. Nichole watched the splash for a few minutes. The noise of the water drowned her whispered response. Then she said more distinctly, "No. I don't want Gregor any more."

"I'm willing to bet that you'll take one look at him when he comes home and be in love all over again."

"Isn't it peaceful here?" Nichole ignored his remark. "I came down here every day and just sat thinking of what I'll do next and where I'll go. Did I tell you that Mr. Namu would help me start a shop for Polynesian imports?" She looked at her watch. "We've been gone more than an hour."

"We'd better start back," Christopher agreed, wishing the conversation would drift back to Gregor, but it didn't. All the way down the mountain, Gregor's name was not mentioned again.

XXXX

"...to hell with Gregor..."

Strong November sunshine bathed the patio of the Holliss home where Kelley sat. Rommey had just joined her. The pocket radio in his jacket played a rock tune. Down the ri-i-ver! Down the ri-i-ver!

"Hey, dig this weather!" he said. "Would you believe that next month is Santa Claus month?" He plopped himself into a chair beside Kelley. "Best beach weather we've had."

Kelley looked glum. "Yes, the third Santa Ana we've had and I can't go down to the beach until this cast is off. What rotten luck! If my doctor doesn't take this off soon—"

Rommey patted her hand. "It won't be that much longer. Just hang in there."

"Oh, Rom, if you knew how much I want to climb over to my rock and run on my beach again and race the seagulls! I can't wait to feel the wind in my face. As soon as I can do that, everything will be as beautiful as it was before, and all this will be a bad dream, nothing more." She pointed to the cast.

Rommey cupped her face in his hands. "Sugar, everything is beautiful right now. Dig that clear sky and that neat ocean!" He stopped suddenly and clapped his hands together. "Here, stand up and I'll show you," he said, coming up behind her and placing his big hands gently over her eyes. "There. Keep them closed, but keep a picture in your mind's eye of what you just saw. Got it?"

"Got it. Hmm, your shaving lotion smells good," she said.

"Never mind my shaving lotion. Just picture what is before you and remember the time when it looked the most beautiful. Color it as rosy as you want, prettier than it's ever been, if you can remember some spectacular day. Okay?"

"Okay."

"Ready?"

She nibbled at his hand playfully. "Ready."

"Good! Then open your eyes. Sesame! There it is," he announced, withdrawing his hands. "More beautiful than you can even remember, isn't it? Look at the pattern that the swells make, and the white caps. Smell that fresh salt air. You should have been with me yesterday in Los Angeles. The smog was so thick that I wore holes in the sleeves of my suit from feeling my way around concrete buildings with my elbows."

Kelley giggled. "Rom, you are something else! You have a special way. Yes, it's beautiful. I guess I'll have to be more patient. Thanks, Rom."

Rommey's eyes glowed. "Right on!" he said, putting his arms around her. Suddenly, his eyes grew misty and he tightened his hold. "Kelley," he whispered, "do you realize how long I have wanted to put my arms around you like this, and—"

She nestled her head on his shoulder as she interrupted him. "And it has always been something! I was so sick before my operation, then the hospital, now this cast."

"You'll have it off soon."

"Well, it better be off before Gregor comes back. I couldn't stand to be at such a disadvantage with Nichole flitting around the way she does just because she knows that Gregor will come here first."

Rommey's expression faded and his arms dropped. "Oh, bummers! Gregor again. Damn, I would like to meet some girl in town who isn't waiting for Gregor to come back. Yesterday, Roy introduced me to some babe who dated Gregor eight years ago, and she's waiting for him because she was always in love with him. Nichole is in love with him. You are in love with him. Nichole has told you what a rat he is and you're still in love with him. God Almighty, I thought you were over that. Here I am, thinking that you finally care for me, and all you want to do is shed your cast so you can chase after Gregor!" Suddenly, he turned to go, adding, "I never seem to know when I'm out of the ball park. I'll see you around." He strode to the doorway.

Kelley stood dumbfounded. Then she screamed, "Rom-mey! Rommey, wait! I didn't know." She lowered her voice as he hesitated and turned to face her again. "Rom, don't be angry. Please talk to me," she begged. "Come sit down."

He answered her curtly. "I *am* angry. I *won't* sit down. You know damn well how I feel about you, and I'm not going to stick around to get hurt."

"I didn't really know. I didn't mean to hurt you, Rom."

His usually soft eyes lost their glow. "You didn't know that I was in love with you?" He laughed bitterly.

She shook her head. "You never actually told me. You never really kissed me. How could I know?"

In two strides, he was at her side. "I'm telling you now," he said roughly. His arms went around her. Hungrily, he kissed her until she melted and clung to him. She trembled with a consuming warmth and listened vaguely to his words. "I love you, Kelley. I can't leave you. I want you. You must know that."

As though the air had grown thin, she breathed with difficulty, "You—you never really—told me, Rommey."

He bent to kiss her again, but his head bobbed up as a voice came from the house. "Someone is calling you," he said.

Kelley drew herself free of his arms and listened. "Guess who," she said as Nichole appeared at the patio door. Nichole hesitated, then asked whether Christopher would be coming for lunch.

"Any minute, Nichole," Kelley answered. "Everything is ready."

Nichole stepped closer, looking from Kelley to the scowl on Rommey's face. "Well, tell Chris that I'll be down at the tidepools," she said.

When she was gone, Rommey drew Kelley to him again. His soft eyes were moist as he gave her a gentle shake. "Do you understand what I'm telling you, Kelley? I'm in love with you." He bent to kiss her again.

When Kelley paused for a breath, she stared at him from under heavy lashes.

273

"You never kissed me like that before," she whispered.

"Humph!" he said. "I was trying to be fair to Gregor because you were so in love with him. I'm not going to be fair anymore, not after what Nichole said he was doing."

Kelley blinked. "What has he been doing?"

Rommey laughed. "Right on! Now we are getting somewhere. You ask her to tell you and then you decide if he is worth waiting for. Kelley, I won't let you marry him. I want you. Can't you understand?"

She felt a smile steal across her face. "Rom, you are really different. Most guys wouldn't care if they stole someone else's girl." She took a deep breath. "Wow! Why have you never kissed me before?"

He held her close again, stroking her back, passing his hand slowly up to her neck where he tangled her flowing hair in his fingers, pulling her head back to kiss her again. Finally, he sighed and asked, "Then I have a chance? I want to hear you say that you love me, too. I know I can make you happy."

Kelley disengaged herself gently from his grasp. She stared at him thoughtfully for a moment. "Want to know something?" she asked as she traced a line across his cheek.

"What?"

"I have seen the man inside you, but I have never seen the man behind your beard."

His head jerked back in surprise. "I'll shave it off today if you'll marry me this week."

Kelley sighed and allowed her gaze to wander to a lone thread of cloud on the horizon. "It isn't as easy as that. I have to wait until Gregor comes back. I just have to, Rom. I really don't know how I feel about him. I'd like to hear what Nichole has to say."

Again there were footsteps. Christopher stepped onto the patio. Seeing his daughter in Rommey's arms, he smiled brightly. "Well, well, what's this?" he asked.

Rommey laughed and held Kelley even more securely. "Would you believe that I want this beautiful girl to marry me?"

"And what did she say?"

"I once had a pretty little filly, a really wild one, hard to corral, but I finally got the lead rope over her head," Rommey assured him.

When Kelley giggled, her father approached and patted her head, saying, "It's good to hear that laugh again, and to see the mischief back in her eye. Rommey, watch out." Then he pointed toward the beach. "Is Nichole waiting for me?"

Kelley nodded and watched her father start down the old wood steps. She found herself hoping that Nichole would be gone.

He could see her small figure in the distance, her jet hair shining in the sun. When Nichole sighted him, she waved and ran toward him, arriving out of breath from the exertion in the shifting sand.

"Guess what!" she panted. "Kim rented her beach house to me. And I got a job at the University, working in a lab with a doctor." She circled him like a child showing her dance steps to her teacher.

Christopher found himself strangely pleased with her performance. "Congratulations. What is his name?"

She stopped dancing. "It's not a man."

"Well, well. A lady researcher?"

She nodded. "I couldn't work with a man, Chris." Her face lost its smile. "I hate men. Didn't I tell you that I hate men?"

Christopher winced. "No. No, I can't say you've ever mentioned it before." He bit his lip. "Hmm. That's not so good."

"I can't help it," she said defensively.

They had started to walk in the direction of the house. "But how could you have been in love with Gregor all this time if you hate men?" Christopher asked.

Nichole stopped and appeared to be staring out to sea. "It started with Rex."

He stepped closer to peer into her face. "Why, Nichole! You are crying!" he said. Without knowing how it happened, he found himself supporting her in the crook of his arm, her head leaning on his chest.

Her behavior had caught him off guard. He lifted his free hand to stroke her hair as he would have to comfort a child. In that split second, his emotions arose in conflict. Her body was soft and warm. He felt that his breath would not come at all; then it came faster. A feeling of guilt came over him, as though he must answer to someone, as though he should not permit himself this happiness. His hand fell to his side. He untangled himself gently, drawing his body away by inches. To his surprise, Nichole clung to him.

Again, Christopher's world hung in suspension. He dared not breathe. In his inner mind, he called out to Vanessa...*forgive me...forgive me...and doubly so if I am guilty of any thought that is not hers also...how interminably long it has been since I have felt someone warm in my arms...Christopher...be careful...don't be a fool....*

Again, he eased himself away gently. "I would have guessed you didn't know how to cry, Nichole," he said.

"Now you know," she answered, stepping backward.

Gingerly, he wiped a tear from her face. "I hope that—that you are not including me in your dislike for men."

She looked up at him. "Oh, no, Chris! You're so easy to talk to, just like my father. I feel comfortable with you."

Christopher winced. Then he nodded, thoughtfully. "I have to get back to the office. Kelley has lunch ready. Come on."

She held back. "No. Thanks anyway. I want to stay here to catch low tide, but—" Her voice dwindled away.

"But what?"

"I want you to see my place. We can talk tonight. Come at seven. I have the best recipe for chili rellenos."

There was not the least change of expression on his face as Christopher nodded, turned, and made his way back to the stairs.

It was exactly seven when Nichole's door opened to admit a handsome middle-aged man of important demeanor and stately carriage; this the prying neighbor noted as she made a clucking noise with her tongue.

The uneasiness that Christopher Holliss had felt as he rang the doorbell dissolved as he sampled Nichole's wine margaritas and the dinner she had prepared. Conversation came easily, but finally he noticed the mantel clock.

Nichole saw him check his watch. "Oh, don't go yet," she begged.

"Got to go. Tomorrow is a working day."

"But I wanted to tell you about today, when I was looking for you at lunch time. I couldn't help overhearing Rommey on the patio. Did you know that he is in love with your daughter?"

Christopher's eyes narrowed as he studied her face. "Yes, he told me that he proposed to her."

"Then Kelley has forgotten Gregor?" Nichole asked.

The uneasy feeling returned as Christopher watched her. Annoying doubts surfaced. Could it be that she simply wanted information? "No. I think she is waiting to talk to Gregor first."

"After what he has done?"

Christopher buttoned and then unbuttoned his coat again. "I don't think she knows the whole story."

Nichole's eyes flashed. "Well, she'll know after I finish telling her. She won't want anything to do with him."

"Don't count on it," Christopher warned. "Kelley lives in a Pollyanna world. She has a remarkable talent for seeing only the things she wants to see. She has an even stronger ability to discount the remainder." He tried to keep annoying questions unspoken in the recesses of his mind, but they popped up one by one... *is she really concerned for Kelley...does she still want Gregor for herself or does she want nobody to have him...this is like playing a game of chess...I'll have to outguess her....*

To accommodate his part of the charade, the words sprang out. "You *may* even see Gregor in the same light as before once he gets here."

She shook her head. "Not a chance. I told you already that I don't want to be under his post-hypnotic suggestion."

"Are you suggesting that he hypnotizes you?"

"I don't know exactly, but you know he could if he wanted to. Hypnosis is among his many talents. But I'm sure you agree that he charms women easily in some strange way, and I think that—" She went on at length.

Christopher's thought drifted off again... *how very strange...I've always regarded Gregor as a son...now he seems more like a competitor...for my daughter's affection and for the regard of this woman....*

Nichole's voice cut through his thoughts. "Chris, you're not listening."

Christopher buttoned his coat again, fumbled for his car keys, and replied quickly, "No, I admit I wasn't. My thoughts were on how pleasant the evening has been and how attractive your house is." He looked about the room, then met her eyes again. "I was also thinking how strange it is that Gregor should have such impact on the lives of two persons close to me."

With a toss of her head, Nichole replied, "Your arithmetic is a little rusty. You've counted one too many, Chris." Then she laughed, and her eyes were still dancing as they said goodnight.

What does she mean, Christopher pondered as he drove home... *that she is not close to me or that Gregor does not have an impact on her life....*

The conversation in the kitchen had started cheerfully but ended a half hour later with Kelley crying in her bedroom.

David had entered the kitchen to help his sister with the dishes. "Move out of the way, Sis, and observe the pro of dishwashers perform."

"I can manage, David. I know that you have to study. I'll do the dishes."

"It won't take that long. Here, you rinse. I'll stack." Softly, he began to hum as he worked, finally breaking into song.

"Oh, taxes, Village taxes! Praise be assessor's name!
We bend our knee with fervent plea, but he raises just the same!

"The city likes to tax us until we are quite broke.
They think we are so very rich, not just ordinary folk!

"They laugh and call us affluent and never tell us why.
They joke about our funny ways but they live here on the sly."

David paused as Kelley applauded enthusiastically. "You like that, eh?"

"That's really cool, Davie! You must be really upset with the city. Is there more? Is it new?"

"Yup. Made it up this week." He reached for his guitar. "How's this?" he asked.

"Little Jack Mayor
Sat with a flair,
Eating his Village pie.
He put in a Frito
And pulled out a veto
To make the Villagers fry!"

"I like your style," Kelley said. "My verses are so heavy."

David continued to strum. "Say, where's Karla?"

"At the library."

"Where did Dad go?"

"I don't know. He just said he wouldn't be long."

"He's been in such a good mood lately."

"Yes, he has." Kelley grew pensive. "We could have such a good Christmas, if only Mom...."

She's going to cry, David thought...*get her mind onto something else....*

"Oh, yes, Christmas! Got something for that, too." His fingers picked out the notes of a carol.

"Joy to the world, tax bills have come!
Let assessors receive our check!
Let every heart prepare the boon,
And heaven and city sing, while the Village goes to wreck,
And heaven and heaven and council sing!"

Kelley smiled despite the moisture in her eyes. "David, you belong on a stage."

"Guess what Roy promised me yesterday, Sis. He said that he planned to take the squalosphere down right after the holidays and that I could go along so that I could do some extra research for my thesis! Roy says he wants to take more movies of sharks feeding."

Kelley's features showed alarm. "David! That's too dangerous! Didn't Gregor tell you what happened when the two of them made their shark movie?"

"Yeah," David answered casually. "Roy had his leg gashed open."

"Did you hear about the day they had some trouble with the decompression chamber and they got the bends? Roy had to be hospitalized."

David nodded. "You know that that is what my thesis is all about, don't you? Nitrogen narcosis. It will be much more meaningful to finish this experiment under real conditions."

"But why is Roy taking more movies? I thought the shark movie was done."

"He is trying to prove a couple things. One is that sharks aren't man's enemy as much as the literature has it." David chuckled over the bewildered look on his sister's face.

"He's got to be out of his mind to go in among feeding sharks to prove a useless thing like that! Good grief! What good will he get from it?"

David laughed again. He shrugged his shoulders. "These days, it's the ultimate. The satisfaction is in doing the impossible, like going to the moon. Personally, I think that he's right."

"Well, how will Roy manage without Gregor? Nobody else can really work as well with Roy. It would be much safer with Gregor."

"Rommey may start diving with Roy. Hasn't he told you? That is, if you would let the poor guy get off on his trip to New York so that he can get back on time."

Kelley's answer was curt. "David, I'm not stopping him."

A pan rattled loudly. "You most certainly are! He has put off his trip three times already just waiting for you to give him some kind of answer. After all, the guy wants to marry you."

"David, I told him that I couldn't make up my mind until I have a chance to talk to Gregor." Her long lashes fluttered with uncertainty.

"*Yes, but,*" David exploded, "he knows as well as you do that Gregor is due to get back. He knows just as you do that the tenant has moved out of Gregor's place. Jesus! Think! The guy's not stupid. He even knows that you go down there every day to see if Gregor is there! It's driving him nuts."

Kelley pressed her lips together nervously. "I, uh, know he is a wonderful person, but I just can't do anything until—"

"How can you hurt him like this? Why, he almost cried the other day when he talked to me about it!"

"You're just seeing it one way, David. Maybe you are too sensitive because of what Kim did."

She had touched a sensitive chord because David exploded again as he answered, "You are so right! You two-faced women!"

"I am not two-faced!" she retorted heatedly.

"What else do you call it? Holding out for your island lover! He is a bum, Kelley. Hasn't Nichole told you?"

"I don't want to hear any more about it!" Kelley shouted, clapping her hands over her ears.

David scowled at her. "You dumb kid! Someone has to tell you for your own good. Mom would if she were here to do it!"

Perhaps David had been a little too strong. However, he had no regrets when Kelley broke into tears and ran to her room, slamming the door behind her.

He started the dishwasher as he grumbled aloud.

"Whether she's my sister or not, I'm not going to stand by to see a neat guy like Rom get hurt! He doesn't deserve it! Now, take me, I guess I knew it was coming, but why do women like to break a man into bits?"

Dr. Quest and Dr. Ornski were attending a seminar in Honolulu. After the last session, the two of them discussed their patient.

"These long absences of his don't help," complained Dr. Ornski. "Anyway, I'm stumped for the time being until we find some kind of breakthrough."

"How about the abreaction?"

"Very severe emotional discharge after each recall. More so each time. He seems to repeat several patterns consistently, followed by profuse sweating and exceptional fatigue, particularly when he describes hearing her calling him that night of the hurricane after the luau."

"Does he still have the sensor?"

"Jerry, he'll die with that thing sewed into his neck. He's not about to let anyone touch it, let alone remove it."

There was a pause. "How much do you think the sensor contributes to the telepathy and psychic phenomena?" Dr. Quest asked.

"It may contribute, Jerry. I still can't decide. Several of the experiences that he has recalled couldn't possibly be in his lifetime."

Another pause. "Then you do think, Ryan, that he is going back beyond his own lifetime?"

Ryan Ornski sighed. "Well, you know, Jerry, that we are still in the dark about his background, his ancestry. If we only knew more. Doesn't anyone know anything?"

"Chris Holliss says he knows nothing and there isn't anyone else to ask, but—"

"But what, Jerry?"

"Well, Vanessa once said something that made me think. Can't remember exactly what it was but it was something inconsistent with her lack of knowledge."

Dr. Ornski sighed again. "It would be easier to put this thing into perspective if only we had more to go on."

"How about the lab in England?" Jerome Quest asked.

"There isn't any lab in England, Jerry. I don't think that's where Pandora goes. I think it's closer."

"Closer?"

"Yes."

"Why do you say that?"

Ryan Ornski rubbed his chin. "Can't say. Maybe it's just a hunch. I'm going to put the pieces together, though, if it takes years. We're going to put it out on a graph first, every detail available. Then we'll feed it into the computer I'm going to have in my San Diego office."

"Oh, you decided for certain then to come stateside?"

"The office on the mainland will be my headquarters. I hope Gregor and I can meet on a regular basis. I have a government grant to do this research."

The telephone rang. It was Gregor saying that he had returned to Honolulu and would pay a visit on the following day.

The clouds were a solid canopy of fire except where the far fringes faded to a warm gray. The sea beneath was a pool of melted orange gold with tiny tongues of flame where the swells reflected the burning sunset dome.

Watching in awe and wonder, Kelley leaned against the open side of the sea wall at Gregor's place waiting nervously for the sight of his tall figure.

A voice inside her seemed to be screaming...*that's him...I'm sure that's Gregor...I can tell his stroke any time...just like him to go for a swim before he does anything else...someone seems to be with him...a girl...probably coming out of the surf at the same time...she's going the other way...oh God...he is coming and my heart is pounding so hard that I can't even move....*

It was true. As he came closer, her trembling paralyzed her and tears wet her cheek.

He was almost close enough to touch before he saw her in the fading light. He stopped with a jerk, peered through the darkness, whispered her name, and then folded his arms about her.

For an instant, Kelley was content to remain in the pleasurably consuming aura of his embrace, feeling that the center of the entire world was made of the two of them and that nothing else mattered.

She wished the moment would never end, and when he spoke, she almost resented the intrusion in the interlude.

"Kelley, I don't know where to begin to explain to you why—"

In a second, her hand was over his lips. "Oh, Greg!" she whispered with a shaky voice. "I don't want you to, not now."

His hand stole over hers. "You're trembling," he said. "It's cold. Come on." He led her up into the warmth of the house.

In the living room, she watched as he picked up an embroidered muslin garment. His skin was tanner than before, his body a trifle heavier, and his pale hair was caught with a band at the nape of his neck. "You look so different," Kelley said. "You've changed."

Even his smile seemed strange when he said, "Stay right there while I change into something dry."

"I can't, Gregor."

He looked at her curiously. "What do you mean, you can't?"

"I have to go. Rommey is waiting for me."

He stepped closer and gathered her into his arms again. "You came all the way down here to tell me that you can't stay?" he accused her softly.

Kelley's eyes became moist. "I've been waiting a long time. You were just going out through the surf when I got here. You didn't hear me call. Rommey's waiting for me. I'll have a hard time explaining where I've been. We have a date tonight."

"Break it," he said as he bent to kiss her.

"You don't understand. He is leaving for New York tomorrow morning, and I just can't do that to—" she began, but his lips sealed hers and his kiss filled the next passing moments until Kelley pulled herself away.

"I have to go. I don't want to, but there's no other way."

He followed her to her car. "Then we'll have breakfast together. A champagne breakfast here at my place. Be ready at eight. I'll come to get you."

"No, no, make it at nine," she insisted as she started the car. "I have to go with Rommey to the airport."

Kelley's face was flushed with excitement when she reached home. Rommey believed her story about the carburetor being flooded, and she felt certain that he took her gaiety as an attempt to make this last evening together memorable.

The next morning, David and Kelley left Rommey at the airport. By ten o'clock, Kelley was on the balcony of Gregor's place helping him to finish the bottle of champagne and the eggs made according to Gregor's island recipe.

She was saying for the third time, "You look different with your hair so long, Greg. I just can't believe it is really you." She reached to touch the lock of hair he had banded at the nape of his muscled neck. His new, white Levis brought a smile to her lips.

He grinned and stretched his long limbs leisurely. "You didn't tell me how you knew I was here," he reminded her.

"Lisa told me," she lied, thinking to herself...*don't tell him that you came here every day.*

"Lisa? Oh yes," he said, "I saw her on the beach yesterday morning."

Kelley leaned forward, making no attempt to hide her surprise. "On the beach? Yesterday morning? When did you get here? Why didn't you call?"

Gregor stood, searched the horizon for half a moment, then fastened his gaze on Kelley. "Everything seems different to me. The Village seems almost strange to me with so many new shops, new people, new feeling. I wanted to get rid of that sensation that nothing was the way it was before. Even the beach is different. Remember how lonesome Black's Beach used to be? Have you been there?"

"Not lately, because I can't walk a long way with this cast. But, I know that the college crowds are taking it over. " ...*I hope he doesn't ask me too much about my leg....*

"And the nude bathing, when did that start? It doesn't seem right."

Kelley laughed. "Look who is talking!" ...*now he'll know that I know....*

"Hmm. Nichole has been talking to you, hasn't she?"

"Yes, and Lisa has been talking to you, or else you wouldn't know much about what Nichole has to say." ...*I don't really want to talk about this....*

Gregor lifted the champagne bottle only to find it empty. He appeared to examine its label as he continued to talk. "Yes, Lisa told me a good bit about Nichole's search for me. I didn't know until yesterday that she had visited our island." He replaced the bottle on the table. "I'd like you to hear my explanation, Kelley. I don't have anything to hide from you."

"I'm not sure I want to hear about it, Greg."

"But I have to tell you! Don't you see?" He seated himself beside her again.

Once more, she placed her hand softly over his lips. "Please. I'm floating on my favorite rosy cloud and I refuse to leave it. You can explain some other time. Right now, let's talk about little things that don't make any sense and lie on our backs in the sand and find pictures in those silly cloud puffs in the sky. Just like we used to, remember?"

"You haven't changed. I'm glad," he said as he gathered her in his arms and pressed her body to his. "Remember when we were kids? I used to call you my laughing elf. You are, still. You are sunshine whenever there isn't any. You make me feel like I'm home after being lost for a long time. I didn't realize how long I've wanted to have you in my arms and to kiss you and kiss you and tell you how much I missed you."

"Then tell me that I won't be alone again. It is so terrible to be alone. Gregor, tell me that you have come back to me, not just to your work or to the Village." Tears welled in Kelley's eyes. "Oh, Greg, don't ever leave me again!"

Tenderly, he took her in his arms, and the half-eaten breakfast went unheeded.

At noon, Gregor took Kelley home. Shortly after Gregor left her there, the doorbell rang. The door opened before Kelley reached it. She drew a sharp breath as Rommey walked in.

He threw his carry-on case on the entry floor, sighed wearily, and sank into a chair. "Chicago is fogged in," he explained. "I'm taking a later flight. A friend drove me back here. Where have you been? I've been calling you for the last two hours."

Kelley blinked her eyes. "I'm sorry, Rom," she mumbled. "I had no idea that—"

"No sweat. You couldn't have known, Sugar. Say, dig that smell of coffee! Man, could I stand a cup of coffee!" He arose as though to get it himself.

"No, no. Stay there, Rom. I'll get it for you." She stumbled into the kitchen. Her hand trembled so much that she dropped the coffee cup. It went crashing to the floor. Kelley stood horrified as the pieces flew in all directions and Rommey came running into the kitchen. He took her hand, overcoming her resistance, holding her despite her squirming.

"What's wrong with you?" he asked. "Why are you so nervous, Kelley?" He held her head and forced a kiss on her lips. Just as quickly, he released her. Leveling an accusing look at her, he demanded, "Where the devil have you been? What have you been doing? Answer me!"

Kelley squirmed under his grip. "You're hurting me!" she squealed.

"I'll hurt you more if you don't tell me what you are up to, Kelley Holliss! You've been drinking! Now, what the—" He drew back, a startled look on his face. "Oh, bummers!" He brought the heel of his hand up to rap himself on the forehead. "How dumb can I be? Gregor came back, didn't he? Well, damn it, didn't he?" The kindly look in his eyes was gone, replaced by an accusing scowl. He took her shoulders in his hands and shook them roughly.

"Rommey, stop it! Okay, I'll tell you! Gregor came unexpectedly. I didn't know he was going to be here!"

"You knew last night. That's why you were so late, wasn't it?"

"There wasn't any point in getting you upset last night," she said angrily, still trying to extricate herself from his grasp.

Rommey glowered at her. "So that's why you were so bubbly last night. All it takes is to have Gregor put his foot in the Village. Damn it all to hell, Kelley, look at him realistically. Why don't you find out how he has been living?" He released her abruptly and his voice rose to a pitch. "I can't believe that is all you think of me, to run to him the minute you think I'm out of the way! You women! You're all hypocrites. What did I do to deserve this again? Why did I let myself fall in love?"

"Please, Rommey, don't shout!" Kelley pleaded as she trembled, in awe of his vent of fury. Guilty feelings overcame her. She searched for words...*what can I say...how can I let him go like this*.... "Rom, listen to me. Let me try to explain. It's the only way I'll find out if I really love you. Don't you see?" She reached to touch his arm.

"No, I don't see!" he shouted. "Hell, if you are that much in doubt, forget it! No woman is going to do that to me again!" He knocked her hand aside, turned, and strode to where his bag lay in the entry.

Stinging from his blow, she followed him, pleading, "Don't leave like this! Rommey!"

His hand was on the doorknob. "*To hell with you, and to hell with Gregor!*" he said as he let the door slam behind him.

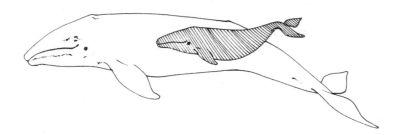

XXXXI

"...autonomic responses..."

In the late afternoon, the sun plunged behind the ponderous cloud that hugged the ocean far out from the land. Despite this, the dome above became tinged with delicate shades of coral. As far as the eye could see, the surface of the Pacific appeared to be strewn with pink cobblestones as the agitated waters mirrored the living sky. Only the rougher water ran in grey streaks. A small craft sped toward its port leaving a dark wake. Small misty sections broke away from the ponderous cloud and sped toward shore spilling patches of rain as they approached Mount Soledad, drenching the roof-tops that lay at its feet. For days, the rain had come and gone. Already slight growths of moss were visible on the roof shakes.

Gregor arrived at Kelley's front door, wet and laughing. "You should see the floods in the streets," he said. "The water can't run off fast enough. Could hardly get through in places. That's why I'm late." He shed his windbreaker and wound his arms around the slender girl.

Kelley's eyes sparkled as she looked up at him. "Greg, it's so good to have you home."

"It's good to be here. How could I have stayed away so long? Where do you want to go tonight? Want to watch the waves come in at the sea wall?"

However, Kelley led him into the room. "Let's just sit in front of the fire. I have a bit of a headache tonight."

Gregor smiled. "Oh, oh! Too much champagne?"

She shook her head. "Nichole came over this afternoon. She talked and talked. It looked as though she would never leave."

"Nichole can give a person a headache, especially when she comes on too strong."

Kelley sprawled on the carpet before the blazing logs, pulling him with her. "It wasn't Nichole's talking alone. Rommey didn't take his plane this morning. He came back here to wait. Got here just a few minutes after I got home from your place." She came to a sitting position, crossed her ankles and hugged her knees. "Well, we had an awful fight."

Gregor didn't answer. He lay on his back completely relaxed, stretching himself lazily. To Kelley's mind came the image of a lion, king of the pride who yawned as he surveyed his domain without concern because he knew himself to be master. There was something about him, she kept thinking... *something different... just being with him does something to me that no one else can do... not the same feeling that I have for Rom...I didn't want to hurt him...poor Rom...he was so upset....*

Gregor's question interrupted her thought. "Just what is this between you and Rommey?"

"He asked me to marry him," she admitted.

There was another period of silence. "What did you tell him?"

"How could I give him an answer, Greg? I've been hoping all this time that you would come back. I've loved you all this time. You don't know how dreadful it is to be lonely. It was terrible! But when I broke my leg, Rom was with me the next day. I don't know what I would have done without him. He is really a neat guy."

Gregor drew up one knee but did not stir otherwise. "You had better not be in love with him. All the time I was gone, I knew that I'd come back to you. I want you, Kelley. You know that, don't you?" He toyed with the strands of her glossy brown hair.

Kelley sighed impatiently. "You turkey! Why didn't you write or something?"

"They didn't mail my letters. I wrote dozens!" He was silent again. "Now that I'm here, you'll have to forget Rommey." He raised his head so that he could watch her face. "I don't want to compete with someone else in your life."

She threw her head back and laughed softly. "Oh, Greg, you are so strange sometimes. You aren't in a position to be very critical after spending almost a year living with a native girl on an island!"

Gregor lifted himself onto one elbow. "It would have been better if you had heard my story yesterday than to have Nichole talk to you. We better get it straight right now! I'll lay it all on the table. Just what did Nicki tell you?"

Kelley shrugged her shoulders. "That you probably thought this girl was the reincarnation of Pandora and that she had you bewitched into an illicit affair. Something like that."

He sat crosslegged beside her and stared. "Good grief! It's a wonder that you even talked to me when I arrived. I didn't realize that Nichole had seen me on the island. How can I even begin to explain the whole thing? Well, let's start with biofeedback. Then I want to tell you more about the laboratory I had there." *...I wish I didn't have to do this,* he thought... *because it isn't going to sound right no matter how I put it....*

"What has biofeedback to do with your leaving me for a year to live with some Polynesian princess?"

Gregor winced under her stare... *could Kelley possibly know that I called the girl Princess just like I did Pandora...how much did Nichole tell her....*

"Everything," he answered. "It will take careful explaining. Concentrate now. Listen and think. Biofeedback is a science that has to do with manipulating your own *autonomic nervous responses*. It is a way toward voluntary control of internal functions. It isn't a new science even though the Western World has just found it." His eyes met hers and held her attention. "Do you follow me?" When she nodded, he continued. "This science has been practiced for centuries by the yogis and swamis of Eastern culture, but it is a slightly different process with these mystics. While I was on the island, I had the chance to meet one of them. He helped me in a way that no doctor could have. He had a treatment for my back injury. He saw me daily for months. We got to be good friends. When he discovered how guilty I was over Pandora's disappearance, he had a remedy for that, too. I can't tell you

285

how terrific he was. He also helped me with my natural drug research. That was the beginning. I had to stay. I made a deal." He continued to stare intently at her, waiting to see if he had gone too rapidly.

Kelley sat deep in thought. Then she said, "Is that why you stayed with the girl? It wasn't because you thought that Pandora had come back to you?"

"Let me tell you about this girl...."

"Please don't tell me her name!" Kelley pleaded. "I don't want to know; I don't want to think about it; I don't want you to mention her again after today!"

That is good, Gregor thought as he sighed with relief...*she doesn't know too much and she doesn't want to remember...that is good*... "This girl was not someone I wanted to live with all my life. She filled an interim." ...*if she had read just one of my letters...she has a right to look bewildered....*

Kelley hugged her knees and leaned forward tensely. "But Nichole said that she was somebody's wife."

His voice grew barely audible. "She was the wife of Mr. Ahkar's young brother who was killed by a shark, after which she became the wife of Mr. Ahkar, more or less automatically. It's the way they do things."

Lifting her eyebrows, she gave a short whistle. "That was quite a switch! Three-way, I'd say. Didn't Mr. Ahkar mind your consorting with his wife?"

"She was only one of his wives. He was her husband in name only. He had been ill for some time and finally died just before I left."

"What will become of her now?"

"She will become the wife of the nephew."

"Don't tell me that nobody was jealous, that nobody got upset over your being there."

Gregor sighed loudly. "Actually, no. This group was structured in such a way that there were no infidelities, so there wasn't anything for anyone to get upset about. You might get the idea that there was a lot of emphasis on sex, but that wasn't so. Rules were so liberal that one became desensitized to it all after a while." He arose to place another log into the firepit, thinking as he did so...*maybe she won't ask any more about the girl....*

"Why have any rules at all? What kind of rules could there be anyway if everybody is—" Kelley threw up her hands as she added, "...everybody's!"

Gregor turned to look at her. "Oh, there were limitations within the group and taboos outside it," he explained earnestly.

"Was there ever any trouble?"

He seated himself again, knees drawn up to his chest. "Only if subsequent husbands or wives were of inferior rank. That made trouble."

Again, Kelley laughed. "Oh, Gregor! How did you fit into a family of royalty?"

He smiled, too, thinking...*the storm is over...the worst is past...whew....* "I was considered on a level of royalty for a number of reasons," he replied smugly.

Kelley doubled with laughter. Like a genie making obeisance to her lord, she pantomimed mock gestures as she recited, "Only make your wish known, your majesty, and your most adoring servant will grant your every desire, your majesty. Only wish it, master, and you will be as rich as the King of Siam on a throne of gold and with a hundred of your children at your feet! Or isn't it quite a hundred, Greg?" She continued to laugh.

Lunging at her, he pinned her with a wrestling hold and they tumbled over and over like two bear cubs until they noticed Christopher standing in the entry.

It was the same kind of downpour at Nichole's beach house as she sorted reports for her work at the laboratory. The sound of door chimes startled her.

She arose, mumbling to herself. "Someone has to be out of his mind to be out in this cloudburst." Opening the door just a few inches, she peered into the darkness. "Chris!" she exclaimed, throwing the door wide. "Come in! Come in! Good heavens, you're soaked!"

"Christopher Holliss hesitated on the doorsill. "Nichole, I had to come. I have to talk to you."

Pulling him in by the elbow, she helped him shed his raincoat which she promptly draped over a chair in the kitchen. "Why didn't you phone? Has something happened? Such an awful night to be out!"

"Nichole, you won't—" he began as he stood ill at ease near the fireplace.

"Oh, please call me Nicki," she implored as she returned from the kitchen. "Come, come, stand nearer the fire."

Christopher backed up to the heat of the burning logs, one hand in his pocket and the other nervously twisting the button of his coat. "Nicki, you won't believe this," he began again as she seated herself on the arm of the sofa. "I've been driving around in the rain for half an hour."

"Oh, mercy! But why, Chris?"

Christopher's inner voice prompted him determinedly... *stop shaking and get it out...when have you ever been wrong...don't lose your courage....* "I had to, uh, organize my thoughts."

Nichole blinked. "Why?" she repeated.

He leveled his gaze at her and held it fast. Confident that she was impressed with his athletic figure, he drew himself to full height. "I'll come right to the point. I—" He reached to where she sat close to him and placed his hand gently on her shoulder. "I want you to marry me." He took a deep breath as she hesitated and was about to speak. However, he held up his hand. "Wait," he said. "Let me finish." He breathed deeply once again. "I'm sure you know that my interest hasn't been platonic. I'm also aware that you haven't given me encouragement." He paused, shifted his weight to his other foot and continued. "Yet, I know I'm welcome here. We talk for hours. We enjoy being together. I find that I can't wait to be with you." He touched her temple gently and pushed back a stray lock of hair.

"Chris!" Nichole said in mild surprise. "Why haven't you—"

"It has been a torture to me, not knowing whether you care," he interrupted. "I have learned to love you, Nicki. I need you." A heavy sigh escaped him and the inner voice whispered words of praise... *there...you did it...don't be afraid to bet on yourself because you win every time if you do...just let her know how much you love her....*

Nichole hesitated and stared, perplexed. "Oh, Chris, why haven't you said something right along? You haven't really—"

"Life won't mean anything without you, Nicki," Christopher interrupted. "I

287

do love you."

Nichole's eyes grew moist. "But, Chris, you never let me know. You've never even really held me in your arms!"

Christopher reached toward her at the suggestion, but Nichole pulled back. "I'm not ready, Chris. I'm just—just not sure how I feel about you. I'm—just not—ready."

For a few seconds, Christopher froze. He drew back a step and glared at her. "You are waiting for Gregor, aren't you?"

"No!" Nichole arose and backed over to a chair where she stood wringing her hands.

Biting his lip, Christopher stood enveloped in thought. His eyes met hers again. "Nicki, tell me if you are waiting for Gregor. The only way I can go on with this is to know that you are finished with him."

"I'm finished!" she insisted. "I'm done with him. It's over." She seated herself again and stared at her hands.

Reflecting on this, Christopher cleared his throat and was silent. Then he sat beside Nichole on the sofa. "How do you know?" he asked softly. "Nicki, have you talked to him? Have you seen him?"

"No! And I won't!" she snapped, suddenly rising to her feet again.

"Then how do you know?" Christopher rose and stood beside her.

"You just have to believe me."

Lord...I wish I could, he thought, *what torture this is...what shall I do now....* "That's not enough," he insisted as he touched her arm. "Talk to him. Find out. You won't know until then. You have to do this for me."

She shook his hand away with a sudden move. Anger flared in her black eyes. "I said I will not see him, Chris!"

Christopher stared at her. The voice was saying...*my God...she is beautiful when she is angry....* "You will! You will see him because I want no answer at all from you until you do!"

She gesticulated wildly with her hands. "How many times must I say it? Gregor means nothing to me."

"Then you won't be afraid to see him."

"I will not see him!" she shouted.

...if she loves me...she will do it if she loves me.... "You will!" he commanded again.

"You can't make me do it, Christopher Holliss!" Her voice broke and her lip quivered.

"We will see!"

"We won't!" she snapped.

Christopher's eyes narrowed...*what will I do now,* he thought...*how did I get into this...what will I do now....* He drew his figure to its full height again and placed his hands on his hips with an air of finality. "Okay," he said softly. "Don't expect me to come back until you do!"

With a surprise gesture, he drew her into his arms and pressed her close for an instant, but Nichole resisted frantically.

"Male chauvinist!" she said loudly as she struggled to be free of his strong grip on her arm. She was even more surprised when he released her with a thrust that flung her onto the sofa. Without another word or a backward glance, Christopher strode out into the wet night.

He kept his word. Christopher Holliss did not return. With each passing week, he became more determined to win the game. He allowed the Christmas season to come and go, but the staggering price he paid in lonesome hours was so painful that he began to regret his own strength.

"...put a face on your dream..."

The record-breaking month of rain ended halfway through January. The water had soaked into the hard adobe as far as the rock layers of the ledge would permit before it seeped into the ocean. The shearing of vegetation from the slopes and the new cuts into the earth from extensive excavation and construction of large buildings disturbed the pattern of drainage under the earth's crust. Many old retaining walls crumbled and foundations of some homes shifted and cracked. Pretty, pebbled gardens had to be dug out.

However, the many varieties of iceplant on the banks drank and swelled, preparing for a spectacular display of spring color. Pepper trees and acacia were covered with a sudden froth of fresh green. The cloudless sky began another long summer season.

On such a day as this, Kelley Holliss lay on her favorite rocky cliff, her head in Gregor's lap. "I wish the doctor hadn't put my leg back into bandages," she complained. "He said I couldn't run in the surf or tumble in the sand."

Gregor stroked the strands of thick brown hair that spilled over his thigh. Playfully, he tweaked the pretty upturned nose. "It won't be long. Be patient. In no time, we'll be jumping off rocks again like we did years ago."

"Oh, Gig, you don't know how wonderful that sounds to me. I just can't wait!"

"You called me Gig! Do you realize that you don't call me that very often anymore?"

Kelley's eyes kindled. "Let's pretend we are kids again. Let's pretend that—"

"With this gorgeous, sexy body lying in my lap, that's hard to do," Gregor interrupted as he gave her shapely legs a playful slap.

"Let's pretend that we've been chasing pelicans and sandpipers for hours and we are going up to Elm's to get doughnuts."

"Then we'll shoot cannons from the pill boxes to sink the Japanese submarines that are trying to attack the Village." Gregor turned to Karla who had just arrived. "Quick, hand me that cannon ball, Karla. We can't let that sub get away."

"Hurry! Hurry!" Kelley said as she sat up and pointed to the sea. "They just bombed the steam railway."

"No, no! Those were the arsonists setting fire to the old hotel."

"Or the sheriffs smoking out the pirates and the opium smugglers from the cave!"

"Or chasing the Chinese crossing the beach." Kelley laughed at her sister's bewildered expression. "Let's pretend we're going to the ice-cream parlor at the Colonial and to browse at Van's book store like we used to do. Remember, Greg?

You took us all the time."

Through all this, Karla looked from one to another. "What steam railway? What hotel fire? What pirates and smugglers? You weren't even born when those things happened, Gregor."

"No, but my grandfather used to tell us the neatest stories."

"Well, you may as well wake up to reality, you two dreamers." Karla placed her hands on her hips. "There isn't any ice-cream parlor anymore. They tore down the book store to build another bank. Pollution has wiped out the sandpipers, and the pelicans have died off too. If the pirates and the Japanese could see how people have exploited this Village, they would be glad that they didn't waste time capturing it! Just look at what they did to Torrey Pines Grade while you were away, Gregor. Did you ever think that those beautiful eucalyptus groves would fall to highrise and apartments?"

Gregor pursed his lips. "My grandfather planted some of those trees. I'm glad he isn't here to see them gone. There was nothing here except low chaparral overlooking the unspoiled beauty of the beach. Grandfather used to talk about it a lot."

"Humph! I wonder what he'd say about putting a cement restroom on the surfers' beach. The city is proposing to put one there, you know."

"Not again! I thought they shelved the idea," Gregor said.

"They did for awhile because the surfers didn't want it. You want to know how I feel about it? Every time a bulldozer scrapes and cuts into the earth, it's like someone is sticking a knife into a friend of mine and cutting away a slice of flesh! Someone is out of his mind to want to spoil the natural beauty of our beach with an ugly, smelly, concrete bulwark. The raw and wild look of our shore is the most precious thing we have. How could anyone put the—the..." Karla waved her hands in exasperation. "...the urgency of his bladder before that? I'm passing a petition to stop the thing. The surfers don't want it. Here, Greg, I know you'll sign it."

"You bet I will!" Gregor took Karla's pen. "It's good to know that someone still cares about this place."

Karla sighed. "I go to all the meetings of the no-growth proponents. We keep fighting to keep things the way they are."

Kelley sat up and raised her hands as though she had a magic wand to wave over the scene. "Wouldn't it be great if we had the power to make time stand still or go back ten years? Now, if I were a powerful genie, I'd do just that."

Gregor gave her hair a tweak. "Back ten years? No! Then you wouldn't be in love with me!"

"Wrong again!" Kelley said. "Don't you know that I've been in love with you as long as I can remember, Greg?"

He gave her shoulder an affectionate pat. "Kelley, if only we could make your idea work, it would be great. I'm afraid we would need an act of nobody *less than God* to keep this place the enchanting hide-away that it has always been. I hope your no-growth group has some success, Karla."

"Well, we're trying! But some people don't care how they spoil the land just as long as they make a profit. And that's not the only disrupting factor. There are the changers who come here and want to find fault because they can't stand to see us complacent and happy, like the guy who doesn't think the place should be so Republican or so Christian, or so white, or so American. There's always someone:

291

students, developers, you name it. Why, Gregor? Why can't people come here and enjoy the place and leave it alone?"

Gregor sighed as he eyed the expanse of beach, the dark pattern of the rocky cliffs that towered over the boiling surf, the line of cars traveling the street above, and the rim of houses that seemed to crowd each other off the ledge. "Face it, Karla. Overcrowding always brings social pressures and economic stress. Be glad that we were here to know how it was before."

Karla frowned. "Oh, turtlepooh! I'm surprised at you, Gregor. That is like playing ostrich. That's Kelley's approach. You can't dream away the problems or wish them gone." She folded her paper. "Why don't you both help me circulate the petition?"

"Give us a copy." Kelley stretched out a hand. "But there's one thing I'm sure of. The human race seems to enjoy groveling in the drabness of life instead of reaching for the sublime. You can call me a dreamer if you want, but I wonder what would happen if everybody tried for one solid week to see something beautiful about everything *whether it is or not.* I mean everything! A nationwide *Say Something Good Week!* I'll bet miracles would happen! Just for one week, if people would say nothing at all unless it was constructive and pleasant! Think of it for a minute. Can you imagine what that would do?"

Karla laughed outright. "*Sure I can!* More than half of the people of the world would be positively speechless for seven days! It would take years for the economy to recover from the breakdown in communication!" She turned to Gregor. "Don't you agree?"

"Yeah, I agree, Karla. We might wake up after the week is over to find neon signs all over the Village streets, an Empire State tower in the middle of town, the trees all cut down and a solid wall of concrete along the shore. But it wouldn't hurt to put a little of Kelley's philosophy to work, too."

As Karla climbed the rocks to head for home, Kelley watched a gull gliding by gracefully, gleaming in the sunlight, coming to rest on a ledge nearby. She watched it for a minute more before she said, "Greg, how would it feel to be a sea bird and not have to worry about petitions and pollution and saving the earth for the next generation?"

He took her by the hand to help her to her feet. "Don't you suppose they know that their earth and the sea are being spoiled? They just can't do anything about it as we can." He put his arms about her. "Come on, let's walk."

He followed the worn path over a jutting ledge and down the next trail until it came to the sand. Gregor's inner voice would not be still...*there is something sad about living on this ledge even though there is something special about it...I can't decide whether this special thing is a blessing or a curse...half of the Villagers live in the future and the other half try to live in the past...they try to continue the dream...the dream of a garden playground for nature's child...but maybe the only way is to sink the Village below the earth for a century and let it come to life on the last day for one pure day of joyful living...yes...I would wish the curse of Teufelhausen upon our Village if I could...if I could....*

Kelley had stopped to watch a small child who was just learning to walk. It stumbled, laughed and prepared for another attempt. Golden-haired and fragile, it captured Gregor's interest also.

"Look," Gregor began, "I've been meaning to ask you—" He cleared his throat and started again. "I've been meaning to ask you about the infant they took into the hospital with you in San Francisco."

Kelley froze in her tracks. "Who told you about that?"

Gregor faced her calmly. "Your father did."

"But—but he promised me! He promised me that he would never mention it again to me or anyone! How could he break his word about a thing like that!" Kelley was visibly distraught.

"Don't blame him entirely. I tricked him into talking. I guessed most of it from one little slip he made. The hospital told me the rest when I went there."

"You went there? Why, Greg? Why?" Her face began to flush.

"If there is any chance that the baby is yours, I should be aware of it," Gregor explained quietly.

About to speak, Kelley swallowed hard instead. "All I had was a cyst. That is all I had and I'm not going to say it again, Gregor!" She swallowed again. "I was due to have surgery. I don't like talking about it."

"Your father said a car hit you and the ambulance found you."

"Yes, I was lying there when they came to get a couple of overdose cases. I'd rather not talk about it." She turned to start back, but Gregor grabbed her arm.

"Kelley, I have to know if I left you pregnant in Hawaii."

She tilted her head backward and closed her eyes. "For God's sake, Greg, you weren't even orgasmic! My arm. Let me go! You are hurting my arm."

"You know very well that that isn't necessary for a man to impregnate!"

She twisted herself from his grasp. "No! No, I don't know anything about anything anymore except that you are upsetting me when everything was going along so well! Can't you understand that you are forcing me to talk about something painful to me? Why are you pressing the point?"

He placed both of his hands on her shoulders. "Because, Kelley, I want that child," he said in a barely audible tone.

"Oh, my God, what next!" She laughed mockingly at him. "Now I've heard everything!" She laughed again. "I can't believe my ears."

"Be serious and listen, damn it!" He shook her roughly.

Kelley pulled away and frowned at him. "Tell me, were there no babies in the year that you were with the island girl, Gregor?"

He shook his head. "You have to let me explain something about—"

However, Kelley interrupted briskly. "I don't want to talk about it anymore." She clapped her hands over her ears. A shiver ran through her, for the ocean breeze had come in together with a light mist.

"Okay," he said as he took her hand. "We'll talk about it later. Let's go back, it's getting chilly."

If Kelley thought that she had dispelled Gregor's concern with the infant, she was mistaken. Several days later, she found how wrong she was.

They had gone to the bluffs where the glider meets were being held. During the lull in activities, Gregor pointed to a blond girl. "Isn't that Lisa over there?

Looks like she's cut her hair."

Kelley nodded. "I don't see her much anymore. She hangs around with the college crowd that uses the nudie beach down below. I'm not sure I go along with that sort of thing." She stopped suddenly, and her face flushed a bit as she met Gregor's glance. She changed the topic abruptly. "Say, are you really trying to grow a beard?"

"Yeah. I wish I'd done it this last fall." He drew his hand over his chin. "They itch when they first come in."

"How long will it take to grow it so it looks like a beard?"

"Oh, not too long. It will be looking good by the time I get back from Honolulu."

"What?" Kelley's eyes flared. "*What did you say?*"

"I've been meaning to tell you that I have to go back to Oahu because Roy wants to sell the fishing boat," Gregor explained calmly.

Kelley sprang to her feet and stood with her hands on her hips. "You will do no such thing! I know very well that Roy can sell the boat without your help."

Gregor rose to face her. "There is something that Roy can't do for me."

"Greg," she repeated, "you know that Roy can take care of the sale!"

He hesitated. "You are making it hard for me to tell you."

"Tell me what?" she flared, trembling in dread of what he might say.

His features remained expressionless as he answered. "The Ahkar family asked me to arrange for something in Honolulu for the princess."

Kelley let out a shout. "The princess? You mean your island harlot? Over my dead body you will! You must be crazy to think that I believe that, Gregor Morghann! Good God! How can this happen to me? Why must something always go wrong? Why?"

She snatched her beach bag and strode to the parked car. Gregor followed and drove, tight-lipped. They were almost home when he tried to speak again. "Kelley, please let me explain. I have to close up a lab that I had there."

"That's a lie, Gregor! How can you possibly tell me that now? Why didn't you tell me this a month ago? What other excuse can you think of? The monstrous gall you have! Telling me that you love me and then telling me that you have to go back to your naked little native!"

"But I do have a lab to close. I gave my solemn word. I can't break it. I have a commitment."

"What did you promise to do? What, Gregor?" She bit her lip and shook her head from side to side. "I'm not stupid! Don't think for one minute that I can't figure it all out. Obviously, the woman couldn't have children or she would have had twelve of them. She wants children. What did you promise, Gregor? To father them for her?" Kelley's laugh was bitter.

"She would lose her rank in the hierarchy if she couldn't bear children," he answered, ignoring her question. "But that's not all of the problem."

"Oh, oh," Kelley moaned. "This is too much. Stop the car. I want to walk home."

"If you would look at it this way...if you would believe that my stay on the island was just an interlude, a passing interlude, nothing lasting for me. If you would just believe that it was the best thing that ever happened to me because I'm finally tired of drifting. I have decided to settle down."

"You're just having a little trouble deciding where and with whom!" Kelley retorted hotly. "Your brown lady or me! I don't want to talk about it anymore."

Gregor gripped the steering wheel with white knuckles. "Let me tell you what I used to think was the ultimate experience. Years ago, my goal in life was to get tubed and to ride my board right on through the wave and out the other end into the sunset before the wave crumbled. You know, I almost did it once? It was just when the sun was setting and the tube was a churning dynamo of gold, smooth at the bottom and crumbling over my head, and I could see the sunset out at the end. I almost made it through that tube, and for a long time, that's all I wanted from life, to be able to come out of a tube into the sunset. I've been doing a lot of thinking. Now I know life holds a lot more. I know what really counts."

"Well, tell me! Exactly what is it you want?" she demanded impatiently.

Sweat stood on his forehead as he said boldly, "I want you, Kelley. And I want to adopt the baby in San Francisco."

Kelley felt herself go white as she fought back tears. She was silent as Gregor turned into the drive at her home. She reached for the door handle, but Gregor caught her arm.

"Look, Kelley, we have to talk this out," he said. "Did you hear me?"

"I hear you," she snapped. "Why do you have to keep bringing the baby into this?"

"Because it could be mine! I've got to know if it's mine!"

"Not a chance! You can be sure it wasn't my child or they wouldn't allow me to simply abandon it! What a dumb thing for you to dream up, Gregor!"

"Kelley, it's important to me."

"Huh! I think I know why it's so awfully important to you. The native girl gave you some great lessons in lovemaking, but she got you worried about whether you're to blame for her being childless. Isn't that it? It's your image of yourself that's worrying you. You really don't care about that baby or about me. It's Gregor you're thinking about. Nichole was right about you."

Gregor winced. "Nichole again! Kelley, she twists things to suit her own purpose. Don't listen to her. I'm going to have to explain some things to you."

"Oh, it doesn't matter! Right now, nothing matters except that you won't believe me. Why don't you ask the doctors at the hospital about the baby they found?"

"I have. They are more confused than I am."

"Then ask me, Gregor Morghann. I'll tell you three things. *It is not my baby! It never will be! If you persist in this, we are finished!*" She snapped open the door and ran into the house. Gregor caught up with her in the entryway.

"Wait, Kelley," he pleaded. "Please listen. You're being hysterical."

"You are so right. Who wouldn't be? You left me for a whole year to go live with some strange brown girl on an island and now you are going back. How do I know that you won't be gone another year?" Tears finally came and poured down her cheeks.

Gregor took her by the arm. "Listen to me, Kelley. I made arrangements to adopt. Does that sound as though I plan to be gone a year?"

Her features twisted in anguish as she demanded, "Tell me, Gregor, did you or did you not get through that tube in the sunset?"

His eyes blinked. "I told you. I wiped out."

"Well, you just wiped out again!" she shouted at him. She jerked her arm free and ran into her room.

Gregor swore as he tried the doorknob. "Kelley! Don't do this! Kelley, listen to me. I have to leave in two days."

She took a book from a lamp table and heaved it at the locked door. "Go! Go! What's keeping you?" she shouted. There was a tense, brief silence, then the sound of Gregor's retreating footsteps. Kelley buried her head in the pillow and cried all the harder.

Christopher almost collided with Gregor as he rounded the corner of the entryway. For a second, the two men stared at each other. Then Christopher said, "Kelley sounded a bit upset."

Gregor smoothed his hair with nervous fingers. "Yeah. Yeah, you can say that again! Whew!"

Beckoning Gregor to the bar, Christopher breathed in deeply. "Women are sometimes hard to handle, I'm finding out," he said. He took two glasses from a shelf. "Would you like Scotch?"

"Is Nicki giving you trouble?"

"How did you know?" Christopher questioned quickly. "I didn't think anyone knew." The bottle he held remained suspended.

"Oh, I have ways of knowing."

With a searching glance, Christopher continued. "I suppose that you know, then, that I asked her to marry me. Right?"

Suddenly, a door slammed loudly in the bedroom wing. The two men exchanged glances. Gregor put a staying hand on the uplifted bottle in his host's grip. "Tell you what, Chris. Let's go to my place and talk while we have a couple."

In a matter of ten minutes, they were drinking chilled Scotch as they scanned the ocean from the balcony of Gregor's place. After filling their glasses several times, they let the conversation drift again to Nichole and Kelley.

"...and even though she takes a long time to make up her mind, once Kelley decides, nothing can change it," Christopher was saying. He shook his head. "I wish I could tell you how to handle her, but I can't."

The ice cubes in Gregor's glass rattled as he gave them a shake. "Well," he said, "I can tell you how to manage Nicki."

"Really?" Christopher glanced at Gregor curiously. "How?"

The ice cubes rattled again. "You have to make some women mad before they become manageable—have a big battle with slapping and hair-pulling and the works."

Christopher blinked, gulped some of his drink and stared at Gregor. "Is that, uh, how you handled Nichole?"

With an amused laugh, Gregor answered, "Oh, no, no! Things have been kept very cool between us. Nicki isn't my type. She may think she is, has lots of style and class and all that, but she isn't for me. Never was."

"That's strange," Christopher mused. "I just don't understand Nichole, I guess. She plays such a cat-and-mouse game that I, uh, I don't know where I stand."

"Well, can't you, ahh—" Gregor hesitated. "Can't you talk it out with her?"

Christopher shook his head. "You won't believe this, but I drove around one rainy night before Christmas trying to get the courage to go to her door and talk to her. Got up to her front door two times, mind you, and chickened out. On the third try, I made myself go in. Took all the guts I had. I couldn't figure where I stood with her. We had such good times together. One minute, she seemed to care, then she scared me off." He brought his hand down hard on the porch rail. "Damn! Damn it all! I'm not the sort of man to knuckle down to a girl's whim!" With a flip of his hand, he seemed to ward off a thought. "I can't stand to be toyed with. You know me, lad. You understand, don't you?"

For a few seconds, Gregor's foot tapped on the floor. "What was her answer, Chris?"

Stroking his chin, Christopher answered softly. "Well, she wasn't sure whether she was still in love with you, as a matter of fact."

Gregor laughed loudly. "Not a chance, Chris! There's never been anything between us."

"She could have used it as an excuse," Christopher interrupted quickly. "I told her to decide and that I, uh, we wouldn't see each other until she did." He rubbed his eyes and stared at the floor. "Maybe I'm too ol—uh, maybe she needs a younger man. She needs to decide."

"Hmm." Gregor drained his glass. "Tell you what. I'll help her. Okay? Let's go for a quick swim just to cool off, and then I'll go talk to Nicki."

In a flash, Christopher held his hand in protest. "Now, don't...uh, don't—"

"Chris, you have to stay a jump ahead of her. I know the games she plays but I'm a jump ahead of her because she doesn't know that I know. Just leave it to me."

"She thinks that you've been goofing off this year," Christopher said. "In a bad way."

"Let her think that. I want her to forget me."

"Then you haven't been? Goofing off, that is."

"Chris, you know me better than that. Remember the ocean plant specimens that I was collecting?"

"Oh, yes, for your pharmaceutical lab in Florida."

"In Texas," Gregor corrected. "The Ahkars' island had swamps filled with varieties I've never seen. There was a swami, a kind of medicine man, who knew every kind and what to cure with it. Chris, I had a field day! They helped me set up a lab, my own lab. I sent for equipment from our company. I trained my own technicians. When I thought I was onto something, I sent it to Neil to finish. He says that we are so far ahead of other companies in the search for natural drugs that they'll never catch up. Had to keep it confidential, even so."

Christopher nodded. "Well, well! I should have known. Did you make any discoveries?"

"Yeah, we have nearly found an antibody that will be effective against gram-negative bacteria as found in compromised immune systems. Possibly several others. We barely scratched the surface. It'll take ten more years to really test the results. Could have done more but for a while, the only animals I had to work on were caged birds. I hate to destroy birds but we did do some avian research. I finally convinced the Ahkar family that avian research can't be extrapolated to human research and they got me mice and monkeys."

Christopher let out a whistle. "You've been mighty busy!"

"Oh, yeah, but let me tell you about the submersible that I invented."

"A submersible?"

"I just applied for a patent, so you have to keep this under your hat, too, Chris. It's a mechanical arm operated from a ship that can probe a half mile under water and retrieve things."

"When did you think of that?"

Gregor laughed. "After I went down for that black box from the plane wreck and found a big octopus sitting on it, not about to give it up."

"You did what! Found an octopus sitting on the box? Now I've heard everything."

"Yeah, yeah! I think he was getting a charge from the signals—trying to make love to it."

Quite amused, Christopher assessed his companion. "Gregor, you really ought to let Kelley know all about these things. She sees it only one way now."

"No, no, Chris. She's got to love me as I come, without the embellishments."

Christopher eyed him keenly. "Ho! Now who doesn't understand about women?"

Outside Nichole's beach house ten minutes later, Gregor listened to her approaching footsteps. The door opened slightly and her voice rang out. "Who is it?"

Gregor pushed the door a bit further. "Nicki, it's Gregor."

Surprised and reluctant, she stood blinking her eyes. Finally, she sighed and said, "Well, come in."

He stepped in casually, hands in pockets as he assessed the small figure in tight flares. "How are things, Nicki?" he asked in a very matter-of-fact tone. Inside him, however, thoughts were racing...*she has gained a little weight...not too much...the flash of those black eyes is the same as always...proud girl...always had a lot of class...wish I knew how to handle this but here goes....*

"You look so different, Gig." ...*gracious sakes alive...he looks like a typical beach bum....*

He fingered the tie that held his hair at the nape of his neck. "You don't like my hair, do you?" ...*I can read her mind...she usually says what she thinks....*

"It's—well, it's so long!" ...*now, just why did he come here....*

Gregor sauntered to the sofa where he deposited himself comfortably. "It was longer when I first got back." ...*when she pushes that strand of hair behind her ear, it means that she is nervous...I've got to do something to make her mad...she's always had a temper...it shouldn't be hard to do....*

She walked around the coffee table still eyeing him. "Is that a beard you're growing? You've been drinking, haven't you? I want to know why you came here, Gregor Morghann. You are up to something." ...*I've got to outguess him...with him, it's always such a challenge....*

"Oh, I just want to welcome you back to Sunday Village since we've both been away." ...*look at those eyes flash....*

"You're lying to me! You want to know why I visited your tropical hide-out and what I saw! Don't play any game with me!" ...*careful, he's up to something....*

Gregor arose and stepped casually around the coffee table to face Nichole. "That's usually *your* technique, isn't it, Nicki? Okay, then, I'll level with you. I want to know what you saw and what you told Kelley." ...*man, oh, man, she is something else when she gets mad...wild like a storm at sea...any man will have a time*

298

handling her....

Nichole's chin went up as she tossed a strand of black hair over her shoulder. "Humph! I saw you and your brown bitch making love under a palm tree on the beach." *...damn him, anyway... how could he turn me down for the likes of that savage....*

Gregor threw his head back and laughed heartily. "Only once?" he asked and he laughed again when her face flushed. "As long as you were spying, you should have waited another day and caught my double performance." *...that should get her....*

Nichole's hand shot out to strike Gregor's cheek, but Gregor caught it and held her tightly by the wrist. "Let me go!" she screamed. "Let me go!"

"What did you tell Kelley?"

"None of your business!"

He gave her arm a twist. "Tell me!"

"Ouch! You're hurting me! I told her that you were an unsound marriage bet, that you need a psychologist and that you would probably go back to your Leilani!"

"Her name isn't Leilani."

"In my language, she's just a savage slut! Let me go, damn you!"

However, Gregor pulled her to him. "Nicki, you're jealous! You're jealous, aren't you? I think you still love me!"

Nichole struggled and beat him with her free fist. "I hate you! I hate you! Let me go! You're hurting my arm! Please let me go, Gregor!"

"But, Nicki, you still love me, don't you?" Gregor pinned her flailing arm, held her close and bent as though to kiss her.

Nichole screamed and broke into hysterics. "Damn you, Gregor, don't do this to me! Christopher Holliss asked me to marry him! Don't do this to me! Let me go, let—me—go!"

"Ahah! You can't resist me, yet you're toying with Chris. Playing games again, eh?"

Nichole continued to struggle and cry. "I—I hate you! I—uh—uh—"

"You don't. You love me, don't you?" He laughed at her attempts to free herself and he tightened his grip.

"I hate all of you!" she stormed. "You men are all alike!" She bared her teeth on his flesh and would have bitten Gregor's forearm except that he was prepared and jumped away from her. Free again, she took magazines and pillows from the sofa and hurled them in his direction as he backed toward the door.

"You tried to bite me!" Gregor exclaimed, suddenly angered. "You little animal!" He rubbed his arm. "You can damned well apologize to me. No lady bites."

"I won't apologize. Get out! I didn't ask you to come here." The magazines kept flying.

"You will come to apologize if you ever want me to talk to you again," Gregor called angrily over his shoulder. The floor shook as the door banged shut.

"Whew!" he said to himself as he drove away. "Taming a wildcat couldn't be harder. She needs discipline from a strong man who can make her respect him. Whew! I wasn't expecting quite such a tirade. I just wonder now if...well, it's her move."

Alone, Nichole stood as if frozen. The sound of the car faded. More than ever, her feelings were in conflict. She threw herself face downward on the sofa and cried.

"Why does he show up just when I want to marry someone else? Oh, Nicki, all those years you've wanted him, and now, what have you done? What's wrong with you anyway? He could be yours and you let him go! Don't let this chance go by. But, suppose he just had too much to drink and didn't realize what he was saying? Wouldn't that be devastating? How would I feel the next day? And suppose Chris found out. Suppose I lost Chris? Would it matter? Would it be worth it to have Gregor for one night? Would it?"

Nichole arose and went to the hall mirror where she faced her image. "Oh, no, Nichole! It wouldn't do for you. Some other woman, not for you, though. Yet, when he looks at me, his eyes do strange things to me and I can't resist him. I could easily forget myself. What does he do to me? Oh, I hate him! I hate him! Why can't I shake it off, this hold he has on me? Chris is right. I don't know my own mind. I need to prove something to myself. But how? By going to Gregor? What about the vows I made not to weaken? Oh, damn! What should I do?"

Nichole dried her eyes, looked at her watch and sighed. "He asked me if I loved him! Come to think of it, he didn't say he loved me! What is he up to, anyway? He only asked me if I still loved him! How dumb can you be, Nicki? He just asked you to come to apologize. He's right. *No lady bites!*"

Having left Christopher swimming in the surf, Gregor went to find him. Perplexed over Nichole's responses and wondering what to say, he did not immediately see Christopher hurrying toward him. When he caught sight of him, he knew instantly that something was wrong. Christopher's hand was clamped over his right forearm and blood trickled between his fingers.

"What the hell did you do?" Gregor asked as he looked at the cut and promptly put pressure on it with his own fingers.

Breathing heavily, Christopher said, "Went down in the surf, elbow first. Damned piece of glass, neck of a bottle that some stupid kid left, was buried in the sand. It's in my back pocket." He turned slightly so Gregor could see. "We'll throw it in the trash. Don't want someone else to do the same thing."

"Yeah, yeah," Gregor said as he hurried Christopher toward the apartment. "Let's get home. You need a tourniquet, the way it's bleeding."

They got as far as the kitchen before Christopher's strength gave out and Gregor eased him to the floor where he lay with his eyes shut.

As Gregor worked to stop the bright-red spurting flow, he swore softly. "Damn, damn," he repeated. "You've lost a lot of blood, Chris. Chris, can you hear me? I'm going to call an ambulance. I can't stop the flow." He continued to apply pressure, mumbling softly to himself. After another minute, he said again, "Chris, I'm going to get help. Your pulse is weak and rapid. Let's not take chances." He went to the telephone, made a call and returned quickly to Christopher's side. It was then that he heard Nichole's voice at the entry door.

"Gig? Can I come in? It's me, Nichole. Gig?" She knocked gently.

Gregor jerked his head around and raised his eyebrows in surprise. "Would you believe!" he said. "It's Nicki!" A look of mischief lit his features.

Christopher opened his eyes and tried to raise himself on one elbow. "I can't let her see me like this, lad. Help me up. I can make it."

However, Gregor shook his head, pushed Christopher back onto the floor and

300

whispered, "No, no! Close your eyes. Leave it to me." Then he called to Nichole. "Yeah, yeah! Come in! Come in!"

Nichole entered timidly, stared horrified at the scene in the kitchen, dropped her purse and kneeled beside the blood-covered figure on the floor. "*Madre de Dios!*" she exclaimed. "What happened?"

Gregor bent over Christopher's prostrate figure again. "I think it's an artery," he said.

Wide-eyed, Nichole stared at Gregor. "He cut his wrist, Gig?" she asked. "Oh, Chris!" she moaned, bending to stroke his cheek. "Gig, did he cut his wrist?" she asked again.

"Give me that ice," Gregor directed. "Yes, damn it, he cut his wrist."

Nichole wrung her hands. "Is it bad?"

"Well, good God, yes! Yes! It's bad! Give me the ice, will you? I can't stop the blood."

As she handed him the package of ice, Nichole blinked back tears. "Oh, Gig, did he do it on my account?" she asked with a catch in her throat.

Gregor sat back on his heels and frowned at her. "Well, hell, Nicki, he didn't do it on my account," he answered brusquely. "Here, press here on this towel, while I make sure the ambulance has the apartment number." He wrapped Christopher's arm with yet another towel and released the tourniquet. "It isn't doing any good," he explained. "Here, press down here."

However, tears had begun to stream down Nichole's cheeks and she wiped them away with both hands, moaning, "Oh, Chris."

"Nichole, will you stop blubbering and press down on his arm," Gregor said as he stood and listened for sounds of the ambulance.

"I can't help it, Gig. I love him!" Nichole sobbed as she showered kisses on Christopher's cheeks and mouth. "I love him, Gig!" she repeated as she looked up at Gregor.

Suddenly, Christopher's eyes fluttered. Gregor put the ice pack on his forehead. "Good, he's coming to," he said. "Chris, I've got an ambulance coming," Gregor reminded.

Christopher's eyes opened wide and he raised himself on one elbow. "Look, I'm not going to be carried out on any stretcher. Here, help me up." With help from Gregor and Nichole, he struggled to his feet and leaned against the counter. In the maneuver, the waste-paper receptacle tipped over and the blood-splattered bottleneck rolled onto the floor.

Nichole gasped and held her hand to her lips. "Oh, Chris! Oh, Chris! Oh, my God! You didn't," she exclaimed as she stared at the piece of glass.

Christopher pressed his lips together. "No, Nicki, I didn't," he finally said. "It happened on the beach." Hearing Gregor's moan, he turned to his friend. "I have to tell her the truth," he said with a shrug.

Nichole's face reddened as she gasped again. She whirled around to face Gregor. "Do you mean to say that this is all a trick?" she shouted. "Oh! Oh! And I fell for it! How could you do this to me, Gig? You, you beast!"

"Nicki, it's no trick!" Gregor caught her arm as she reached to slap his face.

She tore herself away, more furious than ever. "You led me on, Gig! What a miserable, deceitful trick! This is probably catsup and the two of you—

you—" She pointed to the bloody floor and began to sob.

"Nicki, please let us—" Christopher interrupted.

Nichole pivoted about and began to flail Christopher's shoulders and chest. "You men are all alike! I hate all of you, all—all—of you," she sobbed.

Gregor tried to grab one of Nichole's thrashing fists. "Nicki, stop it," he ordered, but she paid no attention.

"I hate all of you," Nichole repeated. "Chauvinists! Chauvinists!" she screamed.

Christopher had circled her with his good arm and had held her to him as well as he could. "Nichole, listen to me. You said you loved me. I heard you. You said so. You love me," he repeated as she continued to pound on his chest.

"Stop it, Nicki," Gregor ordered, reaching to halt Nichole's attack, but she kicked his ankles. "Ouch!" he exclaimed and reached to snatch a full handful of Nichole's thick hair. "Goddamn women," he mumbled. "Nicki, Chris is really hurt! Now, stop kicking." He pulled the thick hair tighter until Nichole screamed and again tried to bite his wrist.

Suddenly, Gregor thrust her over his uplifted knee as he would a naughty child and he paddled her soundly. Just as suddenly, he dropped her to the floor and reached to catch Christopher who fainted with a smile on his face.

Several moments later, the ambulance attendant stopped Nichole from climbing into the vehicle beside Christopher. "I'm sorry, Miss," he said. "Only members of the family are allowed to ride along. Are you his wife?"

"No," Nichole replied as she ducked under his arm and climbed into the vehicle. *"But I will be next month."*

Jerry Quest and Ryan Ornski had frequent conferences. They talked at length one afternoon in the office of the psychiatrist.

"Then you do think there's an explanation for all that's happened to Gregor?" Dr. Quest asked after a while.

Dr. Ornski's perpetual grin grew broader. His fat belly shook as he chuckled. "There has to be, Jerry. In due time, we'll put the pieces together. Pandora is around somewhere. She can't just disappear. From the pattern already established, it's clear that she will keep on finding him."

"If only Gregor would allow someone to analyze that midget instrument he has sewn in his neck, the mystery might come to light."

"Well, he won't allow it. He's afraid to lose contact with her altogether. Secondly, it might not operate the same way if it's removed."

Dr. Quest's long fingers drummed on the desk top. "Maybe it wouldn't. Much of the time, Gregor's judgment can't be questioned."

"Jerry, I'm beginning to wonder if that sensor Gregor has planted under his skin is responsible for even more than Gregor knows."

"Like what?"

"Well, for example, his heightened sexual response when he is with Pandora. That would keep him from allowing anyone to remove the implant."

"But, Ryan, are you forgetting that his sensitive response to her was there even before she sewed that sensor in place?"

"True, true, but *Pandora's* implant might have been in place even then and acted as a contributing factor."

"That's not according to what she said, Ryan."

The psychiatrist sighed. "Jerry, how much of what she says can we believe?"

"Hmm, I see what you're driving at."

"Also, I'm exploring another hunch. Actually, you threw me onto this one when you told me how vague Gregor becomes when he is asked to account for his activities the day after his initial encounters with Pandora."

"You noticed that, too?"

"Yes, I did! He seems to lose a day."

"Are you thinking what I'm thinking? Amnesia of a sort?"

Dr. Quest nodded. "That little instrument, whatever it is, has some strange capability and purpose out of the ordinary. Let me tell you about the black box that Gregor located after that plane went down off Japan. After nobody else could find it, Gregor swam right to it. Heard some signals from an uncanny distance. The bureau I'm working with considers that he might be helpful in decoding and a few other things. They have no qualms about financing this research. All this is very classified information, Jerry."

"I was just going to ask you about that. Gregor can't talk about this then, right?"

"Not this aspect of it. He knows what is classified."

"Hmm. Has some of this taken place while he was on the Ahkars' island?"

"Some of it, yes."

"That creates a problem for him. He appears like such a drifter unless he can explain to his friends what he's been up to. His work has been productive but he can't tell anybody about it and his image is suffering."

"Well, Jerry, he'll survive. He always does. In the meantime, I'm keeping an extensive graph which will go into my new computer and we may make some progress." Dr. Ornski chuckled. "If it takes ten years, we'll get the answers to this, Jerry."

When Karla Holliss overheard David making bets on which of his family would be married first, she relayed the story to Kelley one evening as the two of them prepared dinner.

"David says he has more than twenty bets," Karla confided. "Do you want onions in your salad?" she added.

Kelley looked up from her mixing. "David better exclude me from his betting. I may not ever get married." She licked batter from one finger. "No, no onions."

"Was your quarrel with Gregor that serious?" Karla asked solicitously.

"Yes, it was. I don't even want to talk about it."

"Oh, Kelley, you'll patch it up when he comes back."

"I doubt it. Anyway, he may never come back."

Karla frowned. "Well, what about Rommey?" She handed the salt shaker to Kelley. "Here, salt the potatoes."

There was silence. Kelley fingered the shaker absentmindedly and put it on the counter. She sighed audibly. "I hear that he is dating an old girlfriend in New York. I already salted the potatoes."

"Did David tell you that?" Karla dipped her finger into the bowl to taste its contents.

"No. A friend of mine saw Rom when she went to New York. How would David know anyway?"

Karla looked at her sister curiously. "Maybe I'm not supposed to be telling, but I happen to know that David calls Rom's office in New York regularly, and each time he calls, Rommey seems to step up his date for his return to the Village."

There was another long pause. "Yes, but my friend says that the girl is coming with Rommey."

"Oh, Sis, it could be someone from his office! He told you that they work in pairs like detectives, remember?"

Kelley looked up from her work. "Rom was hurt and mad at me and had every right to be. I may have lost Rommey altogether."

"By the way, do you know that Dad has been calling Gregor fairly often?"

"How do you know that?" Kelley asked quickly.

A mischievous gleam stole into Karla's eyes. "I eavesdrop and check the phone bill. It seems to me that one of your boyfriends wants to beat the other home."

"Huh! How come I'm so in the dark about everything? What else do you know?" Kelley asked, as she stared at her sister.

"Well, I know that Kim had a baby with red hair." Karla's eyebrows lifted and the expression of mischief spread. "Like mine," she added.

"Oh, don't tell me! Do you mean to say that—oh, my goodness! Who else knows? Has David heard?"

"No. It was born in Los Angeles. David will be leaving for officer's training so soon that he wouldn't have time to give it much thought, anyway."

"It won't be the same around here with David gone. There will be just the three of us," Kelley mused.

A curious expression overtook Karla's face. "Sis, why can't you decide between Rommey and Greg?"

"I love different things about each of them."

"For goodness sakes! Decide which things are the most important, Sis!" Karla pleaded.

"I did once, in a dream. We got married and lived together and all, and then I woke up."

"Well?" Karla waited for her to continue. "Well, which one was it?"

"You won't believe this, but I woke up and I still didn't know because my dream man didn't have a face. Really, Karla, I couldn't tell which one I had married."

"Well, if I were you, I wouldn't wait too long before I remembered," her sister replied.

Suddenly, Kelley faced the stark truth... *David is leaving... Karla will be married by April... that will leave Dad and me... oh Lord... I haven't had time to give it a thought... Nichole will come to live in this house... utterly unbearable to me... she doesn't like me... I won't be able to bear seeing her using Mom's things... can't let Dad know... I won't say anything... not even to Karla....*

However, the sudden vision of herself as an intruder in her mother's home was overwhelming. Kelley was overcome by a gush of tears. She ran to the sofa, threw herself on it and sobbed uncontrollably. Karla followed her, knelt by the sofa and put her arm around Kelley's shoulder.

"Cry it out, Sis. I understand," she comforted. "I know how you feel."

However, with each of her sister's attempts, Kelley shook even more with deep-seated sobs that filled the room. "My mother's house! I just can't face it. I—I can't—can't picture Nichole, of—of all people!" she sobbed.

Karla bit her lip and tried to hold back her own grief. "I understand," she repeated. "Just cry it out."

Kelley continued to shake with another hysterical outburst. "I won't be able to stay here," she cried. "Wh—what—will I—I do? Oh, Karla!"

"It will—" Karla began. "We'll get used to it, Kelley. It will all work out. Sis, you have to try to think of Dad, too."

Kelley lifted her head, dried her eyes somewhat, looked at Vanessa's velvet chair and started to cry again. "I just—just can't picture Nichole sitting in Mom's blue chair, and, and—oh, Karla!"

"Kelley, Dad said I could take the chair. I guess he couldn't picture it either."

"And Mom's pretty things, her precious bone china and her linens. It would just kill me to see Nichole touch them, Karla."

"We'll put them all away, Dad says. He said I could have some of it as soon as Jose and I have our place. After all, Nichole will probably get lots of new things, wedding gifts and all. He told me that they would furnish the bedroom differently. Nichole doesn't like blue or French antiques."

Kelley dried her eyes again and sat next to her sister. "Oh, Sis!" she said sadly.

There was a short silence. Karla sighed. "We just have to think of Dad's happiness, too. We shouldn't make it hard for him."

Kelley's features tightened again. "I know, I know, but—" She bit her lip in a vain attempt to control her tears. Her arms slipped around her sister's shoulders. "Oh, Karla, I miss Mom so much!" she sobbed and their tears flowed together for an instant.

It was a brief moment, because Karla took her sister by the hand. "Come on," she said gently. "Come on, Kelley, let's run on the beach before the sun sets, like we used to when we were kids. It'll be good for both of us. We won't get many more chances. And the doctor told you to exercise your leg all you can, remember?" She gave Kelley's hand a gentle tug. "It looks like Dad will be late for dinner, anyway, and we won't be long."

Neither of Christopher's daughters ever knew that he had heard them through the half-open entry door. Upset and saddened, he decided to walk for a while. Two blocks away, he sat on a retaining wall and looked out over the sea.

Christopher Holliss, he said to himself, are you sure you are doing the right thing? Do you realize that Nichole will never be a mother to your daughters? Am I a fool to think that I can keep her happy? Oh, God, what would Vanessa say?

He arose in an agitated state of mind and continued to walk briskly. As he went, he beseeched Vanessa for encouragement. *Or should I call it all off*, he asked her silently... *before it's too late... because I'm not sure I can go through with it... do I love her... yes... but differently, Vanessa... the love that you and I had will last...*

nothing can change that...this is different, Vanessa...I can't put it into words...there aren't any words for it...you gave me your strength and made me think it was my own...but this girl...Van don't laugh at me...it's like being in a circus ring with a wild pony...but I need her...don't you understand...show me what to do...dammit...somehow...some way....

Christopher rounded a corner and almost ploughed headlong into Dr. Kenneth Roper. They both laughed and eyed each other. "Ken! You're usually still on the golf course Wednesdays at this time. What are you doing here?"

Dr. Roper grinned. "Well, I'm just two blocks away from my house, same as you. Got a difficult case that's worrying me. Need to run it through my head. I could ask you the same question."

Christopher sighed and began to walk beside his friend. "You can guess, Ken. I'm having misgivings about marrying a younger woman who is not too much older than my own girls."

The doctor nodded his head. "I see. But if I'm not mistaken, your youngest girl is going to be married soon and leaving. Right?"

"It's Kelley who is so upset. It makes me feel terrible." They had come to the wall where Christopher had rested before. They both sat down and watched the clouds shifting over the ocean.

"Kelley is the one who went off to San Francisco. Right?" the doctor asked.

Christopher looked at him sharply. "Yes," he said, "but then—"

"When you needed her rather badly," Ken Roper interrupted. "Right?"

"Well, uh, yes."

"Look, Chris, the kids leave when they find they have their own lives to live. Of course, that's the way it should be. However, they don't have time to come back every evening to have tea and chat with Dad so he won't have to spend the lonesome hours by himself."

Christopher made a breathy sound with his lips as though his tooth hurt. "That's what I like about you, Ken. You come to the point fast."

Ken Roper's eyes twinkled. "Now, Chris, if you need advice on how to live with a lively, young Latin lady, that's a different thing, and if you'd like to chat about that, come to my office tomorrow. I have some time, old buddy."

Christopher chuckled, but his smile faded again. "I just wish I knew what, uh, what Van would..." His voice broke.

The physician waited, then finished the sentence "...would have said about all this?"

"Uh-huh." Closing both hands into fists, Christopher brought them down hard on his knees. "Ken, every friend's face that I look into screams 'adultery' at me. I can't cope with the guilty feeling I get. Kelley's upset made it worse. I wish I knew what Vanessa would say. Ya' know, Ken, we never talked about this."

The doctor nodded his head in thought. "We should all talk about it, I guess." He scratched his ear and nodded again. "Chris, do you remember the senior physician in our office years back?"

"Oh, yes," Christopher answered after a few seconds. "His wife died in an accident. He got married again shortly afterward. We went with you to the wedding, didn't we?"

Dr. Roper nodded again. "We did. Lots of his friends didn't. There was lots of criticism. Everyone was talking about it. Said it was bad taste, especially friends of his first wife. I remember what Vanessa said to one of them."

Christopher waited tensely. "Yes?"

The doctor rose slowly and stared at the ocean. "She convinced the woman." He put his thumb and forefinger up to the bridge of his nose. "Let me think of exactly how she put it. 'Why should he throw away his brightest rainbow years?' That's exactly how Vanessa phrased it! Somewhat of a poet, wasn't she?"

With a sigh, Christopher nodded. "She always put things into parables and allegories. Had a real literary flair. Used to write me a lot of poetry when I was overseas in the Solomons. A kid on board my ship put one of them to music and we sang it at Vespers. I'll never forget it. Still sing it sometimes when I'm alone."

"I'm listening," Dr. Roper said.

> *"Bridge of ribbon high above, tell me of the man I love.*
> *Band of color, span the sea, and bring him near to me."*
> *The rainbow glistened, sparkled, beamed,*
> *And with this message softly gleamed.*
> *"His touch is the gold of my rainbow bridge.*
> *His voice is the violet on the ridge.*
> *His smile is like the bright green hue.*
> *And his laughter is my softest blue.*
> *His love is the crimson of my bow,*
> *And orange-gold, the after glow."*

As the sound of Christopher's voice died, Ken Roper sniffed and blinked rapidly. "Didn't realize you had such a good voice." He gave his friend a gentle pat on the shoulder. "I have to go now. Donna will have dinner waiting."

Christopher looked at him with a tired lift of his heavy brows. "Uh, Ken, what do—do you think Vanessa would want me to do?"

The physician stared out to sea, sighed heavily and patted his friend's shoulder. "If I knew Van, she'd tell you to marry the girl. Tell you what, Chris, come to the office tomorrow. We'll talk." He turned and started briskly up the grade, leaving Christopher to watch clouds gathering over the horizon.

Just as Vanessa's daughters never guessed that Christopher had heard them, they never would have thought that Vanessa's ghost still pervaded her kitchen. In her grey-blue gown, with her dark hair arranged high on her head, little ringlets falling softly on the nape of her neck, she could have been listening, too. She, too, would have been sad, wanting desperately to comfort her girls, watching helplessly while Christopher stood dejected in the entryway. But the girls left and Vanessa was alone in the kitchen, loitering to touch the blue teapot and her China figurines, wishing that she could dust her precious, hand-painted plates up on the plate rail, bending low over the wilting lobelia in the Dutch planter and caressing Christopher's pipe laid carelessly on the maple bookshelf.

However, as she grieved over each, the room changed slowly to a modern, yellow, glass and chrome enclosure which ejected Vanessa's shadow. She drifted to the blue velvet chair in the living room where she, too, sat and cried.

As she had done so many times before, Kelley ran on the beach with her sister, hand in hand, tripping and splashing and leaving lacy patterns of toes in the damp sand. Soaked and dripping, they flew all the faster over the receding ripples until they felt unrivaled exhilaration within themselves.

Sing, sing, my soul, Kelley's inner self called out...*beat wild my heart...like a white bird...glide and marry the breeze....*

Cool, cool, the wind blows sweet, lifting my spirit, speeding my feet...wild, wild, the waves run free, caressing the sand, caressing me...sing, sing, my soul is fire...the sky is my stage; the sea my choir...mine, mine, this tingling earth, pure element, immaculate birth...heave, heave, mysterious sea...ravish the beaches and call to me...beat, beat— my heart will sing to be a bird with a white wing...and I'll glide with strength and ease until I can marry the breeze....

Where the cliffs finally halted their progress, Kelley rested against a boulder. She made a sweeping motion with her outspread hand. "Look, Sis, can you believe that this astoundingly beautiful place is ours, yours and mine, fresh and singing to us every day? It talks to me when I listen. I feel so—so—so reborn after I come here. Do you know what I mean?"

Karla inhaled deeply and brushed damp strands of auburn hair from her tingling cheeks. "Yeah, yeah, I know. It does the same to me. I always feel like I've gone through the pink softener rinse on the washer cycle, ready for a new start. Ready to forgive the world for its hard edges."

Suddenly, Kelley's expression changed. "If they ever spoil this beach with buildings and clutter, I don't want to be here to see it. I love it so much."

Karla patted her arm. "We all do, Kelley. Ask the kids who surf every day. It changes their sense of values. When I'm down here on the beach, I seem to have more of the things that are important in life. Don't you?"

With a tilt of her head, Kelley answered, "Well, Sis, to tell you the truth—" She gestured to Karla. "Come on, we'd better head for home. That raincloud is heading straight toward us."

"Well? Well, tell me the truth." They began to walk.

"To tell you the truth, I need only one important thing, a man to love me!"

Karla stopped and put her arm around her sister's shoulder. "All you have to do, Kelley, is to put a face on your dream and you'll have a man who loves you. Just put a *face on your dream!*"

The lone cloud had come closer and suddenly showered the Village. The girls began to run again, laughing as they splashed through the ribbons of surf foam. However, the deluge was over as quickly as it had started.

When they reached Kelley's favorite ledge, they stopped to stare seaward. "Oh, look, Sis, there's a rainbow, a big one!" Kelley's hand traced the huge arc.

"Oh, it's a double! See? I've never seen a double rainbow."

"Where?"

"Here, stand here. Right there. See it?"

"Oh, yes! How positively spectacular!" Kelley watched in silence. "You know,

308

Mom used to say that she'd like to live on a double rainbow. Only Mom would think to say a thing like that." Suddenly, the raindrops on her cheek tasted salty.

They watched for a moment more before they returned to the warmth of the kitchen that soon would no longer be Vanessa's.

Standing in the shelter of someone's porch, Christopher had also watched the shower and seen the rainbow. To him, it had been Vanessa's answer. He, too, returned to the pretty blue kitchen where he watered the lobelia, took up his pipe and settled comfortably in Vanessa's velvet chair.

XXXXIII

"...a cap of diamonds for your Sunday Village..."

rom Hawaii, Gregor's flight took him to Los Angeles where he landed late in the evening. Restless and eager to be home, he headed for the Village, arriving well before dawn.

Mindful of Christopher's last warning that Rommey was due to return that day, Gregor decided to swim before daybreak and to cross the bay to the path below the cliff on the other side.

Stimulated by the fifty-five degree water, he swam vigorously. He was out of breath as he climbed the trail that twisted around the jutting shoreline and led to the steps below the Holliss home. When he arrived, the house lay in darkness.

I'm too early, he said to himself...*can't wake everyone at this hour...I'll wait till I see a light....*

He retreated to a place below Kelley's hideaway and settled into the shelter of a protected sandy beach. Impatience dissolved into weariness as he sat on the soft sand wishing for daybreak. The sibilant encore of the receding tide slowly mesmerized him and he struggled unsuccessfully to ward off sleep.

Kelley stood still, not daring to take a breath as the dress was being fitted to her. "Don't make it too tight," she repeated. "I won't be able to dance if it's too tight. You just can't do the swim and the monkey in a binding dress," she said to the figure bending to work on the hem of her long gown.

"Such strange names for dance steps," came the muffled reply.

"We have to have something new. After all, it's 1967! There's another new step, the rock," Kelley added as she glanced critically at her image in the mirror. "You'll think it's awful, Mom, but it's so much fun to do."

"But you won't be dancing like that at your wedding, dear," the gentle voice continued.

Kelley jerked backward, pulling the hem from her mother's hands. "Oh, no!" came her startled protest. "This isn't a wedding dress! It can't be! I thought I was just going to the prom again." Bewildered, she turned back to the mirror. As she stared, the image of a beautiful bride in a long flowing gown shimmered, faded, cleared briefly, then faded again.

"Darn," she mumbled, "if that siren would just shut up, maybe I could see in this mirror and decide, but I can't keep my eyes open, Mom." Kelley tried to stifle a yawn.

"Don't worry, darling," her mother answered, still bending over the hem of the white satin dress. "It will all become clear. The feeling will come from inside, and you'll wonder why you didn't realize it all along."

As the sound of the siren came again, Kelley turned to listen. Her eyelids seemed to be made of lead when she tried to blink. Suddenly, she was sitting upright in her bed in a darkened room.

"Mom, that isn't a siren," she said. "That's our doorbell!"

Confused and frightened by the blurred lines between her dream and wakefulness, she struggled into a robe and headed down the hallway. A familiar voice seemed to be calling her name, but when she inched open the door, a stranger stood there.

There was nothing threatening about the man with neatly styled hair and a handsome, clean-shaven face, but she stepped back instinctively.

It was the seraphic gleam in his dark eyes when he smiled that gave him away. Kelley squealed as she threw open the door and stepped into Rommey's outstretched arms.

"Man of beautiful eyes, how I've missed you!" she whispered softly.

"Not half as much as I've missed you, Sugar," Rommey answered. He kissed her lingeringly, then held her away to peer into her eyes. "Tell me if I got here first. Is Gregor here yet?"

She nestled against his shoulder and let a tangle of thoughts race through her head... *am I still dreaming... prom dresses... wedding dresses... he really did come back to me and I couldn't imagine a more handsome face even in my wildest dreams....*

"Kelley, answer me. I damn near broke my neck to get back before Gregor did. Has he come yet?" Rommey persisted.

"No, Mobe, he hasn't," she murmured contentedly as she breathed the soft scent of his musk cologne.

He sighed with relief, but he tensed again as he held up her chin and looked squarely into her eyes. "Sugar, you know how much I love you, but now I want to hear you say that you love me as much. Me! Me and only me! Understand? I've tried to stay away and I can't. I love you so much, Kelley. Now I want to hear it from you." His voice became gruff. "And don't go telling me that you can't make up your mind until you see that bast—"

She stilled his words with gentle fingers against his mouth. "No, no, Mobe, I won't."

"Right on!" He hugged her again. "Then tell me that you love me."

There was a catch in her voice as she tried to answer. "My dream! Mom said—said—that I'd know when it happened."

"Honey, this is no dream. Hear me?"

Finally, Kelley's eyes opened wide. "Rom, Mom knew it wasn't a prom dress at all!"

"Prom dress? Kelley, for God's sake, are you awake? Listen to me. I'm asking you to marry me."

"Oh, Rommey!" she exclaimed in a voice that threatened tears.

"Sugar, I've been in love with you since the day I found you. Remember?"

311

Kelley was remembering. Once again, she could feel the strong arms gently carrying her away from the turmoil at the love-in. She could feel the warmth of his body, hear his vibrant voice, and see the smile in his eyes. Yes, it was true, she too had known from that moment.

"Oh, Rommey, I love you, too," she whispered. "I opened my eyes that day and saw you and fell in love. It's just taken me until now to realize it."

Abruptly, he dropped his hands from her shoulders and fumbled in his pocket. "Here, I bought a ring in New York, an engagement ring."

She extended her hand, then drew it back. "Let's go down to my special rock. I want you to put the ring on my finger just as the sun comes up."

Rommey chuckled. "Right on! Where else? You haven't changed. Come on."

They went quietly down the steps and over the ledge to Kelley's hideaway. The voice of the sea was the only sound as Rommey slipped the ring on her finger and kissed her tenderly, then passionately. As they embraced, they were silhouetted against the faint glow of dawn for only a brief moment and then they were gone.

Below them in the narrow hollow where Gregor slept, ebony shadows began to dissolve with the onset of the day. Still in a dream state, he opened his eyes to a blurry view of tiny white sea horses tossing frothy manes and advancing in long rows. His eyelids fluttered shut only to lift again as three dolphins cavorted on the crest of the surge, calling him by name.

What are Grandfather's dolphins doing here, he wondered...*they'll never find their way back to the fountain...I'll have to go get them....*

Suddenly, he sprang to his feet, aware of two shadowy figures standing on the flat ledge high above him. He imagined that he saw Kelley in the arms of a man with a clean-shaven face and Apollo-like curls. With a gesture that was outlined against the sky, the man took Kelley's hand and put a ring on her finger.

Gregor hesitated. He raised his hand and uttered a cry, but the figures turned and were gone. "Am I awake?" he asked aloud as he stumbled forward out of the shadows toward the ocean swells. The dolphins and the sea horses were gone. He wet his face with the cold water and looked back at the hill. "Damn it all!" he swore. "Could Rommey have beat me home? How? How?" He returned to the cliff and leaned wearily against it.

"I'll get her back," he said. "I know I can do it. She'll listen to me. She always has." He rubbed his eyelids with the back of his hand. "I'll have to explain about some of the classified things I've been doing. Right now, she thinks I'm pretty rotten. Isn't any wonder. Can't blame her. She'll understand me better after I tell her how wrong Nichole is about me. No matter how I have to do it, I'll make her come to me."

He breathed deeply and squared his shoulders. Fingering the wet knot of tousled hair at the nape of his neck, he decided to take the path back to Kelley's house.

He began to scale the narrow trail that led upward out of the far side of the hollow.

"I know that Kelley loves me," he reassured himself as he took three steps up the grade. "That man putting a ring on her finger—I must have been still dreaming."

"Don't be so sure," a voice came from behind him.

Gregor arched backward as though he had been shot in the back. He lost his grip on the rocky shelf and a loose stone sent him tumbling back to the sand in a heap at the feet of a beautiful woman. Brushing the sand from his eyes, he looked up at a round face with the wistful eyes of a child. She wore a thin blue tunic that clung and outlined the cleft of her breasts and the graceful curve of her neck.

Angrily, Gregor rose on one knee, spitting sand and shaking from his fall. "Good God, Pandora, you scared the hell out of me!" he bellowed at her. He inhaled sharply and pointed to where Kelley had stood a moment before. "That's your doing, isn't it? I can see it all now!" he shouted, but Pandora only smiled faintly as she toyed with the heavy strands of pale hair that fell over her shoulders.

"That's your doing, isn't it?" he demanded again. "Answer me," he said as he got to his feet.

Pandora looked at him imploringly. "Oh, Gig," she sighed.

He didn't soften. He rubbed his skinned knee and berated her loudly. "Don't look at me that way because it won't get you anywhere! As far as I'm concerned, you can go back to your Russian lover or wherever you've been. Don't come to me. Damnation! You've done nothing but disrupt my life. Leave me alone. Why the hell can't you leave me alone?" He gritted his teeth and spit the words out at her. "I don't want you anymore."

"But, Gig," she pleaded, "you must listen to me."

He shook the sand from his hair. When he looked at her again, his eyes were unforgiving. "I'm tired of listening to a woman who comes and goes like a ghost, a deceitful one. Why did you take my car at the luau? Who drove it over the cliff? And don't give me that bullshit about your twin sister! Why didn't you answer me on the escalator? Why did you leave me when I hurt my back that night? Why did you get in my way on the Ahkars' island?" He held up his hand to stop her answers. "Just go away. Don't bother to explain. I can't believe you anyway."

He limped over to the incline. Taking huge steps despite the pain in his knee, he reached the flat trail and left Pandora behind in the cove.

Gregor had gone only a short distance on the mesa when he stopped, swore again and returned to the top of the cliff. At the bottom, Pandora sat cross-legged on the sand in the shadows. The pale hair that cascaded over her shoulders almost cloaked her figure.

"Gig," she called softly, reaching two small hands toward him.

"Oh, for God's sake!" he mumbled, rolling his eyes upward. He climbed back down into the hollow where she sat.

"At least you could talk to me since I made the effort to come," she said sweetly.

"Huh! Why here? Why now? You're up to something again, aren't you? Why this morning?"

"It's not easy for me to find you through all the cosmic chaos and the ultragamma bombardment. The violet blinds me for a while."

Frowning heavily, he repeated, "Ultragamma? Cosmic chaos? Violet? What the hell are you talking about?"

Pandora stared at her feet. "Oh well, let's just say that I came back from—from an experiment for a space shuttle." She arose gracefully and brushed sand from her clothing. "Weightlessness does strange things to you."

Towering over her, Gregor became all the more puzzled. "A space shuttle? But we don't have a space shut—oh, the Russians again?" He ran his fingers nervously through his hair. "Look, Pandora, if it's top secret, that's fine. Just do your things that have priority billing and don't bother me. Obviously, I'm not top priority with you."

She reached to touch his arm, but he drew away. "Gig, don't be so upset," she begged.

"Upset is putting it lightly. Next thing I'll find that you and your friends are using this damned sensor that you sewed in my head as a transmitter of some kind for your shuttle!"

Enduring his glare, she stood patiently. "You really aren't being very nice, are you, Gig?"

"Why should I be nice?" he fumed. "You've caused me nothing but pain. Why do you keep coming back?"

An expression of hurt crossed her face. She hung her head and very deliberately drew a circle in the sand with her toe. "Remember the pact we made? We can never be untwined. Have you forgotten?" She looked up and extended her hand.

Almost fearfully, he backed away. "I—I don't understand. What are you anyway? Are you real or am I imagining things? Tell me what's happening!"

From the recesses of his mind, the words of his grandfather came and spun like a record...*I want him to be a normal, fun-loving kid...not some genius...I want him to be happy...not some genius....*

Gregor groaned as troubled memories continued to circle in his brain. *That night I fell in love with her...what was it I heard the wind say...that I would conquer time...does that mean that I'm to live forever...and the sea said that perfection would come when all the water was on the shore...does that mean it never comes...and the sky said that the universe would disappear and that I would occupy it alone...imagine occupying the universe alone....*

A shudder shook Gregor's frame. "But I don't want to live alone! You," he said, pointing an accusing finger at Pandora, "you did it. Why? Why?"

"The star!" she answered. "Don't you know about the star?"

"There you go again! What star?" Gregor asked with growing disbelief.

She pointed vaguely to the sky. "It was there a while ago. It's gone now. Your beginnings were in the breath of your ancestors' ancestors hundreds of centuries ago on that green lodestar."

"How do you know that?"

"Through my Xionflight. Don't you remember?"

"No, I really d—" Gregor began, but stopped as though suddenly struck with a thought. He scrutinized the figure before him until his fierce glare made her blink and look away. "What else should I remember, Pandora? Tell me something to show me that you are really you."

Again, she drew lines in the sand with her foot, then met his eyes squarely. "Do you remember the night you made love to me? Remember that first time? We touched the star that night."

314

"Good God, Pandora!" Gregor exclaimed. "That's hard to believe. I'm not that different from other men. I think you're programming me again. I'm leaving before I really get mad. Goodbye."

As Gregor turned to go, she caught his arm. "No, no!" she cried out in a panic.

He shut his eyes and clenched his fists. Then he looked back at her and, once again, his resolve melted. "Okay, okay! I can't stand tears. Tell me about the star. What does it have to do with us?"

She released her hold. "Let your mind go back to that night. Think now."

Gregor struggled to sort the images that drifted into his memory. "There was a huge man imprisoned in an icicle of clear emerald, like a tomb. I remember, but I thought it was a dream that I dreamed as we slept in the sand."

"Possibly it was no dream," Pandora insisted.

He passed his hand over his eyes again. Once again, he could see the colossal canyon of jagged, translucent stone. Again, spokes of glistening light blinded him as he passed from one glowing icicle to another across the wide gorge layered with precious stone. The facets reflected his image a thousand times across the valley. When one image spoke to him, it had frightened him.

"Who...who calls me from my sleep?"

"We are only passing through," Gregor had answered quickly.

"What great power of transference have you?" the star-soul asked. *"Are you a mortal?"*

"Yes. We are only passing."

"Wait! Such passion is not for mortals! You are stealing from your guerdon in eternity, and so will I steal from you. I will take a spark of your soul, so I can remember passion."

At this point, Gregor opened his eyes and shook his head as though to rid himself of the memories. "It was a dream. Really weird! It had to be a dream. The voice on the star sounded like my voice." His hand shook as he wiped his brow again. "The image reached over and touched my chest and when he did, he came alive; lost his death-gray color; actually began to glow! I can still remember how his veins began to pulse with blood, how the color came to his lips and cheeks. I could see him begin to gloat over you and I tried to hide you behind me, but he yanked you away. You seemed to be too dazed to struggle. He pressed you to him and bent to kiss you. I screamed at him that he couldn't do that, that you were mine, but he just threw a ring of fire around me and said, 'Then we will be one.' Those were his words. I tried to get through the circle of flames. Instead of burning, the fire immobilized me totally with agonizing pleasure as though we were making love a second time."

"But we did, *mon amour*! We did!" Her arms stole around him.

Once again, Gregor felt himself becoming a prisoner to passion. He held her close to him. "Love me again like that, Princess," he whispered. "Only love me like that again." Gently, he pulled her to the sand. Under her blue tunic, she was naked. His own suit lay discarded. Time seemed to slip back seven years to the time on his hidden patio when the beach melted from under him, when the wind grew still and the sea became silent.

Suddenly, she spoke. "Gig, not here. Not on the beach. I hear—"

He stilled her words with his mouth on hers and held her tighter.

She began to struggle. She reached for the sensor implanted in the back of his neck and pressed with all the strength in her small hand.

A time frame seemed to shift as though someone had spliced a broken film. Gregor's empty arms were clutched to his own chest. Dazed, he struggled to his feet. As he caught sight of her figure in the shadows, his eyes blazed with anger. "What the hell did you do to me?" he demanded as he rubbed his neck.

Frightened by his rage, she begged, "Don't be angry. I put you into a brief moment of flight because—"

"Angry with you? That's putting it lightly!" He threw his head back and laughed bitterly. "You witch!" he shouted. He lunged forward and caught her by her thick hair. Struggling to check his fury, he flung her away from him onto the sand.

Gregor clenched his fists. "Serves me right for trying to make love to an apparition."

"But I heard voices, Gig! And—and daylight is coming. And—and here on the beach, it wouldn't—"

"It was good enough before!" he shouted. "You and your excuses! Don't ever do that to me again! God Almighty, why can't we live like normal people? Why don't we stop all this nonsense and live like everybody else? Look, Pandora, either we do just that or I'd rather end it all right now! See that undertow?" He pointed to the steep beach.

She scrambled to her feet and began to back away. "You wouldn't!"

Agitated beyond tolerance, Gregor grabbed her by her hair again. "Oh, wouldn't I? You'll see!" He forced her to the water's edge. A wave toppled over them.

Pandora thrashed through the backwash, screaming. "Don't do this, Gig! Let me go! Let me go! I promise I'll change! I promise. Let me go!"

Laughing wildly at her shrieking, he dragged her back into the oncoming swell.

Hearing all the noise, two lobster fishermen peered down from the trail above the cove. They dropped their gear and scrambled down to the water.

"You can't swim here, you idiots!" they shouted as they ran to drag Pandora to safety. "Can't you see there's a straight drop-off?"

Somewhat exhausted, Gregor lay prone on the sand.

Standing over him, the wizened fisherman stormed, "Can't you read the damn sign? There's a bad undertow. You tourists! Everybody else knows that you can't swim here. And also, this ain't no bare ass beach, buddy! There's a place north of here for that."

Nonchalantly, Gregor pulled on his shorts. "Sorry to give you a scare."

The younger stranger had been staring at Gregor. "Say, haven't I seen you somewhere before? Seems like I've seen you in the—"

"Look, guys, I'm okay," Gregor interrupted, anxious for their departure. "Thanks anyway."

The fishermen looked at each other. "Lady, are you okay?" one of them asked. "We'll take you home if this bum is giving you a rough time."

Gregor looked sharply at Pandora. "They can really see you! It's not just me, this time."

The older man stared again at Gregor. "Are you some kind of nut or something? Of course we can see her." He gave his partner a knowing glance and jerked his thumb meaningfully in Gregor's direction.

His friend nodded. "Yeah. Speed," he whispered. "This guy's half glazed. Probably doesn't know where he is. Might try it again. Better tell the guard on the next beach."

Gregor straightened and took Pandora by the hand. "Come on, Princess. Let's get out of here." In a moment, they were gone.

Up on the trail, Gregor was the first to break the intense silence.

"I didn't mean to be so rough down there, Pandora. You have to understand what I go through when you leave me as you do. I gotta hear you say that you came back to me because—" His voice broke, "—because you love me and for no other reason. Then maybe I can forget all this nonsense." He put his hands gently on her shoulders. "Say it, Princess."

Eagerly, she wound her arms around his neck. "*Je t'aime! Oui, oui, je t'aime! I am here because I do love you, mon amour!*" She reached her lips to his and they stood there, two solitary figures in the dawn on a cliff. Below, the ocean beat wildly on the rocks.

"That's what I needed to hear," he said finally. "Now tell me that you won't leave...."

"I made you a promise, Gig."

"Then I'll try to forget all the dumb things that you pulled on me, like the time in the riptide, and—"

"I can explain everything, Gig. They came to get me from the yacht in a kind of diving bell."

He eyed her with disbelief. "And at the camp in Baja?"

"I came by helicopter. It was parked behind the hill. The mission was secret. I couldn't tell you about it. I can tell you everything else."

"Everything except why you stayed away so long! You gotta admit that's a pretty rotten thing to do to a guy that you love. I think you're being programmed, right? It has to do with your Xionflight, right? But tell me that you can break away if you want to! We'll take out the sensors and forget the whole business, okay? Then we can live like everybody else."

Pandora shook her head, first yes, then no, then yes again until she broke into sudden hysterics. Her body heaved from her crying as she nestled her head against his chest.

"Don't cry, Princess," Gregor begged. He stroked her thick pale hair. "I won't pry anymore if it upsets you. Come on, we have a lot to do and it's going to be a great day. We'll do all your favorite things. We'll swim and walk the length of the beach and—"

Her face brightened as they continued on their way, hand in hand. "—and barbeque as we did before, and I want to be in your arms as we watch the sun go down. And I want a special Sunday breakfast in bed—with champagne."

"You forget, Princess, that almost every day is Sunday here."

"Yes, yes, I remember." She laughed softly. "When I first arrived, you told me that this was the Village of Three Hundred Sundays."

She stopped suddenly and pointed to the gable of an old cottage.

"Look. Gig! See the beautiful spider web dripping with drops of morning dew. They glisten in the sunlight when the breeze blows."

Gregor studied the magnificent silky design. "Yes, the dew sparkles just like little jewels."

Pandora clapped her hands together. "Yes, yes, a cap of diamonds for your Sunday Village.

The End

Epilogue

The sun was racing to extinguish its fire in the cool depths of the far sea. On the hill, the needles of the twisted pine rustled again in the bewitching wind. Gradually, the tree trunks softened to yield two Indian forms. They yawned, stretched and ambled away, hand in hand, to the whispering surf where they wandered throughout the night.

At dawn, nothing stirred except the hungry gulls and two figures who walked on the ridge.

"It is time to go," the Indian youth said. "Come, Princess of the Sea Village. Come."

The Indian girl hung her head sadly. "Eei!" she wailed. "Shall we not find my brother's spirit, Jaoko?"

The youth shook his head. "Since his tree is cut to the ground, he is lost. It is enough that we have searched through the night."

The girl's face clouded with anger. "Did they cut the tree?" She pointed to the two figures on the ridge.

Sighing loudly, the stocky youth answered, "No, no, not they. It was another who ate the powder of the wild chuga root which separates the mind."

The girl wailed again. "When will they all be gone, Jaoko? What will we do until then, Prince-spirit of the Sea Indians?"

Tenderly, he kissed her upturned cheek. "Do not let trouble shadow the sun, my queen. Our time will surely come soon."

A little fox trotted at their heels as they returned to the tree. Once again, the mystical wind rustled the needles and the ghosts melted into the limbs of the sacred pine.